The Whistle Walk

Ironwood Plantation Family Saga Book One

Stephenia H. McGee

Dear Reader,

The town of Oakville is fictional as is the Ironwood plantation. However, you might find it interesting to know that the name "Ironwood" came from my own family's estate and I used actual names from my ancestry chart for many of the characters. The inside of the Ironwood house is based on Cedarwycke plantation located in Hamilton, MS as well as the descriptions used for the potato house and kitchen. I'd like to say a special thank you to Ms. Susie Wright for allowing me to use Cedarwycke as an inspiration for Ironwood. I even used the unique plantation name for Lydia's family home.

The outside descriptions of the mansion (as well as the photo of the house on the cover) are based on the Herron House, located in Oakland, MS. Although the house was technically built in 1907, the outside still looked like a perfect Ironwood to me. At the time of this writing, it is a lovely bed and breakfast run by Sam and Flora Vance. Thank you both for your wonderful hospitality and for allowing me to use pictures of your home for my Ironwood.

The battles of Corinth referenced in the book are actual events, although everything that happens to Charles and the other characters is fictional. General Earl Van Dorn and several of the generals mentioned are actual men, although the dialogue and interactions with my characters are completely products of my own imagination.

I'd also like to thank all my early readers who helped me correct the historical details in the novel. Any errors are completely my own.

Thank you for stepping into Ironwood. I hope it captivates you as much as it has long captivated me. Happy reading!

One

Cedarwycke Plantation
March 15, 1862

Lydia pinched her nose to stifle the sneeze that would surely betray her hiding place. Drawing her skirts further under her legs and silently berating the hoops underneath it, she forced herself to ignore bits of straw that scratched and poked their way through the layers of material. She only needed a few measly moments to clear her head. Then she would be ready. Why couldn't Mother understand?

"Miss? Miss is yous in here?" The mousy voice of her mother's maid drifted with the dust up to the rafters of the loft. Sally sighed loudly, an uncharacteristic display of exasperation. The day flustered even the mellowest among them. "Miss Lydia, you know your momma gonna be madder and madder the longer you stays out."

Lydia inwardly groaned. As if she weren't aware of that already. She knew she must stop acting like a child, but could not bring herself to relent. She remained perfectly still. After a few moments the girl gave up her search and the barn door slid closed behind her. Lydia let out a long breath of relief and reclined against the freshly cut storage of the horse's winter feed, but her restless mind wouldn't allow her to enjoy her stolen freedom. She would go when she was ready. Not because someone summoned her. Still, if she didn't hurry...

Unfolding her stiff muscles, Lydia stood and brushed her lavender skirts free of dust and clinging straw. She drew her bottom lip between her teeth – a habit Mother said would ruin her smile. If she didn't present herself to be fussed over soon, she'd be accused of blatantly ignoring her mother's instructions. Everyone knew ignoring the mistress of Cedarwycke was completely unacceptable. Such disrespect most especially could not come from her own daughter.

Lydia peered over the edge of the loft, and seeing no one, descended the ladder. *Ladies do not climb*, her mother's voice repeated in her head. *Yes, Mother.* Neither did they do any number of the other things she'd done.

Her shoes landed on the dirt floor and a soft whinny greeted her. Lydia glanced over at her mare, which waited with ears forward and a welcoming gaze. What could a few moments more hurt? Lydia ran her ungloved hand over Snowflake's smooth muzzle.

"Hey, pretty girl. You knew about me hiding up there the whole time, didn't you?" The horse bobbed its head and Lydia laughed at the impossibly implied response. "But you won't tell anyone, will you, girl?"

She placed her cheek against the horse's face and smoothed the hairs along her mane. Unable to stall any longer or risk giving away her secret sanctuary, Lydia bid her childhood companion a good afternoon and made her way back to the house.

She'd barely set foot in the door when her mother's voice brought her steps to a halt.

"You are determined to be the death of me, aren't you?"

Lydia adjusted her features into a composed, yet slightly confused expression, before turning around. "I'm sure I do not know what you mean, Mother."

Mother placed her hands on her slim hips; her bright blue eyes flashing. "Do not play games with me, Lydia. You have been gone since the noon meal!"

Lydia wove her fingers together to keep them from digging into the folds of her skirt. "Forgive me, Mother. I did not intend to give you flutters. I simply lost track of the time."

Mother raised her eyebrows but elected not to argue further. "Get on up to your room."

Lydia turned and started up the staircase, Mother's commands for hot bath water sending the house girls running. She closed her bedroom door behind her, leaning on it for support while trying to gather her strength for what lay ahead. Within a mere moment, a heavy knock vibrated the wood against her back. Stifling a groan, Lydia opened the door for her mother to enter.

"Now, no excuses. I do not care where you've been. Right now we've got to get you bathed."

Lydia nodded. "Yes, ma'am."

Mother looked her over for an uncomfortably long moment. Finally, she sighed and sat down on the patterned quilt spread across Lydia's canopy bed. "Come, sit by me. I need to tell you what to expect on your wedding night."

Lydia's heart shuddered. Oh no. She shook her head fervently, sending half her hair sliding from its pins. Anything but that.

"Come now. I know it is an awkward thing, but a lady must understand her duties to her husband. He will expect you to produce children, and I do not want you to be unaware of how such things are accomplished."

Lydia lifted her chin, refusing her mother's invitation to sit. Her nerves required the freedom of movement. "I already know, Mother. You explained it to me as a girl. When God wishes to gift a married woman with a child, He will place one in her womb. It is later born by expelling through the birth canal, a painful and messy process."

Mother smiled. "Very good, dear. I am surprised you were paying attention. But I am afraid there is more to it than that. The father also has a role in making a child."

She could not have this conversation. Lydia rubbed her temples with her fingers. "Yes, I understand that as well. I do know that it requires both a stallion and mare to produce a foal."

Mother frowned, the lines creasing the planes of her face. "You have spent far too much time in the barns. A lady should not witness the goings-on of livestock."

Lydia crossed her arms over her chest. "It is much too late for that now. Surely a husband and wife will do things in much the same –

"Lydia! Stop that talk this instant. A marriage is not like being a mare..." She fanned her hands in front of her face. "Oh, Lord, where have I gone wrong with this child?"

A knock at the door saved her from one of Mother's rants on Lydia's missing sense of propriety and grace. It came as no surprise Mother wished to marry her to Mr. Harper as soon as possible, lest the man figure out Lydia's knack for clumsiness and lack of social refinement before he was properly shackled to her.

Ignoring her mother's fanning, Lydia opened the door to two young, dark-skinned girls weighted down with steaming buckets of water. They silently dumped the contents into the copper tub and slipped out the doorway. Their procession of several more trips saved her from continuing the conversation.

When the water level reached half full, her mother, having recovered from her feigned shock, pointed a long fingernail at the tub. "Go ahead and get in. No soaking for you today. You've lost the luxury. We need to get you scrubbed." She eyed Lydia's half-loose locks. "And we still have to get all that tied. God blessed you with that thick hair, but we want to make sure it's not a tangled mess in the morning."

"Yes ma'am." She loathed being unclothed in front of others but knew better than to push Mother any further. She shed her clothing and waited for the final bucket of water to flow into the tub. Sally kept her eyes downcast and likely didn't notice Lydia wrapping her arms around her chest to cover feminine parts that still looked as if they belonged to a young girl and not to a woman of twenty years. Sally pulled the door closed behind her with a soft click and left Lydia alone with Mother. Lydia needed to find a distraction.

She pulled her fingers through her hair as she stepped into the tub. "Mother?" She asked, working the soap into a lather and removing the scent of horse from her skin. "When will I get to see the dress?"

Mother's eyes lit and excitement tugged her serious lips into a wide smile. She clasped her hands. "Oh, it's just gorgeous. I'll run get it for you while you finish up."

Mother nearly skipped from the room, pulling the door closed behind her. Ignoring her mother's strange behavior, Lydia sank as deep into the water as she could and tried to let the heat work the tension from her muscles.

She wasn't afraid to marry Charles Harper. Not really. Anyone could see he was handsome, smart, and well-liked. Her father had accepted Mr. Harper's attentions almost gladly. Rumors said he would never marry, since many a debutante had batted her eyelashes in his direction with little notice. Lydia did no such thing, and somehow he noticed where others had always dismissed her. She wasn't really sure why. Her family had relatively little to offer a man of Mr. Harper's stature and she'd never been the belle of any ball. Too skinny for men's tastes and unskilled in the art of charm. She possessed none of the things Mother said drew a man, so why would he choose her? Perhaps the ever-encroaching war had flamed a desire for an heir.

She'd just let her lids fall closed when the door flew open. She let out a startled yelp.

"Mother, you about scared me to – "

Mother waved her hand to dismiss Lydia's protest and held up her prized accomplishment, a wide grin revealing her perfectly straight teeth.

Lydia's breath caught. "Oh, Mother!" she cried. "It is beautiful!"

"Isn't it? I am rather proud of it."

Lydia rushed through rinsing the soap from her hair and hurried from the tub, quickly toweling off and wrapping herself in a cotton robe. "It's perfect. Never have I seen a more beautiful gown." She actually meant it, for once not merely trying to appease her mother. "Is it truly silk?"

Mother nodded. "The best, imported from France. You don't know what it took to get it through those blockades and… Well, never mind. Here, at the bottom, is handmade lace. I had the seamstresses start on it the moment Mr. Harper spoke to your father. There hasn't been a finer bride in all of Mississippi."

Lydia listened to Mother's tumbling words as she ran her fingertips over the smooth material of the bodice, enjoying the feel of it against her skin. The bodice and skirt were made of bright, white silk as pure as the rare snow that fell only during the coldest winters in Mississippi. The silk was slightly gathered at the front hem to reveal the beautiful layer of lace underneath.

"Well, hurry up. I cannot wait a moment longer to see you in it."

Lydia donned her undergarments, and Mother helped her step into the gown. The neckline draped across her shoulders and dipped slightly in the front, showing her collar bone. The sleeveless swathe of fabric left her arms bare. She felt slightly exposed, but also more womanly than ever before. Lydia turned, enjoying the swish of the fabric as she moved. A large bow was tied at the back of her waist and trailed down to the floor. "It's perfect, Mother. Thank you."

Tears gathered in Mother's eyes. Lydia was certain she'd never seen Mother's eyes mist over in all her twenty years. "You look simply beautiful," Mother said.

Lydia threw her arms around Mother's neck. Mother took a deep breath, and after a brief squeeze, unhooked her daughter's arms. "All right now. We don't want to wrinkle it, and there is much that still needs to be done."

Lydia turned and looked at herself in the stand-up mirror. "Just let me look at it for a moment. We have the time." There stood a bride in the most beautiful gown she'd ever seen, made from material her family could scarce afford. Mother would do her best to make her daughter a bride worthy of such a handsome groom. Not that a little powder and lip stain would ever make a beauty out of her. Her stomach knotted. He would arrive soon, and on the morrow she would be a wife tethered to a man she barely knew. All she could do was hope his hands would be as gentle as those honey-colored eyes.

"All right. Let's get you out of it. We need to get your hair in ties."

Lydia surrendered the luxury of the dress and pulled her robe around her before settling into the dressing chair. "Am I to see guests with ties in my hair?"

"Don't be ridiculous child. No one is to see the bride before the wedding."

"Then what shall I do all evening?"

"You will remain in your room."

"By myself?"

Mother pulled the comb through Lydia's protesting hair, yanking on knots with little compassion. "Gracious, girl. The questions. It is not proper for Mr. Harper to see you before the wedding, and besides, your hair is so thick that if I do not get it tied now it will still be damp in the morning. Think of it as a little time to yourself. I should think you would be glad not to have to entertain."

Lydia smiled. True. As Mother well knew. It *would* be nice to have some time to herself. She could even read as long as she liked and no one would say anything to her for it. Assuming she could bridle her thoughts enough to keep them on the page.

"And you will go to bed early. You'll need your rest for tomorrow."

Lydia nodded, though she knew lying abed early wouldn't help matters any. She hadn't slept well all week. "How many are coming?"

"Aside from my cousins and your father's sister, I've invited every family of standing in the county."

She'd guessed as much. They would be there to grieve the loss of a man many a parent had hoped to capture for their own daughters and little else.

"But what with so many of the young men already joining up and gone to Arkansas," Mother said, twisting a piece of hair around a strip of cloth, "I would not expect a large crowd."

Mother's fingers flew through their task, and soon her entire head was tied in tight curls. Mother never let anyone else work on Lydia's hair. She always insisted on doing it herself. Lydia couldn't be sure if Mother enjoyed the time or if she simply didn't trust anyone else to do it correctly. When she married, who would tame her wild mane?

"One more thing," Mother said, breaking into her thoughts. "Your father and I have gifts for you."

"Oh?" She turned in her seat to see the small leather book her mother held out.

"This is from your father. He said it is for you to write down your thoughts and the joys of your new life."

Lydia smiled and unwound the thin leather cord wrapped around the cover. Inside, blank pages stood waiting for her to fill. She felt an excitement well up within her. What would she write? Drawing the little book to her chest, she smiled up at Mother. "Thank him for me. It is most thoughtful."

Mother nodded and pulled something from her dress pocket. Lydia held out her hand, and Mother dropped a delicate piece of jewelry into her palm. She held it up to the fading light to study it. Thin strands of silver swirled together around little milky-white stones that were cut into the shapes of four-petal flowers. "A brooch," Lydia mused.

"Yes. It was my grandmother's. She gave it to my mother on her wedding day and my mother gave it to me on mine. Now it is your turn to wear it."

Lydia blinked back the tears that threatened to spill over. "Why have you never shown it to me before?"

Mother straightened her shoulders. "I have been saving it." Her voice cracked, and she waved her hand. "These are dogwood flowers," she said, pointing to the little tiny stones. "Grandmother said the dogwood flower is in the shape of the cross. White, except on the tips where it looks torn and

9

darkened. That represents Christ's blood. The dogwood reminds us to keep him close." She patted Lydia on the shoulder. "The guests will soon be here. I will see you again in the morning."

Lydia put the brooch next to her comb and smiled at her mother in the mirror. "Goodnight."

As soon as Mother left the room, Lydia pulled on a nightdress and grabbed the gown, holding it up in front of her in the mirror.

Tightness gripped her chest. This gown was far too beautiful for someone like her. She returned it to the hanger.

Lydia sighed and gathered a pen and a well of ink. How well Daddy knew her heart. She untied the bindings of the book and stared at it. What could she write? She couldn't yet blemish the clean pages with her galloping thoughts. No, she must save them for something important. Tomorrow, she would become a wife and the lady of her own home. Maybe after tomorrow she would have something of more consequence to record than the twittering of a girl afraid to wed.

Two

Cedar Hall Plantation

"Bridget, you's gots to light that lamp. I can't see nothin'," Ruth whispered. She rubbed the sore spot on her leg where her shin had found the hard lines of a plank bench.

"Shush," her sister answered. "If they sees the light we might get caught." Bridget shuffled behind Ruth and felt along the kitchen's brick wall. "I found it."

Finally. If someone caught field hands stealing from the kitchen, both their hides would show the marks for it. Of course, if the Harris family fed their people better, she might not have had to risk her skin over one measly sack of flour.

The lingering scent of smoked meat made her stomach growl. Ruth pushed her hand against her complaining innards and willed them to silence. "How you gonna tell which one of them sacks is flour and not sugar?"

Bridget's answer came out in hissed words through clenched teeth. "I don't know. Open them."

Ruth shook her head fervently even though she knew it was too dark for her sister to see it. She must have sensed it anyway.

"Ain't no other choice."

"They might not notice one bag of flour gone, but they's for sure gonna notice if all them bags are opened."

Bridget sighed. "Fine, light it. But turn it as low as you can."

Ruth pulled the match from her skirt pocket. Maybe her sweaty palms wouldn't make it too damp to use. With a flick of her wrist, she scraped the tiny stick against the brick wall. A little flame jumped to life.

Shadows danced across Bridget's drawn face as she pushed the lamp into Ruth. "Hurry up."

Ruth touched the flame to the wick and turned the burner down as low as she could make it go. A soft glow filled the glass chimney and cast a gentle light across the room. Ruth drew a deep breath. She'd never seen the inside of any part of the big house before. Not even the kitchen. Momma said it was a strange thing for a kitchen to be connected to the house. Said she'd never heard of such a thing before. Where Momma came from kitchens were always separate.

"Stop gawkin' and bring that thing over here so I can see them bags."

Ruth hefted the lamp and held it up to the shelf Bridget searched. "Here," she said. "I think this one says flour."

Ruth tilted her head back to see the top shelf, grateful for the reading lessons her grandmother had given them in secret. She'd expected large sacks tied with hay strings sitting on the floor and not small, neat bags lined on shelves. But then everything was strange up here. "That's it. Grab one and let's go." At least it would be easier to carry, and only taking a little eased her conscious.

"Maybe we oughtta get one from the back," Bridget whispered.

"What for?"

"Then they won't notice one from the front's done gone missin'."

"Ain't no need. Just grab the one from the front and then pull one of the others up into its place. Then it looks just the same."

Bridget stretched to her tiptoes, her short stature only allowing her fingertips to brush the bottom of the sack. Even though Ruth was a season younger than Bridget's nearly twenty summers, she was the taller of the two.

"You gonna have to get it for me," Bridget said.

Ruth turned and scanned the area behind her. Her gaze fell on the bench that would surely leave a bruise as evidence of their crime. She set the lamp on the bench and reached for the bag, slipping it off the shelf and cradling it like a suckling infant.

"I got it! Let's go."

"Wait, we gotta pull the other one forward."

Ruth handed the treasure to her sister's waiting arms and lifted herself to her toes. Just a little more. She stretched. There. Got it. Her fingertips grasped the bottom corner of the sack. She should find a stool. No. No time and too much trouble.

"You got it?" Bridget's words came from right behind her back, tickling her neck with hot breath.

"Hold on. I's got it. Just a little more." Ruth shifted her weight back and strained her fingers, the wood of the shelf digging into her bent wrist. With a grunt, she yanked back and slid the reluctant sack forward. Her grip slipped, and she stumbled backward.

"Ugh!" Bridget's feet were right up underneath her. Ruth crashed into Bridget, and they tumbled to the floor, knocking over the bench with a loud crash.

"We's got to go! Someone mighta heard that," Bridget said, her eyes wide. Shadows danced across her face and light sprung up around her.

Ruth pushed her sister's crouching form aside. The toppled lamp spilled fluid over the floor, and flames escaped the glass chimney and scurried along the floor like frightened mice.

Ruth's mouth went dry. She stared at the dancing flames gathering courage and multiplying. Bridget shook her shoulder, breaking the fire's spell.

"Come on! We gotta go!"

Ruth shook her head. "No, we's got to stop this fire. We can't leave."

Panic raced across Bridget's face, but she nodded. They stomped the nearest flames, but the thin soles of Ruth's shoes did little to hinder their advance.

The fire found the dry flour and potato sacks and greedily consumed its way farther along the wall and up the shelves. Black smoke thickened the air. Bridget coughed. She stopped stomping and looked at Ruth.

"We ain't gonna stop it."

If only they had a bucket of water or something that would help them smother the flames. Ruth's gaze darted around the room but didn't land on anything that would help them. Smoke burned her nostrils, searing its way deep into her lungs. She coughed it up reflexively but found no relief.

"We's got to go, Ruth. If they catches us here now we'll hang for sure."

Bridget was right. They had to go. Ruth jumped the flames and threw open the door to the inner house.

"Fire!" she yelled, hoping her single warning would bring help but still allow them to escape. Ruth ran through the fire that licked at her legs and caught hold of her skirt. Bridget waited for her at the rear door, smoke clouding her figure. Ruth dove through the door and out into the night air.

"You's on fire!" Bridget grabbed Ruth and shoved her to the ground, beating at Ruth's skirts with her hands. The flames sputtered and died and the girls lay on their backs heaving in air. Shouts drifted through the doorway on the heels of the billowing smoke. Bridget's terrified gaze found Ruth's.

"Run!" Ruth screeched.

They gathered their skirts in their hands and ran with hunched backs, darting across the open yard and to the safety of the tree line. Ruth pulled Bridget behind a large pine. They peered around either side of the rough bark. Flames now leapt from the windows and tickled the roof. One ember caught, then another. In a few moments, the fire raced along the roof and covered the wood walls. People shouted, their hazy forms scurrying around in the yard.

"What've we done?" Ruth whispered.

Bridget wrapped her in a hug. "We didn't mean to. It was an accident."

Ruth placed her chin on her sister's ruffled hair. "We shoulda never been in there. Now they's goin' to lose the whole place."

Bridget nodded against her neck.

Ruth pulled away. "We gotta get deeper in these woods before someone sees us."

She laced her fingers with Bridget's, and they hurried through the thick undergrowth, briars and thorns tearing at their legs and shredding their skirts.

Ruth shivered. The hard ground poked and prodded her body, making her stiff limbs ache even more. She shook her sister, her form barely visible in the half moon's light. Bridget stirred and rolled to her back.

"You think it's safe to go back yet?" she whispered.

Ruth scanned the woods around them, unable to tell how long they'd been in the woods or how far they'd run before collapsing. "I don't know. But maybe we should start makin' our way back and see what's goin' on."

"Yeah. Can't get no rest against this tree no ways."

Ruth stretched her stiff joints and shook the dirt from her skirt. The smell of smoke drifted to her nostrils and twisted her gut. Maybe her warning had been enough. Maybe they got the fire stopped before it took the house. She'd prayed until the exhaustion overtook her. Surely that would mean something.

Bridget grasped her hand. "Come on. I think we needs to go back this way."

Her sister had a better sense of direction than most, so Ruth followed Bridget's lead through the thick underbrush, her feet tripping on exposed roots.

After what felt like hours, Ruth noticed an orange glow warming the sky in the distance. Sunrise? They must have been hiding longer than she thought. If they could get back home before the morning foreman came, no one would know they'd been out all night.

Bridget squeezed her fingers fiercely. "Ow! You's hurtin' my hand!"

"Hush!" Ruth stilled. The faint sound of shouts drifted to them through the trees. Bridget tugged on her hand, and they made their way through the forest as quietly as they could. The orange glow grew brighter. Smoke. That was no sunrise.

The trees thinned, and she could see it then. The entire house was engulfed in flames, people running frantically around outside. Children wailed. From where they stood, Ruth could see where the blaze traveled along the dry ground, rain-starved grass providing food for its devilish hunger. It traveled beyond the barn and out past...

Ruth gasped. Bridget turned to her with wide eyes. No words were needed. They had to get home. They burst through the trees and into the cleared area along the edge of the yard. Ruth prayed no one would see them, her legs pumping hard and carrying her closer to her greatest fear.

They topped the hill and were greeted by a horrible sight. The cabins had caught fire. The stiff breeze carried it easily from one roof to another. People scrambled about desperately trying to quench the flames with buckets of water from the well, but the tiny splash of water did little to quench the fire pouring from open windows.

"Momma!" Bridget shrieked, racing down the hill and into the chaos below.

Ruth regained enough of her mental abilities to remind her feet to move. Her home stood closest to the big house. The first on the line. The first that would –

No. No, it couldn't be. Flames consumed their two-room log cabin, black smoke billowing from the doorway and through the roof. Ruth scanned the faces running to the well.

"Momma?" Panic gripped her stomach. "Momma! Where are you?" She dashed to the well, grabbing a young girl by the shoulders. "Has you seen my Momma?" The girl shook her head. "Or my little brother?" The girl shook her head wildly, ripping her arm from Ruth's grasp and running away.

More faces streaked past her with terrified eyes and shouts that came from horrified lips. She knew them all, but none were the ones she sought. "Have you seen my mother? Violet! Have any of you seen Violet?"

This was her fault. All her fault. She had to find Momma and little Jessy.

Bridget's scream nearly stilled her heart. She turned to where she'd left her sister standing in shock outside of their cabin.

"Momma!" Bridget screamed.

Ruth dashed to her sister's side and heard the sound that had ripped such a terrified wail from Bridget's chest. Her mother. She could hear her mother's screams coming from inside!

Ruth sprang toward the front porch, but before she could reach it, it gave a terrible groan and collapsed, spraying sparks into the air and sending Ruth stumbling backward. The screams stopped.

"No! Momma!"

No sounds came from inside.

The smoke blackened the sky and rose into the night. The flames consumed everything it touched. The heat became so intense it allowed her no closer. Ruth sank to her knees. She should have gone in sooner. If only she had braved the flames.

How? How could the fire possibly have taken over so much so fast? Her mother and her brother – gone. All because she'd wanted to make a cake for Jessy's ninth birthday. A day he would never see. Ruth's stomach knotted, threatening to retch up its meager contents.

Cool hands gripped her forearms, pulling her up. A voice pricked holes in her blanket of dark thoughts, but she shook her head to make it go away.

"Ruth!"

Her gaze snapped to her sister's face, the fog lifting from her brain. Bridget's eyes reflected the fear constricting her own chest.

"Ruth! Come on!"

Ruth frowned. Where could they possibly need to go? Their home was gone, their family lost.

"Ruth? Is you listenin' to me?"

Ruth squeezed her eyes tight, trying to get herself to think. "What?"

Bridget sank to her knees and put her head next to Ruth's ear. "The cabins are lost. Maybe even the big house. We's got to get away from here before we burn up, too." She tugged on Ruth's arm again. "Ruth, your skin is so hot. You gots to get away from the fire."

The panic in Bridget's voice broke whatever spell she was under. The heat washed over her and she suddenly felt like her skin was covered in biting fire ants. She jumped to her feet. Bridget grabbed her hand and dragged her back to the woods, to the welcoming cool of the tree's shelter. There they huddled together and watched their world burn.

Three

Cedarwycke Plantation
March 16, 1862

Charles Harper paced the floor in the guest room given to him, frustrated with the nervousness gnawing his stomach. He balled his fists at his sides, cursing himself for feeling like a caged bobcat.

It was past time he wed. If his mother were still alive, her harping for him to produce an heir would have long since seen him properly tied to a suitable match. He looked at his wedding attire in the mirror. Many had called him handsome, though he suspected the weight of his name supplied more attraction than his square face and mop of dark hair. Yes, his mother would have loved to see him this day even if it were late in coming.

At twenty-seven, if he didn't start a family soon, there would be no one to leave Ironwood to and continue his name. These last ten years learning to run the plantation on his own had hardly left him time to attend many balls, much less start courting. Besides, vapid smiles and veiled attempts to charm him out of his fortune were hardly what he deemed attractive. He needed a helpmate, not a decoration. But Lydia, she was different. He sensed great depth behind her timid smiles.

Charles tugged on his waistcoat and squared his shoulders, smoothing on the face of practiced composure. Time to go. He strode through the door and down the wide staircase.

"Ah, here comes our groom now."

Charles smiled at Lydia's doting father and bowed slightly. "Good afternoon, Mr. Cox."

"Come now, you'll soon enough be family. Call me Bamber."

"Yes, sir. It is a fine day for the ceremony, and I must say the grounds out back look splendid."

Bamber clapped him on the shoulder. "Mrs. Cox has been rather busy. The poor dear has worked herself into a frenzy making sure all is perfect."

"I assure you she's done a fine job."

Bamber beamed. "Come, it is time we get you outside. The guests are seated and my daughter will come down any moment." Bamber shuffled out the back door and Charles followed behind him.

Long benches lined up under the shade of ancient oaks, filled with ladies in brightly colored dresses and even a few men in fine suits. He searched until he found Mr. Lloyd with his contraption. Charles smiled, pleased with himself that he would be able to take an image and present a photograph to his bride of her wedding day. He made his way to the steps and down the center aisle, nodding at well-wishers and taking his place next to the preacher.

Bamber made sure Charles stood in the proper location, assured the preacher was ready to perform the ceremony, and hurried to gather Charles' bride. Charles couldn't help but smile at the man's joviality. He'd doted on his only daughter. Charles had to repeatedly assure him he would provide Lydia with a comfortable and secure life and would do all in his power to care for her every need. He'd not given the promise lightly.

The small band situated to his left began playing the harpsichord and violin, and Charles shifted his attention to the door from which his bride-to-be would emerge.

The door swung open to reveal a stunning beauty with creamy skin touched pink in the cheeks. She wore her dark hair piled high in a mass of curls. What would it feel like to loosen those tresses from their confines and feel their silkiness in his hands?

She walked forward, clinging to her father's arm, thick skirts swishing across the grass. Her eyes locked on his, and his lips curved. Had she guessed his thoughts? He steadied himself, careful not to allow too much of his feelings to show on his face. Bamber bowed and placed Lydia's slender hand in his. Charles offered her an encouraging smile. She returned a shy one of her own and looked up at him through thick lashes.

He repeated the minister's words and watched her full lips repeat the promises that would bind them together for life. Soon she would be his alone, his lady to return to Ironwood, a delicate creature in whom he sensed a hidden strength that would match his own. A woman worthy of sharing his life's work.

"And now, may I present to you Mr. and Mrs. William Charles Harper!" the preacher announced as cheers erupted from the gathered neighbors.

Charles drew his bride into his arms and placed a feather-light kiss upon her velvet lips. Her face flushed, and she quickly dropped her eyes as the whoops of the men grew louder. Charles chuckled and they walked down the aisle.

Lydia's mother swooped in like a flustered hen, and directed them where to stand. "Mr. Harper, you stand here. Lydia, take your place next to him and your father and I will stand here. Oh, heavens. Where is your father?"

Charles looked at the woman beside him, now his wife. "So, my dear, what did you think of the ceremony?"

She blinked at him with bright eyes, the most interesting combination of blues and greens that reminded him of a restless ocean. "It was quite lovely."

He nodded, wanting to speak to her more, but before he could compose another thought, her mother bustled over and began shifting them around and packing family members around them. Lydia flashed him an apologetic smile, and he momentarily forgot the closeness of strangers pressed against him.

"One, two and..."

Pop

The contraption made an awful racket, and Mr. Lloyd's disheveled head emerged from underneath the black cloth at the back of the large box. "Excellent. Let us try a few more."

Capturing their image required the participants to remain perfectly still, a difficult undertaking for a large gathering and most especially for a new husband ready to be done with the task. Finally, Mr. Lloyd dismissed them.

The crowd shifted, and Charles was swarmed with well-wishing and knowing smiles from older gentlemen. He did his duty and acknowledged their congratulations, ignoring the anxiousness in his belly to be done with the public presentation. When the immediate crowd finally fizzled, Charles took a breath and stepped away from them, eager to take his bride's arm. He scanned the gathering, but his little white dove had disappeared.

The guests milled around the yard, her mother twittering around among them like a hummingbird. Lydia leaned against the tree she'd climbed in her childhood, stifling her desire to shed her slippers and shimmy up to the thick limb just above her head. It would give her the perfect space to observe the ladies strutting around like peacocks, decked out in their brightly colored dresses and fluttering their eyelashes over the tops of lace fans.

The important families of the county moved about in the gardens, the heady scent of newly bloomed roses and gardenias drifting on a slight breeze. They nibbled their noon meal refreshments. The clear sky overhead boasted neither the first cloud nor hint of rain. She couldn't have asked for a more perfect day for her wedding.

The ceremony must have been beautiful. She wished she could remember it. Instead, all she could recall were Mr. Harper's twinkling eyes, his warm hands holding hers, and his smooth voice speaking words that drifted over her like a summer breeze. Then there were cheers, her mother's smile tempered by tears, and a gentle kiss on her lips that made her head swim. Somehow she was posing for a portrait and drifting off into the gardens before she got a hold on herself and started thinking clearly.

Then it all hit her, nearly taking her breath and birthing the need to separate from the press of people that drained her energy like a swarm of mosquitoes drawing blood.

Despite what Mother would think, Lydia slipped away with practiced stealth and allowed herself the space to breathe again. Mother might not notice for a small time, since she buzzed about greeting guests and directing slaves. The reprieve probably wouldn't last long enough for her to refill her reserves, but she would take what little she could get.

Finally allowed a quiet moment, Lydia could appreciate Mother's hard work. White cloth-draped tables topped with various treats dotted the lawn, the grass underneath perfectly trimmed. People laughed and talked as they walked along the garden paths, sat in Mother's prized wrought iron furniture, or gathered under the shade of the large oaks at the back corner of the house, several pairs of colored hands having cleared the benches from the ceremony away. She scanned the moderate crowd looking for the one who stood just a little taller than the others, his thick wavy hair insisting on falling onto his forehead.

"Shouldn't the bride be amongst her guests?"

Lydia startled. How did he sneak up without her noticing? "I was, uh, I was just looking for you."

Mr. Harper lifted an eyebrow. "Were you, now? Looks to me like you are hiding."

Lydia crossed her arms over her chest. "I am not hiding. I am taking in the scene, that's all. And I'll have you know I *was* looking for you. I can get a better view of the crowd from here."

He smiled and wrapped his arm around her waist. "I like knowing you were looking for me. And here I am."

Her heart stumbled over its next beat, and she chided herself for being unnerved by his touch.

"You look stunning, my dear."

Heat crept into her cheeks. "Thank you, Mr. Harper. My mother created an amazing dress."

He laughed. "As well as the woman in it."

She stepped out of his arm and turned to face him, unsure of how to respond. "You have not told me where you plan to spend the night. I assume we will be staying here at Cedarwycke?"

He stepped close, his height causing her to lift her chin to meet his eyes. "No. We will return to Ironwood. I intend to carry my bride over the threshold of her new home on my wedding night."

She dropped her gaze to his polished boots, her nervous fingers winding through her skirts and lifting her hem. "Oh, of course." She swallowed against the lump in her throat. "When do you intend to leave?"

Mr. Harper scanned the crowd behind her then returned his gaze to her face, a small smile tugging at the corner of his mouth. "I don't suppose your mother will let me you whisk you away before your father has his speech, so I will have to resign to waiting just a bit longer."

Her mouth fell open, but she quickly snapped it shut. "We, uh, we probably need to get back to the party." She spun on her heels and hurried across the grass. The man undid what little bit of composure she'd fought so hard to maintain. How could he speak in such a manner?

She spotted Daddy standing off to the edge of the back porch, sipping punch. Lydia made her way to him as quickly as she could get through the crowd, smiling and nodding at guests as she passed but not pausing long enough for them to engage her in conversation lest Daddy get away while she tarried.

His face lit up when their eyes met. She threw her arms around his neck. Daddy pulled her close for a moment, and then eased away from her grasp. "Come now, darling. We are in presence of company." The light in his eyes belied his mild chiding. "Are you all right? You look a bit flushed."

"Mr. Harper says we will be leaving soon."

Daddy nodded. "Yes, he told me he wished not to be gone from his plantation for more than one night."

Lydia chewed her lip. "I am afraid, Daddy. I have never been a night away from Cedarwycke."

"I know. Your mother and I should have let you do more. I fear we sheltered you too much." His eyes glistened. "You cannot blame us, though. You are the child we never thought we would have."

Lydia nodded. She knew the story well. Her parents tried for years for a baby but her mother's womb remained closed. Long after they gave up hope, her mother found herself with child. The physician placed Mother on bed rest most of the time she was expecting, and Daddy had feared neither his wife nor his child would survive the birthing.

Daddy squeezed her hand, pulling her from her thoughts. "Mr. Harper is a fine man. You know I would not allow my treasure to go to just anyone. I prayed many a night over this." He gave a curt nod. "Yes, my child, I do believe God will bless this union."

Lydia ground her teeth. God wouldn't be able to bless any union of hers, but she would never shatter her father's heart by letting him know. She gave him the best smile she could muster. "Thank you, Daddy. I trust you have done what is best for me. You always do."

His eyes glistened. "Now, I see your poor mother is about to come to pieces, so I think you ought to get back to her."

"Yes, Daddy."

Lydia skirted a table laden with tarts and touched her mother's elbow.

"There you are! Where have you been?"

"Talking to Daddy."

Her shoulders relaxed. "Oh. Very good then. So long as you weren't hiding in that old tree."

Lydia opened her mouth to respond, but Mother didn't give her the chance. "Your father is about to give his speech, and then we will all wish you off. The carriage is already loaded."

"Oh, Mother. I do not understand why we cannot stay here for a few more days. Didn't Daddy stay at your father's house after your wedding? When Mary Hanson married, they spent an entire week at Lone Pine. Why must I go tonight?"

Mother waved her hand. "Enough with the questions. Your husband wishes you to go to Ironwood tonight. I tried to convince him otherwise, but he made up his mind. Your father agreed to the arrangement, so you are just going to have to make the best of it."

Lydia's insides twisted. Why would he want her away from everyone? What if all she knew of him was an act? What if, oh Lord, what if he...?

Lydia's breath came too rapidly to properly deliver oxygen to her brain. Her mother gripped her elbow. "Lydia! Stop that this instant. I will not have you fainting." Mother dragged her up the back steps and into the parlor.

"Sally! Get me a basin of water and a cloth!"

The girl scurried off and returned much quicker than should have been plausible. She bathed Lydia's brow and cheeks in the cool water. Mother frowned. "And after I spent all that time powdering your face."

As soon as Mother determined she wouldn't faint on the lawn, she hurried Lydia back onto the porch where her father and new husband were already waiting. As much as she wanted to savor her father's parting words so she could hold them in her heart for the days ahead, she could barely grasp them amongst her galloping thoughts and the pulsing blood in her ears.

Her family and neighbors cheered, and then all too soon Daddy kissed her cheek and assisted her into Mr. Harper's large carriage. At the head of the black carriage stood two matched bays pawing the ground as if they were impatient to return their master home on swift hooves. An old driver opened the door with a sweeping bow, and Mr. Harper helped her climb inside. They waved to the crowd until they rounded the bend.

Lydia watched her home disappear behind the trees and tried to focus her thoughts away from the tightness in her stomach.

"Are you well, Mrs. Harper?"

"What? Oh." Lydia placed a hand at the base of her throat. "Forgive me, I am not yet used to the title."

He chuckled. "Of course. But I do like the way it sounds."

Lydia smiled, the excitement and humor in his voice quieting her discomfort. He did seem to be a good man. Sweet, generous, and quick to laugh.

"How long will it take us to return to your plantation?"

"Two hours or so if we keep at a good trot. This drought keeps the roads compacted, so we should have easy travels."

Two hours. All that remained until her marriage vows became real and her new life began. Lord help her. Only two hours left of the only life she'd ever known.

Mr. Harper did his best to engage her in conversation, and she tried to calm the rolling in her stomach and answer his questions, though she feared she did a deplorable job of holding up her end. The time passed all too quickly, and they arrived in front of a house she guessed to be at least twice the size of her childhood home. It had grown too dark to see it properly. Mr. Harper leapt from the carriage and offered his hand to help her step down. She slipped her gloved fingers into his large palm and placed her foot on the ground.

A cheer erupted and her free hand flew to her mouth. She scolded herself. Too many times today she'd acted like a skittish young girl. Mr. Harper would have no respect for her at all. She'd been so focused on stepping down from the unusually tall carriage without falling that she had not even noticed the group gathered in the dancing lamplight on the massive front porch.

Curses. She kept forgetting her promise to herself not to let this man get to her. She must keep her guard up. Then it wouldn't hurt so much later when the newness wore off, and he no longer put on an act to placate her.

A stream of dark faces spilled from the front door and down the steps, each one smiling and nodding, several hands clapping. Lydia offered a tight smile and looked to Mr. Harper for an explanation.

He leaned close to her ear. "They are excited to meet the new lady of the house. They've not had one since my mother died ten years back. I believe they feared I may never wed."

Lydia lifted a hand to the people and inclined her head. She'd known Mr. Harper lived alone at Ironwood, his parents both having died of influenza not long after its completion, but she'd not been aware of his people's obvious admiration of him. This gathering did not seem required, but rather brought about by their own free will. Mr. Harper appeared both surprised and pleased at their presence. Interesting.

While she stood untangling her thoughts, Mr. Harper swept her off her feet and into his arms as if she were nothing more than a sack of potatoes.

He kissed her briefly on the mouth, dropping her traitorous heart to her stomach and drawing more cheers from the porch. They parted the way for their master and cleared from the front door. Mr. Harper carried her inside and placed her gently on the hardwood floor.

"Welcome to Ironwood, my lady."

Four

The lands of Cedar Hall Plantation

"You hear that?" Ruth whispered.

Bridget stirred next to her. "Huh?" Her groggy voice indicated she'd not yet regained full use of her senses.

"Shhhh. I heard somethin'."

Bridget sat up, sleep falling off her. They sat quietly, barely breathing. Nothing but the sounds of birds twittering in the early predawn light filled the air.

Bridget shrugged. "You probably just heard a squirrel."

"Didn't sound like no squirrel."

"So what did it sound like?"

Voices. Men. But, she couldn't be sure, and she didn't want to rake Bridget's already raw nerves. She shrugged. "Don't know."

Bridget stood and brushed the dried leaves from her skirt. "We better be gettin' on back. The fire shoulda died down by now. We needs to see what's got to be done."

Ruth ran her hand over her matted hair. "I's been thinkin' about that. Do you really think we should go back?"

Bridget's eyes widened. "What you mean?"

"I mean we's the ones that started that fire. If they figure that out, what do you thinks goin' to happen to us?"

Bridget crossed her arms over her large bosom. "And what you thinks gonna happen to us if we become runaways?"

Ruth heaved a sigh. "I didn't say that."

"It's what you meant."

"No, I – "

"Hush!"

Ruth stilled, gooseflesh rising on her arms. She'd heard it too. The voices again. Closer this time.

The sisters dropped to their knees. "That sounds like men. What should we do?"

Bridget's gaze darted around the thick underbrush they'd spent the remainder of the night among. "I don't know," she said. "We can't be called runaways. We ain't left our lands. Maybe they's lookin' for everyone after the fire."

She rose to her feet and stepped out from behind the tree.

"No!" Ruth whispered. "You don't know that."

"Over there!" Someone shouted. "I see a Negro hiding by that tree!"

Ruth grabbed Bridget's arm. "Run! Them ain't none of our people. We need to get back to the big house."

They dashed through the trees, ducking in and out of low hanging limbs, briars shredding their already pitiful skirts. The underbrush thinned and Ruth could see a clearing up ahead. "Come on! I think I see an openin'. We's almost there."

Suddenly Bridget screeched, her hand jerked from Ruth's. A dirty man with greasy hair snatched her sister up against his chest, holding her tight. "I got 'em boys!"

Other boots pounded over sticks and dried leaves. "Run!" Bridget cried.

Ruth straightened her shoulders and stood her ground. "We ain't runaways. We still on Harris lands!"

The greasy head man whistled. "Listen at this one here!"

A thick hand wrapped around her wrist. She looked into the face of a massive white man with a beard reaching to his chest. His eyes were hard. She turned her attention back to the greasy one.

"I said we ain't runaways. We's on our way back to the big house now. We only slept here in these woods 'cause the fire was too hot, and we didn't know how far it was gonna run."

The burly one holding her wrist laughed from his gut, and the hairs on the back of Ruth's neck stood on end. She tried to swallow, but all moisture left her mouth.

Another man stepped through the trees. He wore a floppy hat low on his wide brow, his eyes set too deep into his head. "We don't care none where you came from, or where you think you're going, Negro. You belong to me now."

Ruth tried to pull away from her captor, but he held fast, unfazed by her efforts.

"Come on, boys," the one with the floppy hat said. "These two'll have to do. Don't see any others out here. We best be moving on." He eyed Bridget. "Nice shape on that one, bet she'll bring a good price."

Ruth's heart hammered. She struggled harder, slamming her head back into the bearded chin behind her. The man let out a yowl and let her go as he reached for his face. Ruth darted to the side.

"Run, Ruth!" Bridget shouted. She hesitated. She couldn't leave her sister here with these men. Going for help wouldn't do much good. Mr. Harris might send someone looking for a stolen slave, but he might also start asking questions. He was probably too concerned with the fire to care if one got away.

A hand wrapped around her throat. "You're gonna regret that, Negro." He squeezed hard. She couldn't breathe. Ruth kicked her feet, but the man only hefted her higher, making her toes barely scrape the ground. Her vision started to grow fuzzy around the edges.

"Stop! Don't kill her. Please. I promise! I promise we'll be good!" Bridget's voice sounded muffled, like she was trying to talk under water.

Ruth grew weak, her kicks losing vigor. Bridget wailed again, and then everything went black.

Her head hurt. Pain throbbed at both temples. Ruth cracked open one eye, then immediately squeezed it shut against the searing light. Voices jumbled together around her along with the sounds of stamping hooves and clanging dinnerware. Where was she?

Memories flooded back, and she jerked awake, instantly regretting the sudden movement. Her head swam and her vision threatened to fade again. Ruth struggled to sit upright with her hands bound behind her back. She sat at the edge of a clearing near a tree. Movement to her left caught her attention. A young boy with wide eyes stared at her and a few others huddled nearby. She could only guess where they'd come from. They weren't Cedar Hall field hands.

Her gaze swung back out in front of her. She seemed to be in some sort of camp. Besides the small gathering of people who looked starved and terrified, there were three ragged tents with two horses hobbled nearby. Two of the white men who'd snatched her, Greasy Hair and Big Beard, sat by the fire roasting a rabbit over the flames. Panic gripped her chest. Where was Bridget?

One of the tent flaps rustled, and the man with the floppy hat stepped out, tugging on his breeches. His gaze slid over to her and when their eyes met his lips parted into a yellowed smile. He turned and walked over to the fire, slapping Greasy Hair on the shoulder. Both men laughed.

"So's it my turn now?" Big Beard asked.

Floppy Hat shook his head. "I ain't done with that one yet. When I've had my fill, you can have her."

Bile rose into the back of Ruth's throat.

"How's come you get to have first go?" Big Beard grumbled.

"'Cause this here's my operation. Don't you be forgettin' that. You do your job like you're supposed to, or I'll turn you in to them that was huntin' your hide."

Big Beard stood up, towering over the other two. Greasy Hair flinched and kept his focus on turning the rabbit. "You think you're the boss of me, Byram? I joined this outfit 'cause you promised me easy money. If you get to take pleasure in the goods, then so do I." His beefy face reddened and the muscles in his neck flexed.

Floppy Hat, the one the big man called Byram, looked a little pale, but she had a hard time telling with white folks. He looked to be trying real hard to hide the fact he feared the man standing over him.

Byram lifted his hand. "Now, now, Frank, I ain't trying to spoil your fun. Tell you what. You can have first go at that one." He pointed at Ruth.

No!

She struggled against the coarse rope binding her wrists. Frank grinned and started walking toward her, slow and steady like the lumbering bear she imagined him to be, and every bit as dangerous as ones she'd heard about in the stories. Worse, even.

Her stomach wrenched. Her hands became slick with sweat, and she tugged as hard as she could on the cord that stole her freedom. One hand slipped a little.

Frank stood over her. "Looks like this one's got some white in her. Guess that master of yours likes to play around with the livestock, huh?"

Greasy Hair and Byram laughed.

If she could just get her hand a little farther...

"See now, Frank. I'm fair. Albert, there's a young one over there been tryin' to hide." Frank pointed past Ruth to a girl who couldn't have yet reached her woman years, holding the hand of the captive woman next to her. The elderly woman drew the child to her chest. Frank grinned. "Scrawny thing. Perfect for the likes of you."

"Ain't in the mood."

Frank laughed and turned his attention away from Ruth and the others. She doubled her efforts in pulling free. The rope dug into her skin and blood started to trickle down her fingers. Almost. Just a little more and...

"What's the matter Albert? You ain't into the girls?"

Albert shrugged. "You do what you want. I'm here for the money, and then I'm done. I don't want no part of ravishing children. It ain't right." He pulled the rabbit from the fire.

Frank scratched his head. "But they's just slaves."

Albert stared at him looking like he wanted to say something. His gaze darted to Ruth. The tiniest bit of compassion flickered. She latched on to it and shot him a pleading glare.

Albert shrugged. "Food's done. Why don't you eat first?"

Frank cursed and spat in Albert's direction. "I got a different appetite right now. You boys go on ahead."

Albert didn't say anything more. He tugged the rabbit free of the stick with his knife and slid it on a dented pie plate.

Frank stepped closer to Ruth. She kicked and thrashed, connecting with his shin. Frank reached down and grabbed her hair, hauling her to her feet.

She screamed.

From the side of her vision, she caught sight of Bridget stumbling out of the tent holding her torn dress to her chest. Her eyes were full of fear, and her lip bled. Ruth forgot about the pain in her scalp. She balled her freed fist and swung as hard as she could. Her knuckles connected with the white man's nose and it gave a satisfying crack.

He dropped her. Ruth hit the ground and rolled to her side, breathing hard. She'd never struck a white person before. Now she would hang for sure.

Frank growled and smeared the blood from his nose across his sleeve. He called her a word she'd never heard before. "You gonna pay for that."

Ruth struggled back in the dirt, rocks and branches scratching her legs. He stepped closer and reached out when a gun blast rang through the air.

"What you fellows doing out here?" A man in a wide brimmed hat stood at the edge of the trees holding a shotgun aimed right at Frank.

Byram jumped to his feet. "We's just traveling through. Moving some of Mr. Harris' property down to some family land whilst they deal with that fire."

Should she scream? Yell out that they'd been stolen? She glanced to Bridget. She gave a small shake of her head. Agreed. Best wait to see what this man was about. Likely as not he'd be no friendlier than the others, and her protests would only lead to more trouble.

The man in the hat narrowed his eyes. "Seems like he'd need plenty of help around to take care of all that needs to be cleaned up, wouldn't you think?"

Byram crossed his arms over his thick chest and glared at the man. "What's it matter to you?"

The man with the shotgun spat. His gaze slid over to Frank. "I hear there's a reward on that fellow there."

Frank stepped toward the intruder, blocking Ruth's view of him. She glanced back to Bridget. They locked eyes and a message shot between them. Ruth nodded.

Bridget eased slowly away from the tent and closer to the edge of the tree line. Ruth gathered her feet under her and slowly stood up behind the lumbering form of the big man in front of her.

"What business you got with me?" Frank bellowed. "Who are you, anyway?"

Ruth stepped quietly backward to increase her distance from the thick scent of sweat and liquor drifting off Frank's wide back. Her stomach rolled. A twig snapped under her foot, and Ruth's heart dropped. No one noticed.

"My name's of no consequence to you."

A shot gun blast rattled the air, and Frank dove to the ground. Ruth didn't wait to see what would happen. She broke for the trees and scurried through the bramble as quickly as she could, praying Bridget did the same.

More shots fired, and men shouted behind her, filling the air with curses and the smell of smoke. Ruth tripped on a root and fell to the ground, scraping her hands on the forest debris. She dared a look behind her. No Bridget. She had to be coming! They were almost free. She scrambled to her feet and searched the area around her. No one followed. She could make it to freedom. But she couldn't leave her sister. It wasn't Bridget's fault any of this had happened.

She clutched her hand over her heart and tried to keep the despair from rendering her immobile. All her fault. The fire, her mother and brother, and now this. No. She couldn't think on that now. She had to get them away.

Ruth crept slowly back to the tree line. Where did Bridget go? There. Her sister crouched behind the tent, just out of sight of the man with the floppy hat. Their eyes met. Bridget shook her head and put a finger to her lips. She pointed to the big man just two paces away from her. Ruth crouched low. Silence settled and Ruth tried to control her heavy breathing so it wouldn't give her away.

"Look here now, I got equal share in these slaves, and when we sell them, I'll have a hefty sum. Why worry with hauling me all the way into the law when you could make more from these here than from me?" Frank said.

The man with the gun let out a loud hoot and laughed. Ruth narrowed her eyes at Frank. Whatever he'd done, it must have gotten him in a lot of trouble.

"No, I think I'm going to collect that reward. Can't wait on your share and hang around to see if you're going to run off."

The other two men didn't speak. The man with the gun raised it to his shoulder and took aim at Frank. "Now, are you going to come with me or not?"

Frank looked to Byram, but Byram kept his head down. Ruth crouched lower in the trees and looked to Bridget again. She motioned for her to come on. Bridget pressed her lips together, and after a long moment finally nodded.

Frank dove behind the tent, nearly on top of Bridget as a shot gun blast tore through the flimsy fabric. Bridget screamed and scrambled away from Frank and dashed to Ruth. Ruth grabbed her hand and pulled her through the trees.

"Run!"

They hurried through the brush, a man howling behind them. Ruth pulled Bridget along, desperate to get away while the white men fought. Bridget's hand suddenly jerked out of hers, and Bridget cried out.

Ruth spun around to find Bridget on the ground, holding her ankle and tears streaming down her face.

"Come on! You got to get up!"

"I can't!" Bridget wailed.

"You got to or we are both gonna die!"

Ruth looped her sister's arm around her shoulders and lifted her to her feet. "Can you walk on it?"

Bridget tested a little weight on her foot and immediately buckled. She shook her head, biting her lip. "I'm sorry," she whispered. "You go on without me. Get away from these awful men." The tears crested her eyes and flowed unheeded down her cheeks.

"No. I won't leave you. All we's got is each other now." Ruth pulled on Bridget. "Just lean on me. We can still make to somewhere to hide before they realize we's gone."

They hobbled through the woods, Bridget leaning heavily on Ruth and Ruth fighting through the thick underbrush as best she could. She didn't know if she would be able to support Bridget much longer. They needed somewhere to hide. And soon.

Please, God. Can't you help us?

"Look!" Bridget said, pulling Ruth's gaze from the forest floor. "I see a big tree over there that's fallen. I bet we's can get under there."

Ruth looked to where her sister pointed. A massive oak had uprooted recently, its thick branches snaring on the surrounding woods and preventing it from completely falling to the ground. The tangled mess of limbs created a thick covering almost like a tent. Ruth exhaled a sigh of relief, and they made their way to it.

Crawling on hands and knees, they scooted through the limbs. The wilting leaves still clung to the branches and provided them a thick blanket of cover.

They huddled together on the damp ground. "Let me see that ankle."

Bridget stretched her leg out for Ruth to see. It was starting to swell. Ruth shook her head. "We's gonna have to get you to some kinda doctor."

"How you think we's gonna do somethin' like that?"

Ruth ground her teeth. She didn't know. Even if they evaded the white men long enough, there were bound to be others that would either take them for themselves or send them back to Cedar Hall. "Don't worry. We'll think of somethin'."

Bridget sighed. "I don't see how –"

"Shhhhh!"

Bridget snapped her mouth shut and huddled closer to Ruth. Neither dared to breathe. Footsteps. Bridget looked to Ruth with wide eyes, a whimper escaping her throat. Ruth squeezed her hand.

"I know you's in there." Byram's deep voice called. He laughed, but it was a dark sound with no humor. "Come on, now. You didn't really think that you could escape me, did you?"

Ruth swallowed the thick lump in her throat and tugged on Bridget's arm, pointing to a small hole in the leaves just behind her. They turned over onto their knees and started to crawl out from underneath the tree.

Bridget screamed. "He's got me!"

Ruth whipped her head around to see Byram holding tight onto Bridget's injured ankle, his thick sausage fingers digging into the tender flesh. Bridget wailed as he pulled her backward.

"I told you, you're mine!"

He snatched Bridget from under the cover of the tree, and then held her up by one arm. Ruth scurried out just as his beefy hand landed a slap across Bridget's face. "*I* am your master now. Why do you make me punish you?" He slapped her again, her head rolling back.

"Stop!" Ruth cried, grabbing onto his arm and trying to claw his hand free from Bridget's skin. He growled at her. "I'll deal with you later." He shoved hard, sending her to the ground.

He let Bridget slide to the forest floor and then nudged her with his big boot. "Are you going to run away from me again, girl?"

"No! Please, I'm sorry!"

He pulled back and landed a solid kick to her stomach, and she curled into a tight ball.

"Please! Please stop! You's goin' to kill her!" Ruth screamed.

He stopped with his foot raised and turned his enraged gaze on Ruth. Bridget moaned and he looked down at her, shock flitting across his features. He shook his head. "Why'd you make me do it?" He turned and grabbed Ruth's wrist and twisted until she cried out. "No more lip out of you. You hear me?"

Ruth nodded, the fire shooting up her arm stealing her breath. He dropped her arm and picked up Bridget, throwing her limp body over his shoulder. He held on to her with one arm and grabbed Ruth with the other. Then he took them through the woods and back to the camp Ruth had hoped to escaped from. She saw no sign of Frank and Albert or the man with the gun, only the frightened expressions of the captives who must have been too afraid to run during the commotion.

Byram tossed Bridget on the ground. She didn't move. Byram picked up a rope and tied one end to Ruth's wrist and then linked all the colored people together, Ruth on one end and Bridget on the other, before disappearing into his tent.

When the sounds of Byram's snoring split the silence, Ruth called to Bridget in a harsh whisper.

"Bridget!"

She moaned.

"Bridget, you okay?"

"No, child. I don't think she is." The elderly woman with kind eyes and missing teeth looked at her with sadness. The woman was tied directly to her sister and had been separated from the little girl she'd earlier been trying to protect from Frank.

Ruth crawled over to her sister, the others being kind enough to move with her and allow her the ability to reach Bridget.

Ruth cradled Bridget's head in her lap. "Bridget? Can you hear me?"

A full moon overhead gave enough light for her to see Bridget's eyes flutter open. "I'm sorry," she whispered.

Ruth shook her head, tears spilling over. "Don't you be sorry. This is all my fault. You's gonna be okay. Don't worry."

Bridget gave her a weak smile. "Think Momma'll have some biscuits for us in the mornin'?"

Ruth choked back the sob in her throat and stroked her sister's hair. "Yes. Yes, I'm sure she will."

Bridget smiled, and her eyes drifted closed. Ruth stroked her hair and let the tears fall until her eyes ran dry.

Five

Ironwood Plantation
March 17, 1862

*L*ight fell through the open curtains and pooled on the floor, bathing the huge room in warmth. Lydia stretched under the bedcovers and marveled at her new home. Before the light had fully touched the sky, her new husband had risen, dressed, and began his day. He had promised to return for breakfast, and then show her around the house and the grounds.

She sat up in the feathered bed, exceedingly grateful to be given a room of her own. Mother and Daddy had never shared a room, though she heard some couples did. She slipped her toes from beneath the coverings and felt the thick, green rug that covered the hardwood floor. Had he known her favorite color? Perhaps he'd made inquiries.

She smiled at the amount of thought he must have put into readying the room. On the wall opposite her canopied bed wide enough for two, stood a wooden armoire, larger than she'd ever seen and with more than enough room for her few dresses. She had a desk, a dressing table and mirror, a wash basin and screen, and more space in a single room than seemed practical.

She looked down at her thin nightdress and remembered the night before. She inspected the sheets beneath her. Mother had said a bride was supposed to have a bit of blood on the bedclothes. Would he notice its absence? Her heart raced. She leapt from the bed and pulled the sheets free, hoping to wad them and send them to wash before he thought to inspect them.

Heat rose in her cheeks. Mother proved right. It was nothing at all like what horses do. He was gentler than she expected even though she'd been little more than a stiff board. After their act was finished, he immediately asked she no longer call him Mr. Harper. He'd winked and said they knew one another well enough now to call each other by their given names.

She had to appreciate the fact his disposition was given to humor. Of course, she supposed he was correct but at the same time she feared he would never really know her, her true self, at all. Lydia finished tugging the cotton coverings from the deep recess of the mattress and had them bundled in her arms when a quick knock sounded at the door.

"Ma'am?"

Lydia glanced around the room and decided to dump her armload beside the trunk sitting at the foot of the bed. "Yes?"

"Can I come in ma'am?" said the female voice on the other side of the door. Lydia looked down at her night dress and scanned the room for a robe. She didn't see one.

"I'm, um, not quite ready yet." She hurried over to the armoire and flung open the door. An array of brightly-colored dresses clogged the space. Where had they all come from? She quickly shifted through them. Day dresses, ball gowns in every color, thick heavy taffeta and smooth silk.

"Ma'am?"

"One moment!"

She recognized none of the garments. Then she remembered she'd not even unpacked her trunk. Mother had said her husband planned on surprising her. Did he have this entire wardrobe fashioned for her?

Another tap at the door.

Robe. She needed a robe. She shifted through the clothes again. Nothing she could throw on in an instant.

"Ma'am? You's all right?"

Lydia sighed and padded over to the door and opened it a crack. She looked into the wide face of a dark skinned woman standing primly on the other side. The woman lowered into a slight curtsey, balancing a pile of fresh laundry in her hands. "Good mornin', ma'am."

"Good morning." Lydia stood there, unsure what to do next. Could she simply send the woman away?

"Mightst I come in ma'am? The master has sent me to assist you."

"With what?"

The woman frowned. "With your dressin' and readyin' for the day. He says I'm supposed to assist you untils you find a girl of your own, seein' as how you didn't bring one."

Lydia grimaced and glanced down at her thin covering. "I'm sorry, uh..."

"Lucy."

"Lucy. I'm Lydia."

"Yes, ma'am."

"I, well, I can't seem to find a robe and all I have is this nightdress." She heaved a sigh, heat creeping up to her ears.

Lucy shook her head. "You didn't have someone dress you before?"

Lydia clenched her teeth. They would think her a country farmer's daughter for sure. She couldn't possibly tell Lucy she often ran around without a corset or hoops in simple dresses that allowed freedom of movement. That was what children did, and she was now a woman. She squared her shoulders and widened the door without another word.

Lucy stepped past her, and then stopped at the bed. "Where's your bedclothes, ma'am?"

Lydia paled. "I removed them."

Lucy frowned, but lowered the fresh sheets on to the bed, then walked over to the white pitcher and removed it from the basin. "I done brought up a bucket of warmed water. I's goin' to go fill the pitcher so's you can wash up."

She bustled out and closed the door behind her with a soft click. Lydia scurried over to the wad of sheets. She stared at them. Would they be shown to Charles? Did men still do such things? Before she could contemplate a way to handle the dilemma, Lucy opened the door and walked over to the basin, pouring the water inside. "If you want to be washin' yourself, I'll get your clothes out for the day."

She couldn't choose her own things? Lydia frowned but didn't argue. Life would be different here. She might as well make the best of it. She eyed the dressing screen and slipped behind it, removing her nightdress. She peaked around and saw Lucy digging in the trunk with her back turned.

Lydia quickly washed herself and dried her damp skin with the towel hanging off the side of the basin table.

Lucy draped a pair of stockings, drawers, and a chemise over the top of the screen and Lydia quickly dressed. She stepped out from behind the privacy shield and allowed Lucy to help her into a corset, hoop slip, petticoat, and pale pink dress.

"Now I's goin' to do your hair."

Lydia nodded, swallowing the lump that gathered in her throat.

A knock sounded at the door. Before she could answer, it swung open. Charles stepped in, a large smile on his face. "Good morning!"

She smiled shyly at him, resenting the heat that crept into her cheeks upon remembrance of the night past.

"All finished ma'am. Send for me if you needs anythin' else." Lucy gathered the discarded bed linens and Lydia's nightgown and hurried from the room. Lydia let out a long breath of relief.

One crisis averted, Lydia turned in the small vanity seat to regard her new husband. His gaze drifted to the stripped bed, but his expression revealed nothing.

"Are you ready to go down to the dining room?"

Lydia rose from her seat. "I am."

"After we eat I shall show you the house."

"That sounds lovely."

"And afterward, would you care to go for a ride?"

Lydia brightened. "I would."

Charles lifted his eyebrows. "Good. Then I shall show you the reaches of the plantation. Perhaps we might even enjoy a noon meal out of doors."

He offered his arm, and Lydia looped her hand into the crook of his elbow. Something tingled down her spine, but she chose to ignore it.

Six

Somewhere in the woods of Mississippi

Ruth kneaded the sore muscles in her neck. Her stomach complained at not having any food for the last two days, but she had more important things to worry her than hunger. More times than she could remember, she'd looked back to the end of the line to check on Bridget. Seven others separated her from her sister. She didn't know where they came from. She'd didn't even care to ask. What did it matter where they'd come from when all that mattered was where they were all going?

The two closest to Bridget took turns helping her walk, shouldering her weight. If not for the kind woman and the young boy of about twelve years that kept her sister moving, Ruth feared Bridget might have been left behind. Bridget stumbled along, her drawn face evidence she could no longer muster the sad smile she'd tried to offer Ruth throughout the long day of walking.

They'd started early in the morning when the sky began to gray with the coming light and hadn't stopped for even the most basic necessities. They stayed out of sight, passing through fields and down a lonely road. Ruth hadn't seen the first soul. Not that she expected help to come from any strangers they might pass. The sun began its daily descent, and Ruth longed to stop placing one foot in front of the other if only for a few moments.

Finally, when the procession slowed to the point they were stumbling over themselves, despite how many times Byram cracked his whip at their gaunt bodies, he reined in his horse and moved them into a clearing. He wrapped his thick fingers around Ruth's wrist and dragged her to a large pine, tying her end of the rope securely to it. She sank to her knees, her body too weak to continue to stand.

A moment later he returned to the tree again, securing the other end of the rope around the tree, leaving the captives bound to it and bunched underneath. When he disappeared into the woods, Ruth scooted as close to Bridget as she could get.

"You all right?" she whispered.

Bridget nodded, drawing her knees up to her chest. "I wanna go home."

Ruth gripped her hand, feeling her sister's cold, clammy skin despite the muggy air. Tightness gripped her chest, making each breath hard to bring in. "Don't worry. We's gonna get out of this. I know it. And then we'll head north. I hear there's free Negros up there."

Bridget gave her a sad smile. "Promise me you'll run for it if you can. Run north as far as you can go and live a free life for both of us."

Ruth gripped Bridget's fingers tighter. "We's both goin'. We can make it."

Bridget sighed and lifted her face to the canopy of thin needles overhead. "Promise me."

A sob threatened to escape her throat. She shook her head. The others eyed them. Ruth knew there would be no fight from this bunch. Though kind, they weren't the type to run. Didn't they see? If they didn't try they might not survive.

Byram stomped back to their huddled forms, silencing their conversation. He pulled a knife from his behind his back and examined the way the sun glinted off the blade. His wicked lips parted revealing his yellowed smile. He pointed the blade at Bridgett.

"Soon as I get that tent up, you'll be joining me."

The monster! Ruth strained against her bindings, the rough fibers tearing into her still raw wrists. He deserved no less than to find the fires of the pit. She spat at him. The spittle landed just shy of his worn boots.

Byram laughed. "And when I'm done with that pretty sister of yours, maybe you'll be next. You're not quite as nice to look at, but you still got all the right parts."

Her heart hammered in her chest. The others lowered their gazes, looking at swollen feet and the ground underneath them. She'd have no help from them. If she and Bridget were going to survive, it'd be by her own devices.

Ruth rose to her feet and stepped in front of Bridget as much as her bindings would allow her. "You leave her alone."

Byram's heavy brows pulled together and the muscles in his jaw twitched. "You don't get to say what I will and won't be doin'."

Ruth crossed her arms over her chest to conceal her trembling hands, but pushed as much fierceness into her stare as she could muster.

Byram growled and stepped closer to her. Ruth forced herself to hold his fearsome gaze. Before she could react, his arm swung and the back of his meaty hand smacked across her face, snapping her head around. She blinked away the sting of tears and regained her defiant position. The metallic taste of blood filled her mouth.

Byram grinned. "So, you're a tough one, huh? Well let's just see how tough you really are." He balled his fist and slammed it into her stomach. The breath left Ruth's lungs, and her body immediately crumpled around the pain radiating in her belly. She groaned and fought to regain her footing, stumbling but once again regaining her stance. She leveled her eyes on him.

Surprise flickered across Byram's face, quickly replaced by burning fury. Ruth ground her teeth and held his gaze. "Let her alone. She's no use to you now, anyway. She's too weak." She hesitated, and then straightened her shoulders. "I'll go with you instead."

Bridget gasped from behind her, but Ruth kept her gaze on Byram. Maybe if she could convince him she'd be willing, she could get him to release her from the ropes and she could figure out a way to escape.

Byram lifted his eyebrows. "So now you're eager for your turn, eh? Don't you worry, you'll be getting it soon enough."

He stepped closer and placed a meaty hand on her shoulder, then let it slide down the front of her dress and over her small curves of womanhood. Ruth fought to keep down the bile that rose up her throat and stood still under his touch. When his hand reached lower, she rammed her knee into the place between his legs where men were most tender.

He yowled and jumped back, spewing a string of curses. She watched in horror as he bent over double. He'd never give her the opportunity to escape now. What had she done?

Ruth glanced at Bridget, her sister's eyes wide. "Look what you did! He's gonna be madder than ever now." Bridget hissed.

Her heart fluttered as Byram stood upright again, his breathing labored. In one stride he towered over her. Ruth fought a hard battle with the fear raging in her chest but couldn't contain it.

Byram raised a fist over her head and brought it down with such force that she staggered, blackness edging in around her vision. She blinked rapidly but couldn't free herself from the dizziness. Ruth's knees buckled and she slipped to the ground.

Somewhere far off a familiar voice called to her. She tried to remember who it belonged to. She forced her eyes to open and focus. Byram grabbed hold of Bridget's arm and hauled her away from the others. "No!" Ruth croaked, lifting a heavy arm to stop him. She tried to gain her feet, but the rising tide of darkness sucked her into its depths.

Her bed felt too hard. Had she rolled off and onto the floor? "Momma?"

Why was her throat raw? Ruth swallowed hard and opened her eyes into thin slits. The bright light caused her to become aware of a steady pounding in the back of her head. She moaned and rolled to her back. Rough ground scratched through her thin dress. She closed her eyes and told herself to go back to sleep. When she woke again, she'd be in her own bed, and the nightmare would be over.

Birds twittered overhead and a slight breeze lifted the heaviness of the air. Something scurried over her leg, and her eyes popped open. Massive limbs spread their shade over her, bits of sunlight tumbling down through the bright green needles. Confusion furrowed her brow until the memories flooded her. She bolted upright and immediately regretted it. Her head swam and caused a queasy feeling in the pit of her empty stomach. She clenched her eyes tight and focused on steady breathing until the feeling subsided. She opened her lids slowly to allow them to adjust to the light.

Around her, the others slept curled and huddled together in awkward positions against their restraints. Her pulse quickened.

No Bridgett.

Ruth searched the area for Byram but didn't see him anywhere. If he'd pitched the tent last night, it had already been stowed away this morning. Where, then, was her sister?

She'd just begun to try to rip her hands free of the rope when he stepped out of the woods carrying a short shovel. Their eyes met, and he glared at her. The tiny bit of stale moisture remaining in Ruth's mouth evaporated. Without a word he strode over to the sleeping group and started kicking at them with his boot.

"Get up you lazy lot of weaklings! You ain't worth this here trouble."

The people startled awake, scrambling away from him as much as they could. The young boy that had helped Bridgett yelped when Byram landed a swift kick to his back.

They rose to their feet, eyes wide and white in their dark faces. Ruth stood and studied the hulking man as he cut the rope free of the tree.

"Where's my sister?"

He ignored her, yanking on the rope and sending the people stumbling. He dragged them a short distance through the woods to the road where his horse stood hitched to a wagon. He tied them to it and dug around in the back until he lifted free a long coil of leather. When did he get a wagon? She ground her teeth. If she'd been strong enough to stay awake she could have escaped while he went after it. She pulled herself up on her toes, praying Bridgett slept in the back of the wagon.

Empty, save a few supplies.

Ruth drew a ragged breath and willed her aching heart to ease. Wherever Bridget was, Byram looked like he planned on leaving her.

"I said where is my *sister*?" Ruth hissed through her clenched teeth.

Byram turned on his heel and unwound the coil of leather, sending the whip flying through the air and striking her skin with a loud crack. She cried out and gripped her arm, feeling warm blood slip through her fingers.

"Silence! All of you." Byram bellowed and swung up into the wagon, snapping the reins and sending the horse jumping forward. The wagon lurched and yanked them with it.

Ruth turned to look at the old woman behind her, silently pleading for any sort of answer. The old woman regarded her with compassionate eyes brimming with unshed tears and slowly shook her head. Ruth's heart threatened to render itself into shreds as she left the last of her family somewhere in the forsaken woods of Mississippi.

Seven

Oakville, Mississippi
April 25, 1862

*L*ydia contemplated her life over the last several weeks as she swayed with the gentle movement of the carriage. As April drew to a close, she found that married life had offered more independence than she expected. Charles let her move about freely, going into Oakville whenever she wished and filling her days as she saw fit. For as long as the sweet newness of marriage lasted, she would enjoy the freedom it brought.

They pulled into town and Tommy opened the carriage door for her, offering his frail old arm for support. Lydia smiled and rested as little of her weight as possible on him.

"You needs me to get anythin' whilst you shop, ma'am?"

Lydia nodded and pulled a small paper from her reticule. "Mr. Harper sent this list with items he says we need. I trust you can handle that?"

"Yes, ma'am." His ebony eyes showed a hint of amusement, and she tried not to let it affect her composure. Trying to understand her place at Ironwood seemed a delicate thing.

"Very well." She adjusted the wide brim of her hat to keep the sun's rays from darkening her skin and turned toward the general store.

She visited the bakery and picked out a few peaches from a cart, in no hurry to return home. It was a beautiful day to be outside. She'd just stepped onto the front porch of Willard's to pick out fabric and maybe some new tubes of paint, when she heard a whip crack. She assumed a wayward horse to be the cause of such a sound until it was followed by the most unholy moaning. She couldn't help but turn.

Pain throbbed through most of her body, but Ruth's heart was too numb to care. Startled gasps drew her attention from the dust swirling around her feet to the town that surrounded them. Buildings stood on either side of the street, white people in fancy clothes lining the sidewalks and gawking at them. She had no idea what town they traipsed through. She couldn't even be sure they were still in Mississippi.

Apprehension grew in her gut. Byram kept them out of sight ever since the man with the shotgun showed up, and his two partners disappeared. What were they doing parading down the middle of this town?

"Got fine stock here, folks. Come and see! Fine stock." He bellowed, sending a cold chill up her spine. He planned on selling them.

"Excellent prices! All strong workers. Three hundred fifty dollars for the males and three hundred for the females."

Didn't sound right. She was no expert on such things, but she'd heard enough field hands brag on their price to know Byram was trying to get what he could out of them and be done with it. Especially since he didn't have to split it with anyone anymore. She looked at the people tied to her, but they kept their eyes down.

Byram pulled his filthy hat from his head and ran his arm across his forehead. Ruth watched a few white men in suits step closer, their eyes holding curiosity. The only indication the others felt anything at all was the way they shuffled their feet. Should she be hopeful she might find a decent life away from this monster? Or did a worse one even now step closer, his evil masked by a clean face and expensive clothes?

Her face grew hot. She'd not be something for a man to spill his lust on. She'd die before allowing it. What did she have left to live for anyway?

Please, God. If you care about the cries of slaves at all, show me something so I know you are there.

Nothing.

She squared her shoulders and jutted her chin. No more. She'd die showing these people the demon Byram truly was, if only for the frail hope some soul would see him to justice.

She studied the onlookers. Were any of them capable of compassion? Did they feel anything at all? Byram grabbed her hair and pulled her forward, breaking her contemplation.

"This one here's strong. Good field worker. Got straight legs and a strong back." He sneered. "Make good breeding stock, too."

Breeding stock! She'd not be some man's cattle! Byram reached for her mouth, and she jerked her head away. He quickly grabbed for her again, clamping her jaw in his hand and holding her still. She ground her teeth together.

He pried her mouth open. "Got all the teeth."

He pushed her face away. Rage blackened her heart and clouded her thoughts. They would see. She pulled her head back and spat at him. People gasped. Whether the sounds came from the other captives or the onlookers, she couldn't be sure.

Byram turned slowly, his voice rumbling from his chest. "Yer going to regret that."

Hardly.

A spark lit in his eyes and he pulled the whip from his side. Ruth braced herself for the sickening crack. The leather end tore into her flesh. She reeled back and clasped her shoulder, but she didn't cry out. She would not give him the satisfaction of hearing her pain. She would be strong enough this time. He cracked the whip again and again – how many times she didn't know.

Her legs wobbled. She had to stay up. Her body refused and slipped to the ground. She sat helpless on her knees. The end would come now. She would welcome it.

"Stop!"

A clear voice rang out through the crowd and pushed past the throbbing in her ears. Ruth dared to raise her gaze.

Byram stood frozen, staring at a tiny white lady with a reddened face half hidden under a gaudy hat. Ruth blinked. The woman dressed like the ones she'd once spied coming in and out of Cedar Hall when she'd snuck close enough to see what happened at a ball.

The lady held herself with a posture of authority, but the slight quivering of her lower lip gave away the act.

The lady jutted her chin. "That's quite enough, sir. I intend to buy this one, and I'll not have you damaging her any further."

Byram didn't seem like he paid the woman no mind. Ruth willed her breathing to slow.

The woman dug into a little bag tied at her wrist and thrust a handful of paper into Byram's face. "I'll give you two-fifty for her. She's obviously going to need some work."

Bryam stared at her for a long moment and then sneered. "She's your problem now, lady." He turned and grabbed Ruth by the scalp and untied her ropes, thrusting her toward the lady. "Bet your husband ain't going to be too pleased you spent all your dress money on this here darkie."

Ruth swallowed hard. Had Byram really released her or was it some sort of cruel trick? She glanced around. She might could slip through the crowd and escape to… to what? Where could she possibly go? The woman suddenly grasped Ruth's arm and gently pulled her away. Ruth was too shocked to do anything but follow. After a few paces, the woman released her and stalked down the street through the onlookers who stared with open astonishment.

Ruth hurried to keep up with her. Maybe God had heard her prayer after all. She'd have to take her chances with the bold woman who'd given her money to save Ruth from Byram's fury. She could at least see where the woman lived and what she wanted with her. Ruth figured she owed the lady that much.

The woman glanced behind her, surprise painted all over her milky face. Ruth's brows pulled together. The lady walked faster, almost causing Ruth to break into a trot to keep up.

The lady stopped in front of a giant black carriage and yelled at an old man sleeping on a padded seat on the front.

"Tommy! Wake up!"

His eyes flew open, and he ran a hand over his face. "I's sorry ma'am. I thought – " he stopped short, gawking at Ruth. He snapped his jaw shut.

"We are going home, Tommy."

He turned his focus back on the lady. "Yes 'um." He glanced at Ruth again. "Where do I put, um, where do you want…?" He eyed the large chicken feed sacks stacked next to him in the driver's seat.

"Oh, for heaven's sake. I don't know. I guess she'll just have to ride in the back with me."

What?

The woman flung open the door and climbed in. Ruth looked at the old man. He shrugged and settled into his seat, pulling long reins from a box at the front. What should she do? Surely they didn't expect...

The woman stuck her head out of the door. "Well, come on, get in. We need to get Betsy to look at those cuts. Hurry up."

Ruth stared into her big blue-green eyes looking for any signs of cruelty or insanity. She saw neither. Well, she would cower no longer. This woman would hear Ruth's opinion whether she wanted it or not.

"It ain't proper for a field hand to ride in the carriage with a white lady."

The woman arched her dark brows. "As of now, you are my personal house girl. You will be traveling with me quite a bit, so you might as well get used to it."

House girl? Oh, Lord. Her arm throbbed. No sense in arguing. If she could get a chance to clean herself up, get some rest, maybe even something to eat...

She shrugged and stepped into the carriage. There were two seats covered in bright blue fabric. Ruth sat down carefully on the one across from the woman. She'd get the thing dirty for sure. Would that bring a lashing? It wasn't her fault she was in here. Still, she better touch as little as possible. She drew her feet as far under her as she could to avoid touching the mounds of fabric from the woman's puffy skirt.

The old man hollered at the horses, and the carriage lurched forward nearly tossing her from her seat. She gripped the cushion before she could think better of it. Now there'd be blood stains, too. The woman might not beat her, but her husband probably would after he saw the mess in his carriage.

She looked out the window and tried to get the pounding in her temples to stop.

Lydia took a moment to study the girl gripping the seat like she'd fall from it at any moment. Tall, fine-boned and willowy. Long, muscled arms. High cheek bones, an unusually thin nose. No shoes and filthy feet. If the girl noticed Lydia's gaze, she paid no attention. She was certainly different than the others. Mother's mousy little Sally blended into the walls. All Mother needed to do was flick her wrist, and Sally would appear from nowhere. No, this girl would be just the opposite. The thought loosed a smile on Lydia's lips.

When Charles first suggested she get a girl of her own, she'd imagined one much like Sally. The thought wasn't very appealing, so she'd told him there was plenty of help at Ironwood, doing this or that, and she didn't need another to be her shadow. But this girl was nothing like Sally. She was nothing like any slave Lydia had ever seen. And that intrigued her.

"What is your name?" Lydia finally asked having made her decision to keep the girl.

The girl turned her on her. "Ruth."

"Hello, Ruth. I am Mrs. William Charles Harper of Ironwood Plantation."

She nodded. "Yes ma'am."

"Where did you come from?"

Something flickered across Ruth's features but disappeared just as quickly. "Cedar Hall, in Natchez."

"And how did you wind up in the Delta?"

Ruth closed her eyes and took a deep breath, then stared out the window. When she finally spoke, her voice was hard. "House burned down and fire ate up most of the land with it. We ran off through the woods, tryin' to stay alive." She turned and narrowed her eyes at Lydia. "Not to escape."

Lydia nodded, tending to believe her given how easily she'd followed.

"But them white men, they didn't believe us. Said we was runaways. I don't know if Mr. Harris even knows they took us." She lifted her slim shoulders. "We were too tired to remember much 'bout how it happened, but we ended up with that… man. Then we was here."

She remembered Charles saying something about that fire some weeks ago. Lydia doubted the girl told the whole truth. But, then, what did it matter? They settled into silence, the soft plodding of the horse's hooves creating a soothing rhythm in the quiet afternoon.

Dust boiled from the road unhindered by the slightest breeze, evidence of the dry weeks the land endured. The fine red mist had a way of settling into every crease. Lydia brushed at her skirts, but the stubborn filth insisted on changing her gown's soft pink to old rust.

Ruth continued to stare out of the carriage as outskirts of town gave way to the graceful oaks leading to Ironwood. Lydia cleared her throat to gain the girl's attention, an unladylike gesture Mother often scorned.

"So, you were a field hand?"

"Yes, ma'am."

"Do you know anything about house work?"

"No, ma'am. Ain't never been in the big house."

Well, at least she was honest. "No matter. I'll have Lucy teach you everything you need to know."

"Yes, ma'am." She fidgeted in her seat. "Thank you, ma'am," she said, her voice nearly inaudible.

Lydia lifted her eyebrows. "Nonsense. My husband's been saying I need a girl of my own."

She dipped her chin.

"Besides," Lydia sighed. "That man was a monster."

Lydia closed her eyes and laid her head against the cushion and thought of what Charles would say about her spending her entire allowance on a field slave. He probably wouldn't approve. If it didn't work out, he could always send Ruth to the fields. Lydia opened her eyes into small slits and secretly watched the proud girl in front of her. She soon found herself hoping Ruth would remain with her, although she wasn't sure why.

Eight

"Lord, just look here at this child." The older woman who'd introduced herself as Betsy rested her hands on the bulk of her hips and stared at Ruth like she'd grown wings. Ruth dropped her gaze and shifted uncomfortably. What would she think about a strange field slave in her tidy kitchen? Ruth had no place being here. Not that she had a choice.

Betsy placed gentle fingers under Ruth's chin and coaxed her gaze upward. Betsy looked down with concern and shook her head. "You poor thing. Looks like you done been through somethin' right awful."

The warmth of the kitchen and the yeasty smell of bread felt like a balm on Ruth's battered heart. She passed her tongue over her dry lips and tried to smile. "I don't want to be no trouble."

Betsy released her chin and pointed a pudgy finger at her. "Now look here. I'm gonna get them cuts cleaned up, and then we's gonna get somethin' in your belly. Don't look like you's eaten for a week."

Ruth swallowed the lump in her throat and nodded. "Thank you."

Betsy bustled around the large area, her feet scuffling across the wooden floor and sending a slinking cat hurrying across to the shadows. She gathered her supplies, lowered herself to her knees, and began washing Ruth's arm with a warm, wet rag.

The tension in Ruth's shoulders slowly began to ease, and she took a deep breath. The woman finished cleaning her arm and then wrapped it in a white cloth.

"Now, that should do it."

Ruth looked down at the clean bandage secured around her arm and blinked away the tears that tried to gather in her eyes. Betsy set to work ladling a thick soup out of a large pot hanging over the fire. When the bowl brimmed to the top, she set it in front of Ruth. The steam brought up a delicious aroma, and Ruth remembered the hunger she'd long since learned to ignore.

"Lord, thank you for this here meal and for this precious child you done brought to Ironwood. In the name of our Jesus, amen."

Ruth had been too focused on the food to notice Betsy settled across the table from her.

"Now, eat up."

Ruth brought a spoonful of the delicious liquid to her lips and savored the flavor, trying not to shovel it in too quickly. When the bowl was half empty, she set down her spoon, feeling as if her insides might burst if she tried to down any more.

"My mother used to always pray before we ate," Ruth said before giving thought to her words.

"That's good. We should always thank the Lord for what He's given."

"The master don't mind it?" Ruth fidgeted with the handle of her spoon, not wanting to meet Betsy's eyes.

She laughed. "Of course not, child. What makes you think that?"

Ruth shrugged. Betsy studied her a moment. When she spoke again, her voice was gentle. "Mr. Harper's a good man. He treats all of us fair." She bobbed her head.

Could this truly be a place of safety? Too soon to tell. The kitchen lady probably just didn't know about the things that went on down in the quarters. House Negros were too pampered.

The door swung open and another colored woman swept in, her wide face full of questions. "You hear tell 'bout Mrs. Harper bringin' home a girl?"

The woman's eyes landed on Ruth and her mouth made a little O. She got control of herself and smoothed her bulky skirts, which were mostly hidden behind a prim white apron. She inclined her head. "And you's must be her. I'm Lucy."

"Ruth."

She stood uncomfortably in the doorway until Betsy chided her. "Get on in here and stop gawkin' at the poor girl."

Lucy stepped fully into the kitchen, pulling the door closed behind her. She stood taller than any woman Ruth had ever seen, with broad shoulders and a square jaw. Lucy held her spine as straight as a new sapling.

Ruth eased over on the bench and motioned for Lucy to sit next to her. The woman eyed the place too long before finally sitting down, arranging her skirts around her legs and smoothing invisible wrinkles.

"Mrs. Harper asked that I show you where you's goin' to stay and make sure you's comfortable and have time to rest. She says you gonna spend tomorrow gettin' better and can come to her the next day."

Why would the white lady care if she were comfortable? Ruth's brows drew together. She probably just wanted to be sure Ruth was healed enough to start working. Whatever silly nonsense she'd said about Ruth being a house girl would soon be forgotten. She best get as much rest as she could before they sent her to the fields.

"Well, come on then." Lucy got up and crossed to the door, turning to see if Ruth followed. Ruth rose, scooping up the remaining food her shrunken stomach was too full to eat and returned it to the cook.

"Thank you for the meal, Betsy."

The woman took the bowl from her and wrapped an arm around Ruth's shoulders. "It's goin' to be okay, little one. I'll take good care of you. Don't you be worryin'."

Ruth swallowed the lump in her throat and dared not hope in this woman's kindness. She turned and followed Lucy out the door where they immediately climbed a staircase attached to the outer wall. At the top of the steps, Lucy opened the door and ushered Ruth into a small but homey living space.

Sturdy handmade furniture filled the room, a quilted blanket spread across a sitting bench that appeared to be stuffed and covered in a soft material and large enough for two grown people to sit on side by side. A clean rug covered most of the wooden floor. Ruth scrunched it under her toes and marveled that something so soft should go underfoot. A different life for the chosen few who lived near the white family. She'd always heard it, but now she actually believed.

"This here is our shared space. She nodded toward a door to the left. Me and Betsy share that room there. Your room's back here. It ain't been used in a long while, but it'll do." Lucy opened a door and led Ruth into a nice-sized room with whitewashed walls, a single person bed, a chest of drawers and another rug on the floor.

Ruth's hand went to her throat. Surely they didn't mean for her to stay here? She turned questioning eyes to Lucy. Lucy shrugged. "Likes I said, ain't been used in a long while. Linens will need to be washed, but we's got some fresh ones you can put on until them's clean."

"I'll be usin' this room just tonight and tomorrow whilst I rest," she said, mostly to herself. "But where will I go after?"

Lucy frowned. "What you mumblin' about? I done told you. This here is *your* room."

It couldn't be. "How many others do I share it with?" She could make a pallet on the floor. She had no intention of ousting another from their bed even if it were only for one night.

Lucy put her hands on her hips. "What?" She shook her head. "You ain't listenin'." She narrowed her eyes at Ruth. "Is you missin' some of your sense? I heard of folks like that. Ain't quite right in the head. It's all right if you is, Lord loves all, but I just needs to know."

Indignation brought Ruth out of her stupor. She drew herself to her full height and looked Lucy in the eyes. "I'm not soft in the head!"

Lucy raised her eyebrows.

Ruth crossed her arms over her chest and let her gaze fall. "I just never thought I'd have a place like this."

Lucy face softened slightly. "Well, Mrs. Harper says you gonna stay here with us, and you is to be her new maid. This room here is where you'll stay."

Ruth let a small seed of hope bloom in her chest.

Lucy shook her head. "Unless of course Mr. Harper has other plans."

The seed shriveled and died.

Nine

Natchez, Mississippi
April 26, 1862

*C*harles' cousin slapped him on the shoulder, sending his mug of ale sloshing over the rim and into his dinner.

"So," Matthew Daniels said above the din of the other patrons filling the dining room at the inn, "I heard that bride of yours made quite a spectacle in the center of town."

Charles ran a hand through his hair and raised his eyebrows. "And what sort of gossip have you been dabbling in old boy?" Lydia seemed more the type to keep her head down and avoid attention. Still, she was an exceedingly beautiful woman, and he had left her too long at Ironwood already with his trip to Natchez. Had he allowed her too much freedom? Especially with the war pressing ever closer?

"My brother just rode in this morning. Told me all about how the new Mrs. Harper bought a slave right off the street."

Charles let out a low whistle and leaned back in his chair, his pork and cornbread forgotten. "Male or female?"

Matthew wrinkled his broad forehead. "Female."

The woman was full of surprises. "I told her she needed a maid, but I was planning on getting her one when I got the opportunity. Hasn't been much need for dressing girls at Ironwood."

Matthew settled his large frame on the bench beside Charles. Although five years his junior, his cousin stood a head taller than most men, and with Matthew's near-white blond hair, he was never hard to find in a crowd.

"Yes sir, he said a man came into town driving a ragged bunch through the street," Matthew said, settling in. He gave Charles a serious look. "Most likely stolen stock."

"And my wife walked up to purchase one?" Charles' eyebrows drew together. Stolen property was bound to have an owner coming after it.

Matthew waved to a curvy serving girl and ordered his dinner. When she scurried off, he returned his attention to Charles. "From what I heard tell, the man was beating the disrespectful Negro and it got out of hand. Out of nowhere, this lady comes running into the street demanding he stop. The lady paid for her and took her to a carriage. My brother noticed your symbol on the side and figured it must have been your new bride."

The eldest Daniels brother had not made it to Charles' wedding, as he was in Virginia at the time, so it made sense he would not have recognized Lydia straight away. Though there was a small possibility he'd been mistaken.

"Well, imagine that," Charles said. "I'm sure she's got the whole town's tongues wagging." He'd have to have a word with Lydia upon his return.

The serving girl returned with Matthew's food, and he winked at her. "How about you bring me some of that red eye, too." He turned to Charles "One for you?"

Charles shook his head. Hard liquor soured in his stomach, so he had long since learned to ignore it, opting only for small portions of milder drinks. The girl once again hurried off.

"When are you going to quit flirting with serving girls and find yourself a wife?" Charles jabbed Matthew in the ribs with his elbow.

Matthew grinned around a big forkful of food. "Look whose lecturing me on the appeals of bachelorhood."

Charles lifted his mug and directed it at Matthew. "As you recall, I found myself a wife."

Matthew laughed. "You certainly did. But seems to me I've still got plenty of time."

If Matthew had been the eldest son, Charles' uncle would have seen him wed by now. But as the youngest of four boys, Matthew had had far too little responsibility in his life. Uncle was always too preoccupied with the elder sons to worry much with the wild youth. Charles had taken it upon himself to mentor his cousin as best as he could.

Charles returned to his meal. He'd only gotten in two forkfuls when a man who'd had one too many cups bellowed over the crowd of men and soldiers with an evening pass from their nearby training camp.

"You see that boys? This here fellow don't seem like he's supporting our cause!" He thrust his chin out to an older man sitting at a small table by himself, his rigid back to the fire.

Hisses came from the men in the room and then everything turned quiet, all eyes landing on the man at the table with his hat pulled low over his eyes.

"We don't want any Yankee sympathizers dining with us tonight. So maybe you best be on your way!"

The tension in the room thickened. Charles had witnessed this scene in some form or another several times before. There were many of the older generation that wanted to maintain their connection to the markets offered in the North. New England had factories that needed their tobacco and cotton, and they didn't want to see war destroy all they'd built. Charles tended to agree, but kept his opinions to himself. The war had raged on for the past year, and thus far he'd gone through great lengths to avoid it.

The older man rose from his seat and let his gaze drift over the crowd. The serving girls had disappeared from their midst, likely hiding somewhere out of the way. "You boys are hot on your liquor and your foolish dreams of glory." His voice was touched with an accent Charles could not place.

The boisterous man pointed a bony finger at his opponent. "You would rather we stand by while they destroy our way of life, deny state's rights, and take our property from us?"

The older man stood quietly for a moment, his gaze locked on the one who challenged him. "And who are you to determine that men, women, and children are nothing but your property?"

Several men rose from their seats. Matthew moved to stand but Charles put a staying hand on his arm. Without warning, the younger man swung his fist. The older man moved like one of much fewer years and ducked under the fist meant to silence him. He jumped to the side, his coat tails swinging around him, causing the other man to stumble. Charles and Matthew gained their feet at the same time and covered the distance of the room as two other men grabbed hold of the old man and held him still.

The loud mouth regained his balance and let a fist fly into the restrained man's stomach. He doubled over in pain.

Cheers erupted from the crowd, and Matthew pushed through the throng, Charles following in the wake his cousin's massive size provided. The loud one balled his fist to release another blow, but instead of connecting with the helpless man's abdomen it landed solidly in Matthew's palm with a thud.

Matthew stood between the two men and glared down at the one whose fist he gripped in his hand. "This doesn't exactly seem like the fair way to go about it, does it now?"

The man winced and frowned up at Matthew. "You on the Union side too?"

Matthew flashed his wide grin. "Nope. Signed up to serve in the Confederate army this very morning. But you see, my momma taught me that here in the South we are gentlemen." He looked around at the men gathered around them. "I'm guessing all you fine southern boys had mommas that taught you the same thing."

Some of the men nodded, their gazes dropping to the floor. The two men gripping their captive dropped their hands, releasing the older gentleman. He straightened, tugging on the sides of his coat.

Charles slipped in behind the Union sympathizer and placed a hand under his elbow. He kept his voice low and calm and leaned in next to the man's ear. "I've a feeling these men won't be stayed long. My cousin has a way with words, but I'm afraid even he won't be able to hold off their war fever for long. I suggest we make our exit."

The man gave a brief nod.

Charles stepped backward, the man stepping with him as if they were performing some unrehearsed dance.

Matthew still held the men's attention. "And, my fine southern gentlemen, we know it's not proper to hold an outnumbered man while you beat him, now is it?"

The men grumbled. Charles turned and stepped to the edge of the crowd, skirting around to the back kitchen where he hoped the Inn had a rear door. Matthew's gaze flickered to Charles, and he gave an almost imperceptible nod. Charles had often envied his cousin's ability to command men so easily, but tonight he was grateful for it.

Matthew released his grip and flung down the smaller man's fist, his voice filling the room. "Southern pride runs deep. We will win this war because we are gentlemen of honor! Gentlemen who will fight to save their families and their homes from any threat that comes our way!"

The men erupted into cheers, thrusting their mugs into the air and sending ale and liquor over the hardwood floor. Charles slipped between them and into the heat of the kitchen, glancing over his shoulder to be sure the old man still followed.

"What's happening?" The young serving girl that had brought his dinner gripped his elbow.

The owner stepped up to Charles with questions in his eyes. "I've seen too many fights under my roof this last year. I've lost much of my property." The thin man's voice was strained.

The man behind Charles spoke. "Do not worry, friend. I believe the tide has turned this eve. If you would be so kind as to show me the door, I will remove myself and give you no further cause to fret."

The owner swallowed and nodded, relief flooding his reddened face. "Through there." He pointed to a door at the rear of the kitchen. "There's a small garden out back. Behind it is a gate that will lead you into the alley. Turn left and you will be back out on the main street."

"Thank you," Charles said.

The two men slipped out into the spice garden. When the gate closed behind them and they were left standing alone in the dark, the old man let out a great whoosh of air. "Sir, I must thank you and your large companion. I fear what would have become of me otherwise."

Charles nodded. "What they intended was not honorable."

The man studied him, his features shadowed under the meager light of the moon. "And what is your name, man of honor?"

"I am William Charles Harper of Ironwood."

The man inclined his head. "Major General Franz Kerchner of the United States Army. I am in your debt, sir."

He gave a slight bow and quickly turned on his heel. Charles watched him disappear into the night until he could no longer distinguish man from shadow.

Ten

Ironwood
April 27, 1862

The soft knock came early in the morning. Lydia expected it and had been awake since the first rays of the sun's light touched the earth. Charles would soon return home, and she could only guess at his reaction to her behavior. Today would be Ruth's first day in the house. She must be certain she spoke with Charles before anyone else could tell him or he saw Ruth himself.

Lydia tried not to second guess her impulsive decision. "You may enter."

"Good mornin', ma'am," Ruth said, stepping just over the threshold but no further.

"Good morning, Ruth." Lydia turned from her place at the window. "I trust you had a good rest?"

"Yes, ma'am."

"And your arm?"

She touched the clean bandage briefly and dropped her hand. "Fine."

"Good. Today I'd like to show you around the house, and we can discuss what your duties will be."

"Yes, ma'am."

Lydia lifted her arms over her head and stretched. Ruth turned her eyes to the floor. Lydia watched her a moment, wondering about her thoughts. She'd probably never seen a lady in her nightdress before. "Ruth, why don't you go down to the kitchen and fetch me a pitcher of warm water. Then you can help me lace up my corset."

Ruth tugged her mouth to one side and furrowed her brow. "Yes, ma'am. I'll be right back with that water." She turned and hurried out the door.

"Ruth?"

She returned, poking her head in. "Yes?"

"You might want to take that with you." Lydia pointed across the room to the white pitcher sitting on the wash basin. "Betsy should have some water on the stove. And tell Lucy to come back up with you. She can show you how to lace a corset."

Relief washed over Ruth's face. She grabbed the pitcher, holding it gently against her chest and hurried from the room.

Lydia sighed. What a strange girl. Full of fire one moment and fear the next. Lydia looked out past the front lawn and over the vast fields spreading as far as she could see from her second-story window. The rich earth lay furrowed, ready for the cotton seeds that would soon be planted. Dark-skinned people mingled among the rows, a few guiding plows. A foreman on horseback rode by, occasionally stopping to talk with one of the field hands. Lydia pulled the window open to let in the fresh air, the cool breeze refreshing and carrying with it the delicate scents of nature.

A soft peck on the door called her attention. "Come in."

Ruth entered, carefully carrying the pitcher. Lucy following closely on her heels and watched as Lydia's new help emptied the water into the basin. Lydia stepped behind the screen and quickly washed and put on her undergarments. When she emerged, Ruth held out the corset and Lucy waited by the vanity, comb in hand. The two slaves exchanged a look, and then Ruth stepped forward, wrapping the corset around Lydia's waist.

Ruth fumbled with the lacing, tugging and grunting. Lydia tried to remain still, though it did eventually become necessary to hold on to the bed post to keep her footing. Finally, Lucy came up to help.

"You gotta thread this little ribbon here, see? Then cross it over. That way when you pull on them two ends, it pulls the two edges together, makin' it tight."

Ruth let out a soft humph. Despite herself, Lydia giggled.

"I's sorry, ma'am. We didn't mean no offense," Lucy quickly said. Lydia could see her face in the vanity mirror in front of her. Lucy shot Ruth a disapproving look, but Lydia couldn't see Ruth's response since she was positioned directly behind her.

"Oh, gracious." Lydia shook her head, trying to hide her feelings of awkwardness. It wouldn't do for them to see her flustered over such a silly thing. "I know these things are ridiculous. Nonetheless, it's what is expected." Lydia straightened herself, once again resuming her role as lady of the house. Thankfully, Ruth seemed to know even less about what was expected than Lydia. The thought brought a wave of relief. Maybe with Ruth she wouldn't always have to be on guard against proving herself to be the country bumpkin they probably thought her to be.

Ruth pulled on the strings and Lydia tightened her grip on the bedpost until the two women had everything tied. When they finished, Lucy opened the armoire. "What dress do you want, ma'am?"

Lydia thought a moment. She would just be showing Ruth around the house today, so nothing special. But, then again, Charles would soon be home, and considering her news she might want to look her best. "Let's go with the soft green one."

Lucy nodded and pulled the garment free. Lydia held her arms up and Lucy slid the garment over her head and fastened the buttons. Ruth's gaze followed Lucy's movements paying close attention as Lucy tugged the hemline over Lydia's hoops.

Lydia sat at the vanity while Lucy combed her hair with nimble fingers. Lucy swiftly used the tool to pull through the tangled mess with little compassion for Lydia's scalp. If she didn't stop her, Lydia might not have any hair left to comb.

"I can finish up. Lucy, you may go now. After breakfast I will show Ruth around the house, and then when we are finished, she can help you with the chores."

Lucy looked quickly at Ruth with an expression Lydia couldn't quite place washing over her features before it was hidden behind a polite smile. "Yes 'um," she mumbled and closed the door behind her.

Lydia looked over at Ruth who stared at the new shoes on her feet. She couldn't think of anything else a maid needed to do in the morning. No chance the girl knew how to do her hair.

"Have you eaten?"

Ruth's head snapped up. "Yes, ma'am"

"Well, I'm starving. Run down and tell Betsy I'm on my way for breakfast."

Ruth nodded and darted out the door. Lydia plaited her hair and twisted its long lengths onto the back of her head. She adjusted the pins, hoping it wouldn't be one of those days the heaviness of it gave her a headache. When she finished, she stared at her reflection for several moments. She looked the proper lady. A frown wrinkled her brow. But what did a lady do other than look proper and give directions? Charles, bless him, seemed to want to give her a life of leisure.

Lydia descended the staircase and sat at the place already made for her at the table. She ate her breakfast alone. When she finished, Lucy cleared the dishes and Ruth followed Lydia from the dining room to begin her tour through the house. She'd thought through her speech while she ate and still could come up with little that sounded important, although she doubted Ruth would know the difference. Lydia stopped by the front door, it seeming to be the most appropriate place to begin.

"Your main job is to assist me with whatever I am doing. If I go somewhere, you do too. If I am going to the garden to paint, you set it up. That kind of thing."

"Yes, ma'am."

"If I don't need you for anything, then you can help the other girls with the household chores." She turned to the left, Ruth on her heels. "The windows are washed once a week," she said, pointing to the large parlor windows facing the front porch. "The rugs are beaten once a week as well, but you don't have to do both on the same day."

They stepped out of the parlor and crossed the wide entry back into the dining room where her meal had already been cleared away by curiously fast and unseen hands. "You'll need to help keep the silver polished; it's here in these upper two drawers." She pointed to the sideboard, its carved hunting dogs and scampering fox evidence of Charles' love for the woods.

"Yes, ma'am."

"Then there are those brass things up there that hold the curtains. A pride of Charles' father, I'm afraid. They are a pain to get to but must be shined as well."

Ruth stood gaping up at the massive brass valences that encased the tops of the flowing green velvet curtains on both of the dining room windows. Lydia couldn't blame her. A smile tugged at her lips as she remembered the first time she saw them when her new husband pointed them out the morning after her wedding night. She most likely had the same expression as Ruth. She'd never seen anything similar. Charles explained that his father had had them specially made for Ironwood.

They stepped out onto the back porch. "There's not much you'll need to do back here. But, in case you need anything, the root vegetables and Betsy's canned food goes out here in the potato room. The smoke house is this door next to it." Lydia pointed to the large barn-like structure that was divided in half to both store and cure food. "Out that way," she gestured behind the potato house, "are the barns where we keep the horses and store the cotton. Beyond that grove of trees over there you'll find the cabins where the rest of the coloreds live."

Ruth dug the toe of her still-stiff black shoe into the soft grass. "Is that where I'll be stayin'? Permanently, I mean."

Lydia frowned. She thought she'd been clear in instructing Lucy on Ruth's sleeping arrangements. "No, I'd rather you be here by the house. In case I need you."

A flicker of relief washed over the girl's face, but she quickly hid it.

Lydia nodded back to the kitchen. "As Lucy should have told you, you have a room in the quarters above the kitchen with her and Betsy."

Ruth nodded.

Lydia paused a moment and let the sunshine wash over her. Her stomach felt unsteady this morning. It'd only been a few weeks into her marriage, but... perhaps a babe grew within her? She'd heard sickness was often a part of it. She pushed the thought aside. Birds twittered in the tree tops, and Lydia looked up to watch a sparrow chase its mate across the open sky. When she looked back down, she caught Ruth staring at her. The girl quickly dropped her eyes.

Lydia ignored the feeling in her stomach and continued on with her purpose. "Well, that about covers it, I guess. After you help me dress each morning, replace the water in the basin and make up the bed clothes. I'll let you know if we are going to town or whatever I'll be doing for the day. Otherwise, you'll help Betsy and Lucy do whatever is needed around the house. Just do as they tell you."

"Yes, ma'am." She turned to leave.

"Oh. One other thing."

Ruth turned.

"Charles does not allow work on Sundays other than the necessities. Most of your people attend the chapel, and you're welcome to go if you want."

Ruth's face broke into the first smile Lydia had seen. "Truly?"

Lydia nodded, dismissing Ruth, and returned to the house pondering the look of joy on the girl's face. Did it appear because she mentioned church or the ease of labor on Sundays?

She took a seat in the parlor to watch for Charles and decided it must be the day of rest. Church was much too stoic to garner such a response. They sang hymns, fanned away the heat while listening to the drone of the sermon, and then shared idle chatter outside the doors before returning home for dinner. Never once had Lydia felt elation over the idea of attending a church service. But then, perhaps her feelings came from her lack of understanding about God. He could do all things, yet chose not to. If He saw all things, why would He allow evil to happen? Why wouldn't He be there to protect the innocent?

Lydia shook her head. Enough. That was a door that must remained closed, since no good could come from opening it. She had a good life here. Why worry about such things?

She didn't have the time anyway. The sight of boiling dust alerted her to Charles' return before she even saw the horses. She gathered her skirts and called for preparations to be made for her husband's arrival. The carriage came to a stop just as Lydia opened the front door and positioned herself on the porch to greet him.

The carriage door swung open, and when Charles' eyes found Lydia, a smile spread across his face. Lydia pretended she didn't feel the fluttering in her stomach and offered him a small smile in return. He strode quickly onto the steps and halted just in front of her, close enough that she could smell his aftershave and had to lift her chin to look into his face.

"Hello, husband. I hope your travels have been well."

Something akin to amusement lit his eyes. "Come, I am tired from my trip. Let's go into the parlor and we shall talk."

Lydia pulled her lip through her teeth and followed him as he strode through the door Lucy held open. Thankfully Ruth was nowhere to be seen.

"Lucy, would you bring some tea to the parlor for Mr. Harper?"

"Yes ma'am." The woman nodded and hurried off. Lydia drew a deep breath and smoothed her skirts then followed Charles into the parlor.

She waited for him to speak, trying to figure out the best way to begin her tale.

"I believe these rugs have grown drab. I never replaced them, since they were my mother's, but I do believe it is time for some changes around here."

Lydia nodded, unsure how else to respond. Charles looked at her with raised brows. The unexpected topic unraveled her thoughts. "Um, yes, perhaps I can look into that."

He smiled. Lucy returned with a silver tray and delicate tea set balanced in her hands and set it on the table without any of the cups rattling. Lydia often marveled at how a woman of her size moved with such grace. Lucy dipped her head and retreated from the room, drawing the pocket doors closed behind her.

"Would you care to sit?" Lydia asked.

Charles pinned her with the look that told her she'd been caught. She recognized it as the same one that often fell upon Mother's face whenever she found Lydia in a tree or doing something else a lady oughtn't.

"So, is there something you'd like to tell me?"

Lydia chewed her lip and thought about a response. Suddenly Charles laughed and pulled her into an embrace. He held her a moment and the breath she hadn't been aware she had been holding escaped from her lungs.

She inhaled his scent, a sweet mixture of pine and soap. He spoke against the top of her head. "I already heard all about how my wife strode up to a slave driver in the middle of town, bargained like a man, and left with a hot-headed female."

Lydia pushed back from him, studying his honey-colored eyes. "Are you angry with me?"

He shook his head. "Surprised, yes. Angry, no. I've been telling you to get yourself a helper. I should have known you would do it differently than any other lady."

He smiled at her, running the pad of his thumb over her jaw. "But that's just one of the many things I love about you. However, you need to be aware she's most likely stolen. There may be someone looking for her. Do you know where she came from?"

Yes. "No. She didn't say." She inwardly winced. Why must she lie? Did she fear losing Ruth otherwise?

He kissed her on the forehead. "I have much I need to attend to, but I would like to go for a ride with you. Why don't you go change into a riding habit, and we will enjoy some time together shortly."

Lydia smiled. "I would like that." Though she didn't deserve it. She stared after him as he walked away, leaving the tea untouched. How had she found such good fortune? It would seem that despite her doubts, Father had truly chosen a wonderful man. If only she could keep herself from ruining it.

Eleven

Charles straightened his jacket and strode from the rear door. Did she not know what she did to him? Looking at her flushed face and the way she played with her full lower lip between her teeth quickened his heart and started a flame in his chest. Then when she'd looked up at him through those thick lashes, he could scarcely concentrate on her words. He had to leave the room before he gave into the temptation of scooping her up in his arms and delivering her upstairs. His trip to Natchez had come much too soon after his wedding, but it couldn't be helped. His dealings with the shipping company and securing safe passage for his cotton were imperative.

Charles entered the barn just as the stable boy tossed hay to the pair of matched geldings that were tired from their hurried trip home. "Good morning, Johnny."

The boy spun on his heel, a wide grin splitting his face. "Good mornin' mista Harper. You's have a good trip?"

"It served its purpose. Did you take good care of everything while I was away?"

The boy nodded solemnly. "Yes, sir. I kept Draco's foot soaked in the healin' salts and kept him stabled. The hoof is strong as ever now. He's anxious to be out again."

Charles smiled. "Very good. I knew I could trust him to you."

Johnny beamed.

"How about you get him saddled for me? I need to make some rounds, and when I return, I'll also need Mrs. Harper's mare saddled."

"Right away, sir." The boy bounded off to gather the tack, and within a few moments Charles set out for the fields keeping the stallion reined in at a brisk walk. Draco flared his nostrils and snorted.

Charles chuckled. "You smell those mares you've been denied, eh boy?"

The great stallion bobbed his head, tossing his mane in the air. Charles had to hold tight onto the reins to be sure the horse remembered who was in charge.

He allowed the horse to trot and came to the field to inspect the planting process. "How are we looking, Mr. Peck?" he asked as he settled the anxious stallion next to the foreman's roan mount.

"Looking quite well, Mr. Harper. Seems this drought won't hurt us near as much as I feared. The ground is fertile and planting's been going well."

Charles nodded and looked over the neatly tilled rows.

Mr. Peck removed his hat and ran a hand over his head. "I've been hearing talk that the North will soon be moving into Mississippi." He cast a quick side glance at Charles but kept his focus straight ahead talking in low tones.

"It is as I fear. Though I am holding to hope they will let us be."

Mr. Peck nodded but did not look convinced. "If all remains well," he returned his voice to normal volume, "we should have a good crop this year."

Charles smoothed his hand along the horse's slick neck, giving him a gentle pat. "Let us hope then that all remains as it is for at least long enough to get our shipments out. I have the feeling we are going to need a good year in the face of several lousy ones to come. It is best we prepare now."

Mr. Peck dipped his chin. The man had been with Charles since he'd first taken over Ironwood. Mr. Peck had worked as a youth under his father at Charles' uncle's plantation. When Peck's father died, Uncle sent the man with a strong recommendation. Mr. Peck had proven his worth time and again and could be trusted with the truth of what could soon come upon them. Charles tried to push aside his feelings of foreboding and focus on today.

"Very well, Mr. Peck. Keep up the good work." Charles inclined his head and allowed Draco the forward movement he'd been pawing to receive. He rode through several more fields, and after feeling satisfied that all continued smoothly in his absence with little needing his attention, he gave into the horse's need to have free rein.

Although conventional wisdom warned him against letting a horse run headlong in the barn's direction, they both needed a touch of freedom. He told himself that Draco alone felt the need to quickly return to the house. He squeezed his legs and released tension from the bit. The horse immediately jumped forward, his muscled hindquarters launching them through the air and into a fast gallop.

Exhilaration spread in his chest, and Charles moved in rhythm with the beautiful beast beneath him. They flew across the open land, drawing startled gazes as he approached the field hands. Realizing they would think something amiss, Charles pulled in the reluctant horse and lowered his speed to a casual canter.

Lydia's gray mare stood saddled and tied to the hitching post in the front of the barn when Draco pranced into the yard. Charles tied Draco securely beside her and allowed the two to touch muzzles. He smoothed his hair and stepped into his father's beloved home, finding his bride in the parlor, a book open in her lap.

"Are you ready, my dear?"

She looked up from her reading, a hint of pleasure turning her lips into a slight bow. "I've sent Ruth to collect a traveling meal for us."

Charles nodded and offered his arm, and they walked together through the rear door just as a young caramel-colored young woman exited from the kitchen with a large bundle in her arms. The girl glanced around somewhat nervously, and then puckered her lips. She blew, but no sound came out. Charles lifted his eyebrows and turned his questioning gaze onto his wife, but her focus was locked on the new house girl.

The girl attempted to whistle again, then frowned, straightened her shoulders and took a determined step. Her eyes locked onto Charles before going wide. She wavered only for a moment before confidently coming forward. She paused at the bottom of the step and attempted an awkward curtsey. Charles pressed his lips together to contain his amusement.

"Mr. Harper, this is Ruth. She's... new at house duties." Lydia waved her hand in the air. "But she is a fast learner. I am confident she will do very well."

Charles allowed a smile. "Welcome to Ironwood, Ruth. I hope you find your new home comfortable."

Surprise flickered across her face, but she quickly smoothed her features and gave an impassive nod. "Yes, sir. Thank you."

Lydia hurried forward and took the basket from Ruth. "Thank you, Ruth. I will be out with Mr. Harper for a while. You may continue with your duties."

"Yes, ma'am," she said and scurried back to the kitchen.

Lydia looked at Charles with uncertain eyes. Did she fear his reprimand? How could one woman be so independent and yet seem so fearful? Had he given her cause? He must remember women were more delicate than men.

He smiled. "I believe you did well. The girl seems bright and willing."

Lydia let out a breath. "Yes, I feel she will do well. We get along nicely."

Charles chuckled. She spoke as if she'd introduced him to a visiting neighbor. He offered his arm and decided not to question it lest she clam up. His innocent wife seemed to know little about the ways of the world. He would not taint it for her. If she was happy and liked her new girl, then he was pleased as well. And, if the girl had another owner come for her…well, he would deal with that if the time came.

They strolled to the barn and up to the waiting horses. Lydia gathered her long skirts into her arms and Charles locked his fingers together, offering his assistance. She placed a small booted foot into his hands.

"Ready?"

"Yes."

She bent her knee, and in one movement she jumped, and he lifted. She slid gracefully into the saddle, the gentle mare remaining still as she adjusted her skirts modestly around her legs. She crooked one leg into the lower pommel and smiled down at him.

"It still amazes me a lady can ride with both legs on one side of her horse," he said sliding his hand up the smooth stocking over her calf and gently placing her other foot in the stirrup. He heard her draw in a sharp breath. He allowed himself the touch for a moment longer, pretending the keeper needed adjustment.

"Is the length correct?" he asked, looking up into her flushed face.

"Yes. As I have not grown any since last I rode, it is still in the correct position." A hint of amusement to her tone belied her steady gaze.

"Very good then. Let us be off." He winked at her and swung into his own saddle. Johnny handed him the reins and tied the saddle pack filled with their foodstuffs to the rear of Draco's saddle.

They rode in companionable silence until he guided Draco off the road and into the edge of the woods. The sound of hoof beats behind him silenced. He turned to look at his wife. She sat stiffly, suspicion lighting her eyes.

"Are you coming, dear?"

Her delicate eyebrows pulled together. "Why are we going into the woods?"

"Because it is where I wish to picnic."

"Why?"

Patience. "There is a nice spot within."

Lydia shifted the reins from one hand to the other and eyed the woods again. "Far within?"

The muscles in his jaw tightened and he let out a long breath. "No. It is not far. No need to worry overmuch about snagging your dress." Lydia studied him until he thought he could no longer stand her stalling before she finally nodded and nudged the mare forward. Curious woman.

They wound through the low hanging branches down the narrow path and came out of the trees and into a small meadow bursting with wildflowers. He turned Draco to watch his bride emerge into the clearing. Her face lit and a smile bloomed on her lips. His irritation at her irrational behavior waned, and he offered a smile of his own.

"Do you like it?"

"Oh, it is very lovely."

"So you do not mind that it lies within the wood?" He smirked. He knew he shouldn't goad her. Her moods could quickly turn somber, and he too much relished the look of joy on her face. Still, he could not help himself.

Lydia laughed. "Forgive me. It seemed a strange idea."

Charles lifted his shoulders. "I do not see why. I found this spot years ago. It has long been a favorite place of solitude. And peace."

"And you chose to share it with me?" Her eyes searched his across the heads of the mounts that separated them. Charles tried to ignore the sudden ache to hold her.

"As I have vowed to share all." He tugged the bridle to turn Draco before emotion could cloud his voice and walked through the clearing. Near its center, they came upon a shallow stream that flowed with clear water.

He swung out of the saddle and reached up to help Lydia down. She offered her hand, but he ignored it, placing his hands on her tiny waist and lowering her to the ground. He let his hands linger on her for a moment, and she turned her face up to look at him. Pink tinged her pale cheeks, and he felt his blood warm.

She quickly stepped out of his grasp. "Thank you."

Disappointment scurried through him at losing the connection, but he gave a slight bow and said, "My pleasure."

She busied herself with spreading out a large red blanket and pulling out various items from the pack he offered. She placed miniature meat pies, bread, and cheese out in front of him as he settled in a reclining position on the ground.

"It seems we have enough food to feed several more." He chuckled and popped a small chunk of bread into his mouth.

Lydia frowned. "I told Betsy it would just be the two of us."

Charles reached up and grasped her hand, gently encouraging her to sit. She gathered her legs underneath her and spread her skirts out. Despite the extra fabric meant to cover a lady's legs while riding, without the hoops underneath he could nearly make out the shape of her curved hips as she primly sat on the ground.

"Charles?"

"Yes?"

"I have something I…need to ask you."

"Anything, my dear. What troubles you?"

"Why me?" She kept her gaze on her hands, which twisted in and out of her skirts.

"I'm afraid I do not understand."

The pink in her cheeks grew rosy and Charles reached across to grasp her hand, giving it a small squeeze.

She drew in a breath and her words tumbled out. "I mean, why did you choose me when every young woman in the county vied for your attentions?" She drew her lip through her bottom teeth.

He chuckled. "You caught my attention in a way no woman ever has."

"Oh."

She sounded disappointed. How to explain? He put a finger under her chin and coaxed her face up so he could look into her eyes. "I saw a lady who seemed to possess a quiet strength. Then upon speaking with you, I found a woman with whom I could hold an intelligent conversation. A young woman who found more to talk about than fabric and gossip. Do you remember what we spoke about?"

She nodded, a curl that had slipped free of its bindings bobbing at her ear. "Yes. We spoke of horses."

"Yes. It was then I realized I'd found a woman who could keep my interest, who could think for herself, and who could be a companion."

"You truly thought so?"

"Indeed. And once I began to call on you, my convictions were only strengthened. I knew what I was looking for. I desired a woman who could stand by my side and be my helpmate. I found that and more in you. It is something hard for a man to put into the proper words, but I've been drawn to you since the moment we met." He winked at her. "And the fact that such a woman came with a beautiful face and fetching form only made her all the more irresistible."

Lydia giggled, a light tinkling sound that brought him great pleasure. He would have to strive to tease such laughter from her more often. He reached into his breast pocket and removed a small box. "I brought a gift for you."

Excitement lit her eyes before she turned her gaze downward. "You did not need to do that."

A smile tugged at his lips. "Perhaps. But I wanted to, nonetheless." He lifted the offering to her.

Lydia undid the small blue ribbon and pulled the paper from the box. When she opened it, a melody began to play. She gasped. "Oh, Charles, it's beautiful!"

The carved box inlaid with pearls had cost a good sum, but the look on her face and the way she said his given name was worth ten times what he'd paid. "Do you like it?"

She clutched it close to her. "I do! Thank you."

"I thought perhaps it would be a good place for you to keep your jewelry."

"The box itself is beautiful, but I have never seen one that could play music."

"They have quite a few in Natchez. The music is made by winding the knob at the back of the box. Then, when you open it, a small tube covered in a series of raised bumps turns inside. That is how it makes the melody."

She smiled broadly at him, causing a small dimple in her left cheek to appear.

"I am pleased you like it," he said.

They ate quietly for many moments, enjoying the soft breeze that carried the scents of wildflowers across the meadow. The value of a woman not given to ceaseless chatter was not lost on him. Birds carried on their tunes overhead, and for a few moments Charles could almost forget the troubles going on outside of their little haven.

"Did you have a good trip to Natchez?" Lydia asked, pulling him from his thoughts.

"Yes. I was able to make arrangements with a lawyer who assured me all my shipping will continue through. Even if the North blockades the river, there are certain captains who will make it out to England by whatever means necessary."

"Surely the North would not block a merchant ship on the Mississippi River. Why would they do such a thing?"

Charles lifted a hand to run a finger over her smooth jaw. "This is a war, my dear. They will do whatever they can to cripple the Confederacy. That means cutting off our money by cutting off our supplies coming in and our goods going out. But you do not need to worry. These are the concerns of men."

She turned her face from him. "It seems to me it is a concern of us all."

He rolled onto his back and looked into the clear sky overhead. The weather quickly warmed, and soon it would be too hot to sit out in the open. He did not wish to argue, only to enjoy some time of quiet peace. He didn't want to think about the coming hardships.

"Indeed. It is something we must all worry with. But I pray it will soon come to an end. Many men I've spoken to say it will not last long."

"Would you leave to go fight?"

The concern in her voice made him rise to a sitting position and study her face. Worry lines creased her brow. He lifted an eyebrow. "Would you miss me?"

She pressed her lips together and thought a moment. When she finally spoke, her voice was soft. "I do not wish for you to be in harm's way."

Did she have any idea what she did to him? When he spoke again, his voice was husky. "That is not what I asked."

She fluttered her lashes and looked down. "Yes, husband. I do believe I would miss you."

He pulled her across the half-finished meal and into his lap, breathing in her soft scent. She stiffened in his arms, but when he gently caressed her back, he felt her muscles slowly loosen.

"And what would you miss, my dear? This?" He kissed the tender place behind her ear. She gasped but didn't move from his grasp. He could feel her pulse quicken under the caress of his lips.

"Perhaps," she whispered. "Yes, perhaps this."

A low rumble came from the back of his throat, and his lips found hers. She yielded to him, her arms sliding around his neck. He deepened the kiss and pulled the pin from her hair, letting the long dark braids fall down her back. He pulled his fingers through them to free the soft waves, and then pulled her tight against him.

A soft sound escaped her throat when he moved his kisses to her neck. "Charles." She breathed his name. He began unbuttoning the back of her dress. Suddenly, she was no longer in his embrace, but standing before him, breathing heavily.

"Oh, no. We mustn't."

His chest tightened. "Why not? You are my wife."

She looked at him with wide, doe eyes. "Here? In the open? No, that cannot be proper. A lady shouldn't do such things, don't you think?" She blinked rapidly at him.

"I do not think anyone will happen upon us. In all my years here my solitude has never been broken." He clenched his fist at his side and tried to calm his frustration.

She smoothed her long skirts. "I... I am not sure if I..."

He rose to his feet and wrapped her in his arms, resting his chin on the top of her silky hair. She trembled.

"Be calm, my dear. I will never ask you to do anything that frightens or worries you."

She looked up at him. "Truly?"

His heart ached at the uncertainty in her voice, and he vowed it would ever be true. He would win the trust of this strange and beautiful creature. "Truly, my love. This I vow."

She put her head on his shoulder, and he gently stroked her hair while the wildflowers danced in the wind.

Twelve

*R*uth ran a rag across the shelves of the massive bookcase in the front entryway. She'd never seen so many books. She tried to read the titles, but some were words she'd not seen in grandmother's teaching book. She squinted closer at a long word and tried to see if she could sound out its meaning.

"Ruth? What you be doin'?"

Ruth spun on her heel to find Lucy staring at her with her hands on her hips.

"I's dustin' the bookcase like you told me."

Lucy frowned. "Why was you lookin' so hard at that book?"

Ruth shrugged. "I ain't never seen a big book like that before."

Lucy frowned and walked over to the matching bookcase opposite of her and began dusting. "I'll finish up in the house. Why don't you go out and get a load of potatoes and onions to give to Betsy for supper."

Ruth nodded and handed her rag to the older woman. No doubt Betsy had sent Lucy to do the job, but Lucy didn't seem the type to want to get her white apron dirty in the potato shed.

Ruth didn't mind though. Besides, it would give her a chance to get a little fresh air. She'd already dusted most of the downstairs, and her back was getting stiff from working in all those little crevices.

She bounded down the brick steps at the back of the house and turned toward the building to the right. When she neared the door, she caught sight of a figure by the back corner of the structure. Her heart quickened in her chest. She slowly eased her head around the edge of the brick. A man in a big hat with wide shoulders ducked around the other side. She drew a sharp breath. Had Byram come back to steal her so he could sell her again? Or worse, keep her for himself? Panic rose in her chest, but she fought it down. She must find out. If she spotted him now, she could report him as an intruder and take her chances. If he came for her in the middle of the night... She shook the thought away.

Ruth eased around the side of the building, her back scraping across the rough brick facing. At the back corner she peeked around and found a broad chest inches from her face. She yelped and jumped back, losing her footing and falling on her behind. She scrambled to regain her feet when a hand reached out and clasped her arm. The scream died in her throat when she saw the calloused fingers were darker than the skin on her arm. She looked up into the wide eyes of a man.

"I's sorry. I didn't mean to frighten you."

Ruth snatched her arm from him. "What you doin' sneakin' around like that?" she hissed.

He took his wide-brimmed straw hat off and nervously swapped it from hand to hand in front of him. "I, um, well..."

Ruth crossed her arms over her chest. "Well what?"

He looked so sheepish she nearly forgave him for frightening her. How could a man this massive look so timid? He easily stood a head and shoulders taller than her, and she was by no means short.

"I guess I's goin' to have to ask your forgiveness, miss."

Ruth raised her eyebrows. "Miss? I ain't no white lady." She immediately regretted her sharp words.

He ran a hand over his face. His cheeks filled up and he puffed out a blast of air. "My momma taught me to be respectful of young ladies, no matter what color they's skin be."

Despite herself, Ruth smiled. "I think I might like your momma."

The big man grinned, revealing white teeth that stood out against his ebony skin. "My name's Noah."

"I'm Ruth."

They stared at each other a moment and a strange feeling tingled through Ruth's spine. She wiped her hands on her skirts feeling awkward. She'd never had trouble speaking to people before. Why were words sticking in her throat?

"So, you didn't say why you had to ask my forgiveness."

He dug the toe of his brown shoe into the grass. "It's 'cause I was watchin' you."

"You was watchin' me?"

He pressed his lips together and nodded.

"Why?"

Noah shifted his weight from one foot to the other. "Ain't never seen a girl so pretty before."

Ruth's stomach fluttered, and she felt her face growing warm. She had no words at all now. What would Bridget say? She'd always been the one the young men looked at. Not her. Sadness gripped her heart.

She pulled herself to her full height. "That's right nice of you to say, but you still shouldn't be sneakin' around on people."

"I know. I's very sorry. I was just afraid to talk to you."

Ruth studied the sincere eyes set above his wide nose. He seemed like a gentle giant and maybe even a friend.

"You work up at the house?" she asked.

"I work in the barn. I trim the horse's feet, take care of all the carriages, and fix most of whatever needs fixin' 'round here."

"Well, I's happy to meet you Mr. Noah the fixer." She grinned. "I'm gonna be workin' as Mrs. Harper's maid."

He stuck his hand out, and she let him enclose her fingers in his huge ones. He held on just a little bit too long and her breath caught. She slipped her hand from his and turned to hurry back to get the potatoes before anyone wondered where she'd gone.

"Wait!"

She looked over her shoulder.

"Can I see you again?"

As in courting? She frowned. "Is that allowed?"

He nodded. "Of course."

Ruth swallowed hard. Before she could think better of it, she said, "I'd really like that." She caught his grin before she turned and ducked into the potato room. She leaned back against the wall and told her heart to stop pounding like the hooves of a runaway mule. When she finally felt composed, she gathered the items she needed and made her way through the rose garden and back into the kitchen.

"Well, I was wonderin' if you was ever gonna bring me my potatoes." Betsy huffed without turning around. Her head was wrapped in a thick red cloth and she stood frying something on the hot stove.

"I'm sorry. I got...distracted."

Betsy turned to look at her. "Oh! It's you. What happened to Lucy?"

Ruth shrugged. "She took over dusting in the front hall."

"I shoulda known she'd make you go out there. Don't you let her boss you around. She's always lookin' for anyone she can get to do her biddin'."

Ruth giggled. "It's okay. I didn't mind. I was tired of dustin' anyway."

Betsy eyed her. "You look mighty pleased. Somethin' you want to tell me?"

"Oh, it's nothin'."

"That so?"

"I... just met someone, that's all."

Betsy's eyes twinkled. "Did ya now? Musta been a handsome someone judgin' by that look on your face."

Ruth shrugged. "He said his name's Noah."

Betsy forked a chicken leg out of the grease and set it on a platter. "Noah's a good boy. Many of the young girls have had their eyes on him. He ain't never married, though."

Ruth found a knife and settled on the kitchen stool to start peeling potatoes. Her movements were still awkward, and she took off too many hunks of the vegetable, but she was getting better at it. "He's allowed to marry whoever he wants?"

Betsy didn't answer for a long time. Ruth almost didn't think she'd heard her.

"Child, I don't know what kind of place you came from, but I's sure glad you ended up here," she finally said.

A lump gathered in Ruth's throat, and she fought back the tears that threatened to fill up her eyes. She didn't deserve to be in a place this good.

Betsy cleared her throat. "Noah's a good boy," she said again. "Hard worker, kind, honest."

Ruth finished up the potatoes without answering and took the bucket over to Betsy. The cook handed her a plate of cornbread. "Here, take this into the house."

Ruth shook her head. "I can't."

"Why not?"

"'Cause I can't whistle."

Betsy laughed. "Who done told you you had to whistle?"

Ruth felt her ears growing warm. "Lucy. She said it's a rule that when you carries food from the kitchen to the house you's supposed to whistle the whole way there."

Betsey shook her head. "Well, that's true 'nough, I guess. The first Mr. Harper made the little boys whistle when they brought the food 'cause he kept gettin' little finger holes in his pies."

Ruth widened her eyes. Who would dare stick his finger in the master's pie?

"So Mr. Harper, he said those boys had to whistle when they brought his pies because no boy could lick pie off his fingers while he was whistlin'."

Ruth laughed. "Is you kiddin'?"

Betsy shook her head. "It's as true as the Bible."

"I don't think Mr. Harper will have to worry none 'bout me tastin' his pies," Ruth said, grinning.

"Then you's got no reason to whistle. Now get this cornbread into the house."

Ruth tried a little curtsy, to which Betsy rolled her eyes, before balancing the covered platter on one hand and opening the door with the other. Ruth finished bringing the evening meal in and watched the way Mr. Harper looked at his wife with affection. Ruth served them while they discussed bits of unimportant information, all the while unable to take her thoughts away from the tall man she'd met earlier. She found herself wondering where he took his meals.

"Ruth?"

"Oh! Yes, sir? I'm sorry sir."

Mr. Harper looked amused. "I said you may be finished for the evening. I will see to my wife."

Ruth glanced at Mrs. Harper and saw her pale skin turn bright pink. Ruth ducked her head. "Yes, sir."

She scurried back to the kitchen, grabbed a biscuit and chicken leg off the stove, and hurried to her room before Lucy could find her and give her something else to do. She sank down on her stuffed mattress and ate quietly, being careful not to drop any crumbs that might tempt mice to her bed.

When she finished her meal, Ruth pulled a small charcoal pencil from her skirt pocket. She'd found the writing instrument behind the seat in the parlor. She should have given it to Mrs. Harper, but no one would miss it, would they?

Ruth turned it over in her hands. If only she had some papers. But slaves were not supposed to write. She could never ask anyone for them.

Smooth, whitewashed walls wrapped her in an inviting embrace. They would take the words in her heart. She could tell her story to them. They wouldn't betray her. Ruth crept to the door and looked out. No one was in the shared space. She latched her door and sat on the floor behind it and wrote *I'd only wanted to make my little brother a cake for his birthday.* Ruth stared at the words for a long time, her heart constricting in her chest. The pain and guilt ate at her little by little. She shook her head. This was crazy. If anyone saw her they would whip her for sure.

She clenched her teeth. She had to get the story out. She couldn't hold it any longer. Ruth put the pencil to the wall again and soon the anguish that filled her soul made its way down her arm and into hurried words scrawled across the wall.

Thirteen

June 14, 1862

*L*ydia stood in her room and listened.

The day outside her window beamed with bright morning light. The sky glowed a pristine blue, vivid green trees standing sentry along the drive, their branches unmoved by neither breeze nor critter. Everything stood still. Silent.

Lydia ignored the strange feeling that tickled the nape of her neck. Sound. That would break the uneasy feeling that hung around her like a thick mantle. She started to hum softly. Her mother used to sing it to her as a child. Soon the quiet rumblings in her throat gained momentum and she gave way to the song. The hymn lifted her mood and she twirled around, letting her skirts flow out in a wide arc around her legs.

She stopped. What was that noise? The front door?

She stepped to the window and looked down but saw no horses tied to the post or carriages in the drive. The lightness that had come with her song skittered away leaving only apprehension. Where were all the people of Ironwood?

She hurried out of her room, pulling the door closed behind her. No one worked in the hall, no voices echoed in the empty house. Lydia smoothed her skirts and climbed the upper staircase to the third story ballroom. She stepped inside the long, narrow room. Built into the roof, only the center of the room was tall enough to stand in. The sides had been walled off where the roof pitch was too low. Lydia looked around but found nothing out of the ordinary. She turned to leave. Wait. Something caught her eye.

She walked across the room and knelt down next to the wall. A small panel with a tiny hook blended into the woodwork. Lydia flipped the latch and pulled the tiny door open to look inside. Nothing back there but the dark corners of the roof, a storage space filled with cobwebs and likely crawling with tiny creatures with too many legs. She shivered.

Then something began to glow. A lantern? She looked to the rear corner, far back against the house's outer wall. The light grew until a dark shadow took form.

Her traveling trunk? Who put it in the recesses of the roof?

The light brightened, illuminating the space until she had to shield her eyes. She slammed the tiny door shut and fled the ballroom, her heart pounding.

A door banged shut.

Lydia's hand flew to her mouth to stifle the scream that tried to escape. She dashed down the hall, her skirts swishing and tangling around her feet. Ladies shouldn't run.

She jerked to a halt in front of her bedroom door. It stood wide open. She'd closed it before she went to the ballroom.

Didn't she?

She cautiously stepped into the room, wiping her damp palms on her skirts. She would look under the bed. Just to be certain. Her hands trembled as she reached for the ruffle. Gritting her teeth, Lydia snatched the fabric upward and peered underneath. Nothing. She let out her breath in a whoosh. She was being ridiculous. Enough with acting like a frightened child. She drew herself to her full height and stepped over to her window.

She gasped.

In the front yard stood a man staring up at her. She frowned and put her hand on the glass. No. Not a man. A woman dressed as a man. Long, dark hair flowed free down her back and across a brightly colored top that hugged her body closely. Tight-fitting, dark-colored breeches clung to the feminine curves of her hips and legs.

Their eyes met.

Lydia bolted up in bed, her flailing arms connecting with something solid.

"Ouch!" Ruth hollered, her hands flying to protect her face. "I's didn't mean to scare you ma'am."

Lydia gasped and stared at the girl covering her head with her arms.

"Oh, my. I am so sorry, Ruth."

Ruth lowered her arms and studied her mistress suspiciously for a brief moment before dropping her gaze. She straightened her simple green dress and smoothed the clean white apron across its folds.

Never in Lydia's life had she experienced a dream more vivid. It was as if she had lived each moment. She shook her head to displace the lingering image of the strangely dressed woman in her yard. She frowned and flung the covers off, pushing past Ruth and going to the window. No one stood looking up at her. Of course not.

"Forgive my outburst. I seemed to have had a rather strange dream."

Ruth dipped her chin. "Yes, ma'am. I's brought you some fresh water in the basin."

"Thank you." Lydia stretched her arms over her head and busied herself with getting ready for the day. Her shipments had arrived and she was anxious to begin her new project. "After the morning meal I want you and Lucy to meet me in the front parlor."

Ruth helped her dress and then quietly slipped from the room before Lydia could ask her to help with her combs. Ruth had come a long way these last three weeks, quickly picking up on her duties and displaying keen intelligence, but she still seemed wary of Lydia's hair. Lydia couldn't fathom why.

Lydia parted her locks down the middle and then twisted her hair into a simple coil at the back of her head before securing its weight with several pins. She couldn't manage any fancy styles, but a married woman didn't need them anyway. She could handle at least this one aspect of her appearance on her own. Satisfied, she strode from her room, leaving the haunting dream behind.

The dining room stood empty, no place set for Charles at the table's head. She sighed and seated herself, placing her napkin in her lap. Lucy bustled in placing biscuits, honey, and a slice of ham in front of her.

"Lucy? Do you know where Mr. Harper is this morning?"

Lucy shook her head. "No ma'am. I ain't seen him."

"Very well. Thank you."

Lydia ate her meal in silence, listening to the girls giggle from the other room. Something inside her ached for that type of shared female companionship, but she must push it aside. She must remember her place as Lady of Ironwood. Ladies did not giggle; they composed themselves at all times.

And ate breakfast alone.

She wiped her lips in the dainty way Mother had taught and rose from the table. Her boxes had been delivered and unpacked in the parlor. Wonderful. Someone even moved all the furniture for her. She smiled. They were very efficient around here. One mentioned request and all stood ready.

Feeling determined, Lydia dropped to her knees and shifted the heavy rolled rug across the wood floor. It slid slowly. She took a deep breath and tugged again, forcing the resistant covering into the correct position. There. Perfect. She pulled the twine free. All she had to do now was unroll it out across the floor and...

"Mrs. Harper!"

Lydia jumped to her feet and whirled around. Lucy stood in the doorway with wide eyes. "Oh no, ma'am. Why didn't you's call? We was on our way. You don't need to be on the floor." She shook her head vigorously. "We was comin' to do it. We was comin'."

Ruth poked her head around Lucy's wide frame. A look of amusement skittered across her face, but she quickly hid it. Lydia felt the blood creeping into her cheeks. *Ladies do not sit on the floor.* She clenched her teeth together and inclined her head, indicating the roll behind her.

"We will need to unroll it and position it properly."

The two colored women hurried to fulfill her instructions. Lydia stood to the side and watched them, crossing her arms over her chest and properly waited while they undertook her much anticipated project.

"This here rug sure is nice, ma'am. I love these little flowers. They kinda look like a cross," Ruth said, smiling at her.

Lydia brightened. "Thank you, Ruth. They are dogwood flowers. One of my favorites. And yes, you are right. They do look like little crosses." She eyed the placement across the parlor floor. "I think it's too far to the right. Let's move it an inch or so."

Ruth and Lucy grabbed the edge of the carpet and pulled it to the left. Perfect.

"I think it will look splendid with the new green and white curtains, don't you think?"

"Yes, ma'am," they said in unison. Lydia pressed her lips together. Did they actually agree with her choice or were they only saying what they thought she wanted to hear?

Strong arms suddenly wrapped around her middle. Lydia gasped. Charles buried his face in her neck, once again disregarding all sense of propriety. The girls giggled and slipped from the room.

Charles spun Lydia around to face him. "Well, Mrs. Harper, how do you like the new shipment?"

She couldn't contain her smile at the look of boyish excitement on his face, her earlier sullenness melting away. "I am most pleased. What are your thoughts?"

"I think the look on your face is more beautiful than any decoration." His eyes danced. "And I think I shall buy you anything your heart desires if it will produce such a glimmer."

Lydia's insides fluttered, her heart once again battling with her head. He looked so happy. So pleased to have her. What wouldn't she do to have him always see her the way he did now? It wouldn't last much longer. Would it? When his desire for her cooled to indifference her heart would be rendered to shreds. Her head told her she must protect herself from the pain. Her heart only saw eyes that spoke of love. Could it be?

"Oh, Charles. You are so very good to me." She eased closer to him, ignoring the warnings her mind fired at her. His arms immediately tightened behind her back.

He brushed his lips against hers, and she didn't even care that they were standing the middle of the parlor. "That is because I love you, my dear Lydia."

Her heart thudded. Would he feel the same if he knew the truth? She pushed the thought away. He loved her as she stood here now, and that was all that mattered. "And I believe I love you as well, Mr. Harper." The words slipped from her mouth before she could regain them.

Charles studied her face and then broke into a boyish grin. "I think I may actually believe you. I am beginning to see it in your eyes, and that pleases me more than I can say." He kissed her on the forehead. "I came to tell you I must go to Jackson for a while. I have some business to attend to, but I should return before the month is up."

"You are leaving again so soon? You've only been home a few days."

Charles lifted her hand to his lips and kissed it. He flashed the charming smile. "Are you saying you will miss me, then?"

She nearly giggled, remembering the night after their picnic. "Indeed, Mr. Harper, I believe I just might."

He winked at her and her stomach flopped. The feeling of sickness that had bothered her the last two mornings settled on her, and she swallowed hard. Should she tell him what she suspected? She was only a few days late for her woman's time. But if he were going away for more than just business...

Her brow furrowed. "Does this have anything to do with war?"

"A little. With all that is going on, cotton prices are changing. I need to keep up."

She stared at the new rug beneath her feet. No, she wouldn't worry him. He would probably stay with her, and if her cycle came, he might have missed something important he needed to do. "Please be careful."

He pulled her close, kissed the top of her head, and walked out the door. She stared after him for several moments, and then walked to the windows to watch them load a trunk into the carriage. Without even realizing it, she wandered to the front porch. She tried to push aside the worry that nagged at her. His hurried departure bode ill even though he appeared casual. She would have to pay more attention to what the people said of the encroaching war. She would have to find ways to be more helpful while he was away.

Charles bowed to her before he entered the coach though his eyes said he'd wanted to do more. Lydia swallowed hard. Why must her determination for propriety keep them apart? He was her husband. She leaned against one of the pillars and soaked in the sweet freshness of air laced with the delicate scents of flora as she watched the dust boil up from under the carriage's departing wheels.

She shook off her feeling of apprehension and returned to her duty in the house. Ruth and Lucy had emerged from hiding and were standing on dining room chairs struggling to lift heavy curtains into place. Lucy began to wobble, and before Lydia could reach her, she toppled from the chair and landed in a heap of fabric. Ruth squealed and jumped from her perch.

"Oh! Lucy! Is you all right?" Ruth dug through the tangle of velvet.

Lucy spit and sputtered like a dangling cat when she emerged. Lydia covered her mouth with her hand. Every bit an old mad hen, Lucy's hair stuck up at multiple angles. Lydia burst out laughing, unable to control it any longer.

Lucy stopped her sputtering and stared at her mistress. Ruth looked back and forth between them, and then started to giggle as well. Lucy crossed her hands over her ample chest and mumbled, "It ain't funny."

Lydia fingers clenched at her sides, tears welling in her eyes. "Oh, Lucy! I'm terribly sorry. Are you all right?"

She huffed. "Yes, ma'am. I reckon ain't nothin' damaged but my rear."

Ruth giggled again, and Lucy cut her eyes at the younger girl. Ruth clamped her lips together.

"Oh come now, Lucy. Don't be cross. You aren't hurt. But I must say, with your hair sticking up all over the place and that sputtering sound you were making, you reminded me every bit of one of Betsy's hens when you steal an egg out from under it."

Her face scrunched and her hand flew to her head. After a moment, she allowed a begrudging smile and smoothed the tresses back down against her head. She placed her hands on her hips. "Well, it's still no laughin' matter."

Lydia sighed. "Well, we better get back to work. I've got many projects to get done. When Mr. Harper gets home, I want to surprise him with a new Ironwood."

The girls nodded and got back to work. Lydia smiled. Mother would be proud. She just might make a proper lady after   all.

Fourteen

$\mathscr{R}$uth rose from her bed with the sun and readied for the day. She fingered the cotton on her dress. Betsy pulled several from storage and had given them to her with tears in her eyes. Ruth had wondered about the emotion, but her fear kept her from asking. They were a bit too short but otherwise fit nicely. Ruth had never worn anything so fine.

She looked up at her story which now wrapped around the top half of all four walls. What had she been thinking? What if someone came in here and saw how she'd scrawled all over their pretty white plaster? She couldn't help it. Even if it meant a beating, she had to get the painful words out. She could handle the whip. It didn't compare to the pain in her heart. She'd prayed like Momma taught her to, but still the emptiness didn't go away.

Ruth slipped down the stairs and into the kitchen where Betsy was beating biscuits.

"Good mornin'."

The woman had ears like a cat. Could sense you long before her eyes found you. Ruth stepped up beside her at the big wooden table used for cutting meats and preparing dough.

"Good mornin', Betsy."

Betsy dusted her hands with flour and started feeding the dough through the press. "I got one batch already cookin'. Why don't you check to see if they's done?"

Ruth grabbed a thick rag and pulled the door open, delicious-smelling heat washing over her face. The tops had turned golden, so she pulled the pan free and set it on top of the cast iron stove. "They's ready."

Betsy nodded. "Good. Now get on to Mrs. Harper."

Ruth swiped a steaming biscuit from the tray and hurried out the door.

"I saw that!" Betsy called after her.

She grinned and closed the door behind her, shoving a bite into her mouth that set her tongue to burning. She pulled in the morning air to tame the heat, but June mornings gave little relief from their stifling hot days. Birds twittered as she made her way onto the porch, nibbling her breakfast and making sure her hands were clean before she knocked on Mrs. Harper's door.

"Ma'am?"

No answer. Should she go in? She didn't want to get too close. The lady could be crazy when she woke up. Ruth eased the door open and stepped inside. Mrs. Harper slept soundly, her bed sheets thrown all around her. Ruth almost smiled. Guess she couldn't try so hard to be proper when she was sleeping.

"Mrs. Harper?" Ruth called from her place by the door. "Mrs. Harper? You wanna get up now?"

Mrs. Harper groaned and blinked. Her gaze landed on Ruth. "Oh!" She gathered the blankets under her chin. "I'm sorry. I didn't hear you come in."

"You want to sleep, ma'am? You done told me to get you up early in the mornings."

"Oh. No, no. I'm ready to get up." She slipped her feet out from under the blankets and placed them on the floor. "Mother always says a lady is to rise early to care for her duties," she mumbled.

Ruth pretended not to hear the last part and started gathering Mrs. Harper's clothes. What duties might that be exactly? It's not like white ladies had to do any work. Even the easy tasks around the house were done by someone else. The way she saw it, Mrs. Harper could sleep all day and no one would notice the difference.

Ruth set the bed clothes right while her mistress changed from her nightdress into her chemise and hoop. So many pieces of clothing. How did they keep from burning up in this heat with all those layers of fabric?

"I'm going to make Mr. Harper's rounds today. You will accompany me," Mrs. Harper said as she stepped into the petticoat Ruth held out for her.

Ruth frowned. What kind of rounds could a woman possibly need to do for a man? "Yes ma'am."

Mrs. Harper held up her arms, and Ruth wrapped the corset around her waist, hooking the top closure and threading the loops. She just started to pull it tight when Mrs. Harper spoke softly.

"Do you think we could not tie it quite so tight?"

Did she want Ruth's opinion or just giving her an order? "Whatever you want, ma'am."

Mrs. Harper sighed and waved her hand. "I know. I know. But do *you* think anyone will notice if I don't have it so tight? It makes me..." She hesitated, turning her head to look at Ruth over one shoulder, "uncomfortable."

Ruth lifted her eyebrows. "I's sure wouldn't want to be tied up in that thing."

Mrs. Harper laughed. "Be glad you don't have to be. Yet another thing a lady must do."

Ruth nodded, unsure how to continue. "You wants me to take it off?"

Mrs. Harper seemed to consider the idea, but then shook her head. "No, I don't suppose that would be proper. But maybe we can just leave it looser so I can move around more and still be able to breathe." She smiled showing her straight, perfect teeth.

Despite herself, Ruth grinned. There was something different about this white woman for sure. "I think's that'll work just fine, ma'am. Ain't no one goin' to know the difference."

She finished dressing Mrs. Harper and headed to the barn where she could tell Noah to get Mrs. Harper a buggy ready. How many hours would she have to walk while Mrs. Harper rode? She'd probably have sore feet tomorrow.

She poked her head into the barn and saw Noah's wide back as he tossed hay into a stall. "Mornin'!" she called.

He turned and a grin split his face. "Hey there Miss Ruth. You's come to visit me?"

She dropped her gaze and dug the toe of her shoe in the soft dirt. "I, um, no."

"Oh."

He sounded so disappointed she couldn't help but look up at him. He was staring at her. She tried to swallow, but her mouth suddenly seemed to lack enough spit to do it. "What I means is Mrs. Harper sent me down here to see you."

He nodded. "And?"

She crossed her arms over her chest. "And yes I is glad to see you," she said, the words jumping from her lips like a frog from a hot pan.

He chuckled, and she felt her face grow warm.

"And I'm right glad to see you, too." He walked closer and gave her a funny little bow.

She giggled. "What are you doin'?"

"Tryin' to be a gentlemen."

Ruth stilled. "You ain't no gentleman. You's a slave to one."

The laughter left his face, and he straightened, looking at her with serious eyes. "A man who's got honor *is* a gentleman. He's a man who follows after God and does his best to do right in this here world even though there's lots of evil in it. I don't care if my skin's darker than pitch. In my heart I's will always try to be a gentleman."

Ruth stepped closer to him and studied his face. "You's a rare man, Noah. I's never seen one like you."

He reached out with one of his giant hands and brushed his finger as light as a butterfly across her cheek. Something in her stomach fluttered. She dared not breathe.

He looked down at her mouth, and she thought he might kiss her. She let her breath out in a rush and stepped back. "I's supposed to ask you to get Mrs. Harper's buggy ready."

He dropped his hand and spun on his foot. "I'll get it. It'll be waitin' on her when she's ready."

She watched as he started to walk away. "Noah?"

He turned. "Yes?"

"Thank you for tryin' to be an honorable man. I..." she fumbled for the right word. "Respect that. A lot."

One side of his mouth tugged up. He nodded and turned away. Ruth left through the big sliding doors and made her way back through the rose garden. As she stepped onto the porch, Mrs. Harper came out the back door.

"Oh. There you are. Are you ready?"

Ruth looked down at her shoes and wished she had some better ones for walking. Well, at least she had shoes. She nodded. "Yes ma'am. I done told Noah to get your horse ready."

"But I told you to have him get the buggy ready."

"Yes, ma'am. I did." Wasn't a buggy that strange saddle ladies had where both of their legs went on the same side of the horse? The way Mrs. Harper was looking her…maybe not.

Mrs. Harper frowned. "Oh, never mind. Run get the basket from Betsy."

Ruth slipped into the kitchen and got a large covered basket from the cook and then went to the barn. When she got there, Mrs. Harper was sitting in a tiny little carriage with a small canopy over the single seat. It looked funny hooked behind a big gray horse. Why not just ride the horse?

"Well, let's go. Get in."

Ruth's eyes widened. "In that thing?"

"Of course. Did you expect to ride in a saddle?"

Ruth shook her head vigorously. She had no desire to ever be on the back of one of those creatures. But this tiny thing strapped right behind one didn't look much better.

"I'll just walk."

Mrs. Harper looked at her from underneath her giant bonnet. "You'll do no such thing. Besides, you'd never keep up with the horse. Do you think I'm going to make you run all day?"

Ruth shrugged.

Noah came out of the barn and grinned at her. She shot him a mean look and put one foot on the little step hanging from the side. She climbed in and tried to sit as far away from Mrs. Harper as the tiny seat would allow. What would Bridget think to see her touching skirts with a white lady?

Mrs. Harper snapped the reins and the horse bolted forward. Ruth grasped the side of the seat.

"Have you ever ridden in a buggy before, Ruth?"

"No, ma'am." Besides that big carriage she'd been in the day Mrs. Harper bought her, she'd never been in anything with wheels. But her lack of experience wasn't the issue.

"Are you all right?"

Ruth kept her eyes focused straight ahead. How was she going to explain this to a lady? Still, she had to say something, and Mrs. Harper had yet to raise a hand to her. Ruth took a deep breath and said all at once, "No disrespect, ma'am but dontcha think maybe you shoulda asked Noah or Tommy or one of the other men to come along with you instead of me?" Not that Noah would fit in this thing.

Mrs. Harper tilted her head, looking genuinely confused. "Why on earth would I want to do that?"

Oh good heavens. "Well, I ain't no good with horses, I can't fix no wheel if it gets broken, and I ain't big enough to be much protection." Shouldn't she know all that? Mrs. Harper didn't usually appear to be light on sense, but she must sure be missing some today. She laughed like Ruth said the silliest thing.

They topped a hill and fields full of her own people came into view. Her heart dropped a little. This is where she'd spent most of her life, in fields like this. Tending cotton under the heavy hands of white men on horseback. Part of her felt guilty for where she now sat. What would they all think of her riding around like she was something special?

"Ruth," Mrs. Harper said, breaking into her thoughts. "There is no need for protection. Ironwood is perfectly safe. Noah makes sure everything on the buggy is sound before he hitches the horse up. Now stop worrying. Everything will be just fine."

Ruth dipped her chin but didn't answer.

Mrs. Harper slowed the horse to a walk and eased some of the jostling. They stopped in front of a white foreman on his horse, his hat scrunched down on his head and his broad shoulders stretching the cotton of his shirt. He lifted his hand in greeting.

"Morning, Mrs. Harper."

"Good morning, Mr. Peck. Are the numbers looking good today?"

He spit a stream of tobacco and adjusted his hat. "Yes ma'am. They're all healthy and working steady this morning, hadn't had any issues so far." His eyes fell on Ruth. She twisted in her seat and looked out over the fields. A few of the hands looked up at her curiously. She dropped her gaze.

"And the cotton?" Mrs. Harper asked.

"Growing good enough in this drought. But rain would be a blessing, sure enough."

"Yes, it certainly would. Thank you, Mr. Peck." She lifted the reins.

"Uh, ma'am?"

Ruth looked up from under her lashes at the foreman as he took his hat off and ran his fingers through his hair.

"Yes?"

"Are you going to be taking all of Mr. Harper's ride today?"

Mrs. Harper stiffened. Ruth pressed her lips together.

"Why do you ask, Mr. Peck? Is there something going on during my husband's absence I need to be aware of?" she snapped.

The foreman shook his head. "No, ma'am. We all respect Mr. Harper and not a one of us that would slack any in our duty during his absence." He sat a little straighter in his saddle. "It just might not be safe for you two... " His gaze fell on Ruth, and she squirmed. "Uh, ladies, to be out alone without an escort. I don't know if Mr. Harper would want his young bride driving around the slave quarters alone."

Finally. Someone with some sense. Mr. Peck seemed a decent enough fellow. Did he beat the slaves when no one was watching?

Mrs. Harper's voice softened. "I appreciate your concern. The hands should all be in the fields working under the supervision of your managers. Surely they should not cause me any distress from there?"

Ha. As if *they* were the ones that caused the issues. She had no idea, did she? But then, how could she? This woman had been raised in a fancy house with everything she ever wanted. How could she possibly know anything about what life was really like?

"Of course not, ma'am."

Mrs. Harper clicked the reins and continued on around the side of the field. Ruth clenched her teeth. The wind thrust an invisible hand against her face as if it warned them not to go any further. Mrs. Harper put her hand on her oversized hat and tried to keep it from ripping from her head.

Despite her discomfort with the situation and Mrs. Harper's strange ideas, Ruth secretly enjoyed seeing more of her new home. She hadn't been any further away from the house than to the barn. How many of her people lived within Ironwood? More than Cedar Hall?

Her seat lurched out from underneath her and unseated her rear. She landed hard and her shoulder crashed into Mrs. Harper. Ruth gasped and struggled to right herself, fear making her heart scurry. What had she done?

"I'm sorry, ma'am! I didn't means to hit you like that." She swallowed hard. "I shoulda been holdin' on better. I promise, it won't happen again."

Mrs. Harper blinked at her. She appeared confused for just a second before everything was once again hid behind her mask of superior indifference. She brushed at her skirts. Ruth held her breath waiting to see how many lashes she'd surely gained. It wasn't fair! She hadn't asked to sit in this ridiculous thing next to the white lady. Still, she'd have to be more careful, have to make sure she kept her head about her at all times.

Finally, her mistress spoke, her voice soft. "We hit a hole, Ruth. You are not responsible." Mrs. Harper gracefully swung down the step and looked at the wheel. Before Ruth could gather her senses and decide if she should get down and assist in some way, Mrs. Harper lifted her shoulders and said, "Well, no harm done." She walked around to the big horse and started stroking its nose.

Ruth had no desire to get near the creature, so she stayed in her seat and fidgeted. She couldn't help staring at Mrs. Harper as she regained her uncomfortably close position next to her. Their eyes locked.

"What?"

"Nothin', ma'am."

They continued at a slow pace and soon small, simple homes came into view. They were wooden cabins, made from the hands of the people who lived within. Ruth's chest tightened. As they drew closer, several children gathered in the common area, their little feet stilled in their games and precious faces peeking out from behind the skirts of older girls left behind to care for them. They seemed well-fed. Maybe none of them had ever risked their life to steal flour. Maybe some places were different than Cedar Hall after all.

"Why are they staring at us like that?" Mrs. Harper whispered, not taking her eyes off the small central courtyard.

Ruth tried to hide the frustration in her voice but doubted she succeeded. "Maybe 'cause they ain't never seen no black girl riddin' in a buggy with the white lady before."

Mrs. Harper ignored her comment. She slowed the buggy and raised her hand as if she wanted to wave the children over and then suddenly stopped. What little color clung to Mrs. Harper's face drained from it, leaving her looking paler than a freshly opened cotton pod. Ruth followed her gaze to find a white man coming out of the nearest cabin, tugging on his pants.

Ruth's stomach turned. How stupid to start to think that this place could be any different than home. She clenched her jaw and lowered her gaze.

Mrs. Harper halted the mare. "Why would he be here in the middle of the day?" she mumbled.

Stupid woman. "Ain't no daddies around in the middle of the day," Ruth whispered between the teeth that would not unclench.

Mrs. Harper's nostrils flared, and she snapped her gaze to Ruth. She pressed her lips together and waved for the man to approach. Ruth balled her fists at her sides and wished she were back at the house scrubbing something instead of being forced to sit here. Anger welled inside her chest and made her breaths difficult to draw in. She refused to look at either of them.

"Why are you in the cabins during midmorning? Shouldn't you be tending to a field?" Mrs. Harper asked. The barely hidden bite in her voice drew Ruth's gaze up to judge the man's reaction.

His dark eyes studied Mrs. Harper a moment then slid to Ruth. He licked his lips and thrust his finger toward the cabin. "Got a sick fella in there. Didn't show up this morning, so I had to come down here to check on him."

Liar!

Mrs. Harper's brow creased as if she were considering the truth behind the words. The door creaked and a young girl stepped out on the porch. Ruth's jaw began to ache, and it took all her self-control to keep herself in her seat and not run to scoop the poor thing into her arms. What she wouldn't do to land a punch square in that disgusting man's face.

"You! Girl!" Mrs. Harper shouted. "Is your daddy or your brother in there with an ailment?"

The girl looked at the man, Mrs. Harper, and then Ruth. Ruth tried to show all the words she couldn't speak in her intense gaze.

Be brave! Tell!

The girl hesitated, the fear in her eyes tearing at Ruth's heart. Then she nodded her head, her shoulders slumping.

Mrs. Harper frowned. She looked out at the other children like they might give her the answer she hunted. They would never say a word. None of them even looked up at her.

"Mister, uh..."

"Webb."

"Mister Webb," Mrs. Harper said, her voice cold. "I suggest you return to your post at the field and oversee your job."

He nodded, his shaggy hair bouncing around his shoulders. "Headed that way now since my business here is done."

"Where is your horse?" Mrs. Harper snapped.

He ran his fingers through his long, greasy hair. "Tied up to a tree in those woods so it would have plenty of shade."

"And no doubt so someone else wouldn't know you were here at the cabins."

Ruth startled. Mrs. Harper no longer seemed to care how much hatred dripped from her lips. Ruth suddenly wanted to hug her. Not that she would dare.

The man shifted his feet. He looked at Ruth and her blood chilled. This man was dangerous.

"Well, I'm done here. I'll be moving on now. You be sure to have a pleasant day, ma'am." He dipped his chin and disappeared behind the cabins.

Mrs. Harper snapped the reins, startling the horse and making Ruth grab onto the side of the buggy. They left at a quick trot, passing the next field without stopping. Further and further on they went. Ruth wanted to scream. Would Mrs. Harper do nothing at all? How stupid she'd been to hope otherwise.

They turned down a small trail that snaked through the trees, bouncing the buggy over exposed roots and pushing through low-hanging limbs. They came to a stop at the edge of a small meadow deep within the wood. Mrs. Harper dropped the reins and put her head in her hands. Ruth chewed her lip.

Mrs. Harper gathered herself, a blank expression plastered on her face. They stared at each other for a long time, Ruth hoping that she would say something to show she cared. Disappointed, Ruth slipped down from the buggy and did the only thing she could think of to occupy her trembling hands. She grabbed the reins and secured the horse to a tree, even braving a small stroke on the animal's smooth neck, and then fetched the picnic basket.

When Mrs. Harper finally spoke, her voice wavered. "There was nothing I could do."

Ruth turned her back and walked to the edge of the clearing, looking out over the beautiful things God could make and trying to forget the ugly ones. Tears burned the back of her eyes and she let them fall freely down her cheeks. So much pain in this world. So many hurt and lost and there was nothing she could do. No! She had to find a way. Something.

Your will be done.

The line from grandmother's secretly whispered prayer settled heavy on her heart. To trust in the pain seemed too hard. How could she face it all again now that she was alone?

Mrs. Harper stood beside her. "I'm so sorry. I didn't know. I swear I didn't."

The anger surged again and she no longer tried to hide it. She turned her eyes on Mrs. Harper and let her pain shine through them. She no longer cared the consequence. "White people know and don't care, or they just don't care to know at all. Y'all live in big safe houses where no one comes to take from you the only thing you's have left that's yours to own!"

The mask dropped and Mrs. Harper looked every bit as enraged as she. "Big houses don't save you," she said through clenched teeth, words tumbling from her lips like they had too long been trapped inside. "They don't keep you safe from guests who come to your room in the middle of the night. Their doors are not strong enough to keep them out! And when that big, fancy house is just another place for a party, who is there to protect you or hear your screams when all the adults are dancing and drinking in the ball room? And when it is all over, who can you tell when the man is an old family friend? There is no one to tell and no one to keep you safe when he comes the next time and the next. All you have left is who you are supposed to be!

"No. No one can know when your worth and hope for marriage is based off your purity. Because who would ever want a wife who is tainted? Who could ever love one who is soiled, torn and broken?" Her face deepened to a bright red and her pulse throbbed in a vein on her forehead. Mrs. Harper's knees weakened and she held onto a sapling for support. Her chested heaved.

Ruth lost her ability to breathe. How foolish she'd been. She'd hated people for making up their minds about her when they knew nothing of her soul. Yet she'd done the very same thing. Without thought she grabbed the woman who'd bought her as if she were worth nothing more than livestock and pulled her close.

Mrs. Harper stiffened and then returned the embrace, sobs wracking her body. Ruth held her and prayed. What did God see? Slave and master? Or two of his daughters hurt by a world they couldn't control?

When their tears were spent, Miss Lydia lifted her face from the crook of Ruth's neck and wiped her nose on the sleeve of her fancy dress.

Ruth gathered Miss Lydia's hands in hers. "Maybe you and me have more in common than we's thought."

"Did that... " Miss Lydia's voice cracked. She cleared her throat but no longer tried to hide the sorrow from her eyes. "What we saw at the cabin, did something like that happen to you?"

Ruth took a deep breath. Her voice radiated with pain, but she spoke with a quiet strength she knew came from somewhere other than herself. "Most days, when my daddy was in the fields, the white man would come 'n take from me and my sister what he said was his by right. I never told my daddy 'cause I know he'd try to kill him. I didn't want to see my daddy hanged, so I never said nothin'."

Miss Lydia chewed her lower lip, shame crossing her face. "Was this man the plantation owner?"

"No. His son. He weren't no more than a youth but acted like he owned the place and everyone on it."

Miss Lydia picked at her fingernails. "Do you think...is this something that happens all the time?"

She looked completely terrified of the answer Ruth would give. Ruth almost wanted to tell her that no, maybe it wasn't like that everywhere. But there would be no truth in it.

Ruth sighed. "After my daddy died, Momma told me why I looked so different from my siblings. She said that one of the white foremen used to come for her, and I was the result of that. I's part white."

Miss Lydia squeezed her eyes shut a tear escaping and trailing down her cheek.

Now that she'd started, Ruth let out the words that she never planned to speak to anyone. Especially not her mistress. "When our plantation burned, I lost Momma and my baby brother in the fire. Me and my sister, we ran for the woods. We was safe there for a little while until that awful white man found us and rounded us up. He took a likin' to my sister. Eventually he beat her to death. That was two days before we came through your town. I'd prayed God would save me from that man, 'cause I knew it wouldn't be long before he came for me too. We kept movin', and I kept prayin'. It was all I had left." A small smile tugged at the corner of Ruth's mouth. "Then I heard you a yellin' at him to stop hittin' me and I thought, Lord, what kinda white woman is this?"

Miss Lydia lifted one shoulder and let her lips bow. "I promised myself I'd never be my Mother." Then she laughed, and Ruth couldn't help but join her, glad for the momentary feeling of lightness it brought to her bruised heart.

Miss Lydia grabbed her and hugged her like her sister had always done. "Oh, Ruth, I am so sorry. I'm so sorry for all that happened to you."

Ruth eased back. "Don't you be sorry. You's the answer to my prayer. God done sent you for me. I'll always be thankful for that."

Tears welled in Miss Lydia's eyes, spilling over onto her cheeks.

Ruth shook her head. "It seems to me like evil pays no mind to you's status or color."

Miss Lydia straightened, her tone full of resolve. "I will not let it be so here. As soon as Charles is home, I will tell him what is happening."

Ruth could only pray it would matter to him. He probably already knew. Might have even been down there himself. But she didn't have the heart to tell Miss Lydia. Let her believe the best about her husband. Ruth would pray it would be true.

Thunder cracked overhead, startling them both. They looked up into a sky that had darkened along with their moods and had gone unnoticed. A cloud opened its faucet and dumped buckets down on the helpless women underneath it.

"Hurry! Let's get back in the buggy," Miss Lydia cried.

Ruth struggled to untie the mare and then climbed into the seat, the little cover overhead giving them only a small amount of protection from the blowing rain. Miss Lydia pulled back on the reins, attempting to get the horse to back up. But she'd stopped in the middle of the trees and now couldn't get turned around. The buggy caught on a raised root, and the horse pawed the ground, tossing her head.

Ruth could barely see anything through the sheets of water. How would they get unstuck? She saw only one option. "I'll lead her!" Ruth shouted over the rain and leapt from the side into the quickly gathering mud. Holding onto the horse's bridle, she twisted and backed the mare from the small space. She turned them around in the meadow and put them back on the trail heading out. As soon as she heaved her soaking skirts into the seat, Miss Lydia urged the mare toward the main road.

The wind beat hard against them, ripping the top from the buggy. The horse slid in the thick mud gathering under its hooves. They bounced toward the main road holding onto the sides of the buggy. Ruth prayed Miss Lydia could get them back to the barn in one piece.

The seat suddenly jerked, and Ruth slammed into Miss Lydia. A loud crack told Ruth they would end up walking the rest of the way. They both hurried down to look at the damage, but it was exactly as Ruth had feared. The wooden wheel would take them no further.

"We have to get Snowflake unhitched! We can't use the buggy anymore." Miss Lydia picked up a broken wheel spindle and tossed it in the seat.

Ruth nodded and went to the other side of the buggy. How was she supposed to know how to unhook this thing? She jerked on the harness. There.

If she just unbuckled this here. That's it. The strap came loose. Now all she would have to do is –

Something wrapped around her waist, and she screamed.

"Ruth!"

She heard Miss Lydia calling her name from the other side of the buggy. A hand covered her mouth so close under her nose it blocked her air. She struggled. The man gripped her tighter until she began to panic. Be still! Don't let him see fear. She had to make him think he had her so he would relax his grip. When he did, she would see if she could find a way to strike him.

"Ruth!" Miss Lydia shouted as she rounded the back of the buggy, tripping over her giant skirts, her bonnet gone from her head and her hair hanging wildly from one side. Her eyes widened when she saw Ruth, and she froze.

"Just take yer horse and get on home, ma'am."

Ruth knew that voice. Webb, the man from the cabins. Her stomach lurched.

"I'll make sure this little gal is taken care of," Webb said. He yanked Ruth's arm freeing her grasp from the harness and allowing the rigging to drop.

Miss Lydia stared at them.

"There's your horse," he snarled. "You can get on back to the house now." He tossed the reins at her. The movement broke Miss Lydia from her spell, and she watched them tumble to the soaked earth. When she looked up, her eyes found Ruth's.

And something within their blue-green depths changed.

The man gripped Ruth tighter. In a flurry of sodden fabric Miss Lydia was on them. She lifted a wagon spoke over her head and brought it down with a solid crack against the captor's face. Startled, he released Ruth and focused his fury on the crazy woman in front of him. Ruth stumbled back and watched in awe.

Miss Lydia looked at the splintered spindle in her hand. It's long tapered end sharp and jagged. Webb stepped toward her. Miss Lydia lunged, sending the spike right through the cur's eye!

He staggered backward, blood oozing from his face. Miss Lydia grabbed Ruth and somehow they both swung onto the back of the prancing animal. Why it hadn't bolted when they'd freed it from the harness she didn't know, but she was grateful for it.

An enraged roar erupted behind them and the horse bolted forward. They galloped through the woods and out onto the road. Ruth gripped her arms around Miss Lydia's waist. They sat astride the horse, their skirts hiked up above their knees. They flew past now empty fields and after a terrifyingly long ride finally skid to a halt in front of the barn.

The door flew open and Noah was there pulling at the reins.

"Let go Mrs. Harper! I's got her."

Noah looked at Ruth with frantic eyes. She gently grasped Miss Lydia's hand. "It's all right now. We's safe. You can let go."

Miss Lydia's head rolled back and the reins slipped from her fingers. She slumped and started to slide off the horse. Ruth tried to hold her, but she was too heavy.

"Catch her!"

She slipped into Noah's waiting arms. He cradled the woman like an infant, his gaze asking Ruth questions she couldn't answer.

Ruth dropped to the ground with an awkward movement. "We needs to get her inside and warmed by the fire. You go and take her to her room. I's goin' to get Betsy."

The rain slowed to a steady trickle, and Ruth dashed across the garden not waiting to see if Noah followed her orders.

She threw open the door. "Betsy!"

"Lord, child! What's happened to you?" Betsy swung around from the stove and studied her with wide eyes.

"No time. You's got to help me with Miss Lydia."

Betsy frowned and didn't move. Ruth chided herself. She must remember her place. She straightened her shoulders. "Mrs. Harper's done fainted and nearly fell off her horse. Noah's taking her to her room. We needs to get her in somethin' dry and warm."

Betsy flew into action and followed Ruth into the rain. Noah stood awkwardly on the porch. "I ain't never been in the house before."

Ruth pushed past him. "Up here."

She led him up the servant's staircase and to Miss Lydia's room.

"Where should I put her?" Noah asked.

They agreed on the small settee by the armoire. Noah sat her down, and her eyes flew open. Miss Lydia looked at them like a frightened deer.

"Out!" she shouted. They jumped but didn't move. Miss Lydia leapt to her feet. "Out! Now!"

They all scrambled to the door, but Miss Lydia caught Ruth's wrist. "Not you."

Betsy turned and opened her mouth to speak, but Miss Lydia shoved her out the door behind Noah, slammed it shut, and turned the lock.

Then the two women fell into each other's arms and let the sobs free until none remained.

Fifteen

*R*uth slowly opened her eyes to the morning sun already streaming in through the window. She yawned and stretched her arms over her head. She froze. She was snuggled under the covers in Miss Lydia's room. She leapt from the bed.

Miss Lydia jumped up, knocking her writing utensils across the small table she'd been sitting at. "Good heavens!"

Ruth blinked at her, the memories of their tear-soaked night returning in a gush. She sank down on the bed. "Sorry. I done forgot why I's here." She shrugged. "Sorta spooked me." She offered Miss Lydia a half-hearted smile that wasn't returned.

Miss Lydia straightened the mess, wrapping a thong of leather around a small book and drawing it to her chest.

Ruth pressed her lips together. What a mess. Now that the emotions of a terrible day were over, the lady was probably horrified that she'd allowed a slave to dirty her bed.

"I want to thank you."

Ruth looked up, her brows creasing. "Huh?"

Miss Lydia smoothed her rumpled nightdress, the match to the one hanging on Ruth's slight frame and making her skin wonder at the foreign softness. "I have never..." her voice thickened with unshed tears. She shook her head and cleared her throat, composing her features into the distant aristocratic look Ruth had grown accustomed to.

Ruth offered a gentle smile, and as she hoped, Miss Lydia softened. "I wanted to thank you for talking with me, for understanding and not judging. For being my...friend."

The word hung heavy between them. It carried the weight of truth but tinged with impossibility.

Ruth longed to believe they could be something different than slave and master, and could see the same in the eyes staring back at her. "I thank you, too," Ruth said. "I'd never thought I could tell that story to a white woman and have her understand. Or even care. You's somethin' different for sure, Mrs. Harper."

Miss Lydia giggled. "I think we both know you no longer need to call me that."

Ruth shook her head. "What are the others gonna think if I started calln' you by your given name?"

Miss Lydia huffed. "I no longer give much value to the thoughts of others. Let them think what they will."

Just the same, Ruth knew better than to poke at that snake. "I better be gettin' downstairs. It's already late."

Ruth looked at her sodden dress, still in a heap on the floor. Miss Lydia must have noticed her gaze. "Here. You can wear one of mine."

Ruth shook her head. "No, ma'am. I can't. It ain't proper."

Miss Lydia shot her an annoyed look and flung open the armoire. "Nonsense. My mother gave all the dresses she no longer wanted to her maid."

Ruth considered the claim. She still didn't know much about the way things worked in the big house. It certainly would be better than going down in a soggy dress. Or worse, the lady's nightdress. Ruth shuddered. "Oh, all right."

Lydia tossed her a dark blue dress with a purple bow and grabbed one for herself before ducking behind the screen. Ruth quickly pulled the nightdress over her head and tugged on the heavy skirt. She bent her arms around behind her as best as she could but struggled to get the little hooks into her fingers.

"And now you see why I must have help dressing. It's not because I am lazy."

Ruth stilled. A slow smile tugged on the side of her mouth. "Ain't nobody said you was lazy."

"Of course they would not *say* it. But I'm sure you all thought it."

Ruth's eyes widened.

Miss Lydia waved her hand in the air. "I'll fasten yours and then you can do mine."

Not seeing any other option, Ruth slowly turned her back on her mistress. Miss Lydia grabbed the two sides and yanked, cinching the cloth tight around Ruth's bosom and waist. She gasped.

"Be glad you don't have a corset on under it," Miss Lydia mumbled. She finished the hooks and laces and turned Ruth to the mirror. "See? Lovely."

Ruth looked at the strange woman in the mirror. She had the same features, but no longer looked to be the same person. The deep blue fabric lightened the tone of her skin further, almost making her look like a white woman who had spent too much time under the heat of the sun. If not for the coarse, dark hair on her head, she might even pass as a common townswoman. The idea sent a trail of unwelcomed thoughts snaking through her head. What if she were to run? With a bonnet pulled tight and low and a dress like this...

"What do you think? I think you look wonderful."

The excitement in Miss Lydia's voice brought Ruth's wayward thoughts to a halt. How could she betray her? Especially now?

Ruth sighed. "I don't know. Seems like too nice of a dress to get dirty beatin' rugs."

The smile on Miss Lydia's face faltered, replaced by something Ruth couldn't quite name. Miss Lydia turned away. Ruth quickly cinched Miss Lydia's corset and hooked the row of pearl buttons down the back of her black gown. She should say something. She didn't know what.

As soon as her fingers finished the last button Miss Lydia waved her away. "You better go on now. Tell them I won't be down for breakfast."

"But don't you think you should – "

"Just go!"

Ruth clamped her mouth shut and strode from the room, pulling the door closed behind her. She straightened her shoulders and descended the main staircase, her eyes focusing on not tripping on the folds of fabric that gathered around her feet. No wonder they wore those crazy hoops to hold the skirts out. How could a person walk around all day, much less dance like they like to do, with all this around her ankles?

Her foot hit the last stair, and she heard a gasp. There stood Lucy with a rag in one hand, the look on her face completely stricken. Ruth dipped her chin and scurried off, nearly tripping before she made it to the safety of the back porch. Oh, how would she ever explain this? Lucy already didn't like her.

The morning air still carried the scent of long overdue rain, the damp earth smell reminding her of her childhood. She lifted the skirts to avoid soaking them on the wet grass. A movement to her left drew her attention. Noah stood by the edge of the garden, turning his hat in his hands. Their eyes met and Ruth felt her heart flutter. What would he think of her in such an outfit? The heat rose to her cheeks. Should she speak to him or quickly get back to her room?

"Miss Ruth?"

No escaping now. She swung her gaze fully on him and lowered her skirts below her ankles. "Hello, Noah."

He stood close, forcing her to raise her chin to look into his face. He smelled of fresh hay and cut oats.

"I's been worried 'bout you. What happened?"

Ruth clenched her teeth. How much could she tell him? He must have read her thoughts.

"You can trust me, Ruth. I know somethin' happened. You came back astride a horse and clingin' to the lady, who looked right mad with fear. The buggy's gone and well..." He left the ending open, hoping she would finish it for him.

"We hit a rock or a hole or somethin', and the wagon wheel broke. Then that storm came in and frightened the horse, and the beast brought us back at a full run. I thought we would fall to our deaths tryin' to hang on to that thing in the pourin' rain."

He studied her. "Anythin' else?"

She frowned. Someone should know, shouldn't they? She shook her head. "Not here."

He glanced around at the empty garden and grabbed her hand, pulling her into the barn. "No one in here but us and the horses."

The smell of horseflesh brought back the fear that had gripped her stomach. "What 'bout Tommy?" She whispered, "Or little Johnny?"

He shook his head. "Already gone to town."

"There was a man. A white man. We saw him comin' out of one of the cabins." She swallowed hard.

Noah's face tightened. "What did he look like?"

"Long, greasy hair. Dark eyes."

"Yeah. I know who that is. Name's Webb."

"Yes!"

Noah clenched his fists at his sides. "He came 'round here not too long ago. I was saddlin' Mr. Harper's stallion when he came asking for a job. I could tell right away he weren't no good. Think Mr. Harper saw it too, but gave the man a job anyway."

Ruth wrapped her arms around her waist. "I knew what he was doin' in there."

Noah looked like he might explode from the inside, so she hurried on. "Mrs. Harper gave him a tongue lashin' and sent him on his way. We went to a meadow out in the woods for her to have her noon meal when the storm hit. The buggy wheel broke. We were unhookin' the horse when he came out of the woods somewhere and grabbed a hold of me.

"Somethin' happened then. Mrs. Harper, she done snapped. She came after him with a broken wheel spoke like she was some kinda warrior. She hit him in the head and he let go of me. Then he grabbed for her. I don't think he shoulda done that. She'd gone mad by then. She stabbed him right in the eye, and then pulled me up on that horse. We rode like the devil was on our heels back to the barn."

Noah grabbed her and squeezed her against his broad chest. She let her face bury into his muscles, his grip so tight she feared she might lose her breath, and yet she did not want to draw away. Finally he eased her to arm's length away from him.

"We needs to send some men to look for him."

"What if he's dead?"

Noah ran a hand over his close-cut hair. "Need to know that, too. Don't worry. We'll find him. I'll let you know when I do."

"Thank you, Noah. You's been nothin' but kind to me. You's a good friend."

His eyes softened. "I think you's know I want to be more."

Ruth swallowed the lump in her throat. "I gotta get to Betsy. She'll be worried 'bout me." She hurried from the barn as quick as her skirts would let her. She entered the kitchen and leaned against the door.

"Well, now. This ain't somethin' I expected." Betsy wiped her hands on her apron and raised her eyebrows at Ruth.

"Me neither."

Betsy laughed. "Come here, child. You can help me with this pie crust. Blackberry tarts are Mrs. Harper's favorite, and Johnny done brought me a whole bucket full."

"She said she won't come down for no breakfast."

"Well, we'll see 'bout that."

Ruth slipped on a large apron and tied it behind her back. She washed her hands and dried them on a clean towel before taking her place next to Betsy.

"Just work it like this here," she said, pulling and shaping the dough. "It starts out tough and wantin' to keep itself bound up, but if you just keep gently pullin' and stretchin' it, soon 'nough it'll relax and become workable."

Ruth put her hands into the dough and pulled it the way Betsy showed her. They worked quietly together until they'd prepared several round sections of smooth, flat dough ready for filling.

"Oh, Betsy, I don't know what to do," Ruth said, breaking the silence.

"Well, can't say I'll always have the right words to tell you, but my ears are always open if you want to talk."

Ruth spooned a sweet mixture of blackberries into the center of the dough and folded it over, pinching the edges together and thought of how much she should tell Betsy. She'd already told Noah. She didn't want to turn into a gossip.

"Well, I'm worried 'bout Mrs. Harper. There was a man come up on us in the woods. Gave us a fright. She seems very shaken up 'bout it."

"That why you stayed the night in her room?"

Ruth nodded. Would they be angry at her? She'd crossed another of those invisible lines of propriety that no one spoke of, yet everyone lived by.

"That's good. I'm glad you was there for her."

Ruth tilted her head. "Really?"

"Certainly. Even white ladies need comfort sometimes. They's just don't like to show it."

Ruth gave a short laugh. "That's the truth."

They placed the treats in the oven and settled down on the bench. Betsy looked at her for a long time, emotions playing on her face. It seemed like she had something important to say, so Ruth waited patiently until she finally spoke.

"I had a daughter. She looked so much like you."

Ruth's breath caught. The room, the dresses, the way Betsy had immediately taken to her. It all made sense. "What happened to her?"

"She died of the same sickness that took Mr. Harper's parents ten years back. She wasn't but a girl gettin' close to her courtin' years. So much life left."

Ruth placed a gentle hand on Betsy's arm. "I'm so sorry."

Betsy sniffled. "She wanted to change the world, my Sophie. She said she would show them white people that we's just as smart as them. Show them we feels the same things, hopes for the same things, and loves the same way. She wanted them to see that people were people no matter their color."

Ruth's eyes widened.

Betsy shook her head. "I done told her that talk was dangerous. Would get us in trouble. The place I came from, that was true. But then I's started to see that maybe it could be different here at Ironwood. The Harper's have always been plenty kind to us. Still, I wouldn't let her speak her mind. We argued a lot 'bout it. Then suddenly, my passionate little girl bent on changin' the world was gone. And she done left a hole of hopelessness in her place."

Tears burned at the back of Ruth's throat. "I's so sorry." It was all she could think to say.

Betsy cupped Ruth's cheek in her hand. "And then God drops you in our lives. I's see the same spark in you that I saw in her. And I see you makin' changes 'round here already, even if you's don't know it. Keep at it. This war will bring many changes, too. Of that I'm right certain."

Ruth offered a half smile. "I worry 'bout what it'll mean for us."

"So do I, child." She patted Ruth on the shoulder. "It's time to pull them tarts from the oven." Betsy opened the oven door and a sweet smell filled the kitchen. Ruth's stomach growled.

"You eats one and take some out to the barn for little Johnny and the others. I'd say Johnny deserves one or two of 'em for all his hard work pickin'. Then go see if you can coax Mrs. Harper out of her room with one."

Ruth nodded, but she doubted it.

She wrapped a few tarts in a napkin and walked back to the barn. The air had grown thick and hot, already stifling enough to cause a sheen of sweat to pop up on her brow. The morning grew late and Ruth could not believe how much of the day she'd already wasted without doing much of anything.

She found Tommy and Noah standing close together talking in low tones. She called to Noah and waved to the men. They stopped talking as she approached.

"Betsy made blackberry tarts." She peeled back the edge of the napkin and allowed the sweet smells to escape. She expected smiles of delight, but both men's faces were serious.

"Ruth, I's been talkin' with Tommy."

Her heart fluttered. She glanced at Tommy. Did he know, too? Heavens, what had she started?

"Tommy says he saw a man walkin' the edge of the road on his way back from town. White man with long, dirty hair hanging past his shoulders. He had a hat low on his head, so Tommy didn't see his face. But, when the wagon got close the man looked back at him and then ran into the woods."

That had to be Webb. Not dead after all, as Miss Lydia had so feared. She looked at Tommy. He nodded. "Yep. Thought it was strange the way he ran off. When I got back here and Noah said he was goin' to go lookin' for a man that had bothered you and Mr. Harper's wife, I figured that might be him. I wouldn't worry 'bout it too much, though. If that fellow smarted off to Mrs. Harper, I'm sure Mr. Harper will have plenty 'nough to say to him 'bout it."

Noah and Ruth exchanged a look. She forced a smile that didn't reach her eyes. "I's sure he will, Tommy. Thank you." She handed over one of her napkins. "Be sure Johnny gets one of these, will you?"

Noah nodded and took her offering.

She said her goodbyes and made her way back to the house as casually as she could manage, so as not to raise suspicion. She checked the hall. No sign of Lucy. Good. She couldn't handle the questions the woman was sure to throw at her. She took the back staircase and knocked softly on Lydia's door.

"I do not wish to be disturbed at this time," the muffled voice said through the door.

Ruth took a deep breath. "It's me." She hoped that would make a difference. But would it? She shouldn't read too much into what happened last night.

The door flew open. Miss Lydia looked at her with red-rimmed eyes. She stepped back from the door, holding it open for Ruth. Ruth walked in, and when the door clicked, she turned. "I's got news."

Miss Lydia sank down onto her dressing chair. She closed her eyes and nodded once for Ruth to continue.

"Tommy saw that man walkin' down the road. When Webb saw the wagon, he ran off into the woods. He ain't dead."

Miss Lydia's shoulders drooped. She slowly inhaled. "I thought I'd killed him."

Ruth rubbed her gently on the back. "I know. But you didn't. And he's gone now."

Miss Lydia chewed her lip. "Gone doesn't give him justice."

If only such a thing were easy to grab. Ruth sighed. "Mr. Harper'll be back soon. I don't think that horrible man would dare come back here now."

"I suppose you are right. Still. I cannot stand to know what has happened here. I must tell Charles. I must protect Ironwood."

She said it with such fierceness, with such wildness in her eyes, that Ruth got an uneasy feeling. Not knowing what to say, she turned the subject. "Betsy done made you some blackberry tarts. Ain't they your favorite?"

Miss Lydia shrugged, and the fire in her eyes returned to a haunted vacancy. "I do not want any." She pulled a tight smile across her face. "Thank you for coming to tell me the news, but I do think I may need to rest now."

Ruth nodded and pulled the door closed behind her, worrying that the woman left inside was not the same one who had twice come to her rescue.

Sixteen

Jackson, Mississippi
June 21, 1862

Union Navy in Vicksburg!

Charles scanned the paper and handed the boy a coin. The Union still held Corinth, he read. Confederates had failed to hold it, and the Feds continued to gain strength in Mississippi. For now, Governor Pettus and his legislature sustained their work here in Jackson, and it became a hot seat for war activity. A good reason for him to be here.

Charles moved among the throng of young men joining the cause that burned in their breasts. Some of them nothing but boys. Charles felt the same burn, but the pleading in Lydia's eyes had stayed him thus far. Though he knew it could not last much longer. When he returned home, he would have to discuss his duty with her and pray she understood. He feared his sweet bride tried to ignore all that happened outside of Ironwood. For his part, he had encouraged it. He did not wish to see her worried by things she could not control.

Charles found the door he searched for and stepped inside. People bustled around, many complaining over the outrageous prices. $3.50 for a sack of sugar! He worked his way through the desperate patrons of the general goods store and found the office in the back. Charles tapped on the doorframe, drawing the attention of the clerk seated behind his desk. The man straightened his glasses and gestured for Charles to enter.

"Mr. Harper, I presume?"

Charles gave a small bow. "Indeed. And you are Mr. Smith?"

The thin man rose from his ledgers and offered his hand. Charles gave it one pump and settled into the seat the man gestured to.

"I received your letter. And as I stated in my response, there is little need for cotton now. The Union has the river blockaded. We can get very little out and even then they must go on armed ships."

"I am aware. I have already made arrangements for my shipping. My concern was with sales here in Jackson. What are your interests in my supplying your store with cotton and tobacco?"

The man rubbed the scruff on his chin. "Those things we have. It's sugar, leather and flour we need."

Charles frowned. "What about corn?"

Mr. Smith brightened. "Yes, I would be interested in corn."

Charles had little enough of it, mostly grown for their own table and to feed the livestock, but he'd make sales wherever he could get them.

"I will be paid in gold or silver."

The man shook his head fervently. "I cannot give you that. We are working on the Confederate dollar now. But do not worry Mr. Harper; it is as good as gold."

"I am afraid not. There has yet to be any stability shown in it, and I shall not risk my livelihood upon it."

It took some convincing and a price much lower than he wanted, but when they finally shook hands on a deal, Charles felt a flood of relief. He stepped back out into the heat of the day and continued down the street.

Men were gathered outside the capitol building cheering and straining forward to hear the words of a speaker standing on the steps. Charles stepped into the crowd, his shoulders brushing uncomfortably close to others whose bodies carried the smells of standing too long in the heavy heat.

"Join, men! Join and save your families and your homes from the oppression that the North would lay upon us. You've heard the Vice President! We *are* founded on opposite ideas. Our livelihood is set upon the truth that the Negro is not equal to the white man. Fight to maintain our right to keep him in his natural state of subordination!"

Charles narrowed his eyes. Was not the true issue state's rights? He looked around at the men nodding in agreement. Uneasiness settled in his stomach. He turned and walked back through the crowd, suddenly more anxious to return home.

He crossed State Street and climbed the steps to the Bowman House. His boots clicked across the polished wood floors as he passed under the large chandelier hanging in the foyer.

"Mr. Harper!"

Charles turned to see the clerk waving him over to the large carved desk the man stood behind.

"Yes?"

"You have received a telegram." The plump man shifted through a stack of papers on his desk. "Ah, here it is." He passed the paper over the desk.

Mr. Harper stop Ruth sends word she worries for Mrs. Harper stop Believes her very ill stop

Charles frowned at the paper. "Is this all?"

The clerk shifted through his papers again. "Yes, sir. That is all that has been delivered."

Charles nodded and tucked the slip of paper into his vest pocket. He climbed the steps to his room without another word to the clerk. What type of sick? Fever? Images of his mother in her final moments washed over him. He needed to get home. Further business could wait or be conducted by post. He must return to Ironwood. Charles packed his belongings and checked out of the hotel.

In a few moments his team and carriage came around from the livery. He dipped his chin to Abe, the younger man he now took on his trips for fear the long rides would prove too much for Tommy's arthritic knees. Try as he might to hide it, Tommy's years were catching up to him.

The carriage made slow passage through Jackson; the press of people trying to escape the ever advancing Union troops flooded the narrow streets and overfilled the boarding houses. It had cost him double to secure a private room at the Bowman House.

He settled into the cushions and endured the bumping and swaying of a hurried pace. How many days had passed since his bride had fallen ill? Perhaps he worried too much. Despite how hard he tried, Charles could not keep the image of Lydia lying pale in her bed wasting away from overshadowing his thoughts. Upon her father's suggestion, he'd given Lydia her own room. His own parents had shared one, and Charles hoped one day Lydia would wish to share one with him as well. If she lived long enough to learn to love him.

It was nearly dark the following day when Charles finally pulled into Ironwood. Ruth stood at the front door, waiting on him.

"Good evenin', Mr. Harper. We's glad you made it home."

"Where is my wife?"

"She finally done left her room and she's readin' in the parlor. She ain't hardly eaten for just at a week now. She needs to see you." Ruth turned on her heel and strode away.

Charles didn't have time to contemplate the maid's strange behavior. Without bothering to remove his hat, he pulled the pocket door wide to reveal Lydia sitting with a book spread open on her lap. She jumped, and it slid to the floor with a thump. In a single instant he took in her appearance. Dressed, though hair undone. Color in her cheeks, but dark circles under red eyes. At least it wasn't the influenza.

"Lydia, my love, are you all right?"

She rushed to him, carelessly flinging her arms around his neck and gathering a handful of his hair. He gripped her tightly; his heartbeat thudding against his ribs. He held back his questions, waiting for her to calm the rapid breath on his neck and gather herself.

Finally, she pulled back and looked into his eyes. "Oh, Charles. I did not expect you for many more nights."

He traced his finger along her jaw. *So smooth.* "Tommy sent a telegraph saying you were ill. Your maid says you are not eating. My business in Jackson can wait. Are you sick? Should I send for the doctor?"

She studied his face, uncertainty in her eyes.

Patience. Let her come to you.

He tried to let his care for her shine through his eyes and waited. She looked around like she feared someone watched them. More worry knifed its way into Charles.

She grasped his hand. "Could we talk somewhere else?"

He nodded, not trusting himself to words.

Charles followed Lydia out onto the upper balcony. The cool breeze lifted her loose strands of chestnut hair and teased him with their playfulness. She leaned against the railing and looked out over the front lawn in the gathering dusk. He stood beside her, trying his best to let her begin. Deciding she never would and unable to contain himself any longer, he opened his mouth to speak.

She spoke before he could release a syllable. "I decided to take your rounds and check on the plantation in your absence."

Charles chuckled, relief flooding him. All this worry over her insistence on acting as a man? "I am not in the least surprised. Such independence does not shock me."

"Yet, I hope what I saw during that ride will." Her soft voice almost didn't reach his ears, its hollow sound tightening his chest.

He clenched his jaw. Clutching her shoulders, he turned her around to face him. He concentrated on keeping the strain from his voice.

"What did you see?"

She closed her eyes as if too ashamed to look at him. His fingers gripped her tighter. What had she seen to cause her to react in such a manner?

"There was a man leaving the cabins when all the Negro adults were gone. He said there was a sick man inside. But I saw the little girl on the porch." When she opened her eyes, fire lit their ocean depths sparking them to life. "I know what he was really doing in there."

Charles stiffened. The taking of female slaves was not tolerated at Ironwood, and it certainly wasn't something his delicate wife needed to witness.

"I ordered him to return to his work. He leered at me and Ruth and went to his horse he'd hidden in the woods. I left then and went to the place you showed me. The meadow."

The uncertainty returned to her eyes, and Charles forced himself to relax his features. "Then what?" He asked, the gruffness in his voice undermining his efforts to encourage her.

She drew a deep breath. "A storm came. I'd parked the buggy too deep and couldn't get it turned around. I broke one of the wheels. We were trying to unhook the horse when I heard Ruth scream. When I came around the back of the buggy, he had Ruth in his grasp."

Charles' fist clenched, aching for the feel of the man's skin being pounded underneath them. "Who is this man?"

"Webb."

The wretch he'd felt sorry for and allowed a job, even though he hadn't needed him. He repaid Charles' kindness by taking Ironwood's females? By threatening his wife? The muscles in his jaw worked. When he got his hands around that man's neck –

"I stabbed at him with a broken spoke," Lydia said, breaking into his thoughts.

A tingling sensation crawled up the back of his neck. He narrowed his eyes and studied his trembling wife. Stronger than she appeared. He fought back the rush of pride that briefly filled his chest, too soon replaced again by the worry that increased his blood pressure.

He gathered her in his arms, feeling her soft curves pressed against him. She released a ragged breath, and he stroked her hair. The man got at least some of what he deserved. Brave little woman. She mustn't let guilt cripple her.

"All that matters is that you are safe," Charles whispered, "I could not stand it if any harm came to you. You did the right thing."

She shivered against him and a feeling of protectiveness welled inside his chest. "Do not worry," Charles said. "He will get more punishment when I get my hands on him." He pulled back, his eyes boring into hers. Guilt flooded her face.

He tilted his head to the side and watched her closely, trying to see her more clearly in the meager moonlight. "Is the man still alive?"

She tried to look away from him, but he cupped her chin in his hand. "Did you kill him, Lydia?"

"I wanted to! I wanted him to die!"

"But did you kill him?"

"I feared I had, but he was seen the next morning."

Charles dropped his hand and his fingers curled again. He turned to look out over the dark lawn. "Where is he now?" he asked, his voice tight.

"I don't know. Tommy saw him on the road to town. Everyone was talking about it. He ducked into the woods before Tommy could speak to him. No one's seen him since. I do not know if he lives still, and if so, where he is."

"It doesn't matter. You were strong. And brave. You did only what you needed to do to protect yourself and your maid. No court in Mississippi would find you guilty."

She looked at him, the wariness tightening her lips causing an ache in his heart. "Charles, were you aware of men doing such things in the quarters?"

His shoulders tightened, the tension in his neck causing the muscles to strain. What kind of man did she see in him? "No, I did not. But you can be sure that each man on this plantation will *once again* have a very clear understanding of proper conduct on my property come morning. I promise you, Lydia. It will not happen again, God help me."

"Thank you, Charles," she whispered. A stray tear slid down her cheek, and he quickly whisked it away.

"Come. You need your rest." He wove his fingers in hers and led her back to her room, lighting a lamp from the hallway. He pulled a nightdress from her drawer and offered it to her, motioning to the privacy of the screen. The color rose to her cheeks, and he turned his eyes aside.

She disappeared behind the screen, and he removed his boots and placed them by the door, then pulled his shirt over his head. His fingers brushed the buttons of his trousers, but he decided against it.

Lydia emerged from the screen and gasped. She drew her lower lip between her teeth and he felt his heart rate quicken. Charles drew a deep breath and held a hand out to her.

She stepped toward him and placed her cool hand in his. The stiffness in her body caused an ache. Would she ever desire him? He caressed her shoulder. First she must learn to trust him. He led her to the bed. She silently slipped under the blankets, pulling them to her chin. She gave him a smile that didn't reach her eyes. He lay down beside her and pulled her under his arm, snuggling her body close. He could feel her heart fluttering like a hummingbird against his side.

"Be calm, my love. Just rest."

After several moments, she finally relaxed and nuzzled into his chest. "You are good to me, Charles."

A smile spread on his lips in the dark. Perhaps there was hope yet. He planted a soft kiss on her honeysuckle-scented hair and gave her a small squeeze, not trusting himself to speak. God help him. This slip of a woman threatened to completely undo him.

Seventeen

Ironwood
July 6, 1862

*L*ydia looked at her reflection in the nearly smooth glass. A lovely gown. Mother should be pleased with her efforts. The cream-colored fabric draped gracefully around her shoulders with delicate pink lace brushing her skin. Lucy had wrangled her locks into a heap of curls on the back of her head, one section cascading over her shoulder. She looked as much the lady as possible.

Two weeks of Charles' comfort and company had restored her appetite and healthy complexion. The sickness she'd briefly felt waned, and her woman's time had come and gone right on its heels. She tried to remind herself that though four months of marriage had passed, there was nothing wrong with her if she had not yet produced a babe.

A soft knock drew her attention away from the mirror. "Yes?"

The door opened and Charles entered in a deep gray jacket, stark white shirt, and fitted waistcoat with a perfectly tied black cravat. His black pantaloons fit nicely across his muscled legs, and Lydia felt an unexpected flutter in her chest. A playful smile danced on his lips.

"You look beautiful."

The huskiness in his voice caused heat to rise in her cheeks. She looked up at him from under her lashes. "And you look rather fetching yourself, Mr. Harper."

He bent at the waist in a deep bow. "I am pleased to meet your approval."

She put a gloved hand to her lips to suppress a giggle. His eyes darkened and he drew her into his arms, his lips pressing against hers. She could sense the quickening of his pulse and drew away from him. "We must see to our guests."

Pain flashed in his eyes, and she felt a stab of regret. She laid a hand on his cheek, her eyes offering tentative affection.

He brushed his lips over her cheek and released her. She ignored the disappointment that caused her to release a breath that had unconsciously lodged in her chest. Was she not the one that turned aside the moment?

"Your parents have arrived."

She clasped her hands together. "Oh!" She hurried past him, his deep chuckle following her out the door. She descended the steps as slowly as she could manage. "Daddy!"

Her father beamed up at her. "My darling! You look lovely."

She took his hand and squeezed it. "I've missed you!"

He winked at her and nodded toward her mother standing stiffly at his side. Lydia inclined her head. "Good evening, Mother. Your dress is quite lovely."

Mother smiled softly, wrinkles gathering in the corners of her eyes. They were the first of the guests to arrive for the ball.

A surprise from Charles. For what, she wasn't quite certain. Perhaps an excuse to bring her parents for a visit?

She led Mother around the house, showing her the new items she'd purchased and pleased to see many met with Mother's approval. In the parlor, Mother touched her elbow. "Lydia, you have done well. I see you have grown up quite a bit these last months."

"I thank you, Mother. I have tried diligently."

Mother patted her arm. "And it shows." Then she waved her hand in the air as if fanning away any unnecessary emotions hanging there. "You should start greeting your guests."

They returned to the front entry, the chandelier overhead already lit and twinkling in the late afternoon light. The house girls bustled around, finishing up last minute details before disappearing from sight.

Lydia put on her best face and greeted each guest, a small gathering of family and close neighbors. She wondered what the men would discuss as they gathered in the drawing room since women were not to be *troubled* by such things. By the time Lydia tired of answering questions from well-meaning family on her new life, Charles called for them to ascend to the third floor ballroom.

"Who knew Mr. Harper would be so adept at planning a ball? He never hosted any before now," Mother remarked snapping open her fan.

A trio of violinists sat in the rear corner, their soft music floating across the room. Candlelight danced off the walls and within moments couples began to twirl across the floor. A hand rested on her elbow. "Would you care to dance, Mrs. Harper?"

She smiled up at Charles. "I would love to."

He placed his hand on the small of her back and guided them across the floor. So effortless was he in his movements that she nearly forgot her clumsiness and everything else except for the man in front of her. The dance ended too soon.

"I will come for another dance before long, my dear. For now, please excuse me to men's issues and enjoy your company." He laid a kiss on her hand she wished the glove didn't prevent her from feeling.

As soon as he left, Lydia found herself feeling alone in the vapid company of twittering girls. They fanned themselves, one openly shooting jealous glances at Charles' back. Lydia narrowed her gaze on the bold twit, and the girl had enough decency to let pink flood her cheeks. She excused herself to another group.

Satisfied she'd made her point, Lydia turned her attention to the daughters of a neighboring plantation and tried to appear interested in their discussion. They talked of minor things like dress styles and gossiped about ladies not present. She doubted the men spoke of such trivialities. No. She should try harder. Charles went through such trouble to do something nice for her.

Time passed much too slowly, and Charles did not return for another dance. Needing to escape from the crowd, Lydia passed two neighbors on the stairs with a polite smile. Thankfully they did not try to engage her in conversation. She glanced around, and seeing no one, walked softly to the back door. As it swung silently on its hinges, her gaze fell on Ruth pulling extra candles from the storage bin in the closet under the stairs. Lydia placed a finger to her lips.

Ruth nodded, another secret between them, and returned to her work.

Lydia paused on the back porch, the coolness of the night air giving relief to the heavy heat from the day. A band of crickets played their melody to the moon, and Lydia let the freedom of a starlit night apply a balm to her nerves.

She walked slowly through the garden, removing her gloves to touch the soft petals of delicate blooms. She settled onto a bench and turned her gaze to the heavens, as the soft sounds of music and laughter drifted down from above. Peaceful. And just what her heart needed. An ache settled inside her chest in bitter contrast to the pleasant surroundings. Must she always feel this way?

The crunch of rocks underfoot drew her gaze downward and onto the worried face of her husband. Had she been gone too long already? It felt like only a few moments.

Charles sat beside her and put an arm around her shoulders. He gently brushed at rebellious curls that fell into her face. He looked at her with sad eyes, the disappointment written across his features tearing at her heart. Had she erred again? Of course he would be upset she'd left the gathering he had put together solely for her benefit. She must take care to show more gratitude.

"Oh, Lydia. Don't you know that I love you?"

Her pulse quickened. She nodded, hoping he saw the gesture in the darkness. Oh, she knew he did. How could she not? He had flung open the doors to his heart and tried to invite her within.

"Do you love me as well?"

Her throat constricted. She longed to run from the emotions that burned within her. They could lead only to pain. But what of the pain of denial? He deserved more than that. She searched his face, seeing there all she longed for. "Yes, Charles. I do. With all that I have to offer."

He grasped her shoulders. "Then please, you have to talk to me. Do you think I cannot see it in your eyes? You are detached, distant. Ever since my return, I've known something is wrong. At first I thought you were stressed over the events that occurred during my absence. But now I fear it's much more. Something else eats at you. Little by little it takes you away from me. I cannot help you if I do not know. What I fear I can barely say."

He took a long draw of air, closing his eyes. When he opened them again, the intensity she saw made her stomach drop. "Lydia, did that man hurt you?"

Tears spilled from her eyes. Whatever the consequence, he should know the truth. Charles deserved better than her. She could no longer let him love the false image she'd created. She drew a breath, pained to lose him but knowing she must set him free. "Not him, but another. I am not what you think I am! I am not what you deserve."

There. It was done. He could be free of her now.

Charles ran his hand down her arm, and her heart skipped at his touch, bringing the downward spiral of her thoughts to a halt. His voice was gentle, yet confident. "I love you just as you are. Whatever you've done or whatever happened to you does not change my feelings. It does not change you in my sight."

Could she dare hope? What love could be that strong? Lydia picked at her long fingernails until she trusted her voice enough to speak. Surely he did not understand. "I am not the pure bride you thought you married. I never had that innocence. It was stolen from me long ago." The words came as if from someone else, hollow and detached.

Lydia turned away, unable to face him now that he knew. Unable to look at the repulsion that would replace the love in his eyes. She rose from her seat to flee.

He caught her arm. "Stop, Lydia. Stop." The pain in his voice reflected that which spilled from her eyes as traitorous tears. He gripped her tight. "Please, do not leave me."

She stopped but still could not look into his eyes. She could not trust his words. But she allowed him to pull her back to the bench. She stared at the grass under the folds of her skirts.

They were silent for several moments, and Lydia could only guess the thoughts he did not share. What had she done? It was foolish and selfish of her. She should have let him keep his happiness. Their times were dark, cloaked in the threat of war and hovering destruction. Why could she not allow him the image of the pure bride he so desired? One who belonged only to him?

She began to think of where she would go when he put her away from him. Would Mother be too ashamed to take her home? Would her father allow it? He would be broken when he heard. Oh, she should have thought of Daddy! She could not withstand him knowing. Why could she never maintain control over her mouth?

The silence around them was tempered only by the soft music from above, accompanied by one lone cricket chirping out of rhythm. Lydia dared a glance at Charles' profile. The muscles in his jaw worked, and he stared ahead.

She should not have opened a door she could never again close. Why had she allowed herself to begin to love? Over and over she reminded her heart of the pain that would come from it. And still she gave into the foolish notions of children. He would not want to be married to her any longer now that he knew the truth. The empty feeling in her stomach knotted into terror.

Charles took a deep breath. "When?"

She did not wish to speak of it. But he would have to know it all, now that she'd been fool enough to open her mouth. "When I was young. He was a guest at my parent's house."

"I would see him hanged." Charles' voice was thick and barely controlled.

Lydia slowly shook her head. "He's gone now. Dead and buried three years. It no longer matters, and the truth would only destroy my father. Please, I do not wish him to know."

They sat for many more minutes before Charles finally said, "Thank you for trusting me enough to tell me. I promise I will protect you and no harm will come to you again."

Her breath caught. Hope that refused to die lodged in her chest. He would not tell. He would not send her away. He may no longer love her, but he did not seem to hate her. She could find a way to live with that.

He suddenly drew her into an embrace she thought she would never feel again. *It's only for comfort*, she reminded herself. Nothing more. But as he held her close, her fears of losing him melted with each gentle stroke of his hand. "It is not your fault," he whispered over and over in her ear.

"I am soiled," she said between tears "I am not pure."

He sighed. "We all are soiled in some way, my dear. The Bible says that only God can wash away all that stains us. Only He can make us pure. Have you asked Him to do that for you?"

"No!" She pushed away from him. "How can I? He did not protect me. He did not save me then, so why should I want Him to save me now?" Anger she thought she could control broke free, refusing to stay contained.

"Because it is the only thing that will make you whole again. Not even my love, as much as it may be, can heal you. As much as I want to be everything you'll ever need, this I cannot do for you. Only He can bring beauty from ashes."

"He let this happen to me," she whispered.

Charles stroked her back. "Do not let it rule you. God did not cause the hurt, but He can use it for good. You may not see it now, but someday good can come from this. What men intend for evil He can use for good. Look for the good, my love, and you will find it."

With the stars overhead and her greatest blessing at her side, Lydia opened her heart to the God she had long ago abandoned and prayed for the healing of beauty from the ashes of her heart. When her prayers came to an end, they forgot about their guests and sat together under the stars for a long time in the new peace that surrounded them.

"Come, love," Charles finally said. "I believe we should get you some rest."

"What of the guests?" Lydia shook her head. "Mother will not be pleased."

"Do not worry over your mother. I will make your excuses."

Relief and gratitude washed over her and she allowed Charles to guide her to her room.

He helped her get ready for bed, promising to tell the guests she was not feeling well. Exhausted and yet at peace, Lydia drifted into a deep sleep and found herself again walking in the garden.

She walked past the roses, their sweet smells filling the night air. She paused. Near her bench stood the strange woman dressed as a man she'd seen once before. The woman looked around as if she were as confused at finding herself in Lydia's garden as Lydia was to find her there. A strange feeling of familiarity washed over her. She knew this woman from somewhere. She stepped forward.

"Hello."

The woman drew a sharp breath and turned on her heel, nearly tripping over her own feet. Lydia hesitantly stepped closer, unable to understand what drew her to this woman, yet filled with a sense of purpose.

They stared at each other.

They were about the same height, and the shape of the woman's face reminded Lydia of her own. She might almost be convinced she'd stumbled across a missing relative. Perhaps even a sister, though such a thing was absurd.

The woman rubbed her palms down her coarse pantaloons. Suddenly, her eyebrows shot upward. "Lydia?"

Lydia should have been surprised. Instead, a feeling of great pleasure filled her. "You know me."

"Where are we?" the woman asked.

A smile tugged at the corners of Lydia's lips. "Ironwood. Where else? It is what binds us together, is it not?" A bizarre answer and yet the only one that she could give. The strange sense of knowing, of understanding something incredible was happening, thickened the air around them. There was great purpose in this meeting.

She did not know where the thought came from, but for some reason she knew there was an important message she must deliver. "There is something you must consider," she said to the dream woman, reaching out and clasping her hand. "You must let go and forgive. You must be whole again."

"What?" The woman withdrew her hand from Lydia's. "I can't."

A deep and powerful sadness filled her. She remembered Charles' words. "You must look for the good that comes from the pain. It is not always easy to find. Especially when we don't want to see it. But it *is* there."

Lydia pulled the lost woman into an embrace, suddenly feeling sleepy. "You must look for it," she whispered, her voice near and at the same time sounding far away, as if someone else had her voice.

"I don't know how..." The woman's voice trailed off.

Lydia felt herself being pulled. She struggled against it. There was one more thing she must say. She stepped back, grasping the woman's hands in hers. "For we are his workmanship, created in Christ Jesus unto good works, which God hath before ordained that we should walk in them." A Bible verse she didn't remember memorizing.

The pulling came again, and her hands slipped free. She gave into the feeling.

"No, wait," the woman's voice called to her from somewhere far away.

As if she were floating, Lydia drifted until she settled into the deep folds of the familiar warmth of her blankets, tucked lovingly around her by a husband she didn't deserve. She drifted just to the surface of consciousness, somewhere in the realm between dreams and reality, and wondered about the strange woman in her garden before falling into the recesses of a deep exhaustion.

Eighteen

$\mathscr{R}$uth tucked the quilt around the bottom of her straw and raw cotton stuffed mattress, once again amazed how she had gained such a soft and private place to lay her head each night. The words flowing around her room called for her attention. Dreams of fire and smoke had robbed her of sleep once again. After nights like these, she found letting the words escape from her hand quenched the burn and brought peace. At least for a few more nights.

She didn't have time for that luxury today. Several days had passed since Mr. Harper's ball. The visiting family had finally returned to their home, and now the house girls faced the task of catching up on all the cleaning they missed while tending guests.

Ruth surveyed her space. Satisfied, she descended the outer steps as the first rays of light spread across the dew-covered grass.

"Ruth."

Her whispered name scurried across the quiet morning air. Despite her determination to remain unaffected, her pulse jumped at the sound of the familiar voice. She turned and just managed to contain her smile when her gaze landed on Noah.

He motioned to her. She frowned. He was acting weird. Curious, she lifted the hem of her skirt and stepped across the wet ground. Noah gently took her hand and led her to the potato house.

He left the door cracked just enough to allow the dusty light to touch the rows of Betsy's canned vegetables lining the walls. Ruth put her hand under her nose. This place always made her sneeze.

"What's goin' on?" she whispered, tilting her head back to look into his face.

"The war's gettin' closer. They says there's been fightin' just north of us."

Ruth pressed her lips together. "How you know that?"

"We listen, Ruth. Word travels. Won't be long before they come this way." He shifted his weight back and forth.

"And?"

He sighed. "When they come, if we get the chance, there's some of us that are thinkin' of slippin' behind their lines."

Ruth gasped. "You can't be serious."

"We want freedom. Don't you?" He grasped her hands in both of his, rubbing the rough pad of his thumb across the backs of her fingers.

She did want freedom, didn't she? But he didn't know what he was saying. They might still be slaves, but she knew what could happen to them outside of Ironwood. She'd seen things he hadn't.

Ruth shook her head. "It ain't that simple."

He gripped her tighter. "It is, Ruth. They'll let us pass. They'll let us go north. I's could find work there and take care of you."

She peered up at him. "What is you sayin'?"

He drew her closer until their bodies touched. Ruth's heart fluttered in her chest. "I'm sayin' come with us. Run with me."

Ruth pulled away from him. "I can't. I'm sorry." She turned away from the hurt in his eyes. "I just can't go out there again."

She ran from the potato room and into the back door of the main house. She stood quietly by the door, her hand pressed to her heart. The memories of fire and her sister's screams forced her to close her eyes.

Please God, make it stop.

Noah didn't know. How could he know what it would be like out there? She was safe here. Could start a new life. But oh, she had hoped he would be a part of it. She'd been stupid to let herself begin to have feelings toward a man.

"Ruth!"

Her eyes flew open. Lucy stood with her arms crossed over her chest. "What you doin'?"

Ruth drew a calming breath. "Nothin'."

"Humph. You ain't special, you know. You's still have to work just like the rest of us."

Ruth clenched her teeth. She stomped past Lucy before the woman could say anything more. She heard Lucy snort. Ruth didn't care. She had other things to worry with than Lucy's bad attitude.

Upstairs, she tapped lightly on Miss Lydia's door and turned the knob with one hand, the other balancing a stack of the lady's clean laundry. She stepped inside, turning to pull the door closed behind her.

"Good mornin'. You up yet? Goodness knows that Lucy – "

She stopped short, her heart dropping to her stomach. Mr. Harper sat up in the bed, the sheets falling to his waist and exposing his bare chest. She gulped and dropped her eyes, hastily stepping backward. Her foot caught on the rug and she lost her balance, tumbling to the floor.

"Oh!" Lydia cried from across the room.

Ruth scrambled to right herself, the heat burning in her ears. She grabbed the door, leaving the laundry scattered on the floor. What had she done? If she escaped fast enough would he let her get away?

A deep chuckle froze her.

"Calm down, Ruth."

Good heavens. What should she do now? If she darted away would he be furious she left while he spoke to her? Should she answer? How was she supposed to talk to the master when he lay abed undressed? Her pulse thudded in her ears.

A hand landed on her elbow, and she jumped.

"Ruth, are you all right?" Lydia asked softly.

She nodded, not trusting her voice. Behind her she could hear Mr. Harper getting out of the bed. She squeezed her eyes shut. If only she could get out the door.

Lydia rubbed her shoulder and spoke a little louder. "I think I left my new hair ribbons in the front parlor. Would you mind fetching them for me?"

"Yes, ma'am." She darted from the room and down the hall. At its end, she stopped to calm herself. From now on, she would not enter a closed door unless beckoned. She smoothed her skirt and took her time going to the parlor.

When she entered, Lucy straightened from her stooped position beside a shelf, dust rag in hand.

Ruth cleared the tension from her throat. "Have you seen Miss Lydia's hair ribbons?"

Lucy's jaw dropped, and she stared at Ruth with wide eyes. Ruth's brow creased. Why on earth was Lucy staring at her like she'd suddenly turned green? All she'd done this time was ask if Lucy had seen... oh.

"I, um." She took a deep breath. "Mrs. Harper sent me to fetch her hair ribbons. She thinks she might have left them in here."

Lucy narrowed her eyes. "You's lyin'."

"What?"

"You know you took them ribbons to her room and put them in her drawer yesterday. You did it while I was changin' the sheets."

Oh. That's right. Understanding settled on her. Of course. Miss Lydia already knew that. She wore one of those ribbons yesterday. She'd only sent Ruth on the errand to give her an escape. Gratitude pulled a corner of her lip.

"Well? You gonna tell me what's goin' on?"

"I done told you the truth. Mrs. Harper sent me to find her ribbons. I guess she forgot where they were."

Lucy frowned.

Ruth left the room before Lucy could pepper her with any more questions. She eyed the staircase. She couldn't go back up there until Mr. Harper left. She'd just decided to go to the kitchen instead, when he appeared at the top of the steps. She ducked her head and tried to slip away before he saw her.

"Ah, Ruth. There you are."

Too late. She began to mentally prepare herself for the beating she would get. She remained still and waited for him to come to a stop in front of her. His polished boots didn't have the first scuff.

"Ruth?"

She slowly lifted her gaze from his boots, up to his white shirt and wide-collared jacket, across his jaw that bristled with day old stubble, and finally into his eyes. She swallowed an unwelcome lump in her throat.

"I haven't yet thanked you."

What?

Humor lit his face. "What? You were expecting something else?"

She just stared at him. He became serious again. "My wife told me about the man that came after her in the woods. From her story, I understand you have given her the utmost attention and care. For that, I wish to thank you. There is nothing in Ironwood I treasure more than her."

Ruth gave a slight nod.

"Also, you took it upon yourself to see that I was contacted when you perceived her ill. I am grateful for that as well."

"It seemed like the right thing to do."

Mr. Harper's gaze rested on her too long. "My wife is very fond of you. And you seem to take good care of her. Despite its strangeness, for that you will always have a favored place here." He gave a curt nod and walked away.

Ruth stood dumbfounded. She blinked away the implications of the conversation and grasped the stairway's handrail. She caught movement out of the side of her vision and turned to see Lucy staring at her, displeasure written all over her broad face.

Ruth lifted her chin and climbed the stairs. Outside Miss Lydia's room she knocked loudly and waited in the hall.

"You can come in, Ruth."

She opened the door to find all the clothes picked up off the floor and the bed made. Miss Lydia closed her little leather book she was always working in and put it and her writing utensils in a drawer.

"I am sorry he frightened you. I do not think he meant to."

Ruth sighed. "I's shoulda never come in like that. I guess I just wasn't expectin', well, uh to..."

Lydia giggled. Ruth raised her eyebrows. Color flooded her mistresses' cheeks.

"Well, he is my husband."

"Yes, ma'am."

"Oh, not back to that." Lydia put a hand on her hips. Ruth wondered if she'd been taking scolding lessons from Betsy.

"What?"

"That 'I'll-just-say-whatever-I-think-she-wants-to-hear' nonsense." Something like hurt washed over her pale features, and suddenly Ruth saw the loneliness that mirrored her own heart.

Ruth crossed her arms. "And what you want me do? I's your slave. It's what's expected."

Lydia stomped her foot like a child. "At least be real. I am *tired* of all these pretenses."

"I don't think you's want real. Real can be ugly."

Lydia straightened and indifference painted her features into a smooth, though beautiful composure. Ruth felt a stab of regret.

"I can finish dressing myself. You may go help Lucy with the dusting. The windows also need washing, and the front hall rug will need to be beaten." She turned away.

"Yes, ma'am," Ruth whispered and left the room, wondering if she'd just turned her back on something important.

Nineteen

August 15, 1862

*Ly*dia tapped her fingernails on the desk. Her flowing handwriting, practiced to the point of perfection, covered the pages of her diary. She'd written of the new peace that settled in her chest since her night with Charles in the garden. She'd spoken of her growing love, and she had even made mention – in writing! – of last night's passion. She'd be mortified if anyone ever found it.

A lady's duty to her husband was just that. A duty. And yet, Lydia found something awakening in her she could not understand. It was not born out of fear of a man's touch. Rather, the opposite. Her heart fluttered in his presence, and her blood warmed at his touch. She did not understand the yearning she felt for him to be near her, nothing separating them from being one in body and soul. It could not be a good thing. Would the preacher call it sin? Mother probably would.

And then there was Ruth. She'd thought they'd created a bond, something strange and yet real forged in the flames of shared pain. But perhaps she was being foolish. How could she expect anything different from their relationship?

If only she'd ever seen such honesty from any of her proper friends. But no. They were never open, never willing to show their true feelings. Lydia watched the flame dance on the tip of her candle. Something nagged at her. She was no different. She hid behind the cover of propriety. How could she expect real friendship from a woman she owned? Lydia shook her head. She should let it go. Be the lady they expected her to be. She stood and paced the floor. It was the right thing. The proper thing.

No.

Something more existed between her and Ruth. It would be up to her to take the first steps. Up to her to brave the disapproving looks she would surely receive. So be it.

She found Charles in his study with ledgers and books spread out in front of him. His hair fell across his forehead and tickled the top of his eyebrows. He looked up as she entered.

"Hello, darling. Forgive me for not being much company this evening."

She smiled sweetly at him. "I do. I know there are many things that must occupy your mind. Is it something to do with the war?"

He sighed, leaning back in his leather chair. The clock on the wall began its hourly chime. Charles waited until all seven sounded before speaking. "I'm afraid there is little that is not touched by this war. I've done my best to keep us as far removed from it as I can, but I fear I will not be able to forever."

Fear slid into her heart. She'd never heard Charles speak with such weariness. Her chest constricted. She'd tried to ignore the war. How much longer would she be able to? She crossed the polished wood floors and rested her hand on her husband's shoulder.

He reached up and patted her hand. "Do not fret over it. Ironwood is strong. We shall make it through this. Perhaps not unscathed, but I will do everything in my power to protect my home and its people."

She leaned down and kissed the top of his head, not knowing if she had any words that could help him. He drew her down into his lap and buried his face in the crook of her neck. Lydia wrapped her arms tight around him and forced her fear aside. She did not know if she could bear it if he left. She'd only just found him.

He gave her a squeeze and gently lifted her. "I am afraid if I let you sit here much longer, I shall not finish what needs to be done." His voice was husky and his pupils wide.

She brushed her hand over his jaw. Dare she? She leaned in and pressed her lips briefly against his. She drew back slightly, eyes still closed. "I should like for you to come to me when you finish."

A low sound escaped his throat. "It might be very late."

"You can take your rest in my room tonight." She pulled away from him.

"I've asked before, but I shall again. It would please me for us to share a bedchamber as my parents did."

She inclined her head. "I will think on it more and provide you an answer soon."

His chest rose and fell with slow, deliberate breaths. "Then I shall see you later this evening when my work is done." The sides of his lips rose. "If I can concentrate on these numbers now."

She pulled her lower lip between her teeth and dipped her chin. She nearly passed through the door when she remembered her original reason for seeking him out.

"Oh. I nearly forgot. Charles, would it be okay for me to enter the maid's quarters?"

He regarded her across the room. "For what purpose?"

She lifted her shoulders. "None, I suppose. I just wondered what it might be like to have female companionship outside of the normal dictation of duties." Her heart thudded. Would he understand?

"When this war is over, I will have to see to it that you are allowed more visits with your peers."

Of course. That would be expected. She dipped her chin and grasped the doorknob.

"But until then, I see no reason why you cannot speak with your maid in a less formal manner." He smiled.

"I thank you, husband. You have an uncanny way of understanding me."

"A man studies and seeks to understand that which he holds dearest."

The heat rose in her face. She gave him her best smile and left him to his work.

Outside, the night offered a welcome breeze that belied the oppressive Mississippi summer. Lydia paused to admire the clear night and the stars sprinkling across the black canvas, painted by the hand of the original Artist. His creation never ceased to awe her. Peace settled on her, the soft scents of the garden and the content sounds of the creatures of the dark settling the nervousness in her chest into quiet determination.

She walked down the short cobbled sidewalk the help referred to as *the whistle walk* and to the kitchen. Lydia gathered her skirts and teetered on the narrow staircase leading to the quarters above. The lingering heat from the kitchen seemed to pour through the outer wall. She put one hand on the red bricks to brace herself and gripped the railing with the other. It moved under her weight but held.

She'd have to remember to add that to her list.

At the top of the stairs, a soft light filtered between the planks of the door carrying with it the sounds of conversation. Lydia lifted her hand to knock but hesitated. Perhaps things were the way they were for a reason. They may not want her in their private space, their only refuge from the demands of everyday life. Demands that she herself dealt out each morning from her precious list. She stood on the landing feeling a bit foolish.

Well, she would do what she had come to do. What could it hurt? She knocked firmly on the door.

It swung open an instant later, revealing Lucy with an amusing expression of shock.

"Good evening, Lucy."

She stared at Lydia with her mouth hanging open. Finding her composure, she snapped it shut. "Do you need me, ma'am? I woulda come if you'da sent someone." She glanced around behind Lydia. "Did you send someone and I's just didn't hear?"

Lydia suppressed her smile at Lucy's complete lack of understanding for any reason her mistress could have for standing outside the door. Lucy meant well. She was just too stiff.

"No, Lucy. I don't need you for anything."

She stared at her, clearly dumbfounded. Then she brightened. "Oh, then you must need Betsy. She just went to bed, but she probably ain't undressed yet. Hold on, I'll get her."

"No, Lucy," she said quickly, "That's not why I'm here." Lydia tugged at the folds in her skirt. "I came here to see Ruth."

Disbelief tightened Lucy's features. Her jaw worked.

"But I don't want to bother you," Lydia blurted. Wonderful. She was making a mess of this.

Lucy blinked repeatedly before finding her voice again. "Well, uh, she's in her room in the back."

She stared at Lydia. Lydia stared back, neither knowing what to do next.

"You can come on in if you's want to." She opened the door, and Lydia walked into the small living space.

She'd never been in Negro private quarters before and found she was rather curious. The simple room boasted only a small, shabby couch and a rocking chair resting on a faded rug that had seen too many beatings. Lydia frowned. Ironwood could afford to give them something better. She would have to see to that.

"Do you want anythin', ma'am? I's can run down to the kitchen and fix you somethin'."

"No. I'm fine."

Lucy looked as flustered as a mouse caught in a room full of cats. She didn't know which way to turn. Lydia remained standing in the living room unsure what she should do next.

"Oh. Ruth." Lucy hurried across the small space and knocked on Ruth's door. "Hey, you's got a visitor." She glanced back at Lydia, mischief in her features.

Odd. Lydia had never seen Lucy be playful. A small smile tugged at her mouth, her nervousness bubbling into a strange mix of humor and disbelief.

Lucy crossed her arms over her chest and waited.

Ruth opened the door and greeted Lydia with the same wide-eyed astonishment she'd seen on Lucy's face. Ruth's surprise quickly vanished, and she put her hand on her hip and pointed her finger. "Mista Harper know you's up here in Negro quarters?"

Lucy looked horrified. Her hand flew to her mouth. She glanced at Lydia, wondering if she were going to dole out some kind of punishment for such disrespectful speech. Instead, Lydia felt a small measure of pride. At least now false pretenses fell away.

Lydia laughed. "Yes, actually. He does."

Lucy gaped at her, and Lydia felt certain if her skin weren't so dark it would be a shade of angry red. "Mr. Harper knows you comin' up here at night?"

Lydia nodded.

Ruth just shook her head, and then walked over and gave Lydia a hug. Surprised only for an instant, she gave her friend a squeeze and looked at Lucy over Ruth's shoulder.

Lucy's hand flew to her brow. "Lord Almighty, what on earth is goin' on here?"

"Oh, calm yourself, Lucy." She stepped back, straightening her posture. "I told you. I just came by to see Ruth."

Lucy put her hands on her hips, her death grip on propriety lost. "What for? You's done seen her all day over at the house."

"I came to visit."

Lucy looked dumbfounded again.

Ruth just shook her head. "You know people's goin' to talk. It probably ain't a good idea for you to do such things. They's already seen me ridin' in the buggy with you and wearin' your clothes. What are they gonna to think if they see you comin' up here?"

She was right, of course, but Lydia grew weary of it. Succession tore the country apart. Soon war would descend on Ironwood. If they lost all, what good would their system do them then? "Does it matter what they think?"

Both women stared at her. Lucy frowned. "Seems to me what other folk think is what makes the world turn round."

So, her little quest not only showed her the real Ruth but apparently the real woman beneath the perfectly shined armor of Lucy.

Lydia crossed her arms, mimicking their favored position of displeasure. "I don't care what they think. But if you are uncomfortable with me here, then I will go back to the house." She turned for the door.

Ruth caught her arm. "You mights not worry over it, but everyone else will. I don't wanna see you get hurt."

Lydia smiled. "Ruth, you are always looking out for everybody else. Don't worry about me. Charles knows where I am. He also knows you and I are friends. He may not understand it, but he allows it. Perhaps things have to be the way they've always been if we are away from Ironwood, but here, things can be different."

"I hope you's right. It's a nice dream, anyway."

Lucy sighed dramatically. "I's goin' to bed." She stomped across to the other side of the room, slamming the door behind her.

Ruth clasped and unclasped her hands, the thing Lydia had begun to notice she did when she was thinking something but couldn't say it.

"What is it?"

Ruth pressed her lips together.

"If you really don't want me here, Ruth, I can go."

"No, that ain't it. I knows what you's tryin' to do. And you wantin' to be friends with me despite everything, well..." Her eyes glistened with tears.

Something within her had changed. Lydia could feel it welling up from the place that had once been nothing more than a pit that swallowed any joy she'd found. No more. This night, things would change. Tonight she would allow someone past her walls.

"Ruth, don't you know you are the best friend I have ever had? I'm not willing to give that up just because everyone else says it's wrong. They are wrong. Not us."

Ruth wiped her eyes and pulled Lydia's arm. "Come on. There's somethin' I wants to show you."

Ruth tried to ignore the apprehension clawing at her insides. Miss Lydia made a huge step coming here. She'd thrown aside her place in the world to walk into Ruth's. Of the two of them, Miss Lydia had more to lose by taking to Ruth than Ruth had of returning her attempts. What would the white folk think of it? But, since the only white folk at Ironwood were Mr. Harper and his wife, Ruth released her hold on her fear and swung open the door to her room.

Miss Lydia followed Ruth inside, her wide hoops swishing against the narrow doorframe. She paused, looking very out of place. Ruth had always thought her room a large space of luxury, but it suddenly felt shabby and unfit for the lady standing in it.

Miss Lydia studied Ruth's furnishings with curiosity and a slight look of disgust. Ruth waited patiently for her to discover the reason she'd brought her in here. She lifted the lamp high.

Lydia gasped. "What is this?"

Ruth swallowed the caution begging notice. "My story."

"You can write?"

She nodded. "And read. I know we ain't supposed to know how. But my grandmother worked in the big house. She was really smart, and she picked it up during the white kid's lessons. She taught me. It came so easy. She even found an old story book one of the kids had thrown out and snuck it to me."

"You wrote your story on the walls?"

Ruth dropped her eyes. She'd made a mistake. When would she ever learn? No misbegotten friendship changed the differences between them. How could this white lady ever understand? "I's sorry. I just had to get it out."

"Yet another thing we share," Miss Lydia whispered, but Ruth was already talking.

"I'll clean it off. I wasn't thinkin'. I guess I thought no one would see it. I'm the only one that comes back here. I – "

She stopped. Miss Lydia looked amused and patted her hand. "Ruth, I don't care that you wrote on the wall. I care that you shouldn't have had to. I can get you paper and ink to write with."

Ruth let out a slow breath. "I'd like that very much. I ain't sure why I's got to write. It's just somethin' in me. I's got to get it out. There is peace in gettin' the story outside of me." It sounded foolish. She couldn't expect for anyone to understand the strange thing that happened. How somehow writing those words was better than dreaming them.

Miss Lydia nodded as if they were talking of something as mundane as which dress she wanted for the day. "That's because in your heart you are a writer. So am I."

Ruth stilled. At what point would she stop being surprised at what this woman said? She sank down on the bed. "No. I ain't. Maybe you could be if you really wanted to. But not me. It just ain't meant to be."

Lydia sat down stiffly next to her. Her gaze traveled across Ruth's crude scratching. "What all is here?"

Ruth shrugged. "It starts the day of the fire. I just wrote down all the things that happened to me."

They sat in silence for a while longer. Finally, Lydia said, "I have a book. My daddy gave it to me right before my wedding. I wrote about the day I saw you on the street."

The crickets outside swelled in their intensity. Somewhere from the shadows a lost member of their tribe called to them. Ruth felt a sudden sympathy for the creature.

"Seems kinda strange, us both doin' it. Why you think that is?" Ruth asked.

"I guess because we need to tell the story. Even if no one sees it."

Ruth shook her head. "No, I feel like there's somethin' more. I even feel likes it's somethin' I's supposed to do. There's a reason for it."

"It's strange to hear you speak that way. I thought the very same thing myself."

Ruth smiled. "Then maybe we oughta start tryin' to figure what that reason is."

"It seems there is little choice. Charles says we should look for the good that comes from the ashes of the bad. Ruth, I believe God had a plan all along." Lydia patted her arm and rose from the bed. "It's getting late. I should probably go."

Ruth followed her to the door, opening it to the deepening night. "Thank you."

Miss Lydia turned on the landing, the moonlight washing over her face. "For what?"

"For what you're tryin' to do. For seein' me as more than just property."

Miss Lydia drew a long breath. "Thank you for seeing me for who I really am."

Ruth smiled. "Good night, ma'am."

"Good night."

When Miss Lydia reached the bottom step, Ruth closed the door and returned to her room. She looked at the words wrapping around her like a blanket. One she needed and yet in many ways despised. She pulled the charcoal pencil out from under her pillow, wondering what would have happened if she'd asked Miss Lydia for it instead of hiding it away.

She put it to the wall.

That was the day I met a white woman like none I's ever seen before...

How long she sat on the floor and spilled her heart she did not know.

Twenty

Lydia descended the stairs and wondered if today she would speak to Charles about her suspicion. He'd come to her room as promised sometime late in the night. She'd been asleep but had awakened with the dawn to find his arm draped over her and a sense of peace in her heart. She ran her hand down the length of the banister. Today made two weeks. She'd never thought such a short span of time could mean so much, but a fortnight could mean the difference between knowing if she were with child or not.

Lydia crossed the main hall and entered the dining room, the morning sunlight painting the walls in a warm glow and dancing off the polished silver on the table. She sat in one of the plush cushioned chairs. Her woman's time had always varied, so she couldn't be sure if the delay meant a child grew within her. Yet hope again blossomed in her heart. What would Charles say? She knew it would please him to have an heir.

Lucy entered the room and placed a platter of cut fruits and fresh biscuits on the table. She studied Lydia out of the corner of her eye. Lydia pretended not to notice.

"Good Morning, Lucy."

"Ma'am." She gave a curt nod and strode from the room.

Lydia sighed and lifted her fork, studying the way the light reflected off the smooth plains. Mother prized her silverware at Cedarwycke. It was much plainer than these at Ironwood but had been handed down since her mother's family first arrived from England.

Lucy swept back into the room and filled Lydia's glass with milk. Lydia wrinkled her nose.

"I do not care for that this morning, Lucy, if you would kindly bring me something else?"

Lucy nodded and removed the glass.

"Lucy?"

She turned.

"Have you seen Ruth?"

Her face creased. "No, Ma'am. I assumed she'd be with you."

Lydia shook her head. "No, I thought it strange she didn't come to my room this morning."

"Probably don't think she's got to work like the rest of us no more," she mumbled as she turned to the door, but Lydia heard her.

"Lucy."

"Ma'am?"

"Am I unkind to you? Do you feel you are not treated properly here at Ironwood?"

Lucy's eyes widened and her grip tightened on the glass of milk so that Lydia feared she may burst it. "I ain't never said anythin' of that sort, Mrs. Harper."

"I didn't say you did. However, I did ask if that is how you *feel.*"

Lucy shifted her weight between her feet and looked as if she wanted to bolt. "No, ma'am. I don't think I's ever been mistreated at Ironwood." She took a long breath and looked Lydia in the eyes. "I's came here with the late Mr. Harper. Was born on his parent's place. When we came here, Mr. Harper bought more folks. From whats I heard tell, there are places a lot different than ours. "

Lydia nodded urging her to continue.

"I's always been grateful that we's never been beat or shamed."

Lydia kept her gaze even. "So do you think you are treated unfairly?"

"I don't know what you mean, ma'am. I's done said I know we's treated good here."

How should she put what she really wanted to know? Mother always told her directness was akin to rudeness and that she should strive to deliver her words with a measure of elegance. But with Lucy looking uncomfortable already, she doubted bluntness would make any difference.

"Are you upset with Ruth being here? Do you think she is treated better than you?"

Lucy's eyes grew wider, and she shook her head vigorously. "No."

Lydia lifted her eyebrows.

"Well, I mean, I's do wonder what, exactly, is goin' on with her."

Lydia placed her fork on the polished table. "You mean why I came to visit her?"

"Yes, ma'am. Forgives me, but I's do wonder. Though it's not my place to say so, it just ain't proper."

"You're right. It's not. But I find I am growing weary of what is proper. I sense this war will soon make such things of little consequence."

Lucy looked at her. The intensity on her face caused Lydia's chest to tighten. When she spoke, her words were quiet. "And where will that leave the white folks who live off the sweat of the Negros?"

Lydia swallowed hard.

Lucy shook herself as if coming awake. She dipped into a small curtsey. "Let me gets you somethin' else to drink, ma'am. Your breakfast's gettin' cold." She slipped out the door.

Lydia stared at her plate, but could no longer summon an appetite. The knocker banged against the front door and she jumped, dropping her fork on the floor. Placing a hand to her heart to calm its rapid beating, she rose from her chair.

Lucy had yet to return, so Lydia swung open the front door to three men dressed in traveling clothes and coated with the dust of a long ride.

"Good morning, gentlemen." She recognized the large man in the center but could not place him.

He bowed. "Good morning, Mrs. Harper. It is good to see you again."

Lydia inclined her head. Think! Where had she seen this man before? Charles' ball? No. She would have remembered a man that stood a head taller than all the others. The women would certainly have been chattering about it. The wedding, then? Oh, he was looking at her oddly. She was taking too long.

"And you as well. Won't you gentlemen come in?" She widened the door and allowed them entrance.

The big man spoke again. "Mrs. Harper, let me introduce you to Mr. Willbanks." He gestured to the thin man on his left. Lydia lifted her hand, and he bowed over it. "And Mr. Polk." He nodded to the younger man on his right.

"A pleasure, gentlemen." Lydia lifted her hand to the other man who grasped it and brushed his lips across the back of her knuckles. She withdrew her hand and resisted the urge to wipe it on her dress.

"Matthew told us Charles found himself an exceptionally beautiful bride," Mr. Polk said, lifting his eyebrows. "It seems for once he was not exaggerating."

The heat rose in her cheeks. Ah. Of course. Matthew Daniels, Charles' favorite cousin. How had she forgotten? "You flatter me, Mr. Polk." She turned to Matthew. "Mr. Daniels, if you would follow me, you gentlemen can wait in the parlor while I find Mr. Harper."

She led them into the parlor and saw them seated on her new green settee, which looked meant for a child beneath Mr. Daniels, before pulling the pocket door closed. She turned to find Ruth standing behind her.

"Oh! There you are." She would have to discuss her absence later. "Get some tea and refreshments for the men in the parlor."

"What's goin' on?" Ruth whispered, picking up on the unsettled nature of Lydia's tone.

Lydia straightened her dress. "Nothing. They are just calling on Charles."

Ruth lifted her eyebrows but said nothing. She quickly made her way down the hall and out the back door. Lydia climbed the stairs and found the door to Charles' study closed. She tapped on it lightly.

"Yes?"

She cracked the door and saw him seated behind his desk with more books and papers spread out in front of him. He motioned for her to come in.

Lydia crossed the floor and came to stand before him.

"Hello, darling. I am sorry I had to be gone from you early this morning. It was nearly more temptation to stay than I could stand." The corner of his lip pulled up.

"There are men downstairs to see you."

He frowned and rose from his chair, buttoning his jacket as he came around to stand beside her. "Did they state their business?"

Lydia shook her head. "It is your cousin, Mr. Daniels, and two others."

"Very well." He leaned down and pressed a kiss to her cheek.

"Charles?"

He looked deeply into her eyes. "Yes?"

She swallowed the lump gathering in her throat. She must say it. "I do not want you to go."

He rubbed her cheek, his eyes telling her he knew of what she spoke. "I do not wish to leave you. But you must understand."

She shook her head, fighting against the tears gathering in her eyes. "No. You can better protect us from here. Do not let them take you."

A low sound escaped his throat. "Oh, woman, what have you done to me?" He pulled her into his arms and pressed his lips on hers. She wrapped her arms around his neck. Too soon he pulled back, a look of resignation on his face.

"They are in the parlor," she said, following him from the room. He turned to look up at her from the bottom of the stairs, and her heart flopped.

He stepped into the parlor, and she heard the sounds of masculine greetings and shoulder slapping. Lydia sighed and returned to her room.

She gathered her writing utensils and sat at her desk. Though she stared at the page and longed to write out her fears, she could not focus. She slammed the little book shut and stalked from the room. Feeling like a thief in her own house, Lydia crept down the stairs and positioned herself next to the closed parlor doors. She could hear one of the men talking, but she wasn't sure which. She glanced around the hall and checked inside the dining room. No one.

Lydia eased closer to the parlor pressing her back up against the wall near the door.

"I understand where you are coming from," said the muffled voice. The tinkling of tea cups evidence Ruth had brought refreshments. "We all do. But it's time to acknowledge the corn, Charles. You can't hide from it any longer."

"I am *not* hiding." Charles' voice sounded irritated.

Heavens. She knew it. These men had come to pressure Charles into joining them. Curse this blasted war. Had it not stolen enough already? Every week at church they posted lists of young men lost. Youths who'd rushed off to glory only to find death instead. Now it lurked at her door, disguised as gentlemen in the parlor.

"Charles, I know you are loathe to leave your home. I understand well." The voice of Matthew Daniels. "Perhaps one of her kin can come to stay?"

Who? Her family?

"Her father is elderly and must look after his own plantation. She has no brothers, and no living uncles. I am afraid that is not an option."

Lydia's chest tightened.

"Van Dorn plans to regain Corinth," said one of the other men, she wasn't sure which.

There was a long silence. Lydia held her breath.

"You are certain?"

Oh no, Charles. Do not let them get you with that! Charles had told her the importance of Corinth and its railroad. He claimed it would make the difference in all coming battles in Mississippi, if not the entire war. Regaining Corinth could be what would sway him.

"You will have to give me more time. I will think on it."

Lydia closed her eyes, her breath coming out in a rush. He wouldn't be going. She was sure she could convince him otherwise. She opened her eyes to find Ruth looking at her with her eyebrows raised. Lydia stiffened. She shook her head and grabbed Ruth's wrist, pulling her up the stairs. When they were safely behind her bedroom door, Lydia began pacing.

"What's that all about? You's spyin'?"

Lydia narrowed her eyes. "It was necessary."

"Well, then. So long as it was necessary."

Lydia huffed. "They came to try to convince him to join the army. I had to know what they were saying."

"And?"

Lydia sank down onto her vanity chair and rubbed her temples. "They say they are going to try to regain Corinth. It frightens me. These battles draw ever nearer. We cannot pretend they do not exist much longer."

Ruth sighed. "Miss Lydia, you's the only one's been pretendin'."

Lydia tilted her head back and studied the ceiling. "It's easier that way."

Ruth crouched down in front of her. "I know you's think that. But that stuff is comin' even if you's pretendin' it ain't. Seems to me gettin' ready for it would be smarter than hidin' from it."

"You're right." Lydia straightened and looked down at her friend. "It's time I started figuring out how to protect the people under my care."

"Now that ain't exactly what I meant – "

Lydia waved her hand in the air. "No. You go back down there and see what else they might say. If anyone sees you tell them I told you to wait by the door in case Mr. Harper needs anything."

Ruth pressed her lips together in a thin line but didn't protest. She slipped from the room and left Lydia to her pacing. Lydia stopped suddenly, remembering something she'd discovered a few days prior. She'd thought nothing of it at the time, but it could soon become useful.

She crouched down by the side table at the head of her poster bed. There. She put her finger in a small knot hole. She pulled. It didn't budge. She settled on her knees, frustrated with the wide ring of skirts that fanned out around her. Ridiculous hoops. She wedged her finger in there again and yanked. Her finger slipped free and she fell backward with a thud.

Pain throbbed in her hand. She held her finger up to her face. Red blood oozed from the little scratches encircling her skin. Lydia took a deep breath and looked around the room for something she could use to pry the board loose. There. She lifted the slender metal bar from the hooks on the side of her washbasin, laying the towel aside.

It fit perfectly. Lydia slipped one end into the hole and forced down on the other end. The wood groaned. She rose up on her knees and put the force of her weight behind it.

Something popped.

One edge of the plank had come free. Lydia smiled giddy with her accomplishment. If only she could get the whole thing free in one piece. She turned the bar sideways and wedged it under the loose end. With one hand on each end, she pushed the bar forward, sliding it under the length of the wood.

It cracked and popped free.

"I did it!"

She clamped a hand over her mouth and peered into the dark hole in the floor. The place was only about the width of her hand and about the length of her forearm. It wasn't the largest place to hide anything but it would serve.

Let any Union soldier with his Confiscation Act find anything in there! She slipped her hand inside, hoping not to come across anything with too many legs. About elbow deep, she could feel the rough wood of the ceiling boards below. They were covered in plaster from the other side. Nothing would be able to slip through. She replaced the board and pulled the edge of the side table over top of it. There. No one would ever think to look there.

With a new sense of determination swelling in her chest, Lydia began to gather her treasures.

Twenty - One

Ruth smoothed the blanket over the back of the couch in their living area. Now. Everything tidy and in its place. A knock sounded at the door. Taking her single candle in hand, Ruth opened it wide and let Miss Lydia enter without a word. They slipped into Ruth's room and pulled the door closed, careful not to wake the older women in the other room.

"Here. I brought everything you will need." Lydia splayed out a wooden pen with a tapered end and a metal tip, a small corked jug, and a bound book of pages.

Miss Lydia beamed at her, obviously proud of herself.

"Thank you. But I don't know if I needs all this."

Her mistress frowned. "What do you mean? You'd rather keep writing on the walls instead of in something you can keep? Something you can pass down to your children?"

Ruth swallowed, her mouth suddenly feeling stuffed with cotton. "I ain't thought of that."

"There. See? This will be better. You can write in here, and then you will have it to keep. No one will know."

Ruth picked the book up from the quilt and ran her hand over it. "But I don't think my writin' will look good in here. I knows the words, but I don't always know how they's go together. Or how they's spelled."

"What does that matter?"

Ruth shrugged. "It just does."

Miss Lydia sat on the bed and sighed.

"So you's goin' to tell me what's been botherin' you?" She'd asked twice earlier in the day, but Miss Lydia had refused to answer. She'd waved it away and insisted on keeping herself busy with rearranging all the furniture in the second floor hall. Not that the white lady should be moving around furniture. But no one could tell her no different. Especially Ruth. Her protests had only earned stubborn glares.

"I thought I was going to have a baby," Miss Lydia said finally, her voice sounding a little thick.

Ruth smiled. "That's great."

Miss Lydia's face crumpled, her eyes shimmering with unshed tears. Ruth chewed her lip. She'd said something wrong again. "What? You don't want to have no baby?"

She sniffled. "I do. But my time came today."

So that was it. Ruth sat down beside her and wrapped one arm around her thin shoulders. Had she lost weight? She would have to keep a closer eye on when Miss Lydia ate.

"You's young. I's sure you's still got plenty of time."

"What if he leaves for war and never comes back?" Miss Lydia whispered, her shoulders beginning to shake.

"I don't know. Somehow, we survive. Even when we thinks the pain's gonna kill us. You can't know what the future's got in store."

"I know. But I'm still afraid."

Ruth didn't know what else to say, so she rubbed the smooth fabric covering Miss Lydia's back until her breathing evened out.

Miss Lydia wiped her eyes and offered a faltering smile. "It is nice to have a woman to talk to."

Ruth's throat tightened. She'd never really thought about how lonely Miss Lydia must be. Ruth had Betsy and even Lucy offered some strained companionship. But who did Miss Lydia have? She had no visitors, no one who came to call.

"You know what? I'd like it if you'd write the story for me."

Miss Lydia blinked at her. "What do you mean?"

Ruth gestured to her scrawled writing. "Your writin' looks better than mine. Maybe you could write down what all I tells you, or what I copies from up there."

Miss Lydia brightened a little, though Ruth suspected she'd soon try to hide it. Sure enough Miss Lydia smoothed her features and lifted her shoulders. "If you'd like me to. I suppose I can make that work."

Ruth let out a short laugh. "Yeah. I'd like that."

"Very well. When shall we begin?"

"Don't see no reason not to start now."

Miss Lydia gathered the writing utensils and dipped the pen into the ink, opening the book to the first blank page.

The Story of Ruth

"Now. We shall start at the beginning."

Ruth pulled in a long breath and on a sigh began to tell the story of the night fire consumed all she held dear.

It took a couple of hours. She had to drag the story out, both to allow Miss Lydia's hand to keep up and to steady her own heart enough to stand the telling. When they decided to stop for the evening, Ruth saw her own exhaustion mirrored in the face across from her.

"Shall we work on it some more tomorrow?" Miss Lydia asked as she slipped the writing things inside a little bag and tucked them under her arm.

"Yes. I guess so." Ruth led her to the door and stood with her on the landing.

Miss Lydia patted her arm. "It will be a great thing. A story you can pass on to your children and your children's children."

Ruth nodded. "Goodnight, ma'am."

Miss Lydia's brows drew slightly together. "Well, goodnight, Ruth. I will see you in the morning."

Ruth closed the door behind her and retreated to her room, slipping under her covers and drifting into a peaceful sleep.

The next several days passed in much the same way. After she completed her duties and the older women went off to bed, Miss Lydia would come to her room and they would write by candle light. Miss Lydia remained focused on her story, not wanting to talk too much about anything else.

Ruth had heard Mr. Harper talking with more white men in suits who had come to visit. She'd started to tell Miss Lydia about the shipping blockades and trouble on the river, but after only a few moments Miss Lydia waved her hands like she was trying to fly away and changed the subject.

Ruth waited in the garden for Miss Lydia, thankful the evenings were starting to cool off enough to chase away a small amount of summer's heat. A squirrel circled around an oak tree near the garden, and Ruth watched it chatter. Another joined it, and they chased each other high into the branches, startling a bird from its perch.

"It is a beautiful evening, is it not?" Miss Lydia swept into the garden with her wide skirts and a bright smile.

"Yes. But I's still don't think we should be doin' this here. Out in the open."

Miss Lydia shrugged. "I am tired of doing it at night. It's beautiful here in the garden and the weather is pleasant. I see no reason not to take advantage of it."

"I's got work to do. Betsy needs me to help her, and Lucy's mad she's got to do the cleanin' by herself."

Miss Lydia huffed. "She can stop her bellyaching. She had no problem with it before you came. Besides that, your job is to assist me." She pointed to the bench with a dramatic gesture. "So sit."

Ruth rolled her eyes. "Yes, ma'am."

Miss Lydia giggled and sat beside her. Ruth cast a sidelong glance at her.

"How's come you don't want to work at night?"

She shrugged. "I told you. It's nice out."

"Um hum. And I's suppose that's the whole of it."

Miss Lydia's face turned that funny shade of pink Ruth knew it would. She was still fascinated by how a white person's skin could change colors like that. Miss Lydia ignored the implied question, another thing Ruth knew she would do.

"Let's get started."

"Well, I don't think there's much left. We kept on walkin' after that. When Byram came out of the woods with that shovel..." Ruth's voice cracked, and she cleared her throat. "When he came out of the woods with the shovel, he started pushin' us hard. We walked without takin' breaks, keepin' on back roads with no one passin' us by. I don't remember much. I's just remember prayin' I could keep puttin' one foot in front of the other, even though all I wanted to do was curl up in the dirt."

Ruth told of her pain and her fear, of the long nights with little rest. She waited while Miss Lydia wrote, her slender fingers gliding over the page. When she finally finished, she looked up at Ruth to continue.

"You's know the rest. Ain't nothin' more for me to tell," Ruth said looking up at the swaying tree branches.

"I only know it as I saw it, not as you saw it," Miss Lydia said, pulling her shoulders back and stretching.

They'd been sitting here for some time, and the sun already started to dip below the trees. She'd need to get to the kitchen soon, and Miss Lydia needed to get ready for the evening meal.

"That makes no sense. We's both done saw the same thing," Ruth said, starting to get up.

Miss Lydia shook her head. "No, I was on my way to buy fabric when I saw a striking young Negro woman with fire in her eyes defy a man trying to beat her. I don't really know what you saw. Or how you felt."

Ruth's eyebrows pulled together. "That's how you saw me?"

"Yes. And that's exactly my point. How I remember that day is different than how you remember it."

Ruth had never thought of it that way, but of course Miss Lydia would see the world differently. She glanced down at the book. Miss Lydia didn't just want to write down the events. She wanted to capture the very life and breath of Ruth's story.

A lump gathered in her throat, and she swallowed it down. "I was sore, tired and angry. Losin' my sister, the last family I's had, made me reckless. I didn't care nomore. I didn't want that filthy man touchin' me. I knew I shoulda been acting good, hopin' someone kind would buy me and I'd have a better chance somewhere else. I knew it, but it still didn't matter," Ruth said, returning to her seat. She remembered the way it felt the anger taking over her and burning like the fire that had taken her mother and brother. She'd prayed many nights trying to forget it. Then God answered in a way she wouldn't have expected.

"But I guess God had a plan anyway, 'cause outa nowhere comes this little white lady with a bonnet too big for her head yellin' at that man like she was his master. Ain't never seen no woman stop a man cold like that." Ruth slowly shook her head.

Miss Lydia bit her lip and bent over her papers. Ruth couldn't be sure, but she thought she did it to hide her smile. The light began to fade, casting small shadows across the grass and the last of the summer's roses.

"Then that bold white lady, she comes across the street and offers to take me," Ruth continued. "Lord, I didn't know what to think. Then before I knows it, she's got me ridin' in a carriage with her and tellin' me I'm gonna be working in the big house. I remember tellin' God He sure gots a funny way of doin' things."

Miss Lydia suddenly laughed and pulled Ruth into a hug. "It's the beauty from the ashes! Who would have thought?"

Ruth stiffened. They shouldn't be like this out in the garden where anyone could see. The woman still had no sense. A big heart, yes. But sense? Ruth pulled away from her.

"Miss Lydia, you knows I care for you. But other folks ain't goin' to understand our friendship. With all this talk of war and people gettin' antsy over what's goin' to be happenin' with the slaves, you bein' so friendly with me might get you into trouble."

Miss Lydia studied her. "How do you know all that about the war?"

"I's got ears. I listen. So do all the others. We knows that new president they got up there is talkin' about freein' slaves. I know there's stirring about it down here. I heard the men talkin' while we cleaned up. They didn't pay us no mind, didn't think we know what they's talkin' about. But we do. We know. And we's all listenin'."

Miss Lydia's eyes widened and Ruth regretted her words. No. She couldn't regret them. They were true and Miss Lydia spent too much time hiding from the truth. She needed to know, but now she looked like someone threw water all over her new ball gown. Ruth let out a long breath. Maybe she could have said it a little better.

Miss Lydia put away all her writing things and didn't look Ruth in the eye. "It's getting late. You better hurry into the kitchen before Lucy has a fit. We'll work on this tomorrow."

She scurried off before Ruth could say anything.

Ruth watched her for a moment before rising from her seat and walking slowly back to the kitchen. Noah's words came back to her. What would they do?

If Mr. Harper did leave, would they really run? Should she go with them? She shook her head. No. She couldn't leave Miss Lydia alone.

She wouldn't run. She would stay by the side of the crazy white lady God had given her to watch over.

And hope her heart didn't break in the process.

Twenty - Two

August 21, 1862

" *W*hat's the matter, dear?" Charles asked, dabbing the corner of his mouth with his napkin.

Lydia looked up from the potatoes she'd been pushing around on her plate. "What? Oh. Nothing, I am fine."

He gave her a funny look. "I know you are worried."

About what? What Ruth said yesterday in the garden? About the war? About the sightings of Union troops close to Oakville? About him leaving?

Yes. She worried about all of it. "No, I am not worried."

Charles placed his fork on the table. "You should be. I do not blame you for it. As much as I have tried to keep you from it, I am afraid I can no longer."

Tiny bumps broke out along her arms. She kept her eyes on her plate. "I fear what will happen to us. What will become of Ironwood."

"As do I."

She looked up sharply at the creased face of her husband. She'd not heard him speak so. He always tried to reassure her and tell her Ironwood would be safe. If he doubted, how could she still believe?

"It is why I will have to join in this fight." He looked at her, pain glistening in his eyes. He didn't want to leave her. She could see the truth, yet anger still clawed at her heart. He chose to leave her. Perhaps never to return.

"You would abandon me?" Her voice squeaked, and she hated herself for sounding like a child. Her mind screamed at her to control her emotions, but the fear in her heart rendered such cautions useless.

His jaw muscles worked before he spoke, his voice tight. "You know that is not it. I would go to protect you and this land."

Tears welled in her eyes. "If you would excuse me, I am afraid I am not feeling well."

"Lydia. We must discuss – "

"Good evening, Mr. Harper. I will retire to my room now." She rose from the table and left him looking after her.

She simply could not take it. She'd let her heart crack open and would soon pay the price for letting her defenses be breached.

In her room, Lydia drew out her diary and wrote her thoughts in a hurried hand but it did little to calm her. When the full moon rose over the gardens, she blew out her candle, dressed for bed, and slid under the cool cotton coverings. Where was her strength? How had she let herself become this pathetic creature curled in her bed, afraid of the shadows and fighting back loathsome tears?

Too angry to pray and too weary to think, she sank into a dark sleep.

Lydia bolted upright in bed, sweat soaking the hair around her scalp. The room was dark save the moonlight that poured in through the open window. She got up and crossed the soft rug underfoot. What had awakened her?

The silver light bathed the garden below, a steady breeze bringing in refreshingly cool air for a summer night. Lydia touched her hair. Surely she had not grown chill. Another dream, then? She rubbed her arms, suddenly feeling cold. That had to be it. She glanced at her writing desk, a strange thought working its way past logic. She would write a letter.

She sat at the desk and pulled a loose sheet of paper from the drawer. Uncorking the ink bottle, she paused with the pen hovering over it.

Candles.

Lydia dropped the pen and struck a match to bring forth a tiny dancing flame on top of a lone tapered candle. She sat it on the desk and stared at the sporadic shadows that skittered across the page.

Something bumped in the hall.

Lydia dropped the pen and pushed away from the desk. Her feet rushed across the floor and her hand encircled the doorknob before she had the chance to think. She jerked open the door and looked out into the dim hallway. Her heart thudded. Nothing loomed but furniture.

She must be losing her mind. She sat down at the desk and arranged her night dress around her. She dipped her pen in the ink and began to write.

My dear one,
I have seen you in my dreams.

She paused. What was she doing? Writing a letter to a woman in her dreams? Still, something nagged at her. Yes. Yes, she must. She must write it.

She placed the pen against the paper again.

You come to me and we talk of —

A noise at the door. Her head snapped up, her breath quickening. Hadn't she closed it all the way? It stood open just the width of a few fingers. A tingle ran down her spine. Finish. She must finish.

She wrote faster. Lydia signed her name at the bottom and looked at what she'd written. Satisfied, she folded the paper and tilted the candle to allow a small pool of wax to gather at the fold. She removed the Ironwood stamp from the drawer and pressed it into the seal.

There.

The chair scraped against the floor as Lydia stood studying the paper in her hand. She could not explain her need to write it. Yet she sensed something important transpired. Now what would she do with it? She could not deliver a letter to a woman who existed only within her own head. Her gaze jumped to the board she'd pried up.

The table moved easily, and she pulled the board free. She dropped the letter inside and secured the hiding place. She rose to her feet and saw a shadow pass under the door. Holding her breath, Lydia crept across the room. She eased closer to the door, hearing nothing but sensing more than could be seen. She put her eye to the crack. A rush of air hit her face. She threw the door open. A small figure dashed to the stairway. The woman! She could give her the letter!

"Wait!"

The shadowy figure disappeared. Lydia ran to the stairs, but no one descended them. Her pulse thudded in her temples. She hurried back to her room and looked out the front window, placing her hand on the glass.

The woman stood below looking up at her. She shimmered as if she were made of the heat that rose from a summer's cooktop.

Lydia gasped as the woman flickered and disappeared.

Fearing for her sanity, Lydia dove into bed and pulled the covers over her head. Her heart knocked against her chest. Oh, she wished Charles were here.

His room was only two doors down the hall. Did she dare?

Mother's voice echoed in her head. *It wouldn't be proper.* A lady did not call upon a man. But what of her husband? He'd offered for them to share his room. Why had she continued to decline?

She slipped from the bed and hurried past the shadows in the hall.

Should she knock?

Lydia twisted the knob and eased the door inward on silent hinges. He'd left the dark blue drapes open, allowing silver light to spill through the large window and across the floor, landing on his half-covered form.

Lydia padded over to the bed and stood over him. His hair splayed out over his forehead tempting her fingers to brush it away. Her gaze traveled down from his face to his chest as it rose and fell peacefully. Moonlight caressed the hardened muscles with a small patch of hair at their center. Heat rose in her, and her breath now quickened for a different reason.

She bit her lower lip. Gently, she reached across and smoothed the hair from his face. She'd been a fool. Deciding she would spend every night with him while she still could, she rounded the foot of the bed and climbed in next to him.

He stirred and rolled toward her. Their breath mingled, and Lydia tried to remind herself to relax. His hand came up and ran along her arm.

"I'm glad you're here," he mumbled.

"Me too. I'm sorry."

"Shush. It matters only that you are here." He pulled her into his chest, resting his chin on the top of her head. His breathing soon turned even, and the tension in her muscles slid from her. She nuzzled in and drifted into a dreamless sleep.

She awoke to Charles stroking her arm. Lydia blinked against the light and gave him a timid smile.

"You came to me." The look of wonder on his face pulled at her heart.

"Yes."

"It pleases me greatly." He sat over her, wearing nothing but the sheet that draped low over his waist. The sunlight caressed the planes of his chest, and Lydia reached up to feel the firmness of his muscles under her fingers.

A low sound escaped his throat. Her gaze snapped to his eyes. They darkened and the heartbeat under her hand quickened. She must remember what these touches did to him. It seemed it did not take much to awaken desire in a man.

A small smile played at her lips. Where she thought there would be fear, instead she found comfort in his need for her. Heat rose and spread through her veins.

In one movement he was on her, resting on his elbows to hold his body above hers. He kissed her forehead, her cheeks and finally brushed his lips against hers.

"I would have you stay with me each night."

She took a deep breath, her chest rising until her body touched his, separated only by her thin summer night dress. "It is as I intend."

His mouth covered hers, and she let herself surrender to his love.

Sometime later, when the sun had risen well into the sky, Charles sat in an upholstered chair and pulled on his boots.

"You may redo the rooms however you like. I care only that I shall share a bed with you each night." He shot her the charmingly boyish grin that undid her.

"I shall strive not to make it too womanly."

He chuckled. When he finished tying his cravat, he came to sit beside her on the bed. "Grant is moving 17,000 troops to Iuka, supposedly to keep Price from joining with Van Dorn."

Lydia nodded not sure what to do with the information but knowing it weighed heavy on him.

"The Union troops in Corinth won't leave. They will continue to hold the city because it will cut off major supplies from Memphis to Charleston and from Mobile to Ohio. Those railroads are too important."

Lydia sat up in the bed, pulling the blanket up around her bare chest and tucking it under her arms. "Is that why the Confederates are going to go take it back?"

"Yes. But also because the rumors say it will not be long until the Yankees push farther south. If they come from Corinth, it is not long until they will be on top of us."

Lydia swallowed hard. Charles cupped her face in his hand. "Do you not see why I will have to fight? We have to keep them from coming south. To Ironwood."

She pressed her face into his hand and willed her voice to be steady. "I do understand. It is only my fear that makes me speak against it."

"I promise, my love, I shall return to you."

Resolve filled her chest. She looked deep into his eyes. "And I promise you shall have an Ironwood to return to."

Twenty - Three

*R*uth carried the pitcher of warm water up the back stairs and walked down the hall. She was so lost in thought that she knocked on Miss Lydia's door and waited for several seconds before remembering it'd been two weeks since she'd last slept in there. She continued down the hall to the Master's room and tapped on the door. Her stomach clenched. Despite Mr. Harper's kindness, she still didn't like it that most mornings he'd barely risen from bed when she came. It made her uncomfortable, but at least he'd been clothed.

"Come in!" Miss Lydia's voice carried through the door like a summer bird's chirp.

Ruth balanced the porcelain pitcher in one hand and opened the door with the other, pleased to see Mr. Harper had already gone. "You's sound mighty happy this mornin'."

Miss Lydia sat at her vanity, now moved to sit against the wall near the hearth, brushing her long hair. Ruth wondered at how white women's hair felt as soft as corn silk. She poured the water into the basin.

"I'm going to have a ball." Miss Lydia said, examining near invisible wrinkles at the corners of her eyes.

Ruth put the pitcher down and wiped her hands on her white apron. "You? You wants to throw a ball?"

Miss Lydia shrugged. "Nothing big. It's mostly an excuse to see my parents and have some company while I still can."

Ruth felt a small pang but ignored it. She needed time with her own people. "That sounds mighty nice then."

"I want us to go to town and get some apples. I want to make turnovers." She turned to look at Ruth, her eyes bright.

Ruth raised her eyebrows. "In the kitchen?"

"Where else do you suppose I make them? The parlor?"

Ruth laughed. "You know Betsy would have a conniption fit with someone messin' 'round in her kitchen."

Miss Lydia shrugged. "So she can help us."

"You mean Betsy, me, and *you* is goin' to work in the kitchen together?"

"Yes. I mean that exactly."

"Ha! Better not let Lucy know. She'll be fit to be tied."

"Do you think she'll want to help?" Miss Lydia looked genuinely concerned she'd left Lucy out of her peculiar plans.

"Nope. She'll just be mad you's in there with us."

Miss Lydia made a *humph* sound. "Well that's just too bad. Mother loves apple turnovers, and I know how to make them the way she likes. I'll not be denied the kitchen because it makes Lucy uncomfortable."

"I's got no doubt 'bout that." Ruth giggled and pulled a green dress from the armoire. "This one good for town?" She looked down at her own dress, another of Miss Lydia's, and marveled at how comfortable she'd grown in such finery. Her day dress was no different than her mistresses'. What would folk in town think?

"Yes, it will do fine." Miss Lydia went behind the screen to wash and put on her undergarments. All six pieces of them, including the silk stockings for her legs. How she didn't die of heat stroke, Ruth couldn't fathom. She still had a two-piece dress to put on over all those layers.

Miss Lydia's voice came from behind the dressing screen. "I need you to get one of the men to bring me my trunk that I brought from Cedarwycke. I don't know where they stored it," she said, the sounds of rustling fabric muffling part of her words.

"Yes ma'am. I'll see's that it gets done. You plan on goin' on a trip somewheres?"

Miss Lydia emerged from behind the screen and pushed the half-closed heavy curtains completely back from the window. "There. That's better. No. I am not going anywhere."

Ruth held up the corset and Miss Lydia lifted her arms to have it wrapped around her.

"So then what you needs that trunk for?"

"Storage."

Ruth shook her head. "All right." She yanked hard on the laces.

"Ouch! Don't make it so tight."

"Sorry." Ruth let her take a big breath and push the whale bones out a small measure. "I's still not used to these things."

Miss Lydia glanced over her shoulder and wrinkled her nose. "At least you don't have to wear them."

After Ruth made a decent arrangement out of Miss Lydia's hair and had seen her to breakfast, she went down to the barn to ask Noah for a carriage. When she neared, she found little Johnny perched on the hitching post, studying something in his hand.

"What you got there?"

His head jerked up and he lost his balance. Johnny started to tumble forward and Ruth reached out and grabbed his shoulder to steady him. "Sorry. I didn't mean to scare you."

He grinned. "That's all right." He held up his treasure. "Look here at what I found!"

A black beetle squirmed between the boy's fingers. Its hard, black body shiny in the morning light.

"That's a mighty fine beetle you's got there."

"Ain't it though? Look here at this big horn it's got."

Ruth looked closer. "A grand horn for sure."

The boy beamed. "Is you here to see Noah?"

She nodded. "Yes. You's a smart boy, huh?"

He turned serious, cupping the bug between his little hands. "I know Noah likes to see you. He don't quit smilin' for hours after you's been around."

Ruth's heart fluttered. "That so?"

His brows knitted. "Yeah. But he don't tell me why. You tell him some funny stories or somethin'?"

Ruth giggled. His face lit up. "You think you can tell me one of 'em?"

The doors slid open, and Noah poked his head out. His gaze fell on Ruth, and he grinned. "I thought I's heard talkin' out here. Mornin' Miss Ruth."

She dipped her chin. "Mornin' Noah."

Johnny looked back and forth between them. "Ya'll look at each other funny."

Heat crept into Ruth's face and she looked away. Noah chuckled. "Boy, why don't you find somewhere for that bug and get to work on them stalls?"

Johnny's bottom lip stuck out. "Oh all right. But I want to know what story she done told you when I's get done."

He jumped from the hitching rail and ran into the barn. Ruth looked up at Noah. He tilted his head. "What story he talkin' 'bout?"

She shrugged. "Mrs. Harper wants a carriage to take to town today."

The sun beamed down on Noah's wide shoulders and glistened across his brow. He certainly was handsome. Darker than any man she'd ever seen, his skin was the color of the night sky. But more than the nice lines of his face and strength that stretched his shirt in a pleasing way, Ruth realized it was the lightness and joy in his eyes that drew her to him the most.

"You's got a good soul, Noah of Ironwood," Ruth whispered surprised she'd let her thoughts slip through her lips.

He grabbed her hand and pressed it to his heart. "I'd be good to you, Ruth."

She nodded, feeling the rapid pace of the thumping in his chest. "I do know it."

"I's been wantin' to ask you somethin'. I know it might be fast but with this war and – "

"Good morning everyone, I... oh."

They both whirled around Ruth, dropping her hand and stepping back from Noah.

Noah spoke for her, allowing her a quick chance to recover. "Ma'am. I's sorry. We didn't hear you."

Ruth drew in a long breath but couldn't cool the heat burning in her ears. A smile pulled at the corner of Miss Lydia's pink lips, her gaze darting between Ruth and Noah.

"No, I apologize," Miss Lydia said, "I did not mean to interrupt."

Noah cleared his throat. "Forgive me ma'am. I's got carried away talkin' and hasn't got that carriage hitched."

Miss Lydia waved her hand. "Nothing to fret over. I am in no hurry." She smiled at Ruth, and Ruth wanted to sink into the ground. "I can wait in the garden."

She twirled around and walked off. Ruth and Noah stared at each other.

"I's best be goin'," Noah said.

Ruth nodded, not trusting herself to speak. He disappeared into the smells of horseflesh and hay within the barn. What had he been about to say? Ruth put a hand to her heart. It didn't matter. She had to remember that he didn't plan to stay.

Ruth waited until he came around with the carriage and then fetched the lady. They climbed inside, Noah's hand holding hers just a little too long as he helped her up. They'd made it all the way down to the main road before Miss Lydia spoke, destroying Ruth's feeble hope she'd let the topic go.

"So, is there anything you wish to share with me?"

Ruth took her gaze from the passing trees and focused on the woman across from her. "No."

Miss Lydia raised her eyebrows. "You're not going to tell me anything about that? I know when I see two people smitten with each other."

"Ain't nothin' that can come of it."

"Why not?"

"It just can't."

Miss Lydia studied her for a long moment. "Very well. But know this. It isn't the same. The love of a good man can mend the wounds left by evil ones."

Tears burned at the back of her eyes, and she blinked them away. "I'll remember that."

Ruth turned the subject to apple turnovers, asking Miss Lydia how she'd learned to make them and thereby keeping her occupied for the rest of the trip into town.

When they arrived, Miss Lydia stopped in the bakery for a few pastries, which she tucked away in her large bag, and then chose to walk the short distance to a cart outside of the general store where a man had barrels of apples.

"Brought these all the way down from Virginia, ma'am. Sweetest apples you'll find."

Miss Lydia lifted one of the shiny red fruits and studied it. Ruth let her focus wander and watched as people gathered around a paper nailed to a post. Most likely another list of the dead. Ruth turned from their tear stained faces.

The breeze churned the dust up from the street coating, the ladies' colorful dresses with its reddish grime. It was right over there that Byram had whipped her. She turned her head back to the apple man.

"But that's an outrageous price!" Miss Lydia said, her eyebrows nearly up to her bonnet.

The man lifted his narrow shoulders. "I'm sorry ma'am. But them apples had to go through three lines of Union blockades. Takes a fair amount of bribe money. You won't find no better price for them."

Miss Lydia sighed. "Very well. But I won't be able to get as many as I'd hoped."

He packaged the purchase, and they walked back in the direction of the carriage. Up ahead, people grumbled and a few older men, remnants of those who hadn't already left for battles, began to shout out insults.

Miss Lydia glanced over her shoulder at Ruth who'd stayed the proper two paces behind her. Ruth lifted her shoulders discreetly. They made their way through the thickening crowd and found two Union soldiers mounted on big horses near the end of the street.

Miss Lydia gasped. Ruth stepped up beside her but said nothing. Union soldiers in Oakville was a bad sign. Real bad.

Miss Lydia seemed frozen to her place. Ruth tugged on the sleeve of her dress. "We need to go," she said in a hiss.

"What? Oh. Yes. Let's get home."

They found Tommy alert in his seat, watching the restless movements of the people eyeing the men with bayonets held across their chests. What were they doing? Just looking at the townspeople? Whatever it was, it couldn't be good.

They climbed into the carriage and it lurched forward before they'd even gotten settled in their seats.

Miss Lydia fiddled with her skirts and didn't speak the entire way back to the big house. She was probably thinking the same things as Ruth and neither wanted to talk about them. When they neared the house, a black carriage pulled by a pair of white horses stood parked in front of the steps.

"Daddy! Oh they're early!"

Miss Lydia scrambled out the door before Tommy could make his way around to the side of the carriage. Ruth stepped out slowly, coming to stand just behind her mistress.

"Daddy! I did not expect you until tomorrow." She threw her arms around the old man's neck, more excited than Ruth had ever seen her. Miss Lydia soon gathered herself and adjusted the big ruffled hat on her head. "Mother. It is wonderful to see you. We've just come from town buying fresh apples."

The thin woman with the very serious face glanced around. "We?"

"Oh. Yes, well. I took my maid along to help me."

The woman flicked her cold blue eyes toward Ruth briefly and then ignored her. Ruth dropped her gaze to the ground and clenched her jaw.

"Ruth, send for someone to unload the apples and take them to the kitchen. I will send down instructions on how I want the turnovers prepared."

Ruth nodded and walked into the house, hearing the woman behind her exclaim, "Oh! You are making apple turnovers?"

Ruth clenched her fists. No. She doubted Miss Lydia would be making treats any longer. For all her talk of things at Ironwood being different, things were always the same.

She went to do as she was bid, trying not to let the bitterness in her heart poison her.

Twenty - Four

September 6, 1862

Ruth dusted the bookcase on the left while Lucy dusted the one on the right. With Miss Lydia's mother here, the house was in a flurry of activity. Seemed nothing was good enough for that woman. Ruth would be glad when she left.

"We's got to do them windows too," Lucy said, arching her lower back to stretch out the same soreness Ruth felt in her own. "Mrs. Cox says they ain't clean 'nough for company."

Ruth wrinkled her brow. "I think they's plenty clean. She just likes bossin' folks around."

"Shhhh!" Lucy hissed. "What if someone hears you?"

Ruth sighed. "Mrs. Harper acts different when her mother is here."

Lucy lifted herself onto her toes and wiped the top of the shelf. She'd have to do Ruth's side as well since she was the only one in the house who could reach it. Well, except for Mr. Harper, but he certainly wouldn't be dusting up there.

"Don't matter. We's got to do what they say anyway."

Ruth pulled her bottom lip between her teeth. "Do we?" she whispered.

Lucy spun around and stared at her. "What you mean?"

She shook her head and dropped to her knees to get the lowest shelf clean. "Nothin'"

"See here? This is one thing I mean. All this idle chatter." Mrs. Cox's voice came around the bottom of the steps just ahead of the woman herself.

Ruth cringed. Had they heard what she'd said? Her heart beat faster. No. Couldn't be.

"You heard them talking and whispering in here. Not doing as they should. This house is already lacking. If you don't tighten down on these things, they will soon get away from you."

Ruth risked a small glance up to see Miss Lydia's pale face. "Yes, Mother."

Ruth ground her teeth and scrubbed harder.

"You can't take your eyes off of them for a minute. They are inherently lazy. As soon as they think they can get away with it, they fall slack."

"Now, Mother, I haven't found that to be tru – "

"You are still new. Trust your mother. You can be naïve, daughter. I simply aim to aid you."

Miss Lydia sighed. "Yes, Mother."

They walked from the room with clicking boots against the floor Ruth had just polished.

Ruth glanced at Lucy. She shook her head. They returned to dusting.

A knock at the door startled them both. Ruth rose to her feet. "I's got it."

She opened the door to a man in a gray uniform with his slouchy hat pulled low over bushy straw-colored brows. "I am here to see your Master," the man said briskly.

Ruth straightened to her full height. "Mr. Harper's entertainin' company. You'll have to wait 'til I ask if he will see you."

The man frowned at her. "Very well. Tell him Lieutenant Monroe needs to speak with him."

Ruth shut the door. Lucy gaped at her. "What's wrong with you?"

She pushed past Ruth and pulled open the door. "Forgive her, sir, she's green. Won't you come on in and take some refreshment in the parlor? I'll get you some tea whilst she runs after Mr. Harper."

The man strode in without a word, and Lucy glared at her. Ruth hurried to the back of the house to go up the servant's stairs because Mrs. Cox had announced it wasn't proper to use the main staircase.

She knocked softly on the study door.

"Enter."

Ruth opened the door to the most masculine room in the house, done entirely in wood and leather and smelling of pipe smoke. She gave a small awkward curtsey.

"Yes, Ruth. What is it?" Mr. Harper said over the top of his desk. She glanced at Miss Lydia's father sitting across from him. Both men looked grim.

"There's a man downstairs wants to see you. Lucy done put him in the parlor."

"I will have to greet the guests later. He is much too early. Tell him he is welcome to the gardens or the grounds." He waved his hand to dismiss her and looked down at the papers on his desk.

She didn't move. "Um, well, I don't think he's no guest for the ball."

Mr. Harper's head snapped up. "Then who is he?"

"Say's he's Lieutenant Monroe."

"And now the time has come," Mr. Cox said softly.

Mr. Harper circled the desk. "Mr. Cox, if you will excuse me, I am afraid we will need to continue this conversation at a later time."

The older man grunted and lifted his bulky frame from the chair. "I'll go fetch Mrs. Cox and allow my daughter a little peace." He winked at Ruth as he walked by, and she dropped her gaze to the ground.

She took the long way around the house and by the time she made it back to the parlor, Mr. Harper already had the doors pulled closed. She stepped closer but couldn't make out what they were saying. Something rattled behind her, and Ruth stepped away from the door just as Lucy entered the foyer with a silver tray.

"Here," Ruth said, "Let me get that. I can serve them. You ain't had no dinner yet."

Lucy eyed her suspiciously. "You ain't either."

Ruth shrugged. "I done ate three biscuits this mornin'. I ain't hungry. I can wait 'til supper."

Lucy's brow creased, but she passed the tray to Ruth and left for the kitchen. Ruth struggled to balance it and open the door without spilling anything. She remembered Lucy's past advice. Walk slowly and quietly. Do your job while trying to stay out of sight.

"There's contraband *flocking* behind those lines. Union troops are giving them refuge. Many places around here have already lost a large number of their work force."

Ruth slowly poured the tea, not daring to look at the man speaking. Contraband? Did he mean Negroes? Would they really find safety on the other side?

"Another reason I have stayed," Mr. Harper stated, lifting a sweet from the tray. "My presence here keeps order."

"I understand perfectly, Mr. Harper. It is a problem all have faced, yet they have chosen to serve the cause despite it."

Ruth poured Mr. Harper's tea and peaked up at him from under her lashes. He stroked his chin. "I know the time has come. It is my duty to protect not only this plantation but the lands of my fellow Mississippians."

The soldier slapped his knee and Ruth jumped, nearly spilling the cup. She sat it down and retreated to the door. If she stood quietly here by the wall, would they notice her? She had to try.

"I'm glad to hear it. We are in desperate need of good officers for the march on Corinth. You will be given your own men to lead."

"When will I need to report?"

"They requested I bring you back with me."

Ruth tightened her hands at her sides. Would he leave now? What would Miss Lydia think if he didn't go to her ball?

Mr. Harper shook his head. "It cannot be done. I will need to set affairs in order before I go."

"Very well. But we cannot tarry long." The soldier's gaze shot over and locked on hers. Ruth dropped her eyes.

"Ruth, you may be dismissed," Mr. Harper said. "We can refill our own cups."

She curtsied and slipped out the door. Her stomach knotted. She'd lied to Lucy. She hadn't eaten any biscuits this morning and her worry only caused more complaint in her belly. No time for that now.

Should she tell Miss Lydia first or the others? She'd promised to let Miss Lydia know if she heard anything. Ruth wavered at the bottom of the staircase uncertain what she should do. Voices drifted down from above.

"Now, dear, Lydia is doing a wonderful job. Mr. Harper seems very pleased with her efforts."

Mr. Cox. At least Miss Lydia's father had a heart.

"I never said otherwise. I simply stated she needed to learn to maintain the presence befitting a lady."

She should go. The voices were getting closer. If they started down from the upper floor they would see her here. She moved from the foot of the staircase and around the side near the closet underneath. Ruth glanced at the parlor door. Still closed.

"You make a fine lady."

"Thank you, Daddy."

Miss Lydia sounded tired. Ruth took a long breath. Knowing Mr. Harper would soon be leaving would make it worse. She wouldn't tell her now. Let her have her ball and enjoy it and let her husband tell her. It wasn't Ruth's place.

She hurried out the back door as the three came down the staircase. The day was dark for mid-afternoon, and the air hung heavy with the threat of rain. When she opened the door to the kitchen, the smell of roasted meats and fresh bread made her stomach growl.

"Oh good. You's here. You can carry this other tray." Lucy handed her a silver tray filled with bowls of potatoes, beans and okra.

"Wait," Ruth said. "I needs to tell you somethin' first."

Betsy opened the door for them. "No time. We need to get this on the table. Then you can talk."

Ruth sighed and followed Lucy out the door. Lucy began to whistle.

"Since when do we got to start doin' that again?" Ruth asked.

"Since Mrs. Cox is here," Lucy snapped and then returned to the cheery tune that contrasted with both Ruth's mood and the dark clouds over head.

They set the trays on the sideboards and began placing the bowls of food on the table. Ruth leaned in between Mr. and

Mrs. Cox to put down a basket of hot rolls. She dared a glance at Miss Lydia. Apology shone from her eyes for barely a second before she lowered her gaze to the fine china in front of her.

When they finished placing the food, Ruth and Lucy stood near the end of the buffet. Ruth's stomach growled again. She pressed her palm against it and silently prayed it would stop. Lucy touched her elbow and Ruth looked up to see a soft expression on her face. "You's sound plenty hungry now. I's got this. Go eat," she whispered.

Ruth gave her a small smile of gratitude and hurried to the kitchen before anyone else could stop her. She pushed open the door and scrambled inside. "Betsy! I have to tell you what...Oh."

Noah grinned at her from his seat at the table. "Ruth." He dipped his chin.

"Noah."

Betsy loaded vegetables on a plate and handed it to Ruth motioning for her to sit across from Noah. "Sorry there ain't no meat. Sent it all inside."

"That's all right." She sat down and shoveled a large spoonful of peas into her mouth. Betsy could cook better than anyone.

"You's needin' to tell me somethin'?" Betsy asked.

Ruth swallowed and looked up into their expectant eyes. "There was a soldier here. A Lieutenant. He came to see Mr. Harper."

Betsy put her hand up to her throat and looked at Noah. They exchanged a glance, and she gave him a slight nod.

"We done decided that if Mr. Harper left, there was some of us that are goin' try to get behind the Union lines. Word is they's close," Noah said.

"You really *are* leavin'?" The last of her hope and foolish dreams vanished. "It's not safe!" Ruth dropped her fork, her appetite forgotten.

"We's got to take the chance. Think of it, Ruth. Freedom." Noah's eyes pleaded with her.

"We can't just leave."

Betsy walked around the table and placed her hand on Ruth's shoulder. "Me and Lucy done talked 'bout it. We's too old to try to make that run. And too set in our ways. We gonna take our chances here. But you..." she let her voice trail off, leaving the thought unfinished.

Noah suddenly reached across the table and grasped her hand. "Come with me."

Tears gathered in her eyes. "I can't."

"Come with me. I'll take care of you. I swear I'll protect you to my last breath."

Ruth hesitated, the lump in her throat growing thicker. How could she explain it to him? She had to stay here and take care of her fragile friend. Despite everything. No, none of them would understand.

"I's..." what could she say? Her heart felt like it would pull apart within her.

"Marry me. I'll make you a good husband." Noah gripped her hand harder.

Her breath stopped. His eyes bore into hers. Somewhere from a great distance she heard Betsy gasp and clasp her hands together, but the blood pounding in her ears muffled everything. Tears spilled over onto her cheeks.

"I can't," she whispered.

Noah let go of her hand.

"But – " Betsy started to say something but Ruth couldn't hear it. She jumped to her feet and fled their stares. Her legs moved beneath her, taking her further from the man she could no longer deny she loved. She ran until her lungs heaved, and her sides hurt. She sank to the ground near the edge of the woods at the back of a cotton field, their stalks stripped of every tuff of white. Like gnarled fingers they clawed at the gray sky, hiding her behind their impossible reach for freedom.

Ruth wrapped her arms around herself and let the tears come.

Twenty - Five

September 12, 1862

Charles ran his hand down Lydia's arm, and she suppressed a shiver. If she didn't open her eyes, maybe she could delay this day a little longer.

"I know you are awake." Charles chuckled, playfully shaking her arm.

"No. I'm still sleeping," she whispered cracking one eye to peer at him and then snapping it closed.

"Oh. Forgive me. I was unaware my wife spoke in her sleep."

She giggled. "There is much you still have to learn about me." She opened her eyes and slid her gaze over to him.

Charles grew serious. "I plan to learn anything you are willing to share."

"I shall endeavor to share all with you, husband. It is the good that I have found from the bad. This love I have for you."

His jaw worked, and he cupped her chin in his hand. "I do not wish to leave you."

She pressed her face into his palm. "I know. And I also know you must. I have faith you will not be gone long. Surely the war has nearly run its course."

"So they keep saying. I pray it will be truth."

He rose from the bed and finished dressing. Lydia untangled herself from the bedclothes and wrapped her robe around her. "Soon I'll have to start having a fire made at night. October is nearly on us, and the mornings will soon be getting colder," she mused.

Charles clasped her shoulders. "Autumn can be unpredictable, my love. We never know whether the Mississippi winds will blow hot or cold this time of year. But you can always think of me." He winked. "Maybe that will help keep you warm."

She gasped. "Mr. Harper! You shouldn't say such things."

"Why not? See? It seems I have already caused your face to warm."

She looked up at him. "I will miss you terribly."

"And I you." He pressed his lips to hers, and she leaned into him. Too soon he ended it and pulled back. "I fear I have tarried too long already. They wait for me."

She nodded. "I shall quickly dress and come down with you."

"No. It is better I do not have to ride off and leave you looking after me." He kissed her again. "Besides, I want to remember you here, like this. With your hair falling down your back and your lips reddened by my kiss."

His husky voice caused a stir within her, and she gripped the rough wool of his new uniform jacket. Words would not escape past the lump in her throat.

"I shall write you if I can, but know that every day I am thinking of you."

A tear slipped down her cheek. "And a prayer for you will always be on my lips."

He wiped her tear and kissed her forehead before striding from the room. Lydia watched him go and tried to fill her lungs with enough air to keep back her sobs. She must be strong. She must lead the people of this plantation. But not today.

Lydia didn't know how many hours had passed when someone knocked. She got up from the bed and pushed the hair from her face. She cracked open the door just enough to see Mother standing on the other side.

Mother's eyes went wide. "Lydia!"

She cringed and opened the door wider, turning to let her mother follow her into the room. She sat on the bed to await Mother's reprimand. She found the prospect of her mother's scolding no longer filled her with as much dread as it once had.

"You look a fright!" Mother gripped her chin and looked at her face. "Your eyes are swollen and red."

Lydia shrugged. "That usually happens when one cries."

Mother's expression softened and she tucked a hair behind Lydia's ear. "You have come to love him, then?"

Lydia squeezed her eyes closed against fresh tears and nodded. Yes, she loved him. And with it came terrible pain brought on by the fear of losing him.

"Oh, darling. I did not know." Mother wrapped her arms around Lydia and gave her a small squeeze.

Lydia leaned her head on Mother's shoulder. "I fear he may never return."

"I wish I could tell you that of course he will, but we do not know what the future will bring. But, I can tell you this. Living in fear will only cripple you. You must pray and go on as if he will be returning at any time."

"I will try my best."

Mother rose from the bed and guided her to the screen. "Get dressed, and I will do your hair."

When Lydia pulled on the bright pink dress meant to lift her mood, she couldn't help but allow a small smile. Mother tried. In her way. She sat down and Mother pulled the comb through the tangles of her hair, finally taming it enough to twist it into a coif that left a long piece hanging down over one shoulder.

"I've asked your father if we could stay longer, but he's afraid we've been gone from Cedarwycke too long already."

Lydia clasped Mother's hand. "I thank you for asking. I have enjoyed you staying this last week."

Mother lifted her eyebrows. "Have you? Your father says I am too hard on you."

Lydia smiled. "I know you only try to help."

"I do. I have only ever wanted what is best for you. For you to be everything you have the potential to be. You have made a beautiful lady. Just as I always knew you would, even though you tried your best to convince me otherwise."

Lydia laughed, enjoying the rare moment of teasing. "I did try."

They enjoyed a long noon meal, and then Lydia waved to her parents and watched their carriage grow smaller and smaller until it drove completely out of sight. She sighed and turned back to the house and found Ruth at the door looking at her.

"Ruth. I'm glad to see you." She lifted her skirts and climbed the five brick steps up to the porch.

"Miss Lydia, we needs to talk." Her brow furrowed and Lydia's chest tightened. She didn't need any more bad news today. All she wanted to do was forget the sorrow that dug into her heart. If only for a few moments.

"Let's go for a ride, then."

Ruth shook her head. "No ma'am. We don't need – "

"Then let's go to the kitchen and I'll teach you how to do those apple turnovers. We should have at least a few of those apples left."

Ruth's features hardened. "No. They's all gone."

"Did you try one? They are wonderful, aren't they?"

"No ma'am. Those were only for the white folks."

"Oh." Lydia drew a long breath. "Ruth, I am sorry. I know these last few days have been..." she trailed off not knowing what else to say. For all her words about things being different at Ironwood and their friendship meaning more than what others thought, she had slipped right back into the old ways with ease.

"I's understand."

Lydia clasped her hands in front of her and walked to the swing at the far corner of the porch. "Come, sit with me."

Ruth followed her but stood against the wall near the swing and would not sit. Not that she could blame her. Lydia had proved to be as two-faced as the twittering women she'd always loathed. And now here she sat – the very portrait of a hypocrite.

"Miss Lydia, there's goin' to be a lot of changes 'round here." Ruth shifted her weight from one foot to the other.

Apprehension clawed at her. "What do you mean?"

Ruth looked as if she were trying to decide what she should say. Sighing, she finally shook her head and looked at Lydia with sad eyes. "There's been talk you sympathize with the North."

Her brows knit. "Who says that?"

"Tommy hears things when he goes to town. That's what they's saying. Says you are too friendly with the Negros and don't keep us in our proper place."

"Ha! I do not care what they say." Lydia fell back against the slats of the swing, sending it into a slow arc.

"Maybe you do, and maybe you don't. But you needs to be careful."

"Careful of what?"

"There's men. They look for runaways in the woods."

"We don't have any runaways."

Ruth dropped her gaze to the floor. "Maybe. But they also has been questionin' white folks. Lookin' for anyone who might be helpin' them escape."

A chill traveled down her spine. "I will let the foremen know to be on watch."

Ruth seemed to relax a little.

"Now. Since that's settled, let's go work on some lessons. I was thinking I could help you with your writing skills."

Ruth gave her a sad smile. "No, ma'am. We can't be doin' things like that no more."

Lydia clenched her teeth. "Very well. I shall not visit you in your room anymore."

Ruth looked relieved, and it sent a pang into her heart.

Lydia rose to her feet. Mother was right. She must remember who she was and her place at Ironwood. They would look to her. She would do whatever she must.

"You may bring my meal to my room tonight. I will not eat at that big table alone." She walked past Ruth and ignored the look on her face.

That evening she finished her meal and waited until the house settled into silence. Then carrying only a single candle, she crept down the hall and into Charles' study. His desk loomed like a huge beast. She circled around it and placed her meager light on its polished surface.

She pulled open the top drawer as far as it would go. She felt around at the back. There. Her fingertip brushed a bit of metal.

The back came free. Lydia reached in behind it and pulled a stack of bonds from the hidden compartment. Charles told her where they were in case she had need of them.

He assured her they would be safe here. Yet something gnawed at her. An undeniable need to hide them away in her little secret hole. She replaced the drawer's false back and closed it quietly. She drew the papers close to her chest and retrieved her light.

She would have to move her things back into her own room. She could not take the constant reminder of Charles' absence that his things brought upon her. Lydia moved her side table and lifted the board free. She sat down on the floor, her cotton nightdress giving little warmth against the cool planks.

Lydia cradled the jewelry box Charles had given her, now filled with her treasures. It would be safer here. She lowered them into the dark hole along with the bonds wrapped in a thin cloth.

Safe. In here her treasures would be safe. But where, she wondered, would she?

Twenty - Six

Pocahontas, Tennessee
September 20, 1862

The sun hung high in its zenith, casting harsh light onto the rows of tents flapping against a brisk breeze in their own disjointed rhythm. Charles scanned the scene from the top of his red stallion. They stood a short ways off, still not yet noticed by sluggish soldiers who huddled around small campfires that released lazy smoke curls to mar the pristine sky. At the camp's rear stood a modest white house, from which the family that had once called it home had no doubt been ousted.

Charles would be joining a group of men demoralized by a recent horrific loss under Van Dorn and facing the impossible task of regaining Corinth from Federal occupation. How many of this dirty, ragged group would survive the coming days?

He pulled his slouch hat low over his eyes. They expected him to be an officer. A man with no military experience who'd never been the first to jump into an altercation. They told him he would be a Captain in Company K of the Mississippi 35th. A group of men who called themselves the "Invincible Warriors".

Sweat trickled down his neck and between his shoulder blades. Charles had never been into Tennessee before, but he saw little difference in the Pocahontas weather than it was farther south. The oppressive heat would make their march difficult.

Someone ahead gave a shout and waved their arm at him.

"Time to go, Draco." He patted the horse's thick neck and squeezed his legs against the saddle fenders.

Charles made his way down the hill and met an enthusiastic young man near the bottom. The boy couldn't have been more than sixteen.

"Who goes?" The youth asked, thrusting the end of his bayonet in Draco's direction.

The horse snorted at him and pawed one massive hoof on the ground. Charles stroked his neck to calm him. "You may want to be careful with that, young man."

The boy took a step back and shielded his eyes against the bright sun, sweat rolling down his wide brow and down his sparsely whiskered cheeks.

"Who goes?" he said again, though slightly more wary.

Charles looked down at his new gray uniform covering his arms and legs in stifling wool, brought to him by Lieutenant Monroe, and thought the answer seemed rather obvious. But then, he did have to admire the boy's dedication.

"I am William Charles Harper here to join up with the 35th Mississippi." He squared his shoulders and looked down on the young man in a manner he hoped would show both authority and honesty.

The boy dropped the end of his weapon to the ground. "We've been waiting on you, sir. They sent me to lookout." He puffed up his chest.

The horse snorted again and Charles nearly lost the ability to keep a smile from turning his lips.

"That's a fine horse you got, sir. Mighty fine. I ain't never seen one so red like that. What do you call him?"

"His name is Spiritus Draconis meaning Breath of the Dragon. But I call him Draco."

The boy let out a low whistle. "Well, my orders are to direct you to Lieutenant Monroe, and he will take care of you from there." He turned on his heel in precise military fashion and led Charles to the edge of the camp.

Charles swung down from his saddle in one fluid motion and gripped the reins. "Where are the horses kept? I'll need a place for him and a reliable person in charge of his care."

The youth brightened again. "I can take him to the corrals for you. I tend to some of the horses when I'm not helping cook. We ain't got many, being infantry and all."

Charles studied him. "What is your name, boy?"

He pulled himself to his full height. Tall for his age, Charles thought. Already close to six feet and nearly eye level with Charles. Skinny as a rail but likely to grow into a big man. Matthew had looked much the same at that age, and he turned into a bull. "Private Steven Brame, sir," the boy said clicking his heels together and giving a crisp salute.

"Well, Private Brame, this horse is the pride of my farm. He'll need his own pen and special care. But there's incentive there for anyone willing to care for him up to my standards."

Private Brame grew serious. "You can count on me to do it, sir. I'll make sure he's fit as a fiddle and hankering for nothing."

Charles dipped his chin and handed over the reins into eager hands already calloused from hard labor. "Very well. See to it, then."

Brame directed Charles to seek Monroe out in the officers' tents rear of the enlisted encampment and then led the horse off. Charles turned his attention to the camp, his boots stirring dust up from the worn ground and coating them in a fine layer of gray film. He missed the red dirt of Ironwood already.

Soldiers looked up at him as he passed, some nodding or lifting a hand in greeting. Charles dipped his chin to those who acknowledged his presence despite their obvious fatigue. Their uniforms in various manner of wear, some threadbare or crudely patched, gave evidence of the hard times they'd thus far endured. Guilt washed over him. His stiff new uniform now felt like a badge of cowardice.

His gaze fell on a man with greasy hair grazing the top of his shoulders. A dirty patch covered one of his eyes. The man looked up at him, surprise flashing in his good eye before he dropped his gaze to the fire. Rage bubbled in Charles' stomach like hot acid.

Webb.

In two steps Charles was on top of him, his fist landing with a satisfying crunch in the center of Webb's nose. Webb fell backward off the log he'd been sitting on, his head banging against the ground. He moaned and tried to sit up, but Charles pinned Webb's shoulder down with one knee and landed another blow. When he drew back, fresh blood coated his knuckles. Webb gargled as blood seeped out of his nose and down the back of his throat. Charles centered another punch into the man's face, the thirst in his fists for revenge far from quenched.

Men started to come out of their stupor and began to shout. Charles vaguely noticed them.

Webb struggled beneath him with a pathetic scream gurgling through his red-stained lips. He tried to throw up a hand to block Charles' fist, but Charles threw another blow to the man's remaining eye.

"I'll have your life for it!" Charles bellowed.

Webb sputtered and more thick blood oozed from his mouth. "Help! He's –

The words were cut short by a punch that loosened a few of the cur's teeth.

"After I gave you a chance!" Charles pulled his arm back for another blow, but hands grasped his forearm and wrenched him backward.

Soldiers pulled him to his feet, still snarling at the writhing man on the ground. Webb turned his head to the side and spit out a tooth.

"What is the meaning of this?" a man bellowed from the back of the gathered crowd. The men parted for him, and he stalked up to Charles, his face flushed with anger. Charles assessed the man in the span of a single breath. Thick, dark hair. Long mustache covering a grim mouth.

"I asked you a question, soldier. What reason do you have to cause a brawl in my camp?"

Charles shook off the hands still holding him and tried to compose himself. "I beg your forgiveness for my brash actions, but I – "

"This isn't a church soldier. You'll find punishment, not forgiveness here."

"This man invoked my temper. He worked on my plantation and he – "

The officer snorted. "I'll not have anyone under my command acting in such a manner. Take them both and tie them by the thumbs until I feel like getting them down."

Charles clenched his teeth. He cast a cold glare at Webb. The man sneered at him.

Two soldiers took him by the elbows and led him to the edge of camp where two tall poles were planted into the ground, a thin sapling tied between them. They took Webb first, tying a coarse rope to each of his thumbs and then throwing the free end over the sapling. A stocky soldier tightened the ropes until Webb's arms stretched high over his head and elicited a grunt from his throat. Only then did they tie it off.

"I'll not be subject to such a degrading display. I had just cause for my actions, although they were rash, and I demand to speak to Lieutenant Monroe at once," Charles said as they stretched his arms out in front of him.

They ignored him. A few rough tugs later he found it necessary to lift himself on his toes to relive some of the horrible pressure in his shoulders. He ground his teeth.

"Looks like shue ain't no better san me now." Webb slurred through thickened lips.

The words fanned the flames in Charles' chest.

"Yeah, lots 'o good tha' high-falutin' life does ya now, eh?"

Charles growled. "I'll see you hanged for what you did to my wife."

Webb said nothing. They stood in silence until the sun began to dip behind the tops of the tents and the soldiers began lining up for their hardtack and whatever other loathsome slop would fuel their bodies. Finally, Lieutenant Monroe came to stand in front of him.

"Mr. Harper. I am terribly sorry for the misunderstanding. I was not aware of the situation as you did not give your name at any time during the altercation." He nodded to the man standing a pace behind him and with two quick cuts his arms were blessedly free. When he lowered his hand, pain throbbed through the busted skin of his knuckles.

Charles rubbed his shoulders and studied the man in front of him. "I told the men who tied me up that I needed to speak with you. Is this how Confederates giving their all to your cause are treated?"

Monroe's eyebrows shot up. "*My* cause?"

Charles rolled his shoulders to try to ease the tension and bring back proper blood flow. "*The* Cause. Disregard my poor word choice. That was hardly the point."

Monroe cleared his throat. "Again, I do apologize. If you will come with me, the Major General will see you now."

Van Dorn himself? Why would Charles be brought before the Major General? What could such a man possibly want with him?

Webb moaned. "Wha' 'bout me?"

They ignored him and walked through camp all eyes riveted on Charles. Some first impression he'd made. For a man who prided himself on composure and self-control, he'd let his rage make a fool of him. Still, he would do it again. If only to feel Webb's face under the justice of his hands.

They came to the small house in the rear of the occupied field. Van Dorn stood looking at an arrangement of maps spread out over a simple wooden table, stroking the small patch of sandy-colored hair that snaked down his chin. Several men gathered around. Monroe leaned close to Charles' ear. "They should be finished soon. Then he will speak to you." Charles stood quietly near the door and watched the agitated group with interest.

"We will fake the building of a river bridge here," Van Dorn said, pointing at a paper on the table. "Making the Feds think we have no intention of turning east. Then we will hit Corinth from the northwest. Calvary should have destroyed the track somewhere along the Mobile & Ohio. That will keep them from sending reinforcements. As you can see here – "

"This can hardly be the map you intend on using. Surely you do not plan to base an entire battle strategy on your memory and hand drawn sketches." One man said, his face reddened to the point Charles thought he came mighty close to the color of Draco.

"You will remember your place, Sneed!" Van Dorn bellowed.

Another man placed his hand on Sneed's shoulder. "I'm sure the Major General has his reasons. I did supply him with a proper map of the defense systems around Corinth. Surely this is for a general presentation only."

The man named Sneed glowered but said no more. The sensible one nodded to Van Dorn to continue. The general's eyebrows nearly touched the wavy fair hair on the top of his head. "You would do well to keep your adjutant in hand, Price."

The muscles in Price's jaw worked, but remaining level-headed, he said nothing.

"Get your men to work on that bridge. Make a show for the scouts that have been lurking thinking we aren't wise to them. You are dismissed."

The men dispersed, none bothering to linger their agitated gazes long upon Charles.

Van Dorn seemed not to remember their presence. Charles glanced to Monroe who gave a slight shake of his head. Charles examined the tiny house while he waited, though there didn't seem to be much to take in. A few straight-back chairs, dusty rugs overlapped on the floor, and a trunk in the corner. Where Van Dorn slept, he couldn't guess. There could possibly be a sleeping area behind the door to the rear.

They stood silently for several more moments until Van Dorn finally motioned them over, not bothering to look up from his papers. Charles noted the map and could hardly blame the reaction it had incited.

"Mr. Harper." Van Dorn looked up from his map and studied Charles with a hard glint in his eyes.

"General."

He scowled. "I heard a report that a newly-required officer engaged in brawling in my camp. Have you anything to say for yourself?"

Charles had heard of the general's aggressive, even to the point of reckless, nature. Standing before him now Charles could already see there would be truth in those claims. Here stood a man bent on ambition with a reputation for being married to his desire to claim military fame. Charles would have to choose his words carefully.

"I must ask your forgiveness for the rash nature of my actions." The general opened his mouth to speak, but Charles hurried on before he got the chance while he might yet have time to salvage himself from complete dishonor. "However, I was surprised to see the man who, after begging for a job and receiving a possession on my plantation, then took his pleasure with my female slaves and attacked my wife while she picnicked. As I was away at the time, I learned of his disappearance only after my return, and my anger has had too long to simmer. Thus, it got away from me." He took a long draw of air to refill his lungs after releasing his defense in one breath.

The general frowned. "You are saying this man took advantage of your wife?"

"I believe it was his intent, had she not stabbed him in the eye with a wagon spoke."

The corner of Van Dorn's lip curved upward. "Did she now? Well, that would explain the patch." He stroked his beard, and Charles wondered how he knew such a detail. He was given to believe Van Dorn cared little about the men under his charge. Perhaps the reports were incorrect.

"Very well," the general said. "As you have already served due punishment for causing a ruckus in my camp, we will let it go at that."

"Thank you."

"Normally I am not involved in such matters. However, as Monroe reported your equine skills to me, I have taken a special interest in you. And I understand your justification in your anger. I can't say I wouldn't have done the same." He pointed a finger just a few inches from Charles' nose. "But I'll not have such behavior from one of my officers again. You will conduct yourself properly and dole out punishment in approved order. Unfortunately, incidents outside of this camp cannot be handled within it. Otherwise half my men would be strung up."

Charles gave a curt nod. The general turned his attention to Lieutenant Monroe who was still standing near the exit. "Tell them the man with the patch can stay until the first light of dawn. Then they can cut him down."

Monroe saluted and ducked outside. Charles let himself be satisfied with the thought Webb would get no relief tonight.

"Now. I hear you are an excellent horseman."

"It is a passion of mine."

"Mine as well. I believe we shall get on just fine." Van Dorn chuckled though it lacked any real warmth.

"As I hope, sir."

"Major General."

Charles dipped his chin. "As I hope, Major General."

"I will give you a company of infantry. We are in need of good horsemen to lead. Seems I've lost too many."

Charles ignored the later part of the comment and the apprehension it festered in his gut. "That suits me well, Major General. I thank you."

He gave a small grunt. "You may not be thanking me once you see my plan."

A chill slid through his blood, but Charles let no expression cross his face. Van Dorn stared at him for a long moment, and then motioned to the maps covered with flickering shadows from the lamplight.

"Come see my grand plan. Perhaps you will appreciate it more than my generals."

Charles circled around the table and came to the major general's side, praying that very plan wouldn't land him in the grave.

Twenty - Seven

Ironwood
September 26, 1862

*R*ain fell down in sheets, flooding the garden and washing soil away from the plants. It rained like it was trying to wash the land clean. Two weeks had passed since Mr. Harper left them. Every day Ruth wondered if Noah would keep his decision to leave. So every day she would linger near the kitchen door as she did now, waiting to catch a glimpse of him around the barn. Just a glimpse, then she would go.

She couldn't tell how late it was, not with the thunderclouds obscuring the sky. Past supper, she knew that much, though it was no longer served at any given time. Just whenever Betsy finished cooking, Ruth would take a meal up to Miss Lydia's room and try to get her to actually eat it. She no longer wore a corset. Not that she needed it. She had dropped too much weight already with her worrying.

Movement caught Ruth's attention, and her gaze flicked to the barn. Two silhouettes hunkered against the rain slinked through the doors. Ruth frowned. She waited silently under the cover of the stairwell that led to the quarters above the kitchen. Even through the storm she could hear Betsy singing an old hymn, her soulful voice slipping through the crack under the kitchen door.

Ruth pulled the hood of Miss Lydia's old cloak over her head to protect her from the drips that made their way through the cracks in the planks serving as her shelter. She wrapped her arms around herself and shivered. Just a few more moments, then she would have to give up her watch. He probably wouldn't come out in this anyway.

A group of several more figures appeared around the edge of the barn, ranging in size and shape. Ruth squinted. What were all these people doing going to the barn...? She gasped. The group. This had to be the group planning on leaving. It was happening. Tonight.

She glanced back at the kitchen. Should she tell Betsy? No. She should just go upstairs, climb in her bed, and forget all about the danger they were about to put themselves in. It was their choice. Their need for freedom. She stepped into the brunt of the rain and wrapped the heavy wrap tighter. She made it half way up the stairs before sighing and turning around.

Her feet slipped in the mud. Little rivers that ran like the mighty Mississippi through the garden soaked through her shoes and crept up the hem of her skirt. She shivered and slipped up to the barn, faint light seeping through a small crack between the two large sliding doors at the short end of the building. Ruth put her eye to the crack.

Inside, more than twenty or so field hands sat on hay bales. Some looked at the floor, some glanced around with nervous expressions, and others hunched together in small groups of two or three. All adults. Thankfully, no children. Maybe those with families were smart enough not to risk their lives.

Noah stepped into view, his broad presence gaining the stares of all in the room. Ruth swallowed the lump that gathered in the back of her throat. He began to speak, too soft for her to hear over the rage of the rain and thunder. Many of the people nodded, pulling up packs and bags scattered on the floor.

Before she could convince herself otherwise, her fingers slipped into the crack and she pulled the door open, stepping inside. All eyes turned on her. She straightened her posture and shook the water from her skirts onto the dusty floor. The only sound came from the soft call of a horse somewhere in the back. Her gaze locked on Noah. He broke into a big grin.

Ruth's heart sank, and she slowly shook her head. "I knows what y'all plan on doin'. But I don't think y'all understand the danger you's goin' to find." She slid her gaze over the people in front of her. Some frowned and some seemed as if they wanted to bolt. She looked back at Noah, his face stoic.

"I's been out there. Seen what happens when white men catch colored folk off their lands. Me and my sister..." Her voice cracked, and she cleared her throat. "Me and my sister were still on our master's lands when they took us. Said we was runaways. We were beaten," her eyes fell on a young woman about her age, "given to men's lust, humiliated and tied together to sit in our own filth. Those that survived were drug into town and sold for a pitiful sum."

Some of the people started to mumble. An expression filled Noah's face she couldn't quite place. She shifted her gaze back to the people. "I know you wants you's freedom. But don't think there ain't white men that haunt them woods. Men that'd rather hang you than see you returned to you's plantation. Or men who'd take your women and do what they want with 'em before leavin' 'em for dead. You's might make it to Union lines. But then what? You really think they's goin' to feed you? Let you sleep in they tents? I heard tell slaves without proper papers is sent back."

The people began murmuring again. One young man, probably not too many years past the time his voice deepened and hair sprouted on his thin face, stood up.

"It's a chance we's got to take. A chance at freedom."

"And if you die chasin' it?"

He shrugged. "Better to die for freedom than to live as a slave."

Ruth crossed her arms over her chest. "You ever been anywhere other than Ironwood?"

He shook his head. "Not that I remember. Came here when I's still clingin' to my ma's skirts when they built the new big house."

"Then maybe you don't know how good you's got it here. Other places, you barely get 'nough to eat to keep your stomach from shrinkin' to nothin'. You work all day, every day. No breaks on Sundays. And if you's don't work hard 'nough, or fast 'nough, or maybe you just don't look right to a foreman, you get beat."

The young man shifted his focus to the ground. "But we's still a white man's property. No better than his horses."

"And what if the Union wins this war? You's gonna be granted your freedom anyway. Why risk it like this?"

"And what if they lose?" said gruff voice from somewhere behind Noah, who still hadn't pulled his gaze from her face.

The young man nodded. "Yeah. What then? We's lost our only chance to make it North."

The others nodded their agreement. She knew there would be no convincing them.

Noah spoke up. "We's discussed it for weeks. The decision's done been made. Many will stay. The rest of us, we'll take our fate into our own hands."

"Then that fate may be death."

"But it'll be death as a free people."

Ruth's stomach clenched and she stared into Noah's eyes, trying to beg him to stay but unable to utter the words.

"Come with me," he said.

She pressed her lips together. "I done told you. I can't."

He stepped close to her and she forgot about all the others watching them. There was only Noah with his strong hands and ever gentle eyes. Eyes that glittered now in the flickering lamplight. "You didn't say why."

He gripped her shoulders and stared down into her eyes. Her heart galloped. "Tell me why, Ruth. I's got to know. I'll protect you. You don't have to be afraid of what happened to you before. I swear on my life no man'll ever touch you again or raise his hand to you."

"It's not that." She could scarcely get the words past the thickness in her throat.

He gripped her tighter, confusion in his features. "Why then? Is it 'cause you don't feel for me what I's feel for you?"

She shuddered under the conviction in his voice and in that moment knew that she would never again love another as honorable as the one in front of her. "I owes her my life. I can't abandon her," she whispered.

Shock flashed across his face. He dropped his hands. "You's choosin' the white lady over your people?" His jaw worked. "Over me?"

"You don't understand!"

"I understand. You's made your choice. We's made ours."

"Noah, please."

He drew a long breath. "Maybe you should go now."

Tears welled in her eyes. "Please. Stay here...with me."

He stared at her for a long, excruciating moment. Ruth's breath stuck in her lungs. She'd laid her heart bare.

"I can't. I's promised to lead them."

She swallowed hard and nodded. "And I's promised to protect her as she's done for me. Twice, I's owed her my life. I won't abandon her."

A long moment passed and someone cleared their throat, reminding Ruth they were not alone.

"Then it's settled." Noah said, clenching and unclenching his hands at his sides.

A single tear slid down her cheek. "I guess it is." She turned her focus on the band of runaways and wondered how many, if any at all, would find the new life they hoped for. "I hope y'all find what you's lookin' for."

Ruth spun away from the pain in Noah's eyes and fled into the night, the storm's furry overshadowed by the one in her heart.

Twenty - Eight

Corinth, Mississippi
October 4, 1862

Sweat pricked across Charles' brow. Had an October ever birthed so much heat? If it had, he could not remember one ever so severe. They'd reached Corinth yesterday on tired legs and empty stomachs. How many had dropped from heat stroke on the march he couldn't say, but those that made it to the outer fringes of the earthen fortifications were struggling from dehydration and fatigue.

Charles looked through the remaining cover of woods to the raised grounds of the fortification a hundred yards or so ahead. Sharpened tree trunks burst from the compacted ground like needled teeth from a demon's jaw. Battery Robinett.

He checked Draco's tack again, fidgeting with the harness and the buckles. Everything was well-secured, just as it had been the last two times he'd checked it. Men shuffled their feet around him, examining weapons, gear and each other. Nearly one hundred men were positioned under him, a regiment of men he was not fit to lead. How many would survive this day? Would he?

He'd heard plenty of tales of the gore and glory of battle. He gripped the handle of the sword at his side, his sweaty palms slick against the hilt. He'd heard Union soldiers had walked through the field of wounded Confederates at Manassas severing limbs from bodies and heads from shoulders. A shudder ran down his spine.

"Captain?"

Lieutenant Monroe's voice jarred him from his thoughts. "Yes?"

"General Moore says they finally located General Herbert. Says he was sick. They didn't attack when they were supposed to. The entire plan's run amuck."

That would explain the delays, although not why such a thing wasn't reported earlier. Charles could only imagine how furious Van Dorn would be at the disruption of his perfectly timed plan. Guns had been moved into position a mere four hundred feet from Federal lines. Their four a.m. reveille, meant to signal the Confederate and startle the Union, seemed only to have readied the Fed's for the attack. His mind raced with the thoughts in a single breath.

"What are the orders?"

"There's heavy fighting in the center and left. Moore's ordering us forward." The lieutenant spurred his horse and shot down the line to spread the message. Moments later a blast from the bugle somewhere in the rear brought forth a yell from the men behind him.

Time to move. Charles swung onto the back of his prancing stallion, the familiarity of the saddle and horseflesh underneath him shoring up nerves that threatened to fray.

Charles raised his pistol overhead and Draco lurched forward, nearly thrusting him from his seat. Draco pushed through the woods, snorting as limbs slapped at them and tore through cloth and flesh. A hissing sound sped past him. Then another. The bark of a nearby pine suddenly exploded.

He was being shot at!

Bullets peppered the woods with increased regularity. Two smacked into a tree a mere arm's length from his head. The men ducked behind and around them. Some cowered behind the cover while others raced forward with a near wild-look of glee on their faces. Draco tossed his head and pranced underneath Charles, the mass of him frightened by the hissing sound of bullets and men straying too close to his legs.

"Easy, boy." Charles ran his hand along the horse's mane, his words doing little to soothe the quivering muscles under his fingers. What a prideful fool he'd been! Fox hunting was nothing like war. The stallion was not meant for the battlefield. The smell of equine sweat mingled with the nervous perspiration of hundreds of unwashed bodies, saturating his senses.

They burst forth from the tree line. The looming battery ahead roared to life, belching forth fire that would put a dragon to shame.

Suddenly the horse gave forth a shrill equine scream and bolted. Charles pulled back on the bit and dug a hand into Draco's mane. Blood coated his palm, flowing from a deep gash along the top of the horse's thick neck.

Charles caught movement in his peripheral vision and snapped his head around to see two other mounted officers on his left with Confederate colors flying proudly behind them. He lowered his head and urged Draco faster. Behind him, the famed Rebel yell was no longer something of exaggerated stories but a gut-wrenching cry that would cause the hair on a man's neck to stand at attention.

Musket and cannon fire blackened the air, screeching projectiles narrowly missing his head. Iron hail rained down from above. The ground just in front of him exploded into the air, black earth spraying like a geyser. Draco reared. Charles shifted in the saddle to maintain his hold on the horse when he felt the heaving body under him shudder and begin to sway. He launched himself from the saddle and hit the ground just as the horse fell, the weight of him narrowly missing Charles' foot.

Draco kicked his massive legs and thrashed his head. Then he quit moving.

"No!" The word tore from his throat, lost in the thunder of the cannon fire. He crawled to Draco, running his hand down the smooth muzzle. The horse snorted once and laid still, his big eyes wide. Charles stumbled to his feet, forgetting the screams of the men surging around him. A shell left a massive hole in the horse's tender underbelly. Charles turned away.

He snatched his pistol from where it had fallen and joined the swell of men in the column pushing on to Robinett. Fire fell from heaven and the man to his right shrieked, his body ripped through with shards of metal. He fell to the ground, his gazed fixed above and his mouth twisted at a garish angle. The right side of his face was nearly gone. Charles coughed on the bile that rose to his throat. The boy couldn't have seen more than fifteen summers.

Screams pulled his attention from the mangled youth. Men in blue were nearly upon him! They tore into the lines of Confederate soldiers and were mowing down the regiment that struggled to maintain their advance. Charles leapt forward, his foot catching and catapulting him to one side. Something whistled by as he hit the ground. A bullet?

He lurched to his feet, dashing forward in an effort to regain his position at the fore of his regiment. Men fell around him and still he moved forward. Soon he had to step over them as they piled closer together on the ground. His mind gave over to the madness of battle, firing upon men once called countrymen and his sword sinking into the flesh of fellow Americans. For how long he struggled to survive, he could not say. On they pushed through the ceaseless roar of cannon fire and crashing volleys, choking on dust and death.

Through the five-foot ditch already filled with bodies, past the spikes and up the hill of Robinett they pressed on, sweat and blood staining their uniforms and smoke stealing their breath. Hurling shells hummed overhead, fiery tails blazing behind them in a display that if it had not caused his blood to run cold might have been quite beautiful. The projectiles exploded, showering them in bits of molten metal.

When they breached the fortification, the sun was well into the sky. How many had he killed? How many families would be without a father, a son, or a brother because of him? Charles pushed through the lines and into Corinth with foreign screams too uncivilized to be his own bursting forth from his chest.

He and what he guessed to be twenty or so other survivors of the massacre that had been the siege of Robinett were too battered to do anything other than to keep moving. Simple thoughts throbbed in Charles' mind. Root out the enemy. Take Corinth. Survive to see Lydia again.

They fired into windows of what had once been fine homes, forcing Federals out and to their deaths. Charles ducked behind the whitewashed wall of one such dwelling, his pistol ready.

Shouts rang out through the air as the men scrambled into position. Men in blue uniforms flooded the streets. Charles blinked his thoughts clear. Too many. Fresh troops without a stain on their pressed blue jackets. How many more were embedded within Corinth?

Something jammed hard into his back.

"Don't move, Reb!"

He lowered his pistol slowly to his side, heart pounding in his chest. So this would be his end. Shot in the back while covered in filth. He would never see Lydia or Ironwood again. Would never give her children and raise heirs.

"Move forward."

Charles took one step and halted. The rifle jammed into his spine again. "And drop that gun."

Charles let the weapon slide from his fingers and hit the ground with a thud. He walked out into the street, men in gray being herded together like livestock. His gaze traveled past them to a large building ahead.

The Tishomingo Hotel. He'd stayed there once as a youth traveling with his father. Where once gentlemen had strolled, soldiers were now being dragged inside. Many screamed. Some were missing limbs.

They trudged closer to the hotel, stopping just outside the steps. A Union man shouted something at them, but Charles couldn't make out what he said. Prisoners? Or men to be executed?

A cannon ball tore through the air and slammed into the hotel, wood splintering in every direction and the hysterical screams of women cutting through the fog of his brain. He dropped to the ground and rolled away. Men shouted and everything erupted into chaos. Blackness crowded the edges of his vision. He blinked. Why did he feel dizzy?

Charles rubbed his chest and felt warm wetness. He looked down to see a shard of wood about the size of a stake protruding from his right shoulder. Pain erupted in his chest. He gasped and ripped the offending object free. Blood gushed out and his head swam.

Clutching the wound in his left hand, Charles crawled away from the chaos around him. If he could just reach the safety of cover. He crept to the side of the hotel, willing himself to stay conscious. He must stay awake to keep pressure on the wound.

A dead Union soldier lay on the dirt just ahead. He glanced around. No one paid attention to him. A thought blossomed. Gritting his teeth against the pain, he pulled off his Confederate jacket with its officer markings and tossed it aside. His vision swam. He took a long breath to clear his head and pulled the enlisted Union jacket off the heavy corpse and pulled it on. Nausea washed over him as he thrust his right arm through the sleeve.

His pants. He looked down. They were so dirty the enemy might not notice they were the wrong color.

"Over there! I sees one!" A woman's voice reached his ears but sounded as if it were underwater. He fell back into the dirt and let his tired eyes drift closed.

Hands pulled at him. "Help me get him up. We's got to get him inside and stop that bleedin' before..." her voice drifted away like dandelion tuffs on a summer breeze. Peace came with the darkness. Why should he struggle to stay awake for the screams of death? He felt himself drifting, the warm void calling him to let go of the pain and find rest. The shouts around him grew farther away until only the sound of his thudding heart remained. The light glowing outside his closed eyes grew faint.

And then there was only darkness.

Twenty - Nine

Ironwood
October 5, 1862

"*I* got somethin' I needs to tell you."

Lydia knew that already. It wasn't hard to tell Ruth had something on her mind the whole evening. Candlelight flickered off the walls and danced across the final pages of the story she'd written for Ruth.

"The story is finished, for now, I suppose. Though that isn't the path your thoughts lie on, is it?"

Ruth frowned at her. Lydia placed the cork in the ink jar and rose from her spot at the desk. How late into the night they'd sat here, she had no idea. Time had grown monotonous, dragging slowly into fall. These times with Ruth, when they could pretend the world outside didn't exist, were the only things keeping her from losing her sanity. Or what was left of it.

She glanced at Ruth under her lashes. Couldn't they just keep pretending?

"There is more to the story, Ruth. More you will want to pass on to your children. How will it all end?"

Ruth glanced away. "I don't know whatcha mean. None of us knows what each day's gonna bring."

"And yet, we know what we plan, don't we?"

"I guess so."

"So what is it you plan? Where do you see yourself going from here?"

"Ain't no point plannin'. Life decides for you."

Bitterness Lydia had not seen from Ruth tinged her words. Something was wrong. "What happened?"

Ruth smoothed her skirt and looked at Lydia for a long moment. She forced herself to keep a passive face and wait. She would not ask again. Ruth would only answer when she felt ready.

"Some of the people's done run."

The statement hung heavy in the air between them, a living thing of its own that could be felt, if not seen. Lydia chewed her lip.

"How many?"

"About twenty, maybe more."

Lydia nodded. "When?"

"Last night."

Lydia crossed the floor and looked out the window as if she could find answers in the darkness beyond it. "Impossible. Someone would have told me."

"Like who?"

Lydia whirled around to face her. "Like one of the foremen! Tommy!" She threw her hands in the air. "Someone would have reported to me."

Ruth looked at the floor.

"You knew."

Ruth didn't respond.

"You knew, and you didn't tell me." Her heart clenched. How had she been so blind? Why had she assumed anything different?

"I's tellin' you now."

She glared at the woman she wondered if she even knew at all. "Why didn't you tell me sooner?"

"It was supposed to be a secret. Even now, the others cover it as best they can. You was never supposed to know at all." Ruth's voice was soft, laced with something Lydia couldn't quite determine. Resignation? Guilt?

"I hope they find what they seek." She turned back to the window but could feel Ruth's eyes boring into her back.

"You mean that?"

Lydia sighed. "What should we expect when we buy and sell people like they are nothing more than animals? Why should I be surprised some of them want to see what life they can make for themselves?"

"I told 'em not to go."

Lydia squeezed her eyes tight to trap the unexpected tears that sprang in them. "I thank you."

Ruth rose from her seat and placed a hand on Lydia's elbow. "I's not leavin'."

"I'm not demanding you stay."

"Even more reason why I won't go."

Lydia drew a long breath, annoyed at how ragged it sounded. She straightened her shoulders. "I will try to do right by the people of Ironwood."

Ruth nodded. "That I believe, sure 'nough."

"I am the lady of the house. And for the first time, I know what that means."

Ruth stared at her but didn't respond.

"It's late. You should probably go."

Ruth left her to find her own bed, and Lydia snatched at sleep for a few hours. She rose before the sun began to paint the sky the next morning. Today, she would speak to her people. Today, she would be their lady.

She dressed quickly, forgoing her corset, hoops, and even her stockings and twisted her hair into a simple bun at the nape of her neck. She reached for a bonnet, but then tossed it away.

She found Tommy outside the barn exactly where she expected him to be. He turned to her approach with raised brows.

"Tommy. You will have the foremen gather every person on this plantation and bring them to me. Gather them all. I want every man, woman and child that lives or works on Harper lands in the front of the house within the hour."

Tommy frowned. "But, ma'am they's – "

"I do not care. I do not care what they are occupied with or what is the proper way of doing things. I will speak to my people. Bring them to me."

He inclined his head. "As you wish, ma'am. I'll see that it's done."

She turned on her heel and crossed the garden to the kitchen. A soft voice drifted through the cracked door, so soulful she paused to let the haunting melody wash over her.

There is a balm in Gilead
To make the wounded whole
There's power enough in heaven,
To cure a sin-sick soul.

Lydia paused outside of the door and listened to Betsy. She'd never heard the woman sing before. Such a clear, beautiful voice. Worthy of any stage. The melody did something to her, awakened a response and tugged at her emotions.

Sometimes I feel discouraged,
And think my work's in vain

But then the Holy Spirit
Revives my soul again

Lydia pushed open the door and stared at the woman rolling dough with flour all over her cheeks and a red rag tied around her head, suddenly seeing her for the first time.

"You have a beautiful voice."

Betsy squealed and dropped the rolling pin, her hand flying to her heart. "Oh my Lord. You 'bout scared me plain ta death."

"I'm sorry."

Betsy straightened herself and looked at Lydia with eyes too wise and full of compassion. She nodded to a pan of biscuits sitting on the stove. "I's got some honey, too, if you want to pour it on 'em."

Feeling like a child obeying her grandmother, Lydia entered into the warm glow of the kitchen and plucked a golden biscuit from the pan. The honey was already on the table when she turned around. Forgetting herself, she settled down on the bench and drizzled a line of amber sweetness across her breakfast, letting the flavor erupt on her tongue and deliver a sense of simple satisfaction.

"You make the best biscuits," Lydia said, still chewing her bite in a manner most unbecoming.

"We all got our parts, now, don't we? Mine's biscuits." She grinned. "And chicken."

Lydia studied her. "That's the way it is, isn't it? We are born into our place and nothing we can do or dream changes that. We all have our parts to play."

Betsy wiped her hands on her apron and came to sit across from Lydia as if they were old friends. "Maybe. But the way I's see it, life is like the whistle walk."

Lydia frowned. "The path from the kitchen to the house? How is that life?"

She raised her eyebrows. "You ever watch a kid takin' the food to the big house before?"

Had she? Had she ever taken the time to notice the people that carried her food? "No. I don't suppose so."

"You know what happens, though, right?"

"Of course. They carry the tray from the kitchen to the house whistling because you can't eat and whistle at the same time."

Betsy nodded. "You think the boy, or the young woman, carryin' that pie wants to whistle?"

"I don't know." She squirmed in her seat and glanced at the door.

"Well, whistlin's like singin', don't you think? We do it 'cause we're happy, 'cause it brings joy to a weary soul."

Lydia stared at her, unsure how to respond.

"But them, they whistle 'cause it's what's expected, not because it's what they feel. They put one foot in front of the other down the path they are told to walk. Never once do they step off it. And never once do they stick their finger in the pie."

The cook's words struck an eerie cord and hung in the room like tendrils of fog on a ghostly night.

Betsy shook herself as if coming out of some kind of dream. She stood up and went back to her dough. "I's almost finished with the breakfast, ma'am, if you'd like me to send it in."

Lydia rose from her seat and brushed her skirts. She studied the woman. Was this the same woman who made the meals and bandaged wounds with tender hands or was she someone else entirely? An unconventional messenger with a profound truth meant to stab deep into guarded hearts who never anticipated her thrust?

"I've called the people of Ironwood together. I'll expect you in front of the house within the hour."

Betsy bent over her work, back to the same woman Lydia expected to see and yet at the same time forever different.

"Yes, ma'am."

Lydia strode across the kitchen and pulled open the door, coming face to face with Ruth and nearly stepping into her.

"Oh!" Ruth stumbled back, almost tripping on the big skirts of the blue dress Lydia remembered wearing a lifetime ago when she was but an awkward girl at Cedarwycke. Lydia nodded to her and stepped past.

"Wait! What's goin' on?" Ruth called after her.

Lydia looked over her shoulder. "I'm gathering the people."

Ruth's brows pulled together. "Why?"

She drew a long breath and looked back at the house, speaking to it more than to the woman behind her.

"Because I'm about to stick my finger in the pie."

Thirty

*R*uth watched Miss Lydia walk to the house with a determined step and straight back. She turned to Betsy, who stood in the kitchen doorway with a slight smile and a glimmer in her eyes.

"What's goin' on?"

Betsy's smile widened. "I think she done decided it was time to stop whistlin'."

Had everyone lost their minds? Ruth pinched the bridge of her nose. She didn't have time for this foolishness. "Miss Lydia done called all the people together. You know anythin' about that?"

Betsy raised her eyebrows. "You don't? Seems you always know what all's goin' on 'round here."

Ruth gave a humph and turned on her heel. Seemed no one cared about being clear this morning. People from the fields trickled in and a good fifteen or so walked with her around to the front of the house.

They gathered in the yard, none speaking. Women pulled shawls they should need for October, but didn't in this unnatural heat, tighter around them. Men stuffed their fingers into their pockets. Ruth watched as more came from the back of the house until the entire yard bloomed with a field of ebony faces. Young and old, they stood quietly together and faced the big house with eyes filled with worry.

Ruth shifted on her feet. She hadn't been asked to stand with Lydia. Ruth hadn't even been told her plans. That, more than anything, made her nervous. That woman proved she could do strange things. Not knowing what to expect from a woman who was the soul of contradiction caused her stomach to fill with an uncomfortable squirming feeling.

The sun crested the roof of the house, pouring bright light across the peaks and cascading down the massive front columns. The balcony doors swung open, and the people shielded their eyes to look at the woman stepping onto the balcony.

Lydia stepped up to the rail and surveyed the people in front of her, her face smooth with a quiet determination. Gone was the uncertainty and even the mask of indifference. Here instead, stood a woman of confidence. No longer a lady of leisure.

Something else entirely.

Lydia reached up behind her head and pulled a pin free, her long hair tumbling around her shoulders. Ruth's heart hammered in her chest. A proper white woman did not wear her hair down in public. The stress had been too much. Lydia had lost her mind.

Ruth looked at the people around her. They were all captivated by the sight in front of them, the sun bathing their upturned faces in a warm glow of clean light.

"People of Ironwood!"

Ruth looked back up at Lydia. She placed her hands on the rail of the balcony and looked down on them, her clear voice carrying to every ear. The wind picked up and tugged at Lydia's unbound hair, pulling it back from her face. A face that suddenly came alive.

"Today we make a new path. Today is a new beginning for each of us."

The people shifted, a current of anticipation stirring them from the passion ringing out in her voice.

"Ironwood is more than land and fields, homes, and barns. It is more than the cotton that grows in its soil and the trees that shade its grounds. Ironwood is more than you. It is more than me. Ironwood is not just another plantation fueled by the toil and sweat of bound people with no hope!"

The people shifted on their feet, their eyes darting back and forth between each other and the wild eyes of the woman above them. What did she mean to do? What would Mr. Harper think to see her up there? It was too much for her. This war, him leaving. Ruth's heart constricted.

Lord, help her. She's done come undone.

"*We* are Ironwood. Ironwood breathes! Feel her life! She lives because we work together, each of us with a part. It is only by working together that we will survive. You all know change is coming. You can feel it on the air the same as I can. A mighty wind blows toward Ironwood, seeking to tear us apart."

The people began nodding. They knew. Probably better than her.

"Our culture has told us the path we must walk. It has told us to accept our place and smile while doing it. No more! I *am* Lady of Ironwood. *I* shall say how life will be here. Not them. It is *I* who will care for her people. *I* will see that justice is done and that each and every soul here knows that they are worth more than the sweat of their brows! Created by God. Loved, honored, and valued. *That* is my Ironwood!"

Someone cried out from the back. Suddenly other voices joined them. Energy shot through the crowd, and they strained forward, some even lifting their hands to Lydia as if they could draw some of her passion down.

"Will you stand with me? Will you stay and guard this Ironwood? The Ironwood of my heart? Stay and I give you the promise of fair wage. The pride of knowing the toil of your hands puts food in your children's bellies."

The people began to mummer louder, cheers erupting sporadically throughout their numbers. More than a hundred faces alight with hope. Ruth shuddered and swallowed in the flood of emotions that swirled around her. Hope, excitement, anxiety.

"I give you a choice! Leave if you must. Leave as others already have. I will not stop you. But know that new life begins today, and it begins here! You will not have to search for it in the North. You will not have to fight for footing in a strange new land. Ironwood is the core of change. She is what binds us together. She is our rebirth and in her will we claim our freedom!"

The crowd erupted. Hands flew in the air. Women cried out. Men shouted. Ruth's breath caught and tears swam in her eyes. She'd glimpsed something *more* beneath the surface. She'd known this woman was different from the moment she'd first seen the fire in her eyes that day on the streets of Oakville. It had been hidden under a thick layer of propriety and tradition. Nearly smothered beneath the pressure to be who she thought she must be.

But not today.

Ruth raised her hand and shouted with the others. Today freedom broke open the guarded woman who stood above them. She breathed in life and that freedom poured over the faces below.

Lydia looked intently at them. "Will you stay? Will you stay with me and honor Ironwood?"

The people shouted, their voices filling the air with a jubilant cry.

She nodded and waited for their cheers to quiet. Her gaze roamed over them, her eyes pausing and resting on Ruth.

"It will not be easy. We will always fight against the current. They will not understand. They never understand."

Ruth nodded. Lydia's gaze remained locked on hers.

The people pressed in closer. Lydia swung her focus to the outer edges of the crowd where Ruth knew the white foremen stood. She could not even imagine what they thought of this. Lydia squared her shoulders, seeming much bigger and commanding more respect than her small frame should have been able to hold.

"Foremen! I will need you. I will need you to be men of honor. Men who lead with compassion and strength. Not men who oppress, nor men who allow chaos. But men who can lead a dignified people with respect."

More murmurs from the crowd. Ruth turned to see the scattering of a dozen or so white men. A few seemed intrigued. Some angry, but holding their tongues. None of them spoke. Ruth feared an eruption of rage. Lydia waited. Silence fell heavy on the people.

"I will serve you, my lady. I will lead as you ask of me." A strong voice off to her left. Ruth searched for the face to go with it. A tall man with his chin lifted. Ruth remembered him. The man who had seemed kind. Mr. Peck. The head foreman she'd seen that ill-fated day Lydia thought it would be a good idea to do Mr. Harper's rounds.

"I thank you. Foremen, if any of you doubts he can work under Mr. Peck by the parameters I have given, feel free to leave Ironwood in peace." Lydia's voice carried across the yard, her intentions clear.

Ruth counted seven men who turned and walked off, one spitting on the grass and glaring at Lydia before he strode away. The others exchanged glances but held their ground. Ruth turned back to watch Lydia nod with resolve.

"This will not be easy. Forging a new path means we will have to cut our own way. There will be trials. There will be doubts. There will be fear and uncertainty. But when the times are hard, remember today. Remember that we pledged to work together. We pledged to stand strong. Remember that today we birthed freedom at Ironwood!"

The people cheered and Ruth clasped her hand over her heart. Lydia turned from the crowd and retreated into the house. How long they stood there in the throes of change she did not know. But something had shifted. Life began a new path the day Ruth first met a strange white lady who bought her in the same way she would have bought a new dress.

Where Ruth had once been enslaved by culture, she was now liberated by courage. Bought with a price and freed with a price. Ruth looked around at the crowd. Would they ever know how much it would cost Lydia? How much it already had? Would they ever understand the price that woman had, and still would, pay for them?

She prayed someday they would. And that they would never forget.

Thirty - One

Corinth, Mississippi
October 8, 1862

"*I* think he's wakin' up."

Charles lifted the weight of his eyelids a small slit and then squeezed them tight against the bright light. He drew long breaths, his body slowly bringing every ache, soreness and stabbing pain to his attention until they threatened to send him back into the comfort of the darkness.

Lydia.

The thought of his wife pushed past the cloying call of unconsciousness and reminded him that he must fight through whatever circumstances threatened to keep him from her. He peeled back his eyelids and blinked rapidly, the fuzzy image of a female face slowly coming into focus.

She frowned down at him, part of her wrinkled brow encased in the white scarf wrapped around her head.

"Is you awake?"

He tried to speak, but his tongue stuck to the roof of his mouth. The woman pressed a tin cup to his lips, and he pulled in a sip of tepid water. As the moisture coated his lips, he suddenly realized how thirsty he was. He gulped the liquid, draining the cup.

"More."

She shook her head and placed the cup on a small table that sat between his and another cot. "No more right now. Don't want it comin' back up."

He studied her. A Negro woman but perhaps mixed. What was she doing here? He turned and looked at the four walls surrounding him. They'd jammed at least eight cots into a small single room so as there was hardly room to walk between them.

"Where am I?"

"Tishomingo hospital."

Someone in the room coughed, another moaned. Was he a prisoner? Then he remembered putting on the jacket of the dead Federal. Did they know?

"You's been in and out for a long time. Thought the infection and fever might be the end of you, but you done fought past it. Right now you's in a room with other men the doctor thinks'll make it out of this building alive. You's one of the lucky ones." She pointed her finger at him and put a hand on her hip. Something about her mannerism nagged him, but he couldn't place it. Had he seen this woman before?

He must choose his words carefully. "What happened in the battle?"

"The Reb's were sent runnin'. A few got into the town but there weren't enough of 'em to do much 'bout it. They's all gone now, except for a few of their wounded downstairs."

Charles nodded. It wouldn't be long until someone figured out who he was. He'd have to find a way out of here. And soon.

He swung his legs to the side of the cot.

"What do you think you's doin'?" The woman asked, laying a staying hand on his arm.

"I'm getting up."

"No you ain't."

"Nurse? Nurse?" A man called from across the room, then erupted into coughing.

"Hold on just one second Bill," she said, her eyes never leaving Charles. She leaned closer to him, pushing him into the rough wad of cloth that could hardly be called a pillow. "Now you's stay put."

He said nothing. After a few breaths she swished away, threadbare skirts skimming the wooden floors. He looked down at himself. He wore nothing but his drawers and was scarcely covered by a thin blanket. A clean bandage covered his right shoulder.

"No more signs of infection. Been a plain miracle."

The woman's voice startled him. How had he not noticed her approach? "Where are my clothes?"

"Burned."

"What?"

She shrugged. "Who you think's goin' to wash all them blooded and torn uniforms? Besides, too much sickness spreading. We burned all of them. But don't you worry. You'll get issued new ones. The Lieutenant should be back 'round here in the mornin' to take his records again. You'll be awake for them this time."

A chill ran up his spine. "That's good, then." He'd have to get out of here tonight.

She narrowed her eyes at him. "I's the one that dragged you in from the street."

He stared at her.

"Seems kinda funny to me. What with the hole in your shirt and the way that thing was bleedin'. How's come your jacket didn't have no hole in it?"

No moisture remained in his mouth. He turned his head and coughed. "Water?"

She snatched the cup from the table and crossed to a pitcher in the corner to refill it. What would he say? She'd call him out on his ruse for certain.

"What is your name, nurse?" He asked as soon as she thrust the cup in his direction. He grabbed it and downed.

"What's yours?"

They stared at each other for a long moment, an understanding that dared not be voiced passing between them.

"How did you come to be here, nurse? Seems an odd place for you."

She raised her chin. "I came across the Union soldiers encamped here. They's needed women to tend to their wounded and I took the job."

He raised his eyebrows. "And where did you come from before that?"

"Why you care?"

He looked at her until she started to turn away from him. "You remind me of someone."

She shook her head. "No, I ain't ever seen you before I found you on the street."

"How'd you get that scar?"

She reached up and touched the jagged line that ran out from under her scarf and down her temple. "I don't remember."

He settled back and watched emotions play across her face. She must have sensed the way he studied her. She straightened her back and glared down at him. "You stay in that bed. I'll check on your bandages later." She turned on her heel and darted from the room.

At least he'd stopped her from asking any more questions. He turned his head to the left and looked into a pair of light brown eyes.

"She's a good one. Makes you wonder, don't it? They say that Negroes aren't really human. That all they are good for is hard labor. Then you see one like that and all it does is convince you even more that the Rebels are the real barbarians."

Charles swallowed past the thickness in his throat. "You think all Southerners are barbaric?"

The man shrugged, a bandage similar to Charles' own wrapped around his chest. "More things to wonder about. Let's say there is a man who owns a farm and two Negroes that work for him. Every day the two Negros get up to help him and his six children in the field. Side by side they plow and plant, hoe and harvest. The man needs the help to keep his farm running. If it weren't for those two men, the family wouldn't survive. When they work, so does he. If he eats, so do they."

"So what's the truth, then? Are the Confederates evil or aren't they?"

The solider looked hard at him. "I wonder if there are men who mean well but haven't considered that just as God made the birds of the air and the beasts of the field in an array of color, so too did he make man. What right has one man got to own another? What if God had given me black skin instead of white? I'm the same soul inside. The same man, I reckon. What then? Am I now nothing more than livestock?"

His stomach churned. These were questions that had haunted him often. He did right by his people. Made sure they were fed well and not over worked. Where many abused their slaves, Charles believed happy, healthy people worked better. But still, there were those that had not been born to the Harpers his father had bought at an auction when he built Ironwood. Charles himself had never actually purchased a slave nor sold one. Still, he *owned* all the people of Ironwood. It was a life he'd not tried to question too much, only care for what had been left to him.

"What do you think, soldier?"

The man's words drew him out of his thoughts. "I don't know. I guess it is the only life they've ever known, and I think there are good men out there who try to do right by the people under them."

The stranger's eyes bore into him, and he felt as if the man could see his very soul. "Things to ponder, eh, Charles?" His gaze swung to the door. "That girl there, she needs to leave this place. She thinks she is safe behind Union lines. But someone from her past will soon come through here. And he does not mean any good for her."

Had he told the man his name? The hairs on his arms stood on end, raised by the bumps that covered his flesh.

The man looked back at him. "Think hard on the man you want to be. What legacy do you want to leave to your son?"

Charles could only stare at him. Footsteps came from beyond the cracked door, down the hall and closer to them. The man glanced at the door and then back to Charles, his eyes shining bright with passionate authority.

"When you run, take her with you. She needs you."

Hinges squeaked and Charles swung his gaze to the door to see the woman returning with a tray of steaming bowls. Charles pushed himself into a sitting position, his stomach responding to the aroma that drifted to his nostrils.

"All right y'all. I's got you some chicken soup." She walked gracefully into the room, her walk hindered by a small limp Charles had not noticed before.

She handed him a bowl of soup and a tarnished spoon. Never had he tasted anything so good. He nodded his thanks as she moved off to serve the next man. He turned to comment on the meal to the strange companion to his left. The cot sat empty.

Charles looked around the room. "Where did he go?"

The woman looked at him over her shoulder as she handed the one she'd called Bill a bowl. "Who?"

"The man in that cot." He jutted his chin to indicate the empty bed.

She handed off the bowl and turned to him. It seemed he and Bill were the only ones awake. Two other men slept in their cots, undisturbed by their conversation.

"He was talking to himself while you were gone. Might be infection going to his head," Bill said around a mouthful of food.

She frowned at Bill and sat her tray on the empty cot in question and pressed her cool palm against his head. "Don't feel like you got's fever."

He pushed her hand away. "I'm not sick, woman. I tell you there was a man in that cot with a bandage wrapped around his chest."

She shook her head. "Ain't been nobody in that bed since John left to go back to his unit."

Charles ground his teeth. Did he have a brain injury?

"You eat you's soup and get some rest."

Charles took her advice and tried not to think about the implications of what he'd seen.

Darkness had settled several hours ago. From what Charles could guess, it had to be near midnight. He'd spied a pair of boots and folded clothes on a chair near the door after the nurse left for the evening. He didn't know who they belonged to or how they had gotten there. Someone must have delivered them while he napped.

He placed his feet on the cool floor and padded to the front of the room. Other than a soft snore from one of the men, all was quiet. He slipped into a pair of trousers and a cotton shirt, and then sat in the chair to pull on boots that fit his feet perfectly.

Whether he put on Union blue or Confederate gray he couldn't be sure in the dark, but there was no jacket. He'd make do with the blessing that had been handed to him. He slid out the door and down the hallway. Downstairs, he passed the front desk and men sleeping on the floor. Better not try the front door. Surely a guard would be there.

Charles remembered a door to the rear from his visit here a lifetime ago. He crept slowly past the sleeping men, his boots not giving off any indication of his movement. He placed his hand on the cool of the doorknob, surprised to find it turned easily in his hand. His heart pounded in his chest.

The door swung on silent hinges. He poked his head outside. No movement. He slipped out the door and down a set of narrow steps. He'd done it! He'd managed to get free of the hospital without waking a soul. Now if only he could get –

"Where you's goin'?" A voice hissed from the shadows.

Charles' heart leapt in his chest, feeling as if it would break free of its bony cage. "Who's there?" he whispered.

A dark form materialized from the shadows at the rear of the building. The nurse. Without thinking he grabbed her arm, but she didn't cry out.

"What are you doing out here?"

She snatched her arm free. "The same thing as you, I'm guessin'. Escapin'."

He could barely make out her face in the moonlight. "Why would you want to do that?"

"Why would you?"

An exasperated rumble sounded in his throat. "I don't have time for this." He moved to step around her, but her hand shot out and rested on his chest.

"Look, I don't know where you got them clothes or how you got past them guards but you must be pretty good. And I's certain you ain't no Union soldier."

Charles looked down at her, the strange man's words drifting into his mind. He shook his head to dislodge them. This was mad.

"You're right. I put on a dead Fed's coat to stay alive. Right now all I want to do is get home to my wife so she knows I'm still alive. Then figure out where I'm supposed to be. Can you let me do that? Will you let a man you saved die now?"

She looked at him as if debating on whether or not to scream for help. "He's here. The man that took me." The words tumbled from trembling lips.

"What man?"

Her hand flew to her head. "The one that gave me this scar. He's here. I saw him. He think's I's dead. If he sees me... oh Lord." Her breaths came in rapid spurts.

Compassion flooded him brought on by the man that had forced him to look deeper inside himself than he'd wanted. What kind of man *did* he want to be? He looked at the trembling woman and no longer saw the color of her skin. All he could see was a frightened female in need of protection.

"Come with me to my plantation. I swear no harm will come to you. I'll take you home to my wife. I think you'll like her."

"I don't want to be on no plantation. Not ever again."

"Ironwood is not what you think. I've plans to make changes there. Regardless of what the outcome of this war is. You will be safe there. And once you are free of this threat, you have my word that you may leave any time you wish. I do not lay any claim over you."

Tears slipped down her cheeks. "I pray you's honest. I don't see any other choice. I barely survived being on my own once."

"Then we better get moving."

They slipped quietly along the back of the town and into the woods. Charles could taste the freedom and wondered if the tiny woman at his side felt the same. Where were the patrols? The guards? They saw no one as they slipped into the woods. Charles sent up a prayer of thanks.

Some time later he felt it safe enough to speak. "My name is Charles Harper, in case you were wondering. My home is in Oakville. If we keep to the woods and avoid the roads, we should make it to Ironwood safely."

He couldn't tell if she heard him or not. He pushed a limb out of the way and held it for her to grasp. She stayed close behind him. It would be slow going through the darkness, but they must get as far south as they could before anyone noticed them missing.

They walked in silence for what was probably an hour before she finally spoke. "I thank you, Charles Harper. God's done sent you. I's goin' to believe Him and trust you's a good man."

"God told you you'd be safe with me?"

"That He did."

Peace settled on him. "Then are you going to tell me now where you came from?"

"Natchez."

The sadness in that single word pulled at his heart. He wondered what she'd been through to find herself in Corinth. He tried to push lightness into his voice.

"Well, then I suppose I shall call you Natchez, since you've given me nothing better."

A small giggle bubbled up behind him and he smiled.

"No. I guess since you done gave me your name, I might as well give you mine."

"Indeed, it would make it easier."

After a long pause she finally sighed and said, "My name's Bridget."

Thirty - Two

Ironwood
October 9, 1862

*I*ronwood struggled to walk down the new path Miss Lydia had set them on. Eight who'd danced on the lawn and vowed to stay broke their word and disappeared into the night. Miss Lydia let them go as she'd promised and said nothing about it. But Ruth knew. She could see it cut deeper than Miss Lydia would ever admit.

For the most part, life returned to normal, and they took up the same duties because it was what they knew. But they laughed a little more and dared to hope even when it seemed impossible.

Ruth swiped her rag along the top of the piano and wondered what it might be like to learn to play someday. Could she train her fingers to coax out a melody? Lucy's voice broke into her thoughts.

"I heard there was Union soldiers marchin' through town."

Ruth's pulse quickened, and she turned to watch Lucy absently polish the brass bottom of a lamp as if she'd merely commented on the weather.

"Who done told you that?"

Lucy worked the rag across the surface, her thumbs coaxing a shine from the metal. "Tommy. He saw 'em hisself yesterday when he went for supplies."

Ruth pressed her lips together. That couldn't be good. Already they'd heard the battle of Corinth was a massive defeat. The Confederates failed in their attempt to recover the railways. Nearly every day Lydia decided there was something they needed from town and sent Tommy after it. She never left the grounds anymore.

They all knew the real reason he went. He went to check the lists that came in with weary men and were nailed to the posts. The real reason Tommy went to Oakville was to see if Mr. Harper was listed among the dead.

Every time he returned, Lydia met him on the front steps. But so far no news of Mr. Harper.

"What you think that means?" Ruth asked.

Lucy shrugged and looked up from her task. "I don't know. It might not mean nothin'. They might just be gettin' supplies as they pass through."

"Maybe." Ruth wasn't so sure. If they were here and here in any numbers, then all of Ironwood had plenty of reasons to worry.

"Might be better if they's here."

Ruth frowned. "Why would you say that?"

Lucy sat down the lamp and came closer. "Think 'bout it. Mrs. Harper's done said some crazy things. Men 'round these parts ain't goin' to like that none. You know that. You know they's been comin' after people who they's think are copperheads."

"What?"

Lucy rolled her eyes. "Don't you listen to nothin'? That's what they call it. Folks that live down here but side with the North. They call 'em copperheads."

"Why?"

"I don't know. What's it matter? They for sure done called Mrs. Harper one."

Ruth got a sinking feeling in her stomach.

"So the way I's see it, if the Union troops is here and we is in support of the North, then maybe we's safer with them."

Ruth rubbed her arms against the chill creeping over them and went to poke at the fire, hoping it would push out more heat. When the heat spell had finally broken, October had fallen into a deep chill.

A heavy pounding on the front door caused both of them to jump. Ruth set down the fire poker. "I's got it."

She opened the door and felt all the blood drain from her face. Men dressed in blue uniforms swarmed on the porch and flowed down over the front steps. One unusually tall man proudly stood in the front of all of them, filling the doorway. Ruth drew in a sharp breath and stared at them, unable to get any words to come out.

The man cleared his throat.

"I, um..." she glanced behind her. Should she slam the door in their face? Tell them to leave? What if what Lucy said was right? She shook her head.

"I's sorry, sir. You done caught me unawares." She smoothed the front of her dress. "Good mornin'. How's can I help you?"

The man studied her, his gaze drifting over her dress and back up to her face. Did he wonder why a colored woman wore a lady's dress? Could he tell that Ironwood was different from any other plantation he might have chosen just by looking at her? She caught no disgusting glimmer in his eyes as he looked her over, only curiosity.

"I would speak to the man of the house." He gave a small nod. "If you would be so kind as to get him."

Ruth glanced around behind her. Where was Lucy? How much should she say? She leaned to the side and looked at the men behind him. The officer followed her gaze.

"I don't think the parlor can hold all y'all. You can make y'allselves comfortable here on the porch." She bowed her head and closed the door before he could object, sliding the lock into place. She didn't care what Lucy said. She wasn't letting them in the house.

She turned and ran up the stairs, throwing open Lydia's door without knocking. She sat at her desk, writing. The door slammed against the wall causing Lydia to drop her pen, and it rolled across the floor.

"Ruth! What in – "

"Miss Lydia! Union soldiers. They's on the front porch!"

Lydia gasped and scrambled to her feet. "What should I do? What did they say?"

"They's knocked on the door and asked to talk to the gentleman of the house. That's all."

Lydia wrung her hands and started pacing the floor, mumbling to herself like a madwoman. "I suppose I will have to go and speak to them. It's too much to hope now that they will leave us in peace."

"Lucy says we's might be safe with 'em. Since the southerners done called you a cottonmouth."

Lydia stopped pacing and stared at her. "What?"

Ruth shook her head. No, that wasn't it. She waved her hands in the air, exasperated. "Some kind of snake. Something 'bout southerners who side with the North."

"Copperheads," Lydia whispered.

"That was it." Ruth bobbed her head. "She says it might be good the Union soldiers is here."

Lydia gave her a long look. "There are a lot of things Lucy doesn't understand."

Before Ruth could think of a reply, Lydia spoke again. "How many?"

"Looks like seven or eight out there on the porch. I's not sure if there is more hidin' somewheres else."

A long pause. "Tell them whoever represents them can wait in the parlor. I will speak with them. But I do not wish to be that far outnumbered."

Ruth nodded and hurried down the stairs, opening the door to find the man still standing quietly on the porch, his expression a strange mix of annoyance and amusement.

"My mistress says she'll speak with you, but the others got to wait outside."

He raised his bushy brows. "I will be accompanied by my men."

Ruth shook her head. "No, sir."

The amusement washed from his face and Ruth's chest constricted. He towered over her like a bear. "Then I shall offer you but one compromise. Half of us will come and half will stay. It is the only offer you will receive."

Ruth swallowed hard and opened the door. The officer motioned to some of his men and three of them followed him into the foyer. Ruth closed the door and locked it behind her, unsure if she was locking the danger out or in.

She led them to the parlor wondering where Lucy had disappeared to. She gestured the men into the room, and then pulled the doors together behind them. She pressed her back against the seam of the doors and tried to force her breathing to slow.

Ruth felt each slow thud of her heart pass like time was trying to go uphill through a bog of mud. It must be a half hour by now. Maybe more. How long would she make them wait? Wouldn't they grow more impatient, and therefore disagreeable, with each lost moment?

Lydia swept down the stairs wearing one of her best gowns and looking every bit the proper lady. No more free hair and missing hoops. Ruth wondered how she'd gotten everything fastened alone.

Lydia nodded once and Ruth opened the door, letting Ironwood's lady enter with all the regal air she imagined a queen might. These men would do well not to underestimate this one. They had no idea the type of woman that fortified that fancy dress.

Ruth pulled the door closed and positioned herself against the wall. She would not leave Lydia alone. This was not the time to worry with Lucy's protocol and tea trays. These men didn't need tea anyway.

"Good morning, gentlemen. I am Mrs. Charles Harper. My husband is away and I represent Ironwood in his absence. What brings you to our humble farm?"

The tall man gave a slight bow. "Good day to you, madam. I am Captain Edward Thomas, third in command to General Rosecrans, United States. We have come to request the use of your splendid home as a temporary lodging for my officers and myself."

Ruth's stomach clenched. Lydia didn't flinch. "And what do you gentlemen expect with your accommodations?"

There was something in her tone. Something dangerous. Ruth looked at the other men in the room. Two of them exchanged glances and sideways grins.

Ruth ground her teeth. She'd heard of the President's Confiscation Act. Free rein to take whatever property they wanted. There'd also been whispers of the army committing "unfathomable acts" against women. Ruth glanced at Lydia. She remained the picture of gracious calm, though Ruth knew there was more to her question.

The officer knew it too. He shot the two men a disapproving glare. "Meals, clean linens and the use of your third floor."

"The ballroom?"

He shrugged. "It affords a prime view of the encampment."

Ruth clenched her hands at her sides, willing her pulse to calm. Even while they came to the door like gentlemen, they'd already defiled Ironwood with their unwelcome advance. Lucy was wrong. There would be no safety here.

Lydia blanched. "What encampment?"

"Our troops will settle in the flatland just below the house."

Lydia's composure slipped. "But those are our fields! Soldiers will destroy all hope of our crops. We have not yet finished our harvest, and I need that to pay ... Never mind." She bit off the words through clenched teeth her pale face growing rosier with each word.

Captain Thomas stiffened. "Our presence here provides you a measure of safety. Perhaps you would prefer we chose another location and left your plantation to the mercy of battle?"

Battle.

The word crawled through Ruth's veins. Battle would bring death. And fire. Visions of her burning home rose in her mind, and she began to shake. She wrapped her arms around herself. One of the men noticed her and looked on her too long. She dropped her gaze. Strong. She would have to be strong. Lydia would need her.

Lydia rose to her full height, little that it was, and spoke as if she were a man and she were the one with the upper hand. "If I allow you to stay, and my girls and I prepare your meals and tend to your linens, then do I have your word you will leave Ironwood unharmed?"

He gave a curt nod. "To the best of my ability, you have my word that it will be so."

"So be it. I shall hold you to your word on your honor as an officer."

"Then we are agreed."

Lydia nodded. "How many do you plan to keep here?"

"I shall require my own sleeping space. My seven men can be divided among what other rooms you have."

Lydia gave Ruth a look full of meaning. "Ruth, give the Captain my room. We will put three in the blue guest room and two in the green one. Have Tommy bring in sleeping pallets and set up the other two in the drawing room."

Confusion swept over her but she did her best to conceal it. "Yes, ma'am."

"Captain, you can determine which man sleeps where."

His brow creased. "Why are my men going on pallets in the drawing room? Surely in a house this size you have more sleeping chambers."

She smiled sweetly at him. "I have offered you my personal bed, Captain. Surely you do not begrudge me holding rooms for myself and my girls to sleep in?"

He eyed her cautiously. "No. I suppose I cannot."

"And of course you understand if I wish to leave my husband's room undisturbed since he may return at any time."

The muscles in his jaw worked, but he said nothing. She smiled at him like she had no idea why he seemed perturbed, the perfect picture of the beautiful but dense woman he no doubt expected to find here. Ruth suppressed her grin.

"Now if you gentlemen will excuse me, it seems I have a great deal to tend to. Ruth will see you to your places." She inclined her head and glided from the room with more grace than Ruth had ever seen her display. The woman was a contradiction, indeed.

Lord, help us.

What did she have planned? Why was she giving up her room and what was that about rooms for her girls? They had rooms over the kitchen.

Ruth led the men up the stairs and tried to remain calm. With so much uncertainty Ruth could know only one thing for sure.

Lydia was up to something.

Thirty - Three

"*T*ommy, I want you to gather up some men and get them to the house. I need several things moved. Ironwood is now occupied." Lydia glanced around the rear yard from her place on the back porch but saw none of the men in blue. She wanted desperately to pretend it had been a dream and that Ironwood was not under occupied hostility, but she had no time for such childishness now.

Tommy's eyes grew wide in his aged face. "I's seen the soldiers. More of 'em marched in and went through the primary field. Mr. Peck done told me to report to you. I was comin' to do just that."

The cool October air swirled around them as if it were as agitated by the intruders as she. Lydia tried to control the thoughts clamoring in her head and focus on the man in front of her. "I am aware. They intend to camp here, and I shall have to house the officers."

He stared at her.

"It is the only way I can hope to leave Ironwood unharmed. They have burned many plantations. Sherman comes through like a wildfire, destroying everything in his wake. I will protect Ironwood, and this is our best hope."

He nodded solemnly. "I knows you'll do what's right by all of us. We trust you."

Warmth blossomed in her bosom. "I thank you. Knowing that means a great deal to me."

"What you need me to help you with?"

She chewed her lip, checking off the list on her fingers. "I am moving the girls into the house with me, so they will need help moving their things. See if you can find additional locks to put on the first floor bed chamber. I will also need three sleeping mats placed in the drawing room."

"Yes ma'am. I'll see that it's all done." He turned to leave, but Lydia reached out and clasped his arm.

"One other thing," she whispered.

He leaned close and she could smell the scent of horse and hay on his skin.

"The Captain will soon be taking over my bedroom. I have packed a trunk they will assume I am moving into where I'll be staying. Let them think that. But somehow, I need you to hide it for me. Somewhere safe."

His brow wrinkled and he searched the garden beyond as if it held the answers he sought. "I don't know any hidin' spots that might work for a full-sized trunk, ma'am."

"Well, we have to think of something, I need to – "

She stopped short, the memories of a strange dream descending on her with perfect clarity. The ballroom. The tiny little door. It had called to her, filled with light, as if it were something of great importance. She couldn't explain it but knew she must trust her intuition.

She leaned closer to Tommy's ear. "Upstairs, the third floor. On the left wall, about middle of the room, is a small access door. It's difficult to see. You might not ever notice it if you were not looking for it. Take the trunk there. Find somewhere behind that door to hide it."

He looked at her with uncertain eyes.

"Please, Tommy. I cannot explain to you why, but I know it is vital that I get that trunk safely away from anywhere the soldiers might see it."

"Yes ma'am. I'll figure out a way to get it passed 'em."

Relief flooded her and she inclined her head. "Thank you Tommy, I know I can always rely on you."

"Ma'am, they's somethin' else you needs to know."

Something in his voice caused a feeling of dread to settle on her like a wet shawl. How many more things could go wrong? *Oh, Charles. Why did you have to leave?* How could she do this on her own?

"What is it?"

"Three more of them foremen left. They said they might come back after Mr. Harper comes back and this place is back to... normal."

She cocked an eyebrow. "Is that so? That's what they said?"

Tommy shifted his gaze to the ground. "Well, that's not exactly what they's said."

"So what was it then?"

"They said the lady done gone mad and would run the plantation to the ground. They wouldn't stick 'round to take orders from a power-hungry female."

Heat rose in her face. Crazy indeed. All she did was for the good of the people. But they were too blind to see it. "Is that all?"

"Yes, ma'am. They's said they would come back to work when Mr. Harper came home and got a proper handle on his wife." He cringed as he said it. From fear of her reaction or from insult on her behalf? No matter. She would remain in control.

"Very well. That is their choice. I would not have any stay who resist my lead or the new ways of Ironwood. We work together by consent, not force."

Tommy's eyes glistened. "And for that ma'am, you's got the hearts of every colored left on this here land."

A small smile tugged on the corner of her lips. "As they have mine. Now, there is much to be done. I fear we have little time. Tell the people to remain strong. We must bear up under this yolk. We will survive it." She tried to fill her words with more conviction than she really felt, hoping her words would prove true. Their very lives depended on it.

"I will." He dipped his chin and descended the steps looking spry for a man of his years. Lydia turned her attention to the kitchen. Time to inform the others they would be moving.

She descended the steps and placed her foot on the walkway. The whistle walk. She smiled and strode down it. Her path would be one of her own choosing.

She found Betsy in the kitchen, but instead of being in her usual place with her hands in some sort of dough, the round woman paced back and forth, her eyes studying the contents of the shelves lining the wall.

"What are you doing, Betsy?"

The woman turned to look at her with despondent eyes. "They's come. They's come to take Ironwood from us."

"As long as I breathe they shall do no such thing."

Betsy blinked at her but said nothing.

"Gather your things. Tell Lucy to do the same. You, Lucy, and Ruth will be staying in the house with me. I want us close."

"Why?"

"The officers will stay in the house. We will tend to their needs."

"What needs?"

"Make their meals, do their laundry, change their linens. We will serve them to the best of our ability."

Betsy gazed at her with those wise eyes, making her have to resist the urge to squirm beneath their intensity. "You's gonna serve them men? It's not befittin' your place as lady."

Lydia lifted her chin. What did such things matter anymore? "I shall. What Ironwood needs out of its lady now is any protection she can afford them. The Captain has given me his word that Ironwood will be spared."

"Ah. So we do what we must."

"Yes."

"I's still don't like it. Strange men in the house."

Lydia sighed. "Neither do I. But we shall stick together. You and the girls will sleep in the room Charles' parent's intended to be a nursery. There is no upstairs door there. Tommy is having a new lock placed on the bedroom door below it. The two rooms will give enough space for the four of us and provide a manner of protection with only one door to guard."

"So you's done thought this through."

"Yes. We must hurry now. I fear the men will grow impatient. I have Ruth showing them the house, but they will not be stalled with such things for long. I need you to find Lucy. Where has that woman disappeared to? I haven't seen her all day."

Betsy pressed her lips together and looked away.

Uneasiness swelled again. "What?"

"I don't know if I should say."

"Why not?"

She ran a hand over her short-cropped hair, devoid of its usual brightly-colored scarf. "You's made so many changes 'round here. They bring us hope." She paused and studied Lydia, as if at odds with herself. "But even good change can be frightenin' to some."

She grew impatient. "And?"

"Lucy, she's pretty set in her ways. She likes to know her place and know things be done properly." Betsy shrugged. "It's just her way."

"There is little use for what is proper now. We have to do what we must to survive."

"As we's always done."

Her soft words hung on the air, the crackling fire in the hearth the only sound. Would Lydia ever truly know what life was like for them? She felt like a child pretending. Dressing and playing a part she hardly understood.

"I am sorry. Security and the promise of a new future is all I can offer. I am doing my best." Her voice cracked on the last word, and she hated herself for it. What good would her best do? But she could offer nothing more.

Betsy crossed the floor and placed her hands on Lydia's shoulders. A gentle gesture that only months ago would have seemed completely foreign but now felt only natural. "You's strong and kind. I don't think them men have any idea who they's dealin' with." A smile tugged at her lips.

"Perhaps. But what does this have to do with Lucy?"

Betsy dropped her arms and walked to the fire, staring into the dancing flames that cast scurrying shadows across the floor. "She was afraid of them men. Afraid of what them bein' here would mean."

"We are all afraid of that."

"She couldn't stay."

"What do you mean she couldn't stay?" Frustration boiled out of her. How many more would choose to abandon her? And Lucy! How could she with all her talk of safety with the Union? "I don't understand."

Compassion glistened in Betsy's eyes. "As soon as them men came to the door she came to me. Said she couldn't stay here to see what happened. She needed to go."

Lydia shook her head hard enough to loosen a pin from her heavy hair and cause a lock to slip free. "No! She told Ruth the people called me a northern sympathizer. Lucy said we would be safer with the Union troops near in town. Why, then, would she leave when they came? Of all of us, wouldn't she be glad to see them here?"

Lydia's breathing became hard, pent up anger she tried to contain seeping out as sweat from her brow. "Were her words nothing but lies?"

"I don't know, ma'am. I wish I did. All I can tell you is I's as surprised as you."

"She can't have gone far. I shall retrieve her."

"But you's said they was free to choose."

Lydia ground her teeth. "Lucy is not like the others with wild fantasies of a glorious freedom on the other side. She is more logical. Practical. She knows the dangers of going out on her own. What would possess her to do such a thing? I can convince her she needs to stay. Surely she was acting out of fear not reason."

Betsy watched her pace the floor, her long gown sweeping around her legs and pooling behind her like a silken waterfall.

"Ma'am, I don't think chasin' after her would be the best use of your time right now. We needs you. The people needs to see you under control not chasin' after Lucy. We's talked. This here ain't no real surprise. She's talked 'bout leavin' since that first group done gone."

"But she's not the type to run." Even as the words slipped from her mouth, she wondered at her own audacity. What did she know of the woman? Lucy always answered in the manner expected. She did as she was told. She lived under the strict ideas of propriety and structure. Maybe her heart longed for something different. How could she possibly begin to judge the inner heart of a woman she really never even knew?

Betsy waited as if reading her thoughts.

Lydia ran her hands over her skirts and took a long breath of the air that always seemed filled with the homey scents of food lovingly prepared. "Then so leaves another from the walk."

"Yes. It seems so."

"And you? What will you choose?"

"My path is here."

Lydia lifted her brow. "And you do not wish to leave the walk as well?"

"I's already have."

"What do you mean?"

Betsy opened her arms wide and gestured to the expanse of the kitchen. "I don't got to step off the walk to whistle a new tune. I love my home, and its people. You done brought freedom to us, and I ain't got to go after it." She winked at Lydia. "'sides, I'm too old and too fat to go a runnin' through the woods."

A ridiculous giggle bubbled up out of her. "Oh, Betsy. I am glad you will stay. The captain would not be pleased with the meals I would make him."

Betsy laughed. "No, I reckon not."

When their giggles died, seriousness settled once again on Betsy's features. "You think he'll keep his word?"

"It is the only hope I have."

"And you think he'll act with honor?" The tightness in her voice betrayed the very concern Lydia had tried to bury.

Her hands tightened at her sides. "I shall see to it that he does."

Betsy watched her for several moments and then gave a single nod. "Likes I said, they best not underestimate you. But what can a woman do?"

One man bore scars of her fury already, if he even still lived. She would do whatever she must.

"We will do their washing and mending. I will even polish their boots, if it keeps my Ironwood safe. We'll be their cooks and their maids. But anything more they try to take from us and Lord help me, I will poison their food and stab them while they sleep."

She spun on her heel and left Betsy staring after her in disbelief.

Thirty - Four

October 14, 1862

The captain eyed her with a cold stare. Five bottles of Charles' good wine from the cellar already sat empty on the dining room table. She was tired, her back sore from spending the day washing their clothing and mending their socks. She'd cleaned their messes, carried in their meals, and stood by the table to refill their glasses when they ran low. Four days they'd sat in her house doing nothing but smoking cigars and drinking too long into the night.

Four days of catering to their whims – which grew ever more frivolous. One of the men eyed her with a glimmer in his gaze that made her skin crawl. She'd give them no more fuel for their foul tempers and impure thoughts.

"As I said, Captain, I am afraid no more wine can be brought up tonight." She held her ground, forcing herself to hold his stare and keep her face impassive.

"And I say I shall drink my fill."

Lydia glanced to Ruth, who shook her head ever so slightly. She returned her gaze to Captain Thomas. "My husband says a man too many in his cups risks losing himself to dishonor, and then finding that upon sobering he has created regrets that cannot be undone." Her voice remained soft, but she knew the underlying warning shone in her eyes.

Captain Thomas toyed with the stem of his glass and looked down the table at his men. Lydia tried not to hate the man sitting so self-righteously in her husband's chair. The Captain's presence only made Charles' absence sting more.

Oh, Charles. Where are you?

Still no word from him. Her only solace was that his name had not appeared on the lists of the dead. Not yet.

The men's boisterous laughter died down as they turned to their commander. Ruth glared at her.

"Do you doubt our honor, then?" he said, still looking at his empty glass.

"I mean no disrespect, Captain. I merely wish to help you remember the men under your charge are your responsibility and that even the best men can be turned to scoundrels with too much drink."

Lydia held her breath. He pushed back from the table and stood to look down at her, making her tilt her head all the way back to see into the face towering over her. She must not falter now. If she lost ground here, she would never regain it.

"So now not only am I dishonorable, but I neglect my responsibilities as well?" His hot breath washed over her, threatening to turn her stomach.

She inclined her head and tried to remember all Mother's lessons on the guile and charm a lady could use to gain men into her favor. How she wished she'd listened closer. "Forgive me, dear Captain. I am but a simple woman who does not always know the proper way to command words. Such is for men to do." She smiled sweetly at him and some of the redness from his face drained. He narrowed his eyes but returned to his seat, his gaze not falling from her.

"I wish only to implore your good kindness to not let drink rob you of the ability to remain the protectors we women need." She forced the words past the constriction in her throat.

He let out a low sound in his throat and looked over his men. One grabbed Ruth's hand and was attempting to coax her into his lap. Something lit in the Captain's eyes. He slammed his hand down on the table.

"Lieutenant!"

The man dropped Ruth's hand, and she scurried out of his reach, standing with her back pressed against the wall, her chest rising and falling a little too quickly. The candelabra in the center of the table boasted only the nearly-spent candles of a meal lasting long past practicality. The Captain glared over it to the younger man three chairs removed from him.

"You will do well to remember you are on duty and this is not a brothel. Conduct yourself accordingly."

"Yes, sir." The man lowered his eyes to his plate.

Captain Thomas turned his focus back to Lydia, his eyes less glazed than they had been only moments ago. She prayed that clarity would work in her favor.

"Mrs. Harper, sometimes a lady can see what we men often overlook. You have been a most gracious hostess."

She let the breath escape her lungs in a rush and forced the best smile she could muster. "I thank you. Now, if you like, I had my cook prepare a cobbler for you for dessert." Hopefully the thought of a treat would turn his mind from the wine.

He smiled. "Splendid. Yes, bring it in to us."

She glanced to Ruth and motioned for her to follow her out of the room. As soon as the door closed behind them, voices and laughter filled the room. Ruth crossed her arms over her chest.

"I don't like that one bit. You's almost made that man get ugly. What would we have done then?" Ruth hissed through clenched teeth.

A year ago Lydia might have felt ire, or at least disbelief, rise upon hearing a colored woman speak to her that way. But that was a lifetime ago. Now she served as a maid in her own house, working side by side with Betsy and Ruth. The color of her skin made no difference. Strange how she always thought being equal would make them like her. She'd never considered giving up her place to be like them.

She grabbed Ruth's arm and led her out of the house. "I couldn't let them keep drinking. That would only make them bolder and more dangerous."

"Maybe you shoulda just told him there ain't no more wine."

"And if he discovers I lied? What do you think would happen then?" Lydia shook her head. "No. Then he would start looking for other things we might be hiding. I can't have that."

"It's like standin' in a mound of dry grass holdin' a burnin' match over you's head. Sooner or later somethin's gonna fall and light everythin' on fire," Ruth said.

They descended the steps into the clear night, a chorus of frogs singing their tune, oblivious to the wars waged by men. Lydia rubbed the sleeves on her arms, wishing she'd thought to grab a cloak.

"We will just have to step carefully and try to keep peace for as long as we can. It is our only option."

They hurried into the kitchen and retrieved a large pan of cobbler from Betsy.

"Them's the last of my peaches," Betsy said.

Lydia looked at the tray in her hands. "How are we on supplies?"

Betsy wagged her head. "We's a lot lower than we ever been, and it's only October. I don't know how we gonna make it through the winter."

Ruth huffed. "Especially not with them men eatin' like they do."

"She's right. Betsy, start stretching our food as much as you can. I won't see our people starve while they feast."

Lydia turned on her heel and strode from the warmth of the kitchen out into the chill of the night, warm cobbler she wouldn't get to eat balanced on one arm and her feet once again traveling the whistle walk. Ruth opened the door for her, and she placed the tray in the middle of the table of boisterous men.

Lydia's skin crawled with the sounds of their raucous laughter. Grinding her teeth together to keep honest words from reaching insulted ears, she cut each man a portion of the dessert and handed it to Ruth to pass out among them.

"We need some entertainment don't we, fellows?" One of the men, whose name Lydia didn't care to remember, said as he raised his arm in the air and gathered the others' attention.

"Here! Here!" cried the youngest-looking of the bunch. He couldn't be much older than Lydia, if that. He might have been considered handsome if not for the dark circles under his gleaming eyes.

Lydia shot a glance at Ruth. Her jaw worked, but she kept at her task placing the last piece of cobbler in front of a dark-haired man who kept his gaze on the table.

The captain pushed back from the table and rose to his feet. "Yes! Some entertainment."

The men cheered. Lydia removed the pan from the table and set it on the sideboard, her eyes communicating to Ruth to slip out the door. Ruth skirted around the room and came to her side. Lydia's fingers brushed the doorknob.

"Mrs. Harper!"

She turned slowly and kept her face impassive. "Yes, Captain Thomas?"

"My men call for entertainment."

She inclined her head. "As I have heard, sir. But such things were not part of our agreement."

His face darkened.

Lydia held his gaze. She could not show weakness. But neither must she show defiance. A delicate balance, that if tipped, could prove disastrous for all of them.

"She could leave the pretty maid. I'm sure she wouldn't mind keeping us company," one of the men called out. The others laughed.

Lydia's fists clenched at her sides, but she kept her focus on the captain. How much these men tried would depend on him. She batted her eyes. "Ruth does not know how to play the pianoforte and neither does she have a good singing voice. I am afraid she would do little good as entertainment."

The men burst into more laughter, the darkness in it raising the hairs on the back of her neck.

The captain put up a hand and the men quieted. "Perhaps you could play for us, then?"

"Forgive me, but I am tired. Perhaps another night."

She turned and grasped the door again, pulling it free.

"Wait."

She lifted her chin and focused on her breathing. Ruth crossed her arms over her chest. Lydia prayed she wouldn't open her mouth. "Yes?"

"I will have my men and myself well-cared for. Remember what's at stake." The low threat in his voice turned her fear into seething anger.

Ruth's cold fingers clamped down on her arm, and Lydia realized she'd taken a step closer to the leering Captain. Composure. She *must* remain calm.

She kept her words even. "And well-cared for they are. Served by my own hand in every area we agreed upon. As I said, I shall hold you to your word."

He narrowed his eyes at her. Silence hung on the room. Before he could say anything more, Lydia dropped into a curtsey. "Good evening, gentlemen. I trust you can see yourselves to your beds."

They ducked out of the room and across the hall to the bedroom Charles' parents had built for themselves on the lower floor so as not to tax the elder Mr. Harper's failing knees with too many trips up the stairs. Lydia slid the two bolts on the door closed with trembling fingers.

"Let's pray that keeps 'em out," Ruth said. She hugged her arms around herself. "They's gettin' restless. I don't know how much longer until one of 'em forgets to act like a gentleman."

Lydia wanted to deny it if only to calm Ruth's fears, but she knew too much truth hung on the words.

Oh, Charles. We need you.

Lydia listened at the door, waiting to see if any of the men followed. Heavy footsteps in the hall. Near the door.

Both women sucked in a breath and tensed. The footfalls came closer. Lydia glanced at Ruth. Would he knock?

Silence.

The footsteps retreated.

"I'm going to get Betsy," Lydia whispered.

"What? No. She'll be along soon. She always stays late in the kitchen."

"This isn't the time for her to worry about having everything clean for the morning. I fear what may happen tonight. I want her in here with us."

Ruth pressed her lips together. Finally, she nodded. "I'll go."

"No. They will hesitate to do anything to the married white woman whose house they occupy." She stared into Ruth's eyes. "But they won't with you."

She bristled.

Lydia gave her arm a reassuring squeeze and slipped the bolts free. The hallway stood empty. "Keep everything locked. I'll be right back," she whispered.

"Hurry."

Lydia slipped out into the hall on silent slippers, feeling like a criminal in her own house. The shadows in every corner took on an ominous feel. Where there had been only peace and warmth, there now lurked danger and fear. She would forever blame them for destroying the sanctity of her home.

Lydia slipped out onto the back porch unseen and into the darkness, turning to pull the door softly closed behind her. She turned to find a dark figure on the porch.

She barely contained the scream that tried to rip from her throat.

The figure stepped closer. "Mrs. Harper?"

Betsy.

Lydia gulped in air and grabbed the woman's arm. "You nearly scared me to death creeping up on me like that."

"I ain't creepin'."

"Never mind. Let's go."

Lydia led Betsy through the dark house. Voices came from the dining room. She couldn't be sure how many of them were still in there, but she didn't want to come across any of the soldiers in the dark. With any luck, the rest would be upstairs.

She tapped softly on the door.

"Who's that?"

"It's me, Ruth. Let us in," Lydia whispered to the wood.

Metal scraped on metal as she disengaged the locks and pulled the door open. Lydia slipped inside with Betsy on her heels. Ruth secured the door and turned to face them.

"What's goin' on?" Betsy swung her gaze between Lydia and Ruth, wrinkles gathering in the center of her brow.

"Them men's done drank too much of Mr. Harper's good wine and done forgot they sense." Ruth stood rigid, her fists clenched at her sides.

She'd been right. They were living in a bundle of tinder waiting for a spark. "Let's get some rest. You girls head up to bed," Lydia said.

They exchanged glances but didn't say another word. Ruth lit a single candle sitting on the bedside table and opened the narrow door in the rear corner that led to the small upstairs room that had been built to be a nursery. Lydia tried not to let the thought it would never hear infant cries undo her.

They looked at her with worried eyes. Lydia forced a calm smile onto her lips. "Good night, girls."

The women ascended the narrow staircase, the last of the tiny light following them until only the faint glow of her single lantern remained. Ruth had left the door open. She briefly considered closing it, then decided against it.

She removed her gown, hoops and petticoat, leaving on everything else. If she needed to dress in a hurry, she'd be ready.

Lydia sat on the bed and pulled her hair free of its pins, letting it fall free in waves down her back. She shivered. The fire in the hearth already glowed low. It wouldn't keep the chill out much longer.

She pulled open the small drawer in the bedside table, removing an object she'd discovered upstairs in Charles' study only that morning before hiding it away here. The pistol felt heavy in her hands, its cold steel hard. She turned it over and studied the mechanisms.

A small vile of powder remained in the drawer along with five caps she'd found with the gun. She pointed the long barrel at the door.

All she would have to do was pull the hammer back with her thumb. Then the trigger. One shot. It would have to be enough.

She lowered the weapon, glad for the comfort it brought. She would defend them. Lydia slipped the cold steel under her pillow and pulled her knees to her chest.

Sleep finally came in snatches, carrying with it dreams of creeping shadows and haunting laughter.

Thirty - Five

October 15, 1862

Thunder rumbled, rolling through the house and pulling Lydia from her dreams. She tossed in the bed and pulled the covers tighter around her to ward off the chill. Another boom.

Lydia shot up in bed. Not thunder.

She leapt from the mattress, the covers binding her feet and nearly causing her to fall on the floor. She yanked her foot free and threw on her gown, not bothering to put on her hoop or petticoats underneath it. She fumbled with the buttons behind her back, only getting half of them fastened.

Another crash. The walls rattled. Forget the cursed buttons.

She grabbed her slippers, pulling one on as she hopped across the floor. No time to fight with the buttons on her boots. "Ruth!"

Betsy stumbled through the staircase door and into the room. "What's happenin'?" she screeched.

Gunshots. Too close to the house.

"They're fighting!"

Ruth crashed into the room, her hair sticking up in all directions. Lydia flung open the curtains, but the slight tinge of pink in the pre-dawn sky did not illuminate the grounds enough to give her any clue what happened in the yard.

She pushed past the two women, not registering anything they said and fumbled with the bolts on the door. Finally they came free and she threw open the door. Cannon fire. The sound rattled the walls and reverberated in her ears.

She flung open the front door. The shouts of men and screams of pain flooded over her. Where were they? A whistling sound proceeded a shadow that hurled across the yard, collided with the magnolia tree, and severed its trunk.

Lydia gasped. Hands grabbed her shoulders and flung her backward. "Get out of my way!"

Captain Thomas pushed past her and out on the front steps, shouting curses to the sky. Lydia slammed the front door and secured the lock. Then she ran down the hall to the rear of the house before she could stop to consider the consequences of her actions.

The back door stood wide open. How many of them had run out? Cracks of bright light exploded in the space beyond the door. She should close it, barricade herself inside. But she could not control her urge to see what evil frolicked in her garden.

The sight that greeted her on the rear porch filled her chest with raw fear. Men lay bleeding and crying out with their arms outstretched. Shouts carried on the wind like wounded birds, their calls meaningless. Gray and Blue swarmed together like angry hornets across the trampled mess that had been her roses.

Gunshots cracked through the air, splintering the morning and bathing it in flashes of unnatural death. Lydia put a hand to her mouth, unable to tear her eyes from the horror unfolding before her. Surreal, as if a troop of actors decided to surprise her with a private show. A man screamed, blood erupting from a hole that exploded in the front of his gray jacket. His mouth gaped open and he fell to his knees, then face first into the dirt. Others stepped over him as if he were nothing more than a fallen log.

Lydia's blood ran cold. One step. Then two, three. Before she could stop herself, she'd left the cover of the porch and stepped into the nightmare. Screams from all directions. Some in agony, others in rage. Somewhere behind her, someone called her name. It floated to her ears like a storm-blown butterfly, muffled and shattered by the chaos around her.

Something grabbed at her skirt. A man lay on the ground, his bloody hands smearing red streaks down the ruffles of her dress. He looked up at her with desperate eyes clouded with pain.

"Margret! Oh, my Margret!"

She shook her head, words lodged in her throat. He pulled at her, and she dropped to her knees beside him.

"Hush now. You need a doctor." Lydia scanned the area around her. Men ran for cover. Some were hiding behind the barn, muzzles of rifles poking around the corner and spitting fire. Somewhere in the back of her mind she knew she had to move. She could not stay out in the open. The man grabbed her hand.

"Oh, Margret." He propped himself up on one elbow. "I thought I'd never see you again. I needed to see you again…" His words dissolved into coughing, and he pulled at her, his frantic eyes lost to the vision only he saw.

"Doctor!" Lydia screamed. "We need a doctor!"

No one stopped. No one turned to her cries. The metallic smell of blood burned in her nostrils and only then did she notice it seeped from the corner of the young man's mouth. Her heart clenched. This boy couldn't be more than sixteen years. His ashy blonde hair hung across a smooth forehead that had yet to bear the wrinkles one earned from years of worry. She reached down and brushed it away from his face, ignoring the blood that smeared with it.

"I'm so sorry Margret. Please tell me you forgive me." His eyes pleaded with her.

Lydia placed her hand on his cheek. "Hush now. Of course I do. I forgive you. Don't you worry now."

Relief flooded his face and he dropped down flat on his back. Lydia knelt there beside him while the chaos raged around them.

"Thank you, Margret. You were always… my girl." He turned his head aside and coughed up blood. Tears filled Lydia's eyes. "Always…my girl. I'm sorry I won't be able to get you that little farmhouse like I promised." He choked on the last word as blood bubbled up and gargled his words.

Tears slipped down Lydia's cheeks. She placed her hand on his chest and felt his labored breathing.

"Miss Lydia!"

She could hear Ruth's screams, but she couldn't tear her eyes away from this boy. His gaze was locked on her. "I love you, Margret." He heaved with a wretched cough. The tears clouded her eyes until she could no longer see the blurred face in front of her. His body shuddered beneath her hand and then lay still.

Hands grasped her shoulders and pulled her to her feet. "Get up! You's got to get up!"

A cannon blast shook the ground and sent her ears ringing. Ruth yelled next to her, but she sounded more like she was under water somewhere off in the distance. "Let's go."

She spun Lydia around to face her, the whites of her eyes impossibly large in her caramel-colored face. Black smudges of soot darkened her cheeks and forehead. Why on earth had she smeared herself with soot?

Ruth shook her. "Lydia! Gets a hold of yourself!"

Lydia blinked rapidly and stared at Ruth. "What are you doing?"

"We's got to get into the house! Bar the doors!"

"Why?"

Ruth shook her again. "Look around you! Death's done come for Ironwood."

Clarity hit her like a slap to the face. Battle. Here, on her land. She looked back at the scene around her. Bullets flew through the air, whistling their song of death. Cannon blasts from somewhere out in the fields tore their land asunder.

She looked to the barn. Several men positioned themselves behind it, shooting across the garden to those gathering by the kitchen. She didn't take time to consider which men belonged to which side. It did not matter.

She surveyed the scene with clear eyes. There. Dark faces huddled by the potato shed. More, looking through the window of the kitchen. She sprinted to the top step of the porch, hiking her skirts near to her knees to avoid the cumbersome fabric.

"People of Ironwood!" She screamed at the top of her lungs. Would they hear her above the roar of rage around them? She waved her arms over her head.

Ruth tugged on her arm. "We's got to get you inside!"

Smoke thickened the air, the sun finally making its slow appearance above the trees and casting hazy light onto the ruins of her garden. The people did not move from their spots. They did not hear her.

"Lydia!" Ruth pulled on her again and she snatched her arm free.

"No!"

Lydia darted down the steps her, skirts in her hand. She ducked her head low and ran for the kitchen knowing it would be a miracle to reach it without a bullet lodged in her flesh. How she'd made it in the open so far she did not know. The hand of the Almighty must have been shielding her. She'd have to remember to thank Him.

Her feet slipped on loose rocks, and she nearly tripped over a bloodied arm detached from its owner. Her stomach convulsed, but she did not allow it the luxury of emptying its contents. She flung open the kitchen door to find several people huddled on the floor.

"Come with me. We must get to the house."

A woman with a wailing infant in her arms sobbed. "We's won't make it!"

"Get up! All of you!" she screamed at them, grabbing the nearest child by his arm and hauling him to his feet. "We have to get to the house!"

The woman with the baby stumbled to her feet. She looked weak, the infant in her arms too small. She was too soon after child birth to be huddling here. A bullet busted through the wall and lodged in the center of Betsy's chopping table. The people screamed and scrambled to their feet.

Lydia pointed to the house. "Run! Keep your head down and run to the house. Ruth will take you inside!" They scrambled past her with their heads down. They plunged into a sea of madness, scurrying for their only hope of survival past the rain of bullets. Lydia watched several of them make it to the porch, and Ruth usher them inside. Only the woman with the baby remained.

She clutched the wailing child to her chest. "I ain't gonna make it!"

"Yes you are!"

Lydia pulled the child from her and tucked it under her arm, careful to cradle his head in the crook of her shoulder. She wrapped her other arm around the woman, ducked her head, and half ran, half dragged the struggling mother with her to the porch. Only when they reached the safety of the steps did she realize the buzzing of bullets had ceased.

Lydia pressed the child back into his mother's arms and gently nudged her into the house. Ruth looked at her with wild eyes.

"Get all the people into the upstairs hallway. Sit them down and keep them away from any windows. They should be safe up there. Keep the doors locked and have some of the men barricade the front door. I'm going for the others."

Ruth pointed across the yard. Men in uniform scrambled to reload, a mighty gust of wind sending their powder flying free of their weapons before they could get them properly loaded. Lydia locked eyes with Tommy and gestured him to hurry across the yard. A line of people dashed out from the barn, leaping over fallen soldiers and dead shrubbery, diving into the house on frightened legs and with heaving lungs.

Lydia pushed them all inside and bolted the door behind her. "Get them upstairs."

"All y'all come with me!" Ruth rounded the fifteen or so frightened people and herded them up the staircase.

Lydia turned to Tommy. "We need to get these doors barricaded."

He gave a grunt, and they each fetched a chair from the dining room. Lydia wedged one under the front door latch and motioned for Tommy to do the same at the rear door. There. That should keep them out for –

A loud crash and the sickening sound of shattering glass dashed her hopes. Lydia ran for the parlor. Shards of glass littered her green dogwood rug and glistened in the morning light like tiny diamonds. Did nature not know this was a day of death? The cheery sunlight and mild warmth were out of place with the screams from the pit of Hades.

A boot crashed through the busted window, crunching the diamonds under its black soles. Above the boot, blue pants, and then a bloodied Union jacket. Her eyes drifted up farther, panic rising in her chest and stifling her intake of air.

Blood dripped down Captain Thomas' forehead from a nasty gash at his hairline. It snaked its way down and to the side of his nose. He wiped his sleeve across his lips, painting his mouth a gruesome red.

"Thought to lock me out, did you?" He snarled.

She took a step backward. "We are only trying to stay safe, we –

"Enough!" He bellowed. She fell silent. One small step backward. Another.

"I've had enough of your trickery. Tell me, did you send word for the Rebels to come here?"

"What?" He thought she sent for them? How could she have done that? And why would she have brought this bloodshed to Ironwood? "I did not! I have been here with you the entire time."

He sneered at her. "You could have sent one of your slaves to send a message. Is that it?"

She took another step backward, feeling behind her for the wall. If she could get out the door, she might have a chance to make it into the bedroom and lock the door. "I swear! I had nothing to do with it. I wanted to keep battle *away* from Ironwood. Not bring it here."

He crossed the room in three strides and reached her before she could turn and flee. He grabbed her shoulders and pushed her up against the wall, pinning her with enough force to make her cry out.

"I don't believe you. You're a cocky one. Got a little too much mouth on you."

She turned her face away from him. "Let me be. I wish only to protect my home."

His chuckle held no mirth. "And now you have brought its downfall. You thought you could bring those Rebels before dawn and slaughter my men while they slept."

"I swear. I did not. I had nothing to do with it."

He grabbed her chin and forced her to look at him. "I will burn this place to the ground."

Her eyes rounded.

His gazed dropped to her mouth. She clamped it shut, her rapid breath coming hard through her nostrils.

"Maybe I should get a taste of you before I leave you to burn."

She struggled against him, but he held her firm. A scream tore from the depth of her soul and slammed into his face.

"I think I would let the lady go, if I were you." A voice, heavy with accent, said. Then she heard the soft click of a gun.

Captain Thomas released her and spun around to face the long barrel of a revolver leveled at him. The man wore the same blue uniform, but he carried himself as one who was used to people obeying his commands. He trained his weapon on the captain's face.

Another man came in behind him, his gaze darting back and forth between the two other men. Lydia held still against the wall, her hands trembling.

The man with the gun spoke to the soldier behind him, his eyes never leaving Captain Thomas. "Arrest this man and have him bound."

The soldier hurried to do the older man's bidding, and Captain Thomas surrendered without a word. Only after they dragged him back out the shattered window did her savior lower his weapon. His eyes studied her.

"Am I correct that this is the home known as Ironwood?"

She nodded, unable to get words to form in her mouth. He gave a curt dip of his chin and turned on his heel. He stuck his head through the window frame.

"Sound the retreat! I want all of our forces removed from this land!"

Lydia's breath caught. The man turned back to her, no doubt wondering at the tattered state of her appearance.

"Are you Mrs. Charles Harper?"

"Yes." She blinked rapidly. Who was this man? "How did you know?"

The man smiled and bent at the waist into a bow. "Major General Franz Kerchner, madam."

"You... called them off of Ironwood."

He studied her, something in his expression melting confusion into compassion. "And they shall not return. You have my word that Captain Thomas will be dealt with and your home will receive no further occupation from Union soldiers. We will leave this place in peace."

Her heart hammered in her chest, and her knees could no longer hold her weight. They buckled beneath her. He grabbed her elbow and steadied her, leading her to the couch and lowering her to sit.

"I do not know how to thank you." She gazed at him, not daring to question why he would do such a thing lest he change his mind.

"Is your husband about?" he asked gently.

She shook her head.

"When next you see him, tell him my debt is repaid."

"Repaid?"

The man nodded, his sharp eyes alight. "I found myself in a precarious position at an Inn a couple of months past. Your husband and his companion took it upon themselves to see my life was not forfeited that day. Were it not for their wit and bravery, I might have found myself under the war-fevered hands of inebriated southern youths."

"Oh?"

"Indeed. I am pleased to meet the wife of the most honorable man I've ever met. Give him my regards." He bowed again and strode back out the window, barking orders before his foot hit the porch.

Lydia bowed her head and let tears run free down her cheeks.

Thirty - Six

October 16, 1862

Lydia wiped the blood from her hands onto her last clean rag. Soon it would join the pile destined for the cleansing flames. The wounded men covered nearly every inch of the main entrance, spilling out from the door and onto the front porch. Scents she could not even identify burned in her throat and reminded her that death dealt with men equally, with no regard for the banner under which they fought. Blue and gray faded beneath crimson. She knelt beside a man near the age of her father and bathed his head with a damp cloth. He scarcely stirred beneath her touch.

A voice from the lawn drew her attention.

"Ma'am? The lieutenant sent me to talk to you."

Lydia turned to find a haggard soldier, his hat in his hands.

"Yes, what is it?" She rose to her feet and ignored the pulsing pain that drummed in the back of her skull.

"We are in need of more wagons."

"There are two more buckboards in the lower cotton barn, but I fear that's all I have left."

The soldier nodded solemnly but did not move. Lydia sighed, fatigue drawing her muscles tight. "Is there a problem?"

"Well, we already found those. The lieutenant said that you wouldn't mind us using them, since you'd already allowed us the others. 'Sides he figured the Yanks had already taken some, so we'd better grab those two before they took off with them too."

Lydia smothered her annoyance. "What, then, would you have me do?"

The soldier shrugged, his frayed gray uniform hanging from gaunt shoulders. "Don't know, ma'am. We've loaded all the dead. All's left now is to get these wounded up. Reckon they'll have to walk or stay here."

She could not sit here much longer among the death and wonder if somewhere out there Charles languished in another home distraught by another battle. Did compassionate hands care for him? Was there another lady who tended him as she tended these? She studied the soldier in front of her. What would she ask of the lady that nursed her Charles?

She would ask for him to be sent home.

She nodded with resolve. His life would mean more than his horses. "Take my carriages. These men have more need of them than I."

The soldier dipped his chin. "The Confederate Army thanks you."

The two carriages were brought around to the front of the house. The smaller, the one she often used for town, stood attached to a pair of geldings Charles would have never paired. The larger one, the one in which she first traveled to Ironwood, stood with its matched bays as if waiting to carry her and Charles on a pleasant autumn outing. The constriction in her throat tightened, and she found herself in front of the bays, stroking their soft muzzles in an attempt to calm the agitation they suffered.

"Easy, now. Easy. You have a noble task ahead of you, dear ones. See that they make it home. See that they find their way to their families again," she whispered.

The horses bobbed their heads and settled, a breeze of determination lifting their manes and sending the thick tresses dancing. They would do well with their charge. The bloodlines of Ironwood were strong. These equine soldiers would do their duty well.

She patted them and turned to watch as men limped up inside the carriages, stifling moans and clutching to still-raw wounds. Would they make it to safety? Where would they go from here? They were questions she could not answer. This was all she could give them.

She smiled at them, offering a word of encouragement where she could, and waved to them as they pulled away. With a heavy heart she returned to the porch, stepping carefully over spots of blood. Ruth emerged from the front door.

"Tommy's been down to the quarters. Most of 'em are still together. Roughed up a bit, but nothin' that can't be fixed." She stood with her shoulders erect, the picture of calm authority.

"I have a new job for you, Ruth."

She raised an eyebrow.

"There is still much I do not know. Things I do not understand about your people. I've tasted only the smallest portion of your life. If I wish to lead Ironwood on a new path, I must not allow myself to slip back into the old ways."

Ruth's brows drew together, and Lydia held up a hand to stop her words. "I will need you to speak for the people. You understand me, and you understand them. I will need your help."

She put a hand on Lydia's shoulder. "I's here."

It was all she needed to say. Lydia inclined her head and walked into the house. Men in uniform wandered around as if they had nowhere else to be. Come sundown, they would return to the lower fields and to their encampment. An encampment Major General Kerchner had assured her would break in the morning.

How long would it take her to feel safe again? She shook her head as if the motion would dislodge her fears. She must be strong. She must pray and look for the beauty that would surely rise from the ashes smothering them.

As dusk fell, silence settled onto Ironwood – the only sounds the whispering winds that snuck through busted windows and crept along the halls leaving subtle secrets in their wake. Ironwood drew in a shuttering breath and let the wounds of the souls inside find the troubled rest of a quiet night.

Thirty - Seven

October 17, 1862

Ruth stood on the balcony and watched streams of blue uniforms flow from Ironwood like the remnants of a flood. They drifted around the house, through the yard, and down the road farther than she could see. There had to be hundreds of them. Maybe even a thousand. Too many to count. Not that she wanted to.

Sunlight filtered through the remaining leaves on the oaks, casting patchwork shadows on the silent men who passed beneath them. Ruth's gaze traveled over the ranks and came to rest on a man sitting tall on a black horse; his hat removed and tucked under one arm. His shoulders were set like a man determined to see his orders fulfilled to the letter. She studied him, wondering why he'd come to their rescue and at the same time too grateful for it to really care what his reasons might be.

He turned his face up as if he could feel her stare upon him. Their eyes locked. He tilted his head as if to offer her a bow from the saddle. She dipped her chin. The Major General placed his hat snuggly on his head and eased the horse into a slow walk, falling in beside the men.

A small breeze ruffled the trees, freeing tawny leaves from their final cling. Ruth stood and watched until the last intruder disappeared from her sight. Other than trampled grounds and the lingering smells of smoke, the Major General had ordered all trace of their presence removed. Bodies from both sides had been carted away. The outnumbered Confederates reveled in the victory gifted to them.

As the sun climbed lazily higher and settled into its peak, Ruth drew peaceful air into her lungs and steadied herself for the day ahead. She slipped back into the house, mentally going over all the tasks she would need to accomplish to get the house back in order. The colored people could return to their homes, many of which had been spared by the grace of the Almighty, and she would see to it that they were rationed supplies from the storehouses to replace what had been stolen from them. Somehow, she'd become the one they looked to for answers. Lydia seemed pleased to turn over the care of the people to her, placing her as the speaker for their needs. It would be a big responsibility but a challenge she looked forward to fulfilling.

If only her family could see her now. Ruth, once a field slave, now the freed manager of nearly one hundred liberated workers. The woman who would stand as representative between black and white. Her blood had set her with one foot in each race, and now it would help her bridge the gap between the two.

She walked down the main staircase, purpose filling her veins. It would be a road filled with trials and errors, bumps and frustrations, but one worth walking. A soft voice trickled down the hall from the parlor and Ruth followed it to find Lydia softly singing as she swept broken glass from the floor.

Trials are dark on every hand, and we cannot understand
All the ways God would lead us to that blessed promised land;
But He guides us with His eye, and we'll follow till we die,
For we'll understand it better by and by.

Ruth rested her hand on the door frame and smiled. Yes, there would be much work to be done. And much they would struggle to understand. But they would do it together. Ruth stooped down to position the pan for Lydia to push the shards into, her voice joining in the song.

By and by, when morning comes,
When the saints of God are gathered home,
We'll tell the story how we've overcome,
For we'll understand it better by and by.

Lydia smiled at her and they swept the rug clean. When the last shard was whisked away, Lydia looked out over the muddied yard.

"Do you think Ironwood will survive?"

Ruth stood beside her and draped an arm around her slender shoulders. Shoulders that seemed too small to hold up the weight they had to bear. But Ruth knew that, in their own way, these shoulders were stronger than those of any man born to spend his days in the fields.

"Ironwood will survive anythin' that comes her way. Ironwood breathes with the life of the people in it. People who done been made strong by the lady that leads 'em and loves 'em even when the rest of the world wants to condemn her for it." Ruth squeezed her tight. "Don't you fret. I think we's goin' be just fine. I pity any poor man what thinks he can pry this place from you."

Lydia laughed, a genuine sound that came from deep within her. "As do I." She straightened her skirts and brushed her hair back from her face. "Well, let's get to it. There's plenty of work that needs to be done to erase the stain from our home."

Ruth nodded and followed her through the house as they discussed what orders would need to be given out and who would best be equipped to handle each task. Side-by-side they worked, scrubbing, cleaning, and mending, until the day passed with the rhythm of their labor.

Thirty - Eight

October 27, 1862

Ruth surveyed the scene around her, satisfied with the amount of work that had been accomplished in such a short time. Young men and boys with rakes and hoes worked to return the gardens to their proper order, and Lydia walked among them thanking each one with a smile. When Betsy called for luncheon, Lydia ordered it served picnic style on the back porch Ruth had just finished scrubbing clean.

"Come eat, everyone!" Lydia called, taking one of the platters from Betsy and setting it on a small table.

Soon the people were all gathered on and around the porch, plates of fried chicken and cornbread in their hands and sweet tea in their glasses. Unexpected tears gathered in the back of Ruth's throat.

"What's wrong?" Lydia settled into a cushioned chair and motioned for Ruth to sit with her. "Aren't you hungry?"

Ruth sat and listened to the tinkling laughter of two children chasing one another in front of the steps. She glanced over at

Lydia and saw a smiled tugging at her lips. They were slow in coming, but the sad smiles more often graced her features than they had a few days ago.

"Do you think we'll ever have little ones running through the yard like that?" Lydia asked.

Ruth lifted an eyebrow. "Together?"

"Of course." She said it as if anything else would be completely ridiculous. It was a thought that should have made Ruth smile, but instead she felt only sadness settle on her heart.

"I don't know," Ruth said, her voice straining past the constriction in her throat. She took a single chicken leg from the tray and returned to her seat to nibble on it. She'd thought Lydia had let the conversation drop when she spoke again.

"I see things in my dreams." Lydia said with a strange far-away look in her eyes.

When would she cease to be surprised at the things that came out of this woman's mouth? "What kinda things?"

Lydia pulled her bottom lip between her teeth. "People, mostly. They are strange dreams. I see a woman that looks like me, but she's dressed like she is a man. I've seen Charles and I together, and a little boy with dark hair who dances while I play the pianoforte."

Not sure what she should say, Ruth watched her. Too much stress had surely messed with the poor woman's mind.

"And then I see that little boy playing with another little boy. His skin's dark, much darker than yours, but he has your eyes."

Tears pooled and Ruth blinked them away. "Them's just dreams. They don't mean nothin'."

Lydia tilted her head, the fire Ruth thought might never return lighting her eyes. "I think they do. I prayed that God would give me peace and show me a future for Ironwood. I asked Him to give me a legacy of family and love in this place.

A heritage of hope. I think those dreams are just that. A sign and also an answer to those prayers."

Ruth stared at her.

"That's why I'll leave my trunk there. For her." Lydia mumbled.

Ruth shook her head. She hoped Lydia got the future she dreamed of. She prayed Mr. Harper would return, and Lydia would someday meet the little boy she so longed for. But there would be no boy for her. Her tattered heart had loved and lost too much to be able to stumble down that path again. No, her future would be guiding the people of Ironwood. They would be her family and –

Her thoughts jerked to a halt.

No. It couldn't be.

Ruth rose from her chair, her hand flying to her heart. Did her mind play tricks on her? Had too much stress also caused her mind to break?

"Oh my!" Lydia jumped to her feet, her plate tumbling from her lap and clattering on the floor. The people stopped chattering and all their eyes turned to the man standing at the far end of the garden.

His presence seemed to fill the entire space, his large frame as big as the tree he stood underneath. Ruth's heart pounded in her chest. His eyes locked on hers, and her knees felt weak. She took a few steps forward and braced herself on the large white column at the top of the stairs, unable to do more.

Noah.

He strode across the yard, his eyes never leaving hers. Her heart hammered in her chest. Why had he returned? If he asked her to go again could she resist?

Three more paces. Two.

He stopped in front of her and for the first time she looked down on him. He held out his hand. She hesitated only for a moment, and then stepped down two stairs to place her hand inside of his.

"Why'd you come back?"

Pain flickered in his eyes. Not the words she'd wanted to say. How many times had she imagined what she would say if she ever saw him again?

"Marry me."

Air refused to fill her lungs. "What?"

"Marry me. Be my wife. I's fulfilled my promise and took the people north and to safety. I tried to start a new life, but, I can't live without you. Ruth, I knows I can't give you much. But I promise to love you, protect you, and honor you every day of my life."

Tears streamed down her face. He'd returned. For her. She felt as if the heart pounding in her chest would burst free at any moment. He stared at her. Oh! He needed an answer.

She threw herself into his arms. He stumbled back a half step and then twirled her in a circle. "That a yes?"

"Yes!" She buried her face in his neck and clung to him like she would never let him go again. Finally, he set her on her feet.

Only when her shoes hit the ground did she hear the cheers around her. She blinked and looked around at all the people gathered. Their faces were alight with joy. Her gaze landed on Lydia. Her hands were clasped in front of her face, but they could not hide the huge smile that erupted from either side of her fingers.

She pulled away from Noah and looked into his face. "Where's we gonna live?"

He shrugged his big shoulders. "Anywhere you want."

She glanced again at Lydia and then back at Noah. "I can't leave Ironwood."

Noah frowned. "I figured you's gonna say that. I'll stay even if it means we's never gonna be free. All that matters is that I's with you."

"And who says you will not be free?" Lydia said, coming to stand at the top of the stairs. "There is much you missed while you were away, Noah. The people who call Ironwood home do it by choice."

Noah's eyes darted to the faces of the people eating on the porch with the plantation's lady as if seeing them for the first time. Confusion puckered his brow. Several of them nodded.

"Miss Lydia done asked me to speak for the people. To help her as we work together to create a new Ironwood. One where's the people earn they wages."

His gaze darted back to Lydia. "Truly, ma'am? You's done this?"

"I have."

He gave out a sudden whoop, swinging Ruth into his arms again. "Then I'll build us a home right here!"

Lydia's eyes twinkled. "As long as you don't mind me coming to visit."

He grinned. "You's welcome any time."

He looked down at Ruth nestled in his arms and slowly lowered his lips to hers. Heat erupted in her chest, and she clung to him deepening the kiss and ignoring the cheers in the background. He was hers.

He finally broke away, a glimmer in his eyes. "I'm thinkin' we's gonna need a weddin' right soon."

Lydia clapped her hands like a child. "Yes! Oh, and it will be beautiful. We can do it right here in the garden. Boys! We will need to get these furrows out of the dirt and see if we can find some new flowers before they are all dead."

Ruth giggled. "It ain't gonna be today!"

"Tomorrow, then!" Noah said.

Ruth shook her head. "You's crazy. How we gonna do that? There's too much that needs to be done – "

Lydia waved her hand in the air, cutting Ruth off. "No. We'll not wait for work to be done. Each day is a gift. Love while you can. Marry the man tomorrow."

Joy spread through her. A bride! She nodded once. It was all the consent they needed. The small gathering cheered again and Noah pulled her close.

When his lips fell on hers, the rest of the world faded away.

Thirty - Nine

October 28, 1862

*L*ydia tugged the corset tight around Ruth's waist, the irony of the moment coaxing a giggle from her throat.

"You ain't gotta make it so tight!" Ruth fussed, tugging at the corset to try to create space between it and her ribs.

"Oh, but I do. But don't worry, I won't lace it up as much as you always did."

Ruth tried to give a derisive snort, but it dissolved into laughter. "Don't know how you managed to breathe in this thing."

"Now you see why I try to get away with not wearing one."

"Sure do."

Lydia tied the strings in place and picked up the gown from the bed. Ruth frowned at the garment for the third time. "That's too fancy."

"Ha! It's either this or my wedding gown. And if you think this ball gown is too fancy, you'd faint to see what my mother made for my wedding day."

Lydia looked down at material the color of fresh butter cream, almost on the verge of pale yellow. Ruth gazed at the mounds of fabric, a hint of longing peeking through her stubbornness.

Lydia prodded the crack in Ruth's defense. "Every bride should wear a gown on her wedding day."

She held it up for Ruth to step into, the long layers of fabric that gathered on the floor when Lydia wore it, grazed the carpet perfectly on Ruth's taller frame. She wouldn't need to worry with those silly hoops anyway. Lydia hooked the buttons down the back and guided Ruth to the mirror.

A single bow nestled at her bosom, slightly fuller than Lydia's own, filling out the gown beautifully. The smooth fabric draped down over her shoulders, finishing in delicate lace that danced along the crook of her elbow. The same lace lined the bottom of the bodice dipping down in the front to accentuate her narrow waist.

Lydia smiled. "It fits you beautifully. I say this ball gown is perfect for a wedding dress."

Ruth stared at her reflection with tears gathering in her eyes.

"What? You don't have to wear it if you don't want to."

"It ain't the dress. It's the most beautiful thing I've ever worn. Oh Lord, and I thought all them dresses you put me in were too much." She shook her head. "But I thank you for being so kind to me."

Lydia wiped away a stray tear that slid down Ruth's cheek. "What, then?" She said gently.

"I just..." She drew a long breath to steady herself. "I just wish my family could be here today. That I had someone to share this with."

Lydia sighed and pulled her into a hug. "I wish you did too. I am so sorry. I know it is not the same, and we can never replace them, but we will be your family."

"You is. I wish you's could have met my sister. I think she would have really liked you."

Lydia smiled.

Ruth turned back to the mirror. "Now what we gonna do with this wild hair?"

Lydia plucked a comb from the vanity. "We are going to make it look beautiful. Now sit."

A half hour later they descended the stairs arm in arm. Two women joined by fate and by nothing less than the hand of God.

Oh, Charles. I wish you could see this.

The steady ache for him never disappeared. She couldn't count how many times prayers for his safe return settled on her lips. She mumbled them at all hours, the petition always on her heart.

They stopped in front of the rear door. "Ready?"

Ruth nodded, wrapping the light cotton shawl around her shoulders. The fickle Mississippi autumn had given them the gift of a mild day. Lydia opened the door to the back porch, and the sound of music drifted in. Someone had produced a guitar and played it with adept fingers. The people gathered around. There were no chairs to seat them, but they stood on either side of the yard, leaving a short path from the porch to the large oak under which stood Noah.

Despite his best efforts, Tommy had not been able to find a preacher from Oakville willing to conduct their ceremony. By the grace of God alone, on his return home he'd come across a freed colored preacher headed north along with the colored Union troops he served. He'd agreed to stop at Ironwood to do the marriage. Ruth's marriage would be legal by Union laws.

The guitar played a soft tune, and the beautiful notes danced on the cool afternoon breeze. Ruth stepped past Lydia and onto the porch. Lydia followed her to the top of the steps and then paused to watch the ceremony. Noah's face seemed it would nearly crack in two from the smile that split it.

Dressed in simple but clean pants and jacket, his white shirt fell open at the neck with its homespun cotton seeming whiter against his ebony skin. Ruth glided down the steps and across the ground that had been raked clean of stray leaves.

She came to stand before the preacher, a wiry man with an honest face. "People of Ironwood Plantation, he said "We are here to see these two married under God."

Cheers came from the onlookers, and Lydia smiled.

"It was God who designed the marriage. He said that a man would leave his father and mother and be joined to his own wife. That the two of them would be one. This day we here'll witness the joinin' of two souls in the holy bonds of marriage."

The people clapped and nodded their heads. A young man shouted an enthusiastic "amen" from somewhere to her left. These people were little like the somber faces that had gathered around when she wed Charles. Where they were reserved, these people were boisterous. They wore their joy like a badge of honor. Perhaps it was. Fought for and won.

"Do you, Noah, take Ruth to be the wife at your side? The only woman in your bed and the mother of your children, if God chooses to bless you with 'em?"

"Yes."

The preacher nodded and turned to Ruth. "And Ruth, do you take Noah as your husband? The only man you give yourself to? To be the helper by his side?"

"I do."

"Do you both promise to remember your vows, to hold each other up in times of struggle, to bind up wounds of sorrow when they come? Will y'all remain faithful in the times when joy overflows and in the times when trials threaten to overcome you?"

They stared into each other's eyes, and Lydia's heart stirred with the fractured memories of her wedding day. She could not remember the words, but she'd never forget the promise in the honey-colored eyes that bore into hers on that day.

Lord, please bring him back to me. I will try with all my heart to be the true wife that he needs.

"Then by these here witnesses and the powers granted to me by the United States Army and God Almighty, I declare Noah and Ruth to be husband and wife!"

Noah swept Ruth into his arms and planted a solid kiss on her lips, tilting her back. When he finally righted her, she seemed flushed with joy. Lydia smiled, her heart feeling as if it swelled too much to be contained in her chest.

Betsy came to the front of the crowd and presented Ruth with a new broom with its handle wrapped in ribbons. She placed it down in front of the couple and gave a nod. They grinned and clasped hands, leaping over it in a single stride. The people cheered their consent and swarmed around the couple.

No rings were exchanged. Only this simple gesture that spoke their bond to the community. Bound together for the remainder of their days by their own choice and by the love in their hearts. Lydia prayed Ruth would find Noah to be the good man she expected he was, and that his unwavering love would heal the broken places in Ruth like Charles' love had done for her.

She watched them with joy and held tight to her hope that joy would abide.

Forty

The gravel crunched underneath boots that were now worn nearly thin. He'd lost count of how many days they'd traveled through the woods, surviving on what they could scavenge and the rare handout from kind strangers. Never had Charles known hunger, cold, or pain as he now did. And knowing it, he understood life more deeply.

The sharp intake of breath drew his attention to the girl behind him. She'd been thin when he first met her. Now she looked like she would blow away if the wind stirred. Her dress hung threadbare and her cheeks sunk in. He would have to see that she was fed and well-rested before she continued on her way.

"This here's your home?"

"That it is. This is Ironwood."

She eyed him cautiously.

"What?"

She shrugged. "You just don't seem like the type a man that's got a place like this."

"I don't?"

She gave a small smile that told him she thought he might be a few marbles short of a full set. He turned to look back at the house as he approached and a frown creased his brow. Wagon ruts furrowed the lawn. The front fields had shown signs of trampling, but he'd told himself he was reading too much into it. Now his heart began to quicken. He walked faster.

Bridget hurried along behind him. "What's wrong?"

As they drew closer to the house, his fears thickened. Gunfire had torn hunks from the columns and one of the front parlor windows was covered with a pitiful quilt, flapping against the slight breeze. He ground his teeth, suddenly afraid of what he would find within.

"Looks like somethin' bad done happened here."

Charles clenched his fist and stepped onto the front porch. The sound of cheers erupted from somewhere around the side of the house. They paused. Bridget looked at him and lifted her brows, but Charles couldn't provide the answer she sought. He pushed open the front door.

Home.

His throat tightened. He'd thought he would never see it again. Had feared it wouldn't be standing when he finally returned. Likely he would face severe punishment as a deserter. He would gladly take it for the peace of mind of knowing Ironwood remained. He would return to his duty soon enough.

The sound of laughter drifted down the main hall. Whose, he could not be certain. He looked back at Bridget.

"Perhaps you should remain here a moment until I can assess what has happened here."

She gave a small nod and sank down on the lowest step of the staircase, exhaustion evident in her features.

Charles walked down the hall to find the rear door standing open. And there on the porch stood the light of Ironwood.

Lydia.

Relief flooded him, causing his heart to flop. Safe. She was safe. Her back was to him, long hair flowing freely down to the small of her back. Peace spread through him like a warm river, and he walked quietly through the door.

Lydia watched the new couple and tried to swallow down the fear that threatened to consume her. Would she ever feel the joy of the arms of her beloved husband again?

Can you hear me, Lord? How much longer will you tarry? All I ask is for some news. Please, just let me know he's still alive —

Someone touched her elbow, cutting her prayer short. She drew a breath. Erase the emotions. Put on the smile they will want to see. She began to turn to greet whoever had come late to the wedding. Be the lady they…

The world skid to a halt and all air left her lungs.

Charles.

He was alive!

Air slammed into her lungs and released as a squeal.

"Charles!"

She threw her arms around his neck, covering his rough cheek with kisses. "Oh, Charles! You're home!"

He wrapped her tight against him, his body too thin. His heart pounded in rhythm with hers, a desperate call to echoed love. She ran her hands over his back and then pushed away from him cupping his face in her hands. Was he really here?

Please, don't let it be another dream.

She couldn't stand for it to be another vivid dream that disappeared into the mists. He felt real beneath her touch, his face rough with weeks of growth.

"Have you truly come home to me?" she whispered.

"Yes, lady of my heart. I have come home to you."

Tears slipped down her cheeks. "How long?"

He gave a gentle smile, and she knew he could not stay long. But he was here, and her prayer had been answered. So many prayers answered.

He drew her tight against him and lightly brushed her lips with his. "Did you miss me, Mrs. Harper?" he asked, his light words belied by the thick emotion in his voice.

"Indeed, Mr. Harper I fear I did."

"Oh?" He placed a feather-light kiss on her mouth, his warm breath sending tingles down her spine.

"Indeed." She pressed into him and kissed him as if she might never see him again. Somewhere in the distance she heard giggles and a few cheers. Charles drew her against him, and if her heart were not soaring, she might have feared she would be crushed underneath the grip with which he held her.

Finally he pulled back, laughing. "My dear, I do believe we have an audience."

"I do not care," she breathed.

"Oh, my dear one, how I love you so."

"And I you, husband." She buried her face in his chest and let the tangle of tears of joy and tears of relief soak his filthy shirt.

He stroked her hair until she could regain control of her emotions. She straightened herself, drawing away from Charles only enough to see the people but remaining pressed against his side, his arm tight around her waist. The people watched her intently, their gazes shifting between her and Charles. How would they respond? Would they rejoice in his return or fear he would undo what she'd fought to bring upon Ironwood?

Her gaze locked on Ruth.

Ruth smiled and gave a slight nod.

Lydia lifted her chin. "People of Ironwood! My dear husband has returned to us whole!"

They shouted their happiness for her, and she glanced at him, relishing the mixture of confusion and joy on his face. There would be much to explain.

"I have made many changes, Charles. There are some things you and I will need to discuss."

He gave a nod. "Indeed. There are changes I must make here as well. Though it seems I happened upon some manner of celebration."

Lydia beamed. "Oh, you've come just in time to enjoy refreshments in honor of Noah and Ruth's wedding."

Charles chuckled. "Well, I am pleased I didn't miss the refreshments. You and I will have time for discussions after I've had a chance to remember the taste of Betsy's fine cooking."

She giggled and pressed herself closer to his side as he lifted a hand to the people.

"Oh, I nearly forgot." Charles turned from the crowd and looked down into her face. "I've brought someone home with me."

Lydia tilted her head. "A solider in need of our care?"

He chuckled. "In a manner of speaking." His eyes danced with amusement.

"Be clear, husband."

He tucked a stray hair behind her ear, his eyes speaking to her more than words would ever be able to convey.

"I was wounded during the battle and – "

"You are wounded! Where? Let me see!"

She lifted the hem of his shirt, which he quickly pushed back down. "My dear!" He chuckled. "Do not fret. I am well."

She frowned at him. "I shall see this wound."

He grew serious. "And I will show it to you. But you have not yet let me finish."

"Very well."

"I was wounded. I managed to slip on a Federal coat in order to disguise myself."

Lydia gasped, but he held up a hand. She let him continue.

"A nurse found me and took me inside the hospital, even though she suspected my ruse. If not for her, I probably would not have survived."

Lydia placed her hand on her throat. "And she returned with you to further care for you?" Who was this woman? Did she have intentions with her husband?

Charles cupped her face as if reading her thoughts. "She was in trouble. When I found a way to escape, I knew she had to come with me. I had to save her as she saved me. I could not let that poor girl travel on her own. I told her I would bring her home to my wife, who I was certain would care for her."

"Of course." She placed a kiss on his lips. "Where is she?"

Charles gave her a squeeze and stepped inside the house. He returned with a girl in a ragged dress that hung from her gaunt frame, a swath of cloth twisted around her head, its long tail falling down over one shoulder. She glanced around the gathering, and her mouth formed a little O.

Ruth's scream pierced the silence.

Forty - One

*R*uth's heart pounded in her chest. Noah grabbed her shoulders, but she shook him free. Chills ran down her spine. She was seeing a ghost.

A ghost, there on the porch.

She picked up her skirts and ran up the steps, pushing past the confused faces of the Harpers. Her breaths came in rapid succession.

Alive.

She reached out a trembling hand, afraid the ghost would disappear under her touch. Her fingers touched the warm skin of a face she thought she'd never see again.

"You's alive!"

Bridget nodded, choking on words that Ruth could not understand. It didn't matter. All that mattered was the living miracle that stood in front of her.

Ruth wrapped her sister in her arms, and they sank to the ground in a heap of fabric and tears. When Ruth could breathe again, she held Bridget out away from her.

"How? I saw him... I saw..." her voice cracked, and she could not push the words past the lump in her throat.

Bridget shook her head. "I know. I's so sorry. He went out in the woods, and I followed him. I done found a shovel and thought I could knock him in the head and then get everyone untied. I thought I could save us."

Ruth glanced up at Lydia, who stood wrapped in Charles' arm and staring down at them with wide eyes. Ruth stood up and pulled Bridget to her feet.

"You was so brave," Ruth said.

Bridget wrapped her arms around herself and looked at the Harpers with worried eyes. Ruth rubbed Bridget's back. "You's safe here."

Bridget looked at Mr. Harper and a strange expression crossed her face. It was something closer to trust than Ruth had ever expected Bridget to show a white man. He nodded to her.

The people gathered around close, pulling in to see who this strange girl was that had caused such a stir. Noah pushed past them and stood beside Ruth, worry in his eyes. She took his hand and gave it a squeeze. There would be much she would have to share.

Bridget drew a long breath. "So I followed him into them woods. But he heard me before I could get a good swing on him. He musta hit me pretty good, 'cause when I woke up I had this here cut on my head. I think he musta thought I was dead." She reached up and touched a scar that ran from underneath her scarf and down the side of her temple.

She shrugged. "I didn't know where anyone was. Everyone was done gone when I made it back to the camp."

"How'd you make it out there on your own?" Ruth asked.

"I only had to walk for one day when I found a camp of Union soldiers. They was in pretty bad shape. I showed 'em how to bandage a wound right, and they kept me. I went with them up to they's hospital and worked there."

"God done brought us miracles today," Ruth said. She squeezed Noah's hand. "He done brought me my family."

Bridget nodded. "I saw Byram come to the hospital. I had to run. Mr. Harper took me with him."

The people all looked at Mr. Harper with wonder. He gave a small shrug.

Tears streamed down Ruth's cheeks and laughter bubbled up within her. She looked at Noah. "Noah, this here is my sister. Bridget, Noah is my husband."

Bridget's eyes flew wide. "Husband?"

She grinned. "Yep. You's just missed it. That's why I's in this fancy dress."

Everyone laughed.

"Speaking of dresses," Lydia said. "I think I have just the right one for Bridget. Green would suit her nicely. Don't you think so, Ruth?"

Bridget turned her big eyes on Ruth, and Ruth laughed. "There's a lot you's gonna have to learn 'bout Ironwood."

She grabbed Bridgett with one hand and reached her other out to Lydia. "If you'd not saved me that day, I wouldn't be here now to see my heart done made whole again."

A tear slid from Lydia's eye. "It's I who should thank you. You've saved me more than I ever did you."

Charles chuckled. "The Lord works in some strange ways. It would seem we all needed saving in one way or another."

The wind picked up and blew across a new Ironwood. One ready for the changes that would come, her people strengthened for the challenges ahead. Mr. Harper wrapped his arm around Lydia, and she smiled up at him, a different woman than the one he'd left.

Ruth drew Bridget close and led her into the house behind the Harpers, her new husband on her heels.

Ruth knew there would be plenty of hard times to come. War still raged beyond their lands and the future remained uncertain. But they would make their way, a people brought together by hope.

Today they would dance and forget all that separated them. They would whistle the tune of new life, new hope, and a new Ironwood.

Epilogue

"*M*ista Harper! Mista Harper!" Ruth bounded down the stairs as quickly as her swollen belly would allow. Betsy said she was only days away from the birthing, but she had to be here for Lydia today.

They said the white ladies had a hard time birthing children. She'd seen the truth in that today. Lydia was too small for the babe that grew in her. But Lydia didn't seem to know she wasn't supposed to be strong enough. They'd all feared she wouldn't make it. But Ruth knew Lydia possessed a strength the rest of them would never fully know beneath the surface.

"Ruth!"

Mr. Harper paced the floor at the bottom of the stairs, no doubt overcome with his nerves. He'd made it in from his regiment a scant few hours ago, and his wife's wails had torn through Ironwood for near on two hours now. Twice, he'd nearly broken down the door to get to her, and both times Betsy had shoved him from the room.

Ruth stopped and grinned at him her, hand drifting to her lower back to rub at the muscles that always seemed to be sore. "You's can go up now."

"And the babe?" He grasped her shoulders and looked like he might shake her.

"They's both doin' just fine."

He let out a long breath and dashed up the stairs, taking them two at a time. By the time she made it back up to the room, he was already sitting on the edge of the bed with the tiny bundle in his arms. He beamed down at his wife.

Lydia laughed, her wet hair plastered to her face from the pain of bringing new life into the world. Pain that now seemed forgotten. The babe in Ruth's own belly put his feet against her ribs and pushed, nearly stealing her breath. He wouldn't wait much longer to join them.

"Since you have yet to ask, I have brought forth a son."

Mr. Harper looked up from the tiny face with surprise as if he couldn't believe he'd forgotten something so important. "A son," he repeated, staring back down into the tiny face. "So you were right it would be a boy."

"We should name him Robert, after your father."

Mr. Harper grinned like a boy who just got a stick of hard candy. "Welcome to Ironwood, Robert. We hope you like your new home here."

Ruth settled her hand on her stomach and watched the new little family, the peace in her heart growing. If this little boy grew up with a heart like his momma, well, then the rest of the world better go on and get ready. The Harpers of Ironwood brought change. They forged their own paths and made their own ways. They were a people of convictions and dreams and hopes that reached past their time. Like the ironwood trees that grew wild all over this land, they were stronger than they seemed – and this would forever be their home.

Dear Reader,

I hope you enjoyed the first story of Ironwood. I'd love for you to take a few moments and leave a review. It means the world to an author to get feedback from readers!

Stick around for a few more pages to meet Emily in an excerpt from book two. Emily grew up an orphan, so she never expected to inherit Ironwood Plantation. When she discovers an old diary hidden in the attic, her life becomes entwined with her Civil War ancestor. Soon Emily begins to wonder how a woman long dead can keep showing up in her dreams...

For more about the Ironwood books and the upcoming Magnolia Belles series, visit me at www.StepheniaMcGee.com

Heir of Hope
(Ironwood Plantation Family Saga - Book 2) – Summer 2015

The Magnolia Belles Series
Discover the grandeur and haunting history of Mississippi's iconic landmarks. Each stand-alone Belle story tells of tragedy, redemption, love and family steeped in southern culture.
Ranging from the 1840's to the 1880's these books feature strong women who take on a tumultuous time in our nation's history.
Coming Fall 2015

Excerpt: Heir of Hope

Chapter One

My name is Emily Burns, and this is the story I never intended to write.

Back when my life made sense, I dreamed of being the next breakout novelist. But this isn't the masterpiece I visualized presenting to publishers. Nonetheless, perhaps if I put it on paper, it will stop burning in my mind and pushing its way into my dreams.

Maybe if I get it out, I will finally have some peace.

So, where to start? When writing fiction, they say the *proper* thing to do is to drop you somewhere in the middle of the action and let you figure out what's going on. That's called a hook. Well, since this isn't fiction, I'm going to commit a cardinal sin and do something entirely different. I'll start at the beginning – the time at which my very predictable, ordinary life got turned upside down.

It began just one day after I first ventured south of the Mason-Dixon Line at the start of a relaxing retreat full of writing – the long anticipated chance to finally start my novel. That's where life handed me something far more interesting than even my overactive imagination could have produced.

My thirtieth birthday found me alone, over-worked and generally fed up with my life, and I needed out. No more excuses. Time to get serious about that book. So despite my boss' protests, I cashed in my vacation time and packed my bags for two gloriously free weeks.

Fast forward a few phone calls and a short flight later, and I settled into a remote cabin nestled in the towering pines blanketing the northern Georgia mountains. I've always loved the mountains. Still remember camping once when I was a kid. That summer held the last good memories of my parents. So anyway, I'd taken the first step and gone to a happy place. Then came the most important of all moments in writing. Starting.

I stared at my computer for a good twenty minutes. Checked e-mail, played games and posted results to stupid quizzes on Facebook. Okay, so maybe the cabin wasn't *that* remote. I couldn't get *too* far from civilization because every writer needs the internet. You know, for research.

I took a deep breath. Time to get to work. Put the proverbial pen to page. Or, rather, fingers to keyboard. The blank page stared back at me. I drummed my fingers and narrowed my eyes at the flashing cursor's impatience. I'd taken three classes and read all kinds of "How to Write and Sell your Novel" books. I could spout all the rules on point of view, creating tension, and developing plot. I knew the fundamentals. How, after all that, could my computer screen still be blank?

And so there I was, angrily tapping the backspace key because yet another opening line just wasn't enough of a "zinger" to make me the next best-seller, when the doorbell rang.

Ordinarily this wouldn't, pardon my cliché, make me jump out of my skin. Even people without friends expect to hear the familiar *ding-dong* once in a while. There's always the UPS man, Girl Scout or political activist to account for. But here in my rustic paradise, I didn't think I even *had* a doorbell.

I cracked the door open and peered out. A round-faced, bespectacled man in a grey suit stood on the porch. He smiled warmly. I eyed him suspiciously, mentally shifting through any of the cabin's contents that might serve as a weapon. He looked harmless enough, but a woman alone in the woods could never be too sure.

"Miss Emily Burns?" The man's thick southern drawl coated each word in a sticky layer of gentlemanly charm.

"Yes?"

"I've been looking for you. You're not an easy woman to find." He lifted a hefty manila envelope.

I recoiled behind the door, ready to slam it in his face.

He took a step back. "Forgive me. My name is Buford Cornwall, and I am a lawyer from Oakville in Itawamba County, Mississippi. I'm here to talk to you about your estate."

I eased the door open further, but still kept my hand on the knob. "Ita-*what*-a?" I looked at him like he'd just escaped his padded cell. "Estate?"

"It-uh-whum-buh. And I'm here to talk to you about the estate your great-aunt left to you."

"You've got to be mistaken." I said, knowing this poor fellow had trudged through the red dirt in his tasseled loafers for nothing. I wasn't the kind of gal to have any sort of estate.

"No, no. I'm quite certain. Took me quite a bit of research, but I tracked you all the way through the child welfare system. Then, wouldn't you know it, found you on Google."

I frowned. Good old Google. Who needed private investigators anymore when anyone could be hunted down on the internet? "Well, Mr. uh – "

"Cornwall. Buford D. Cornwall. But you can just call me Buford."

"Right. Mr. Cornwall, maybe we'd better talk about whatever it is you've got in that folder." I studied him a moment longer until my curiosity overpowered my cynicism, and then stepped back from the door to allow him entrance to the one bedroom cabin I hadn't bothered cleaning. I eyed the dirty dishes in the sink, hoping he didn't notice the pried-open soup can still sitting on the counter.

He hustled in without hesitation and let the bulk of his frame settle into one of two wooden chairs at the small table that served as both a dining space and my writing desk. It protested with a slight groaning sound. I fought the urge to do the same.

Shuffling my papers around like they were something important, I gave myself a moment to collect my thoughts. My parents died when I was ten. My father grew up in the system. My mother never knew her father, and her mother died of cancer when Momma was twenty-three. I had no relatives. I know because surely *one* of my three social workers would have diligently looked for some before dumping me into New Jersey state child services.

"Mr. Cornwall—"

"Buford."

"Buford. I'm afraid I don't understand. What estate?"

He opened the envelope and pulled out a large color photograph. "This one."

His pudgy fingers pushed the image toward me. A house. No, not really a house. More like a mansion. One of those old southern mansions on Civil War movies. White columns and everything. I looked back up at Buford, not quite sure what to make of it.

"You're joking, right?"

He looked confused. "No ma'am. This here was the home of Miss Adela May Harper. Your great-aunt." His voice softened slightly when he spoke her name, but then quickly returned to its smooth, yet business-like drawl.

I shook my head emphatically. "No, I don't have any relatives."

Buford raised a fuzzy eyebrow. "Miss Adela was your father's aunt. She told me so herself. Two months before she died, when she made some adjustments to her will."

My forehead wrinkled as I sorted out the implications of Buford's simple statement. "But my father said he grew up in the system. He didn't have a family."

Buford nodded slowly and looked at me for what seemed like a very long moment. "Your father's mother, Adela's baby sister, dabbled in some, well, not very nice things. She brought home boyfriends that were less than reputable. One night, probably after having been beaten again, your father ran away. He was fifteen. Adela said she reported him missing, but they never heard from him again."

I studied a knot-hole on the plank surface of the table. "So, if that's true, how'd you find me and how are you even sure you've got the right woman?"

"Adela never gave up looking for Jonas. The day she came to me to change her will, she finally got a lead on him. Said he'd gone north and changed his name. Took on the last name of some poet or something."

A reluctant smile tugged at the corner of my mouth. Robert Burns. His favorite.

"Anyway," Buford continued, "She said she'd found out he'd married and had a child, a girl, but he and his wife died twenty years ago in a car crash. She didn't know the girl's name. Only knew Jonas's pseudonym and that his daughter would have been roughly ten years old when her parents died."

I studied Buford's teddy-bear brown eyes, but declined a response. He seemed sincere, and all his information checked out. Still, it was a lot to accept just yet. I nodded for him to continue.

Buford cleared his throat and leaned into the slats of the chair. "Since she had no children of her own and Margret was her only sister, Adela said the girl would be her only heir. She asked me to start looking. So I did. But the good Lord took her home just days before I found something." He paused and leaned forward.

"Adela left everything to you."

"Everything?"

He nodded, his clean-shaven, caramel-colored double chin mashing together. "Yes. The house and all its contents and the remaining balance in her checking account." He pulled a paper from the folder. "Which totals just over seventy-five thousand, as you'll see here."

I tried to swallow but found my mouth severally lacking the necessary moisture to do so. "And you're sure it's me?"

The lawyer grinned revealing even, white teeth. "I'll just need you to sign a few papers, please." He pushed a fancy pen across the table.

Five minutes later, I wished Buford a good trip home and closed the door. I'd promised to look over all the documents and meet up with him in a few days. It looked like I'd be traveling deeper south than I'd intended.

When Buford disappeared down the drive, I gathered the papers from the folder and stepped into the bright May sunshine. Thick, warm air settled around me and I inhaled a deep breath of the clean air, letting its release from my lungs drag some tension from my body. I sat down in one of the two rockers on the small front porch and listened to the birds twitter before opening the envelope again.

I pulled out the glossy photograph of the house. Absolutely beautiful. I studied it closer. Paint chipped and hung in flakes in several spots and one of the front shutters sagged. Not that it mattered. I'd probably still get a hefty sum out of it. A small seed of hope began sprout tentative roots. Maybe, for once, something good was about to happen to me.

I placed the photo on the side table next to my glass of lemonade and fished for another paper. The last will and testament of an aunt I never knew existed. Short and direct, it confirmed Buford's story. Adela Harper left everything in her possession to the daughter of her nephew, Jonas B. Harper, living under the name Jonas Burns. I stared at Daddy's name. What did the B stand for?

I laid the copies of bank statements on the table and removed a photocopy of a news article. Where did she find this? I ran my finger over the small picture of the pile-up.

> *Crash Kills Three, Wounds Two*
> *A drunk driver took an exit ramp onto interstate 81 last night around 10:00 pm meeting one car head-on and causing two others to crash. Jonas Burns, 33, a factory worker, and his wife Morgan, 30, a teacher, were both killed instantly in the head-on collision. Samantha Kelly, 57, rear-ended the Burn's car and was taken by ambulance but died before arriving at the hospital. Authorities say the drunk driver and his passenger both sustained significant injuries but are expected to recover. Their identities have not yet been released. The police say the driver will be facing DUI charges and possibly...*

Enough. I already knew how the story ended. The paper knew the facts, but didn't really know anything. Only I knew how Daddy saved for months to take Momma out to a fancy restaurant in the city for their anniversary. How pretty Momma looked in her new yellow dress and how Daddy's eyes shone. The paper gave no mention of them kissing their little girl for the last time and leaving her at her best friend Amy's house. No, those weren't the things that made news.

I placed the paper face down. It represented the first dark cloud in a series of thunderstorms that had caused my irreparable damages.

"Enough of the past," I said to the massive pines surrounding the cabin. They swayed in agreement. I needed to figure out my next steps for the future. I tapped my fingers on the armrest. I could use some guidance. Some advice. But who would I call?

If I was still the praying type, I might have implored the Almighty. But God and I were no longer on speaking terms. So what? I could do it. Get a plan, steam-roll through. No reason to change tactics now.

Step one. I was already off work, so obviously step one meant traveling to Oakville to sort through all this. Step two would be to cash in the bank accounts, put the house up for sale, and head home. With that kind of money I could take a year off and really sit down and do some writing. A break from my stuck-up boss would do me wonders.

I went back inside to scout plane tickets I couldn't afford. But, then again, seeing as how I'd just come into a fortune maybe I could. A smile tugged at my lips. Today was the launch of a new future.